BLUE STARS

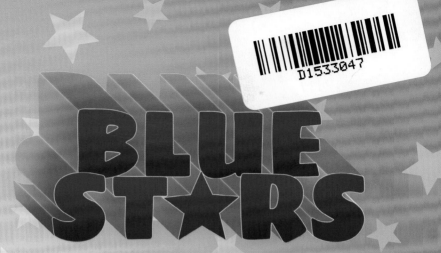

BLUE STARS

THE VICE PRINCIPAL PROBLEM

MISSION 1

KEKLA MAGOON
and
CYNTHIA LEITICH SMITH

illustrated by
MOLLY MURAKAMI

CANDLEWICK PRESS

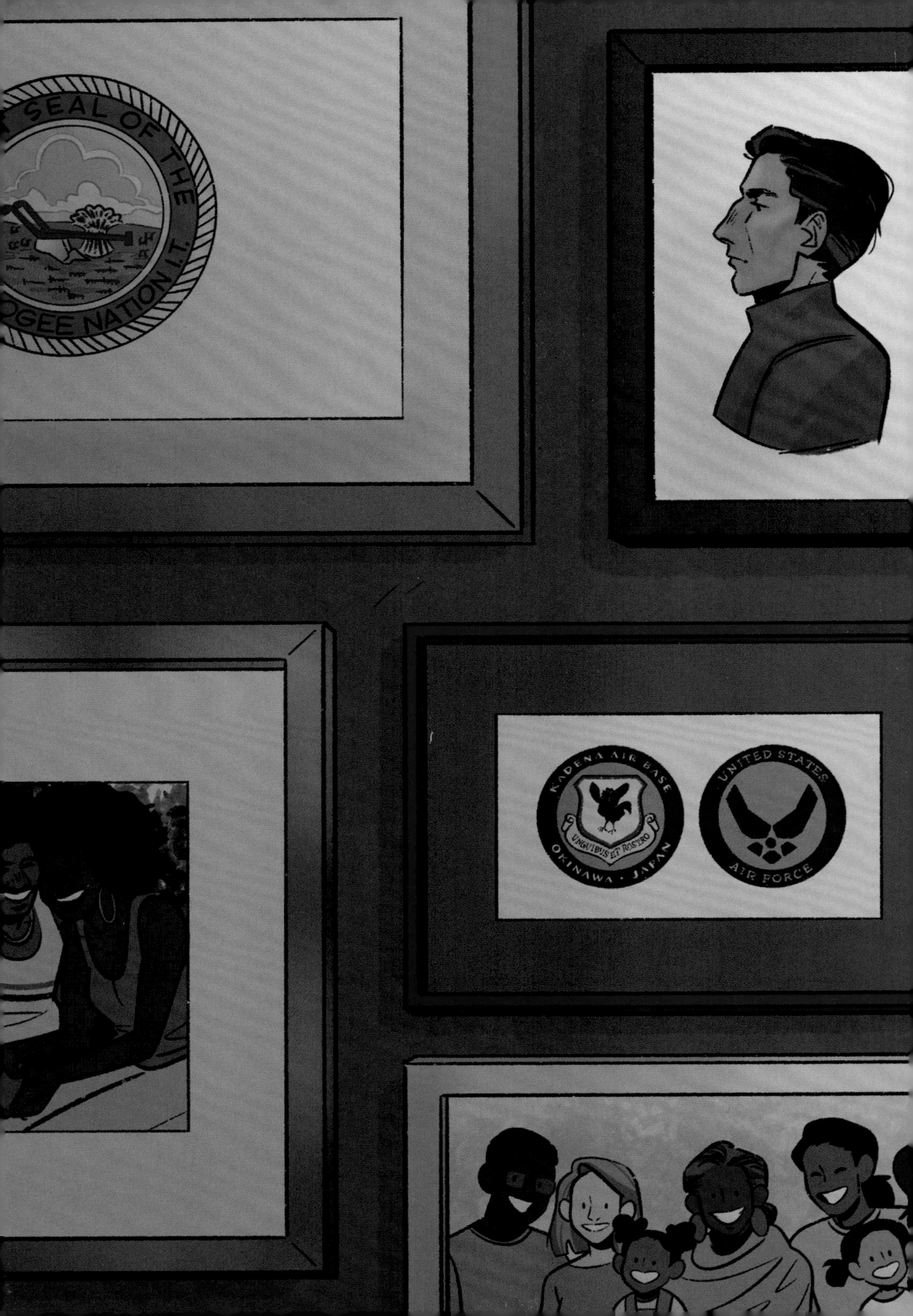
SEAL OF THE
NATION I.T.
KADENA AIR BASE
UNGUIBUS ET ROSTRO
OKINAWA · JAPAN
UNITED STATES
AIR FORCE

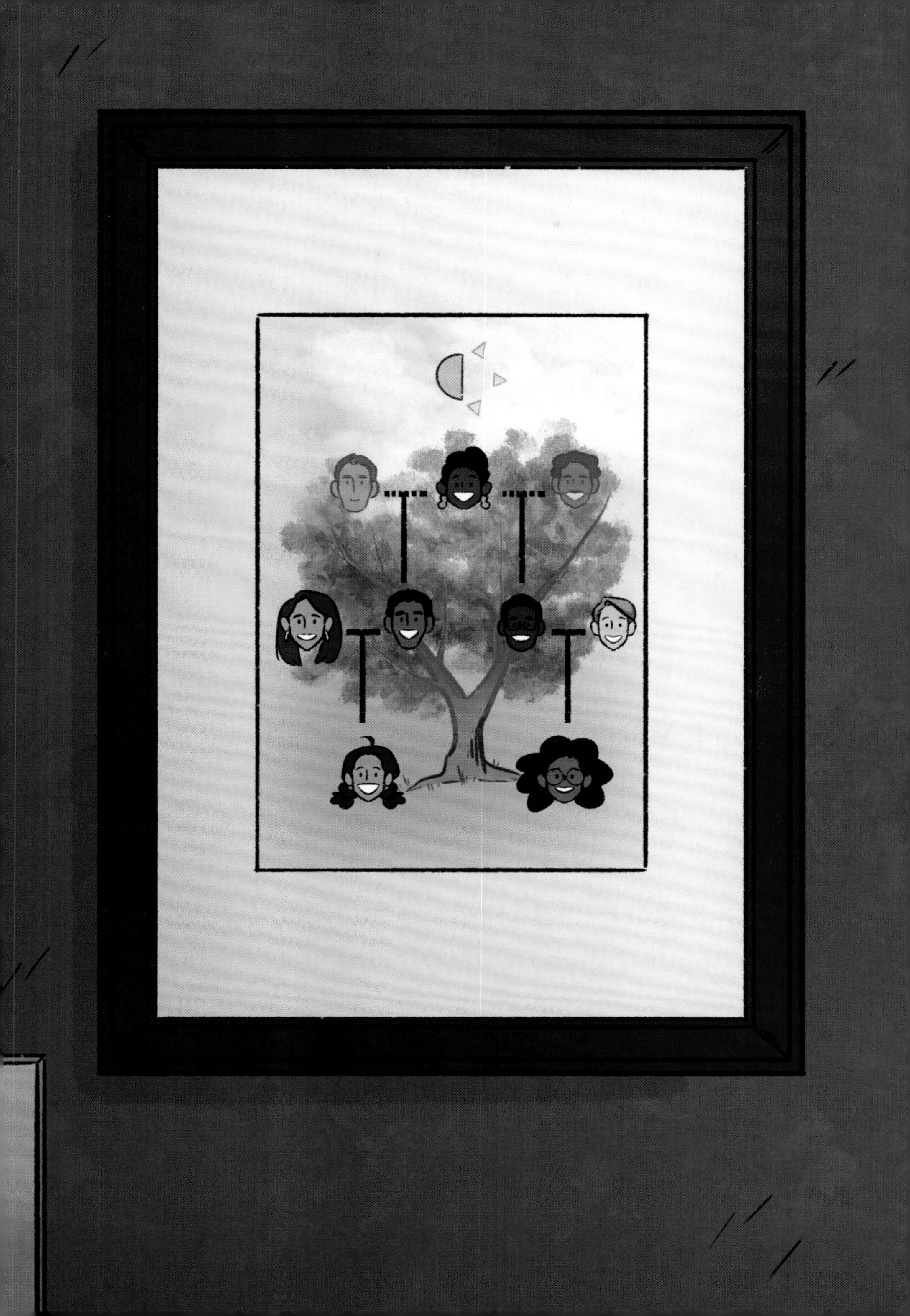

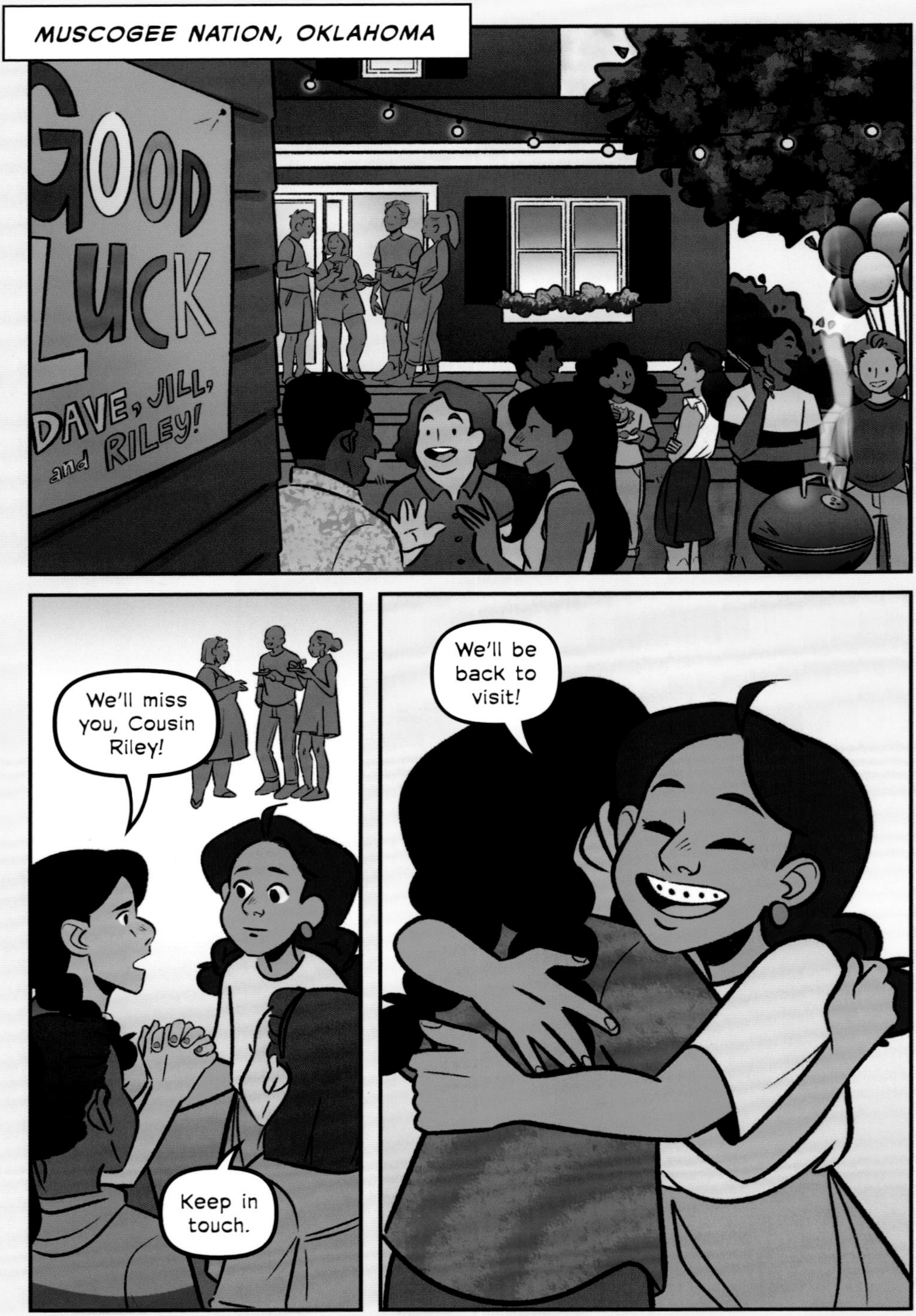
MUSCOGEE NATION, OKLAHOMA
GOOD LUCK DAVE, JILL, and RILEY!
We'll miss you, Cousin Riley!
Keep in touch.
We'll be back to visit!

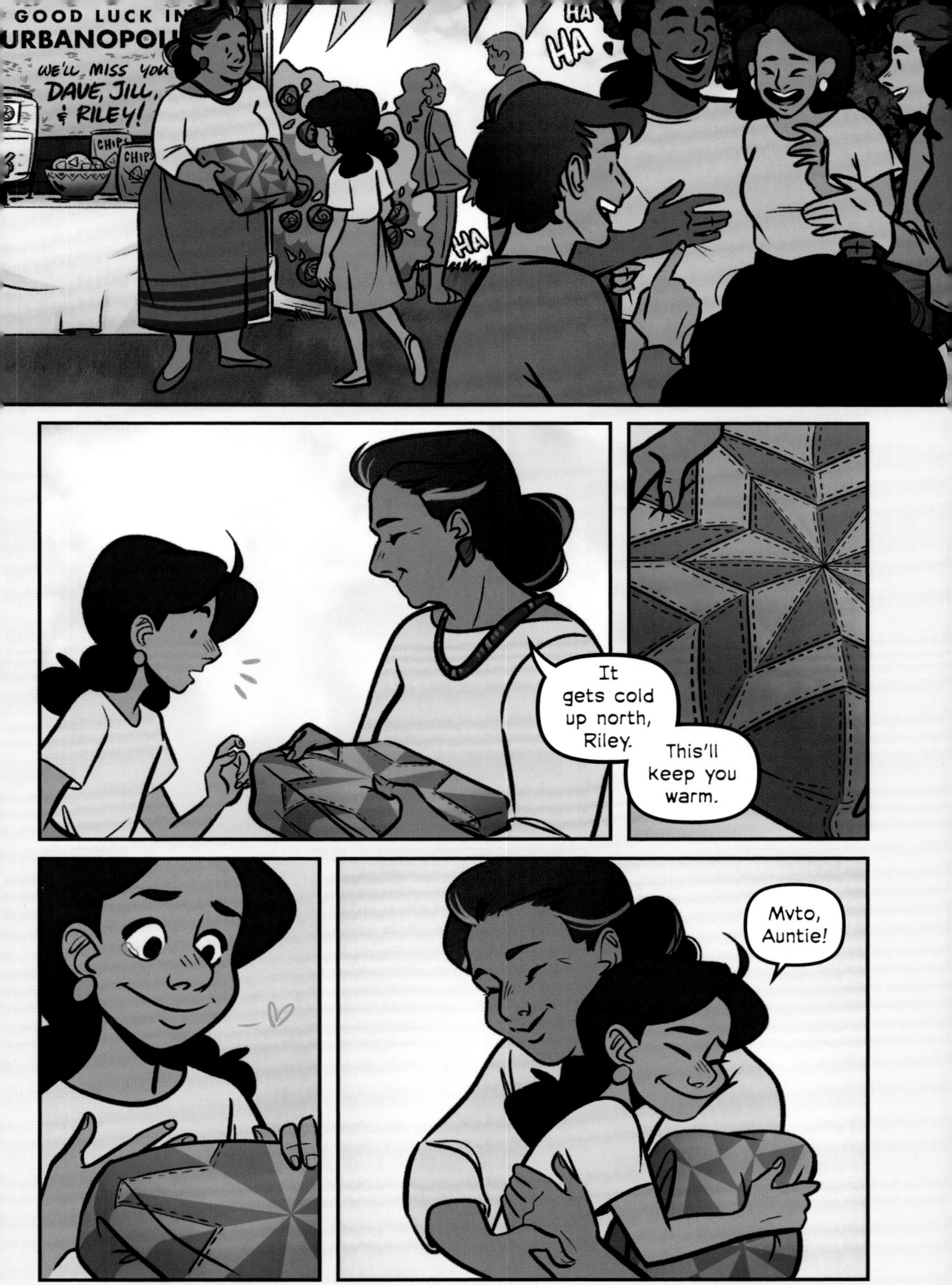
GOOD LUCK IN
URBANOPOL
WE'LL MISS YOU
DAVE, JILL, & RILEY!
CHIPS
CHIPS
HA
HA
HA
It gets cold up north, Riley.
This'll keep you warm.
Mvto, Auntie!

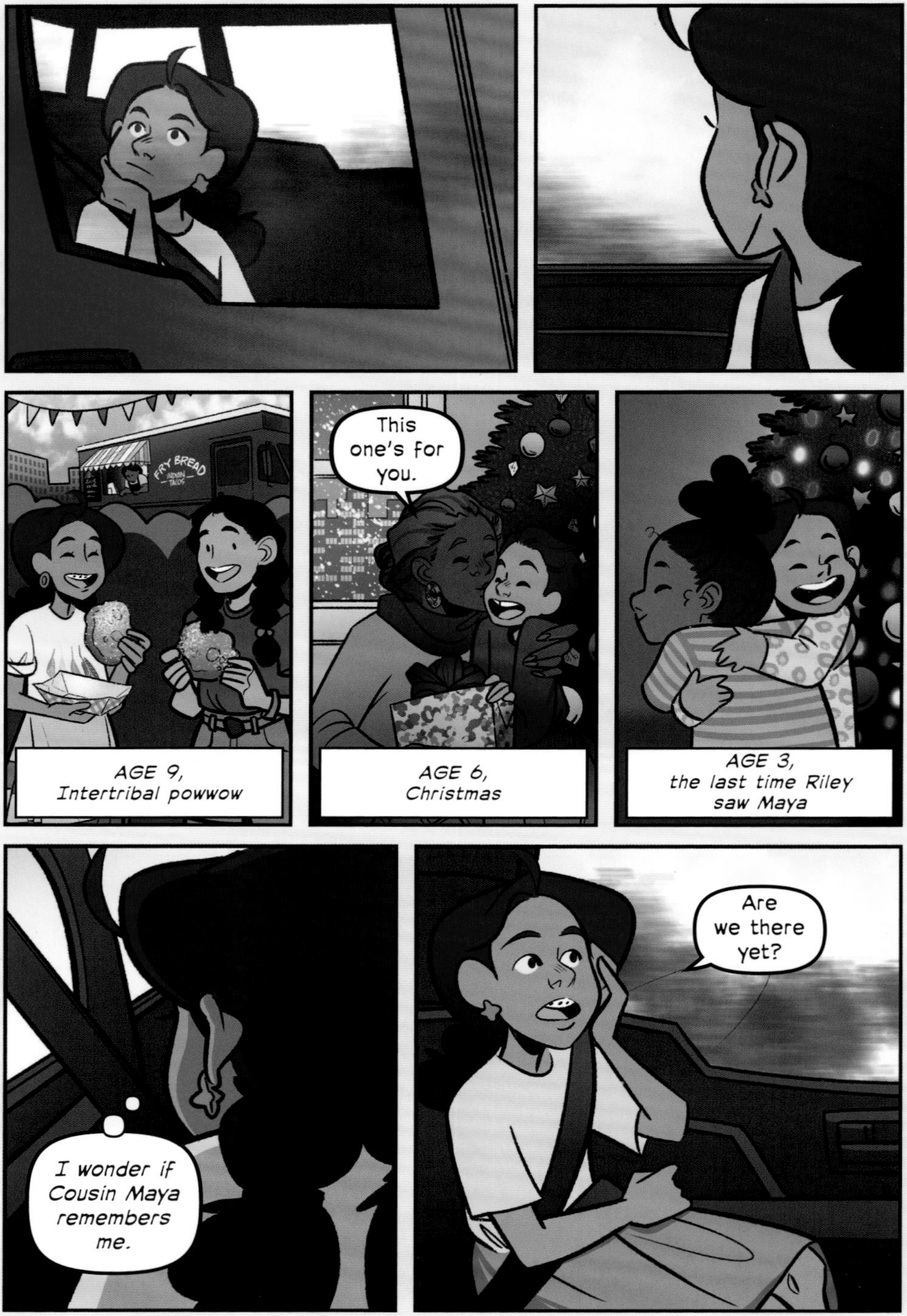
FRY BREAD
INDIAN TACOS
AGE 9,
Intertribal powwow
This one's for you.
AGE 6,
Christmas
AGE 3,
the last time Riley saw Maya
I wonder if Cousin Maya remembers me.
Are we there yet?

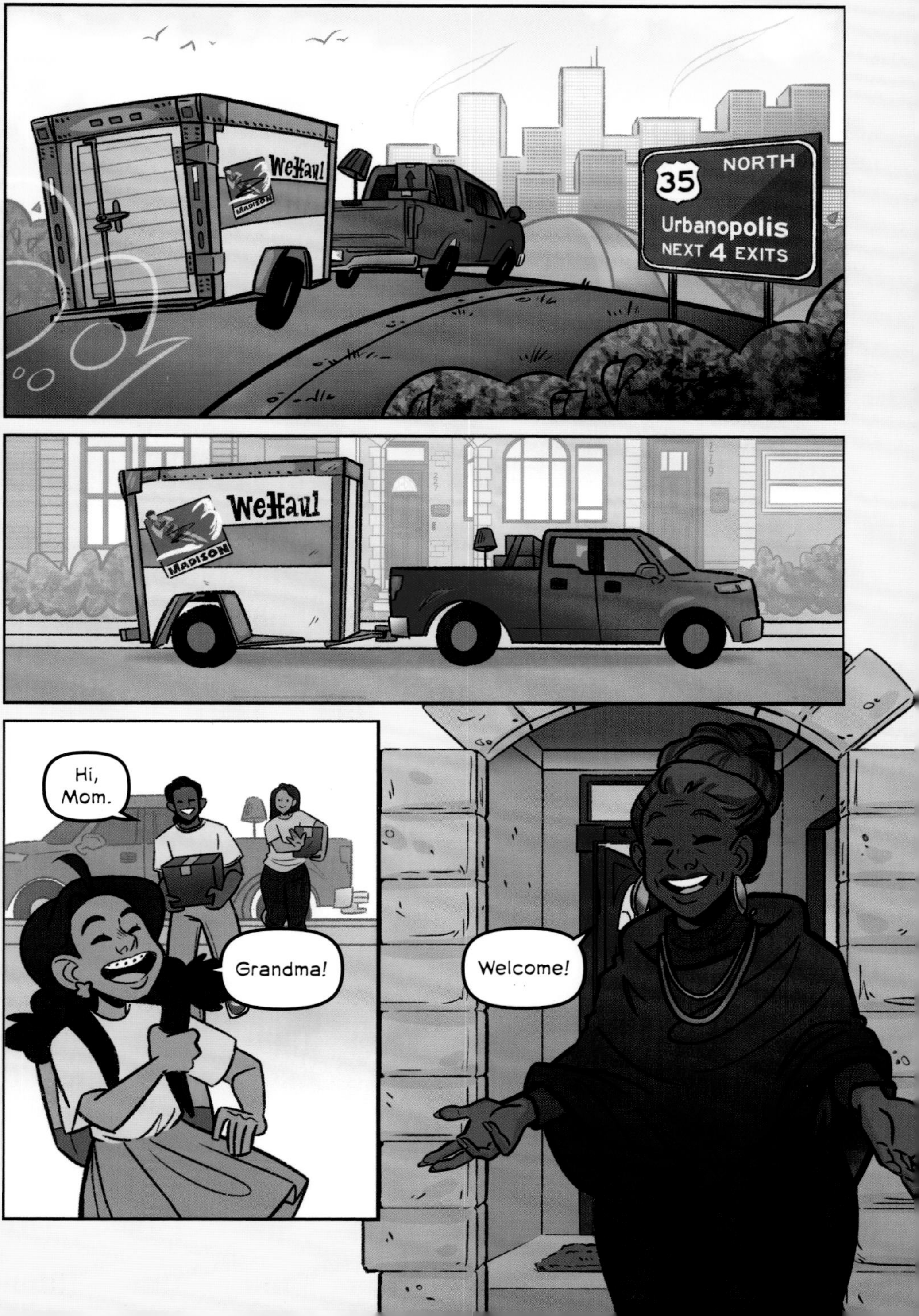
WeHaul
MADISON
35
NORTH
Urbanopolis
NEXT 4 EXITS
WeHaul
MADISON
Hi, Mom.
Grandma!
Welcome!

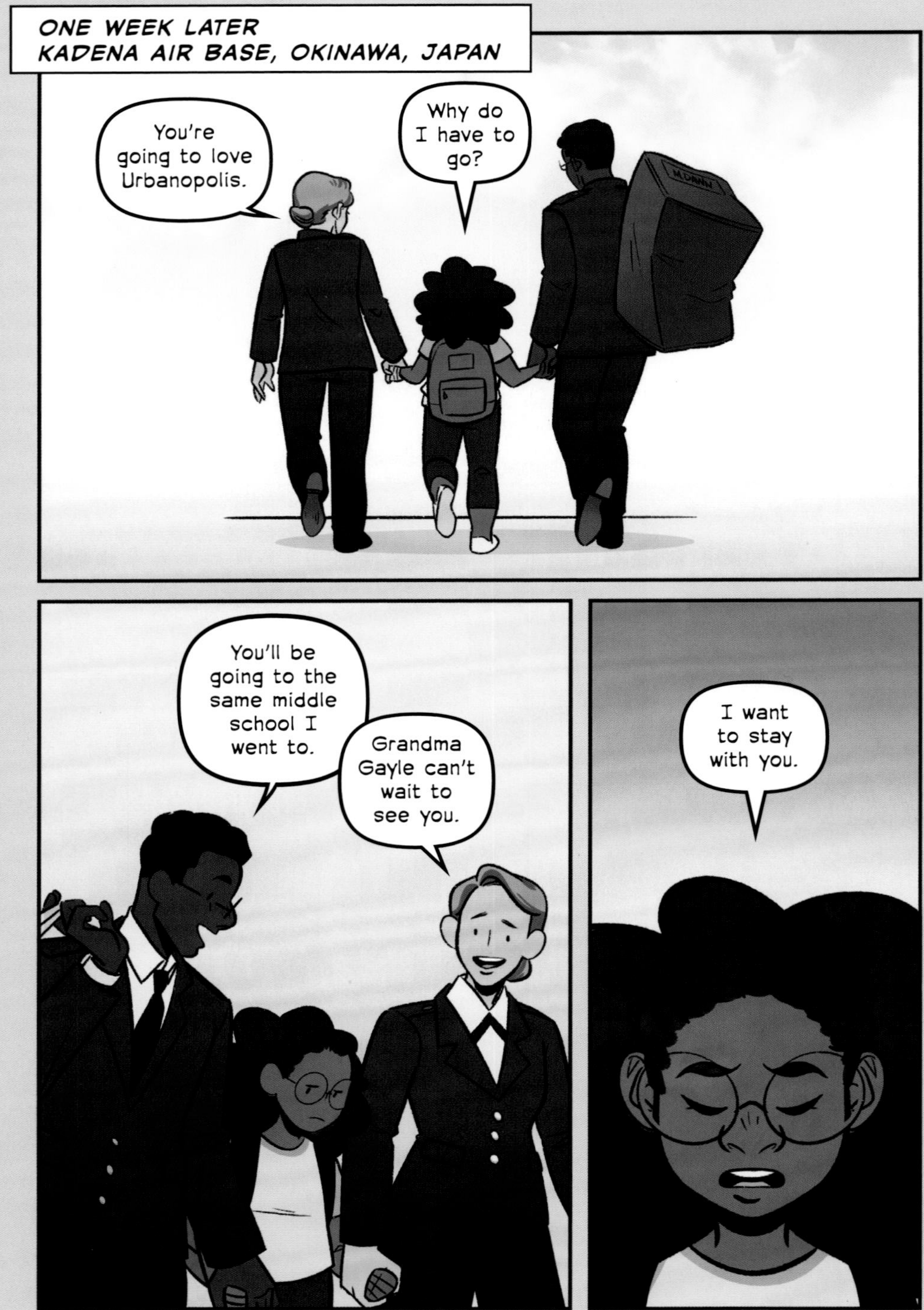
ONE WEEK LATER
KADENA AIR BASE, OKINAWA, JAPAN
You're going to love Urbanopolis.
Why do I have to go?
M.DANN
You'll be going to the same middle school I went to.
Grandma Gayle can't wait to see you.
I want to stay with you.

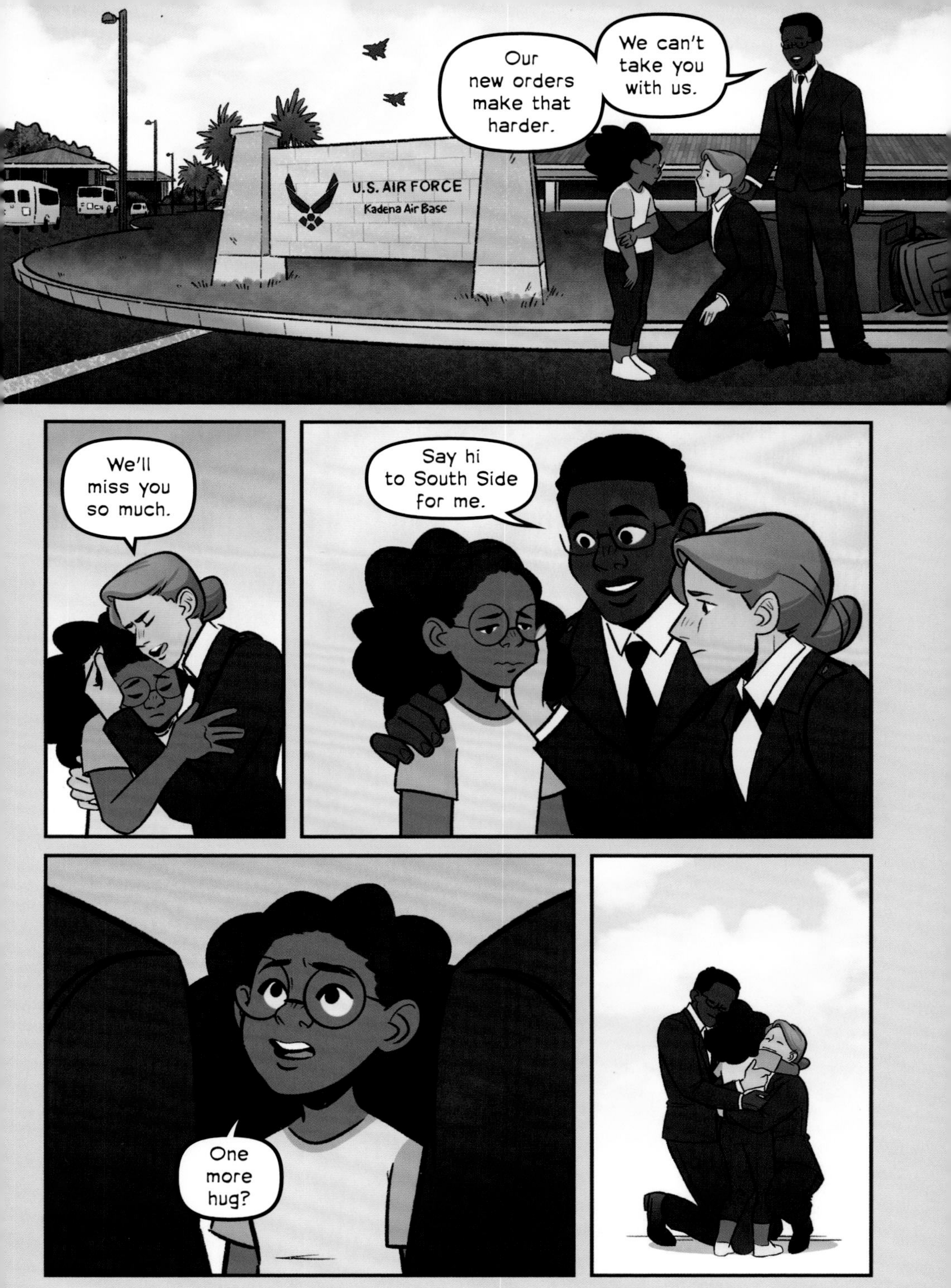
We can't take you with us.
Our new orders make that harder.
U.S. AIR FORCE
Kadena Air Base
We'll miss you so much.
Say hi to South Side for me.
One more hug?

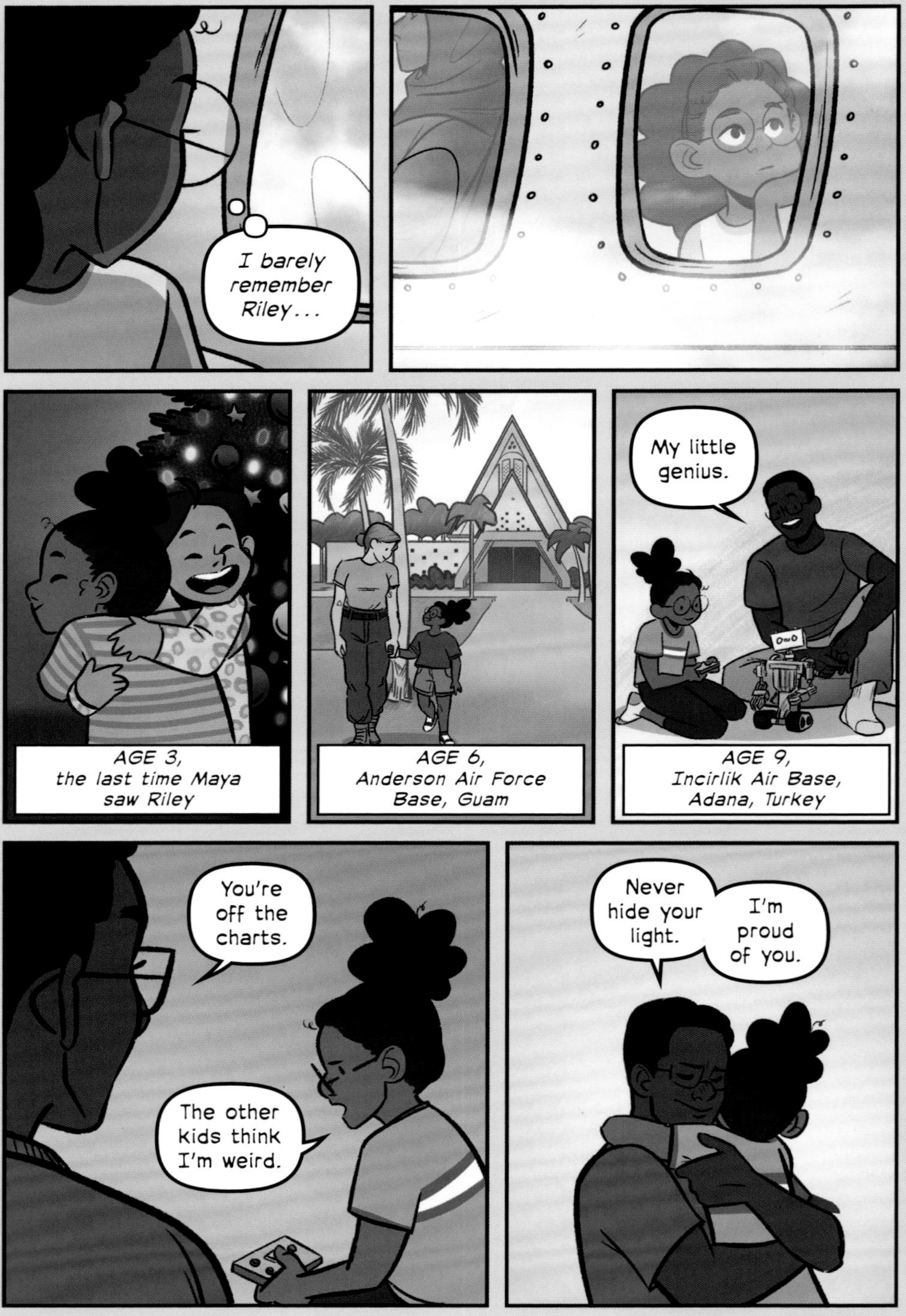
I barely remember Riley . . .
AGE 3, the last time Maya saw Riley
AGE 6, Anderson Air Force Base, Guam
My little genius.
AGE 9, Incirlik Air Base, Adana, Turkey
You're off the charts.
The other kids think I'm weird.
Never hide your light.
I'm proud of you.

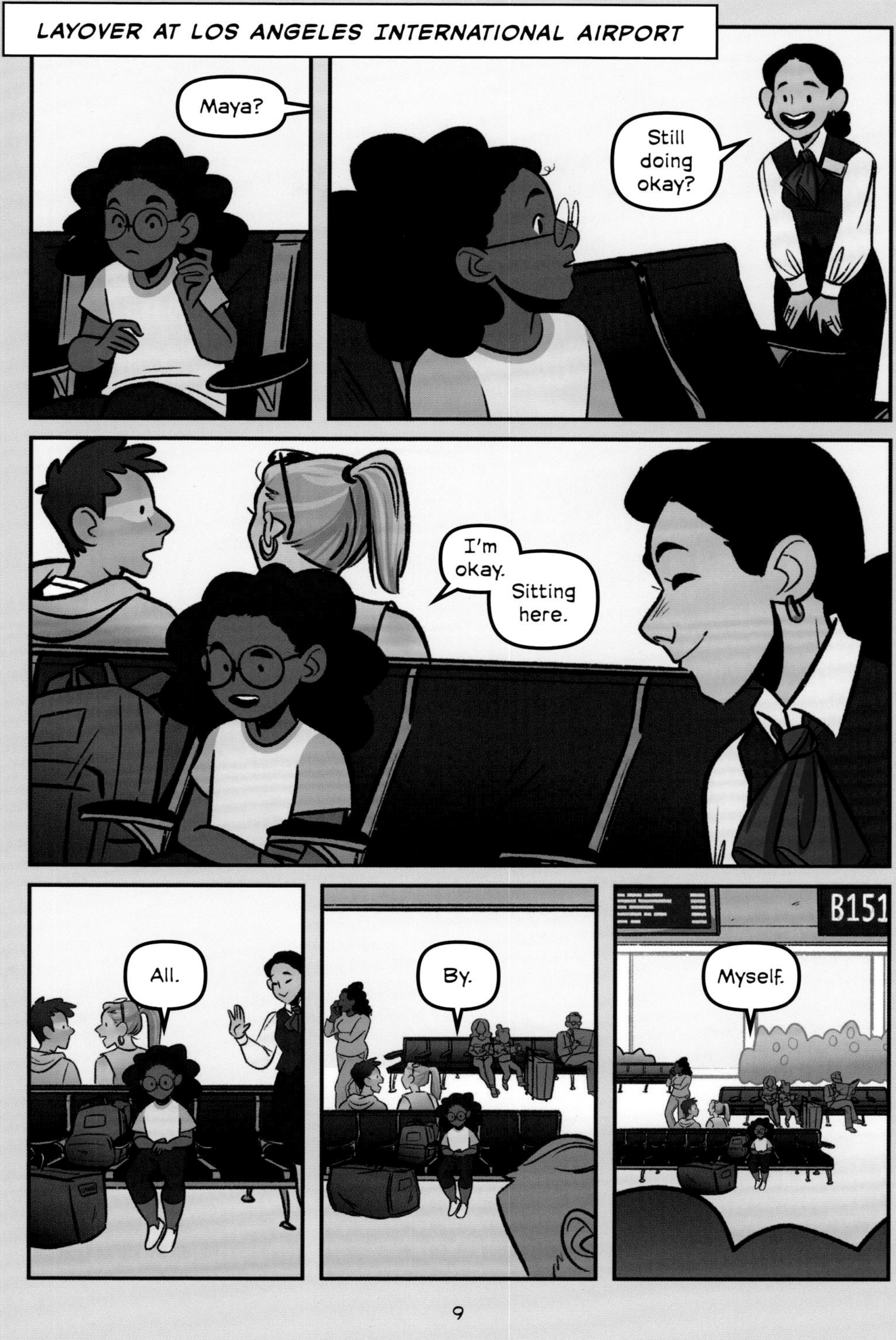
LAYOVER AT LOS ANGELES INTERNATIONAL AIRPORT
Maya?
Still doing okay?
I'm okay.
Sitting here.
All.
By.
Myself.
B151

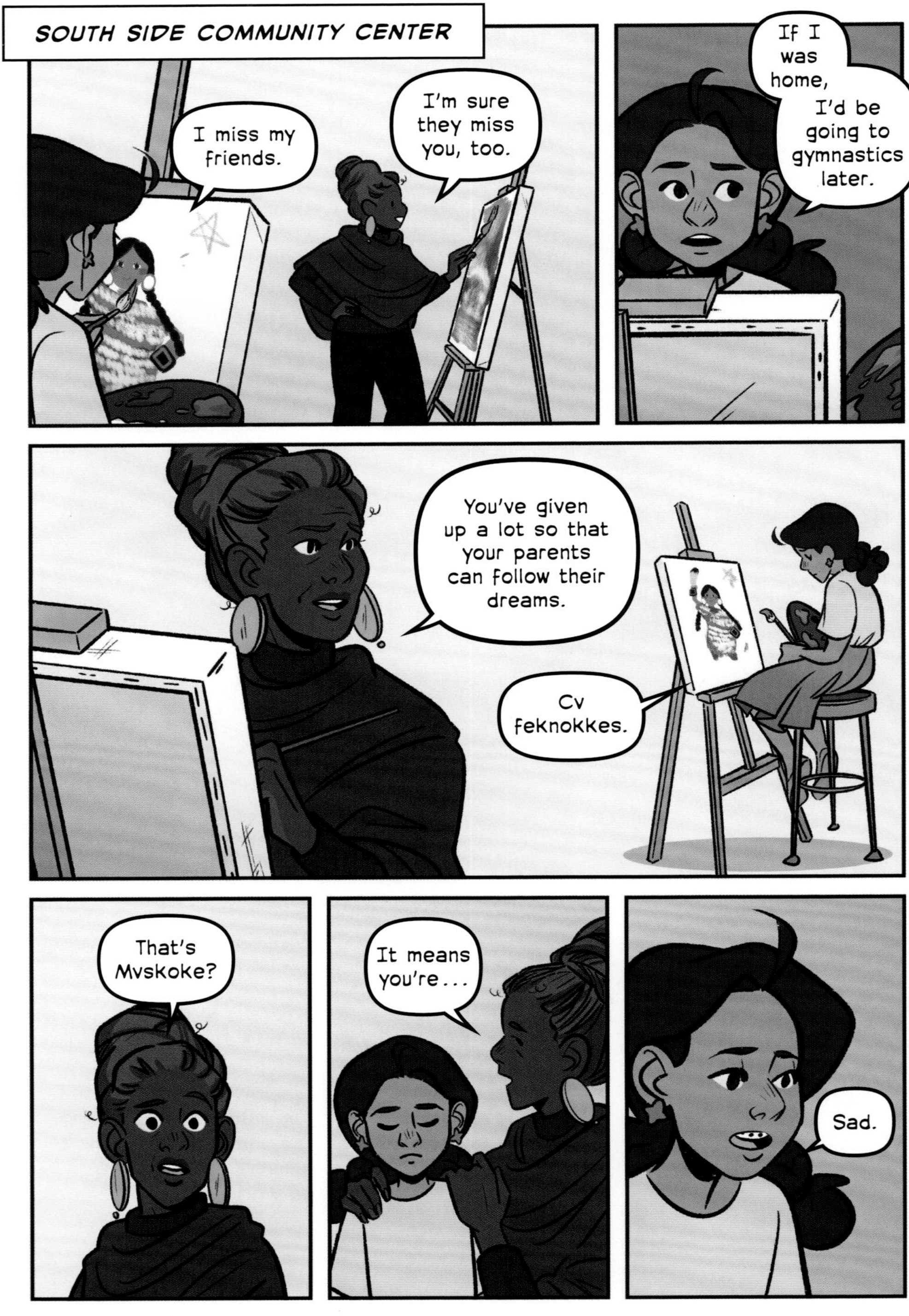
SOUTH SIDE COMMUNITY CENTER
I miss my friends.
I'm sure they miss you, too.
If I was home, I'd be going to gymnastics later.
You've given up a lot so that your parents can follow their dreams.
Cv feknokkes.
That's Mvskoke?
It means you're...
Sad.

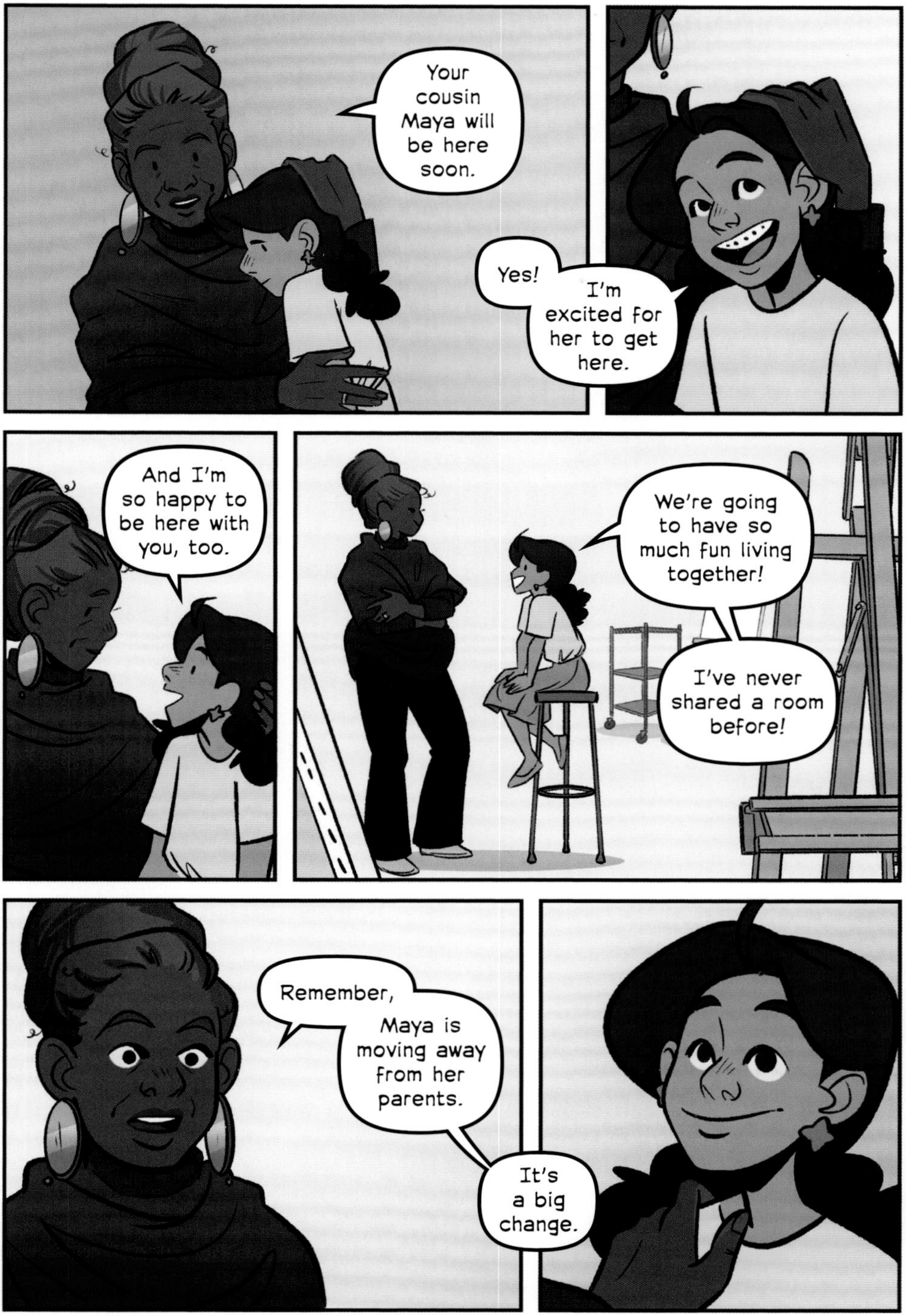
Your cousin Maya will be here soon.
Yes!
I'm excited for her to get here.
And I'm so happy to be here with you, too.
We're going to have so much fun living together!
I've never shared a room before!
Remember,
Maya is moving away from her parents.
It's a big change.

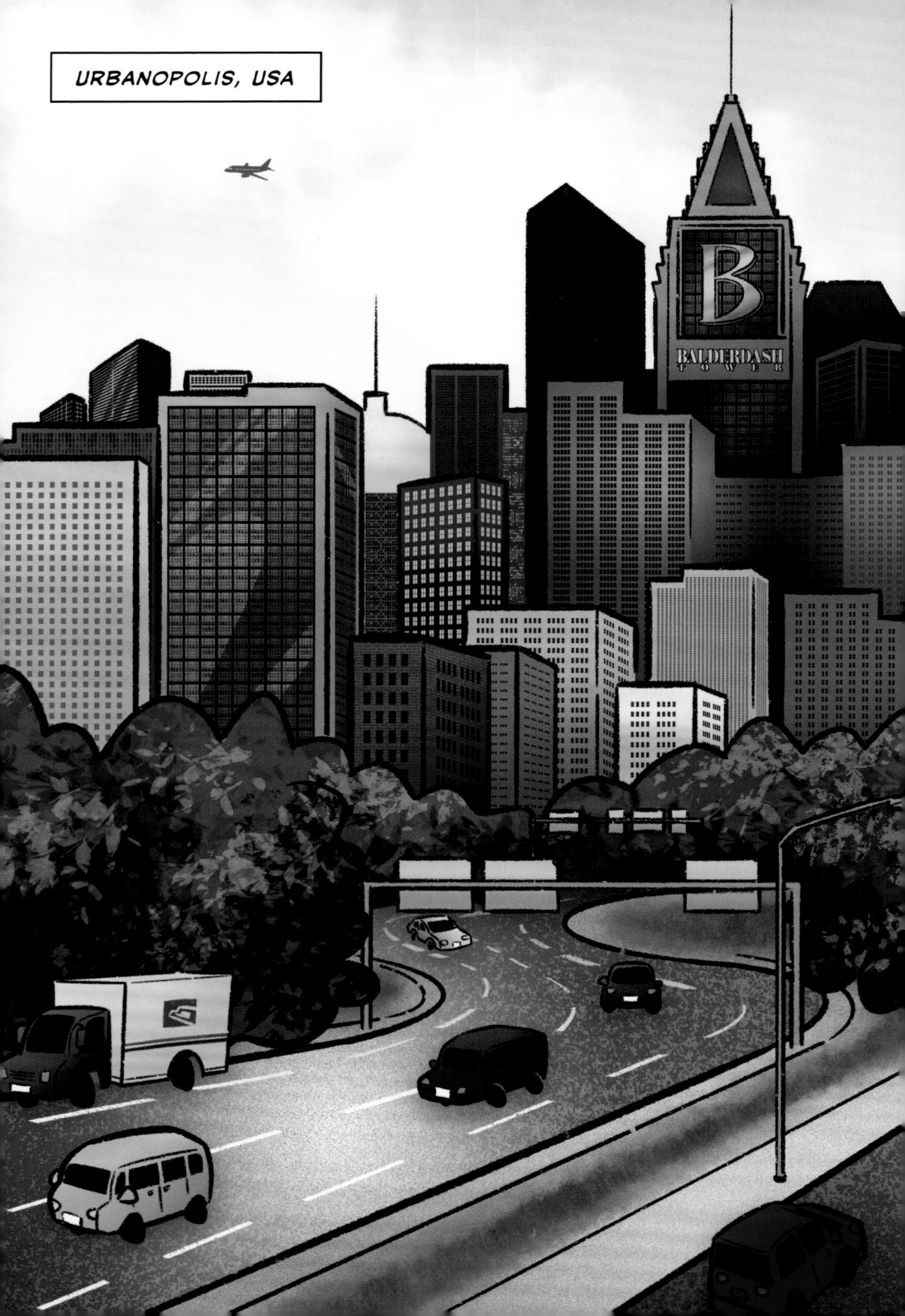
URBANOPOLIS, USA
BALDERDASH
TOWER

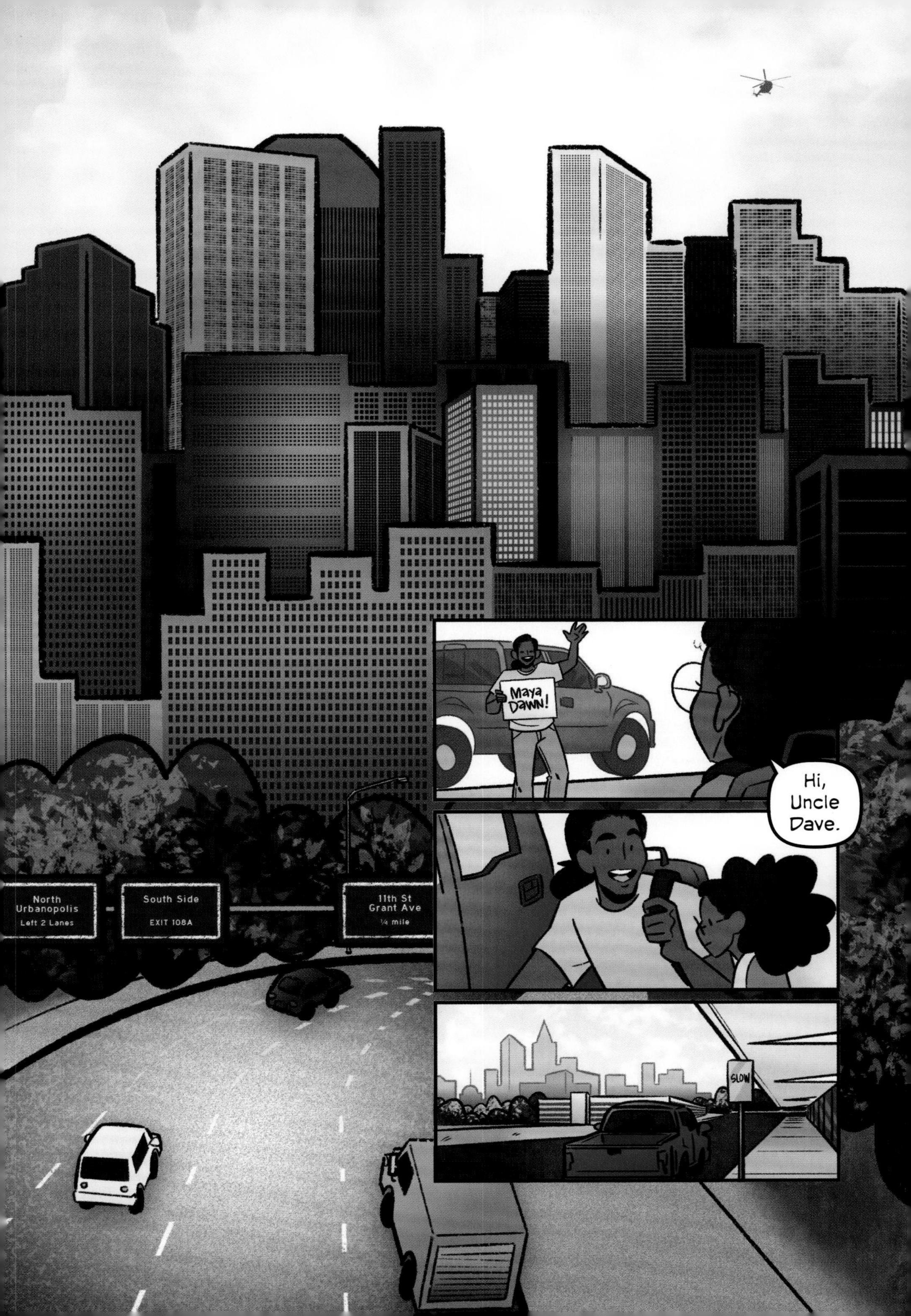
North Urbanopolis
Left 2 Lanes
South Side
EXIT 108A
11th St
Grant Ave
¼ mile
Maya DAWN!
Hi, Uncle Dave.
SLOW

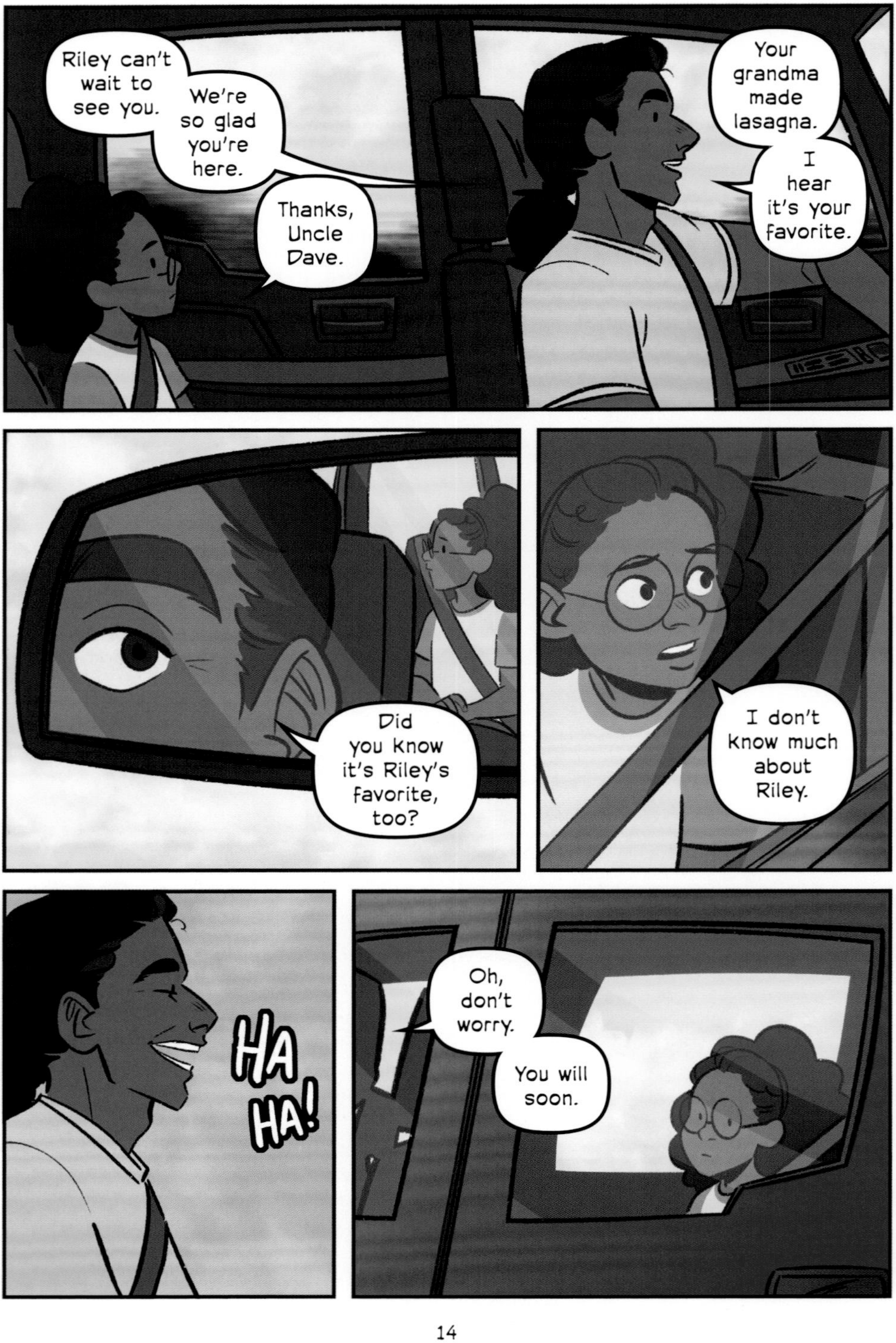
Riley can't wait to see you.
We're so glad you're here.
Thanks, Uncle Dave.
Your grandma made lasagna.
I hear it's your favorite.
Did you know it's Riley's favorite, too?
I don't know much about Riley.
HA HA!
Oh, don't worry.
You will soon.

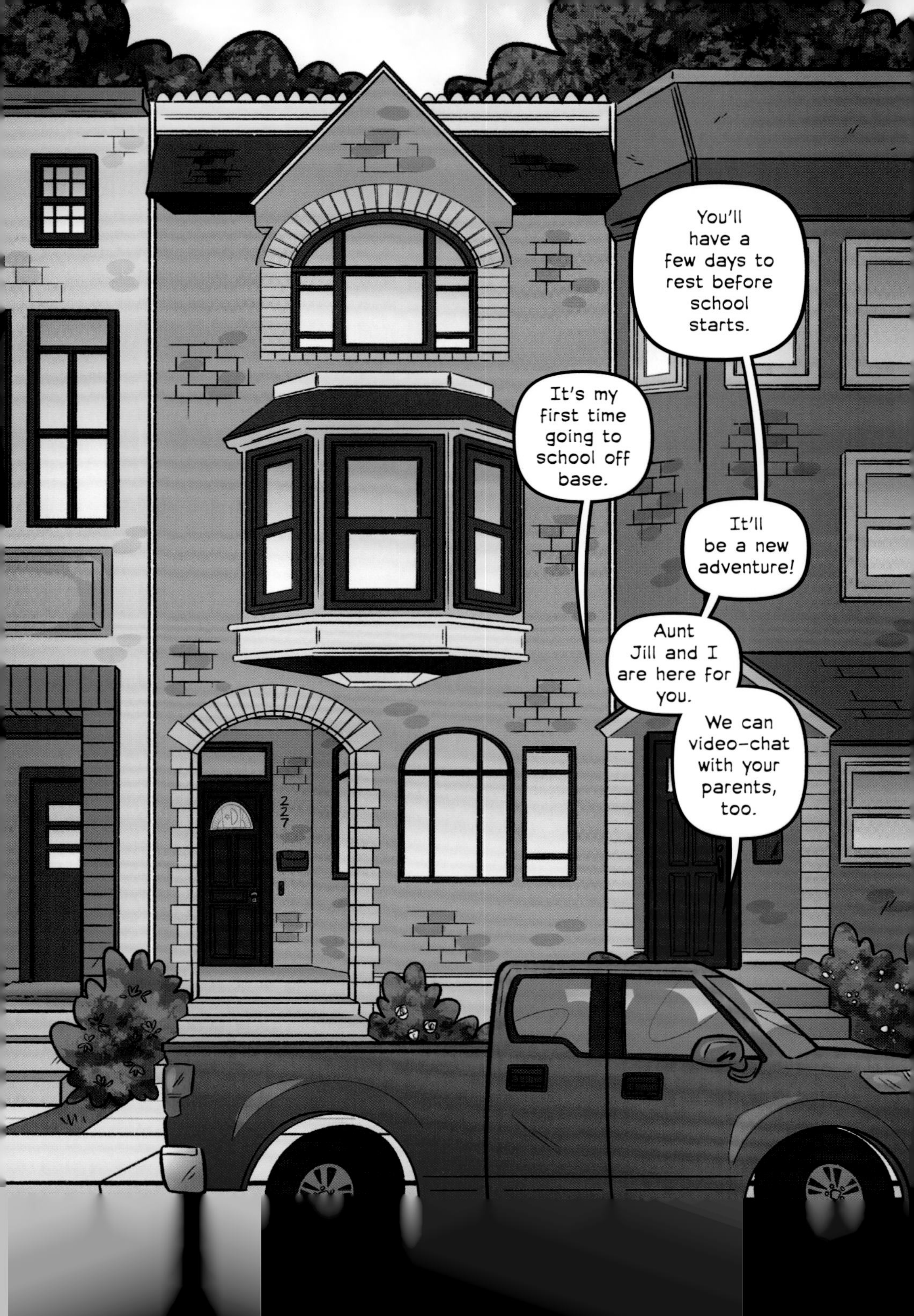

It's my first time going to school off base.
You'll have a few days to rest before school starts.
It'll be a new adventure!
Aunt Jill and I are here for you.
We can video-chat with your parents, too.
227

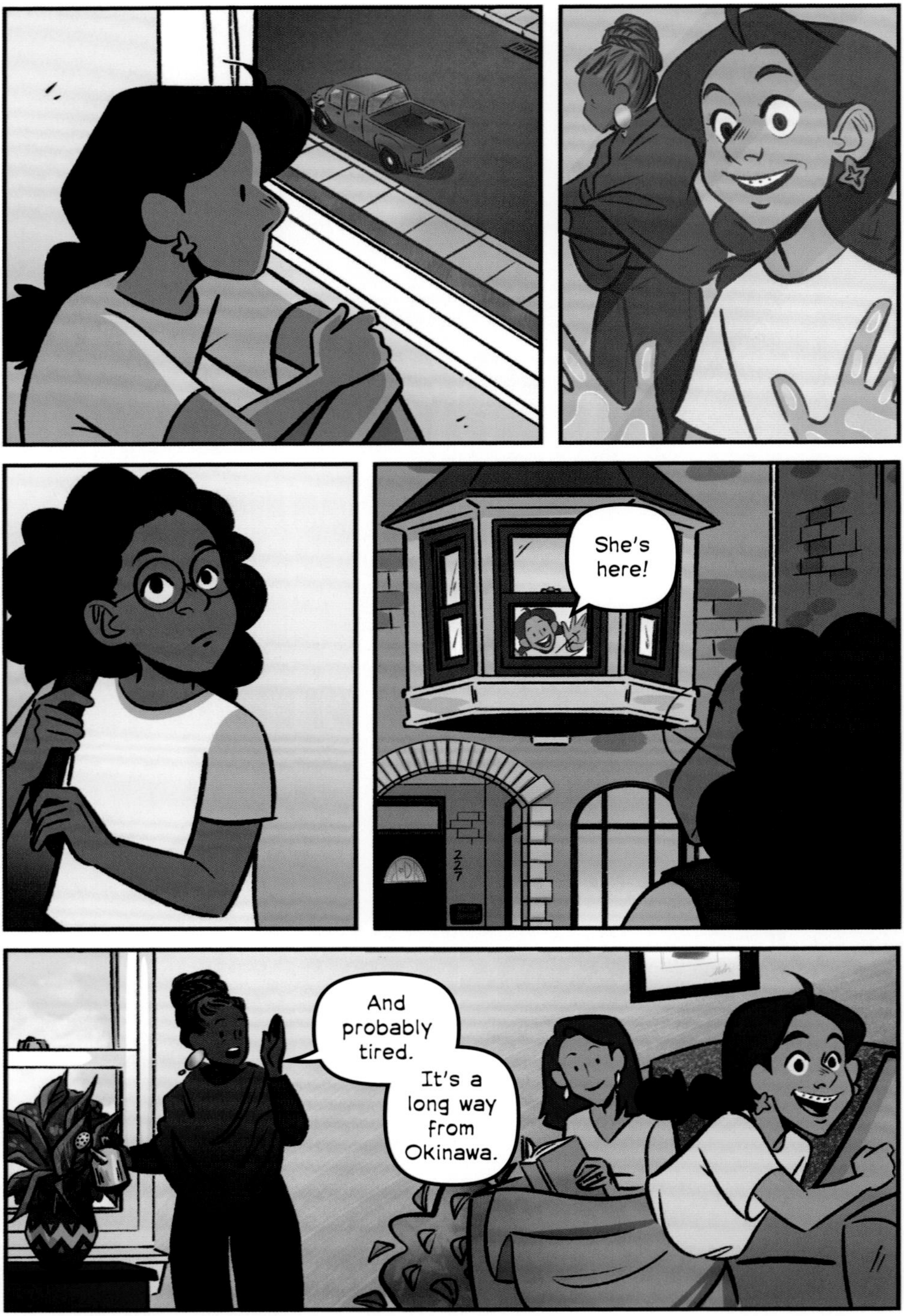
She's here!
And probably tired.
It's a long way from Okinawa.

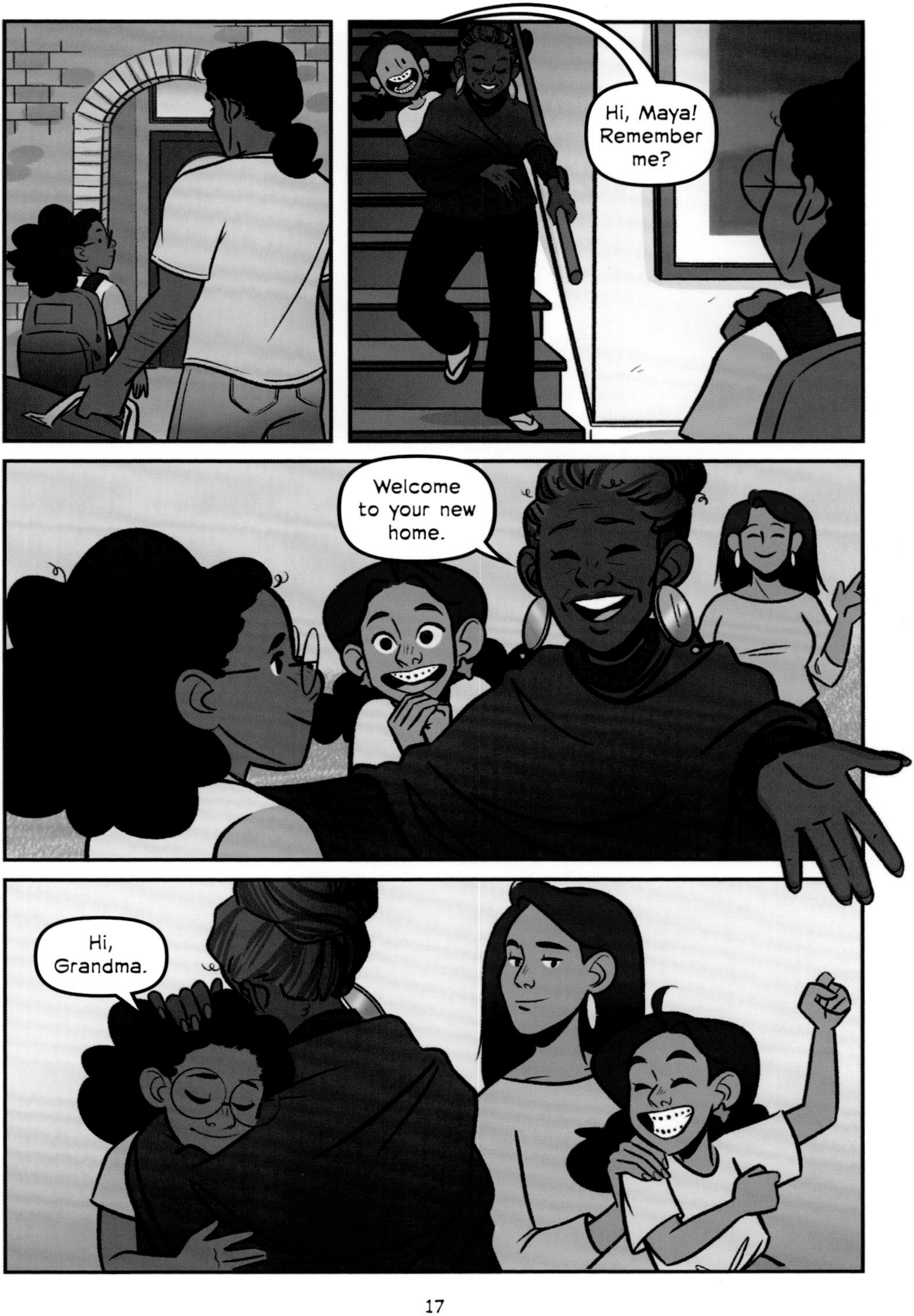
Hi, Maya! Remember me?
Welcome to your new home.
Hi, Grandma.

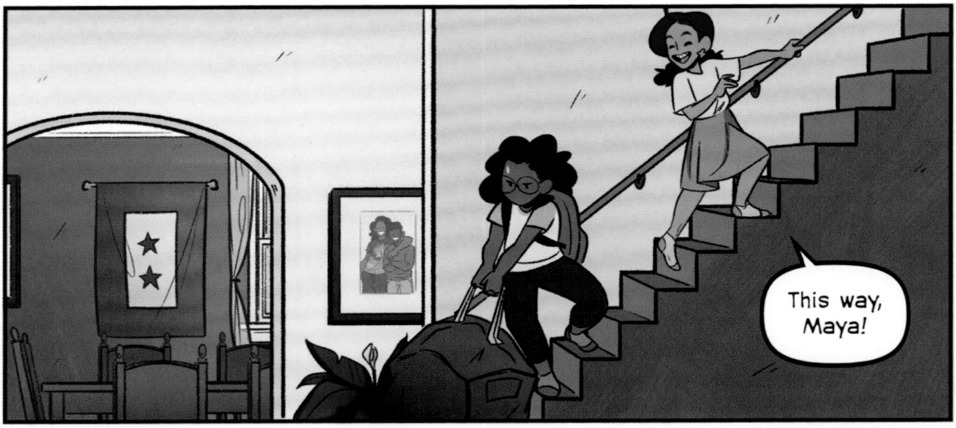
This way, Maya!

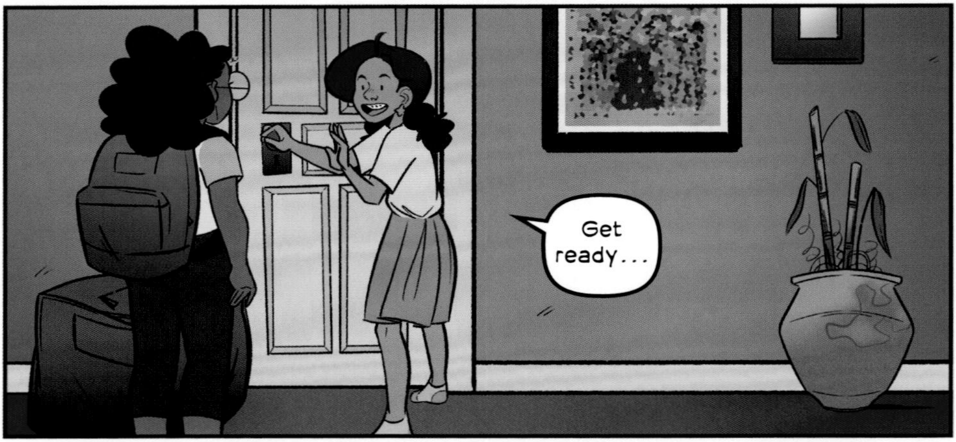
Get ready...

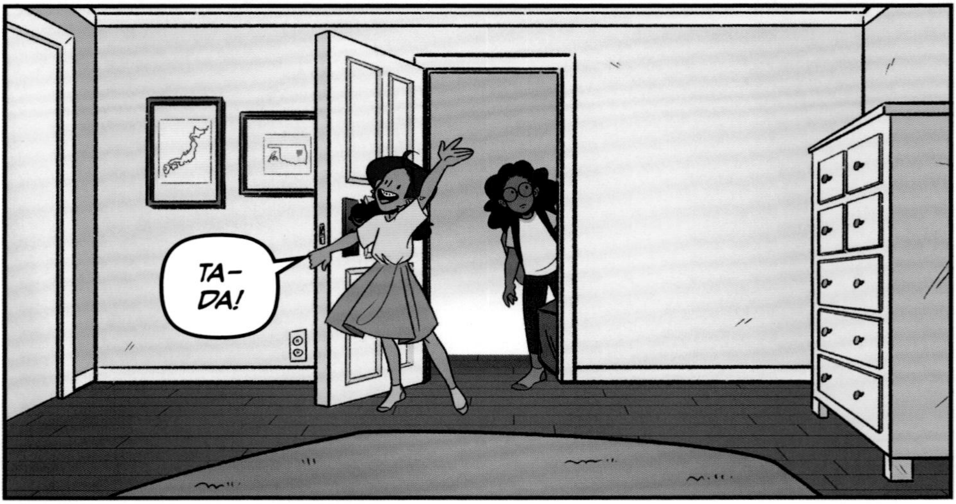
TA-DA!

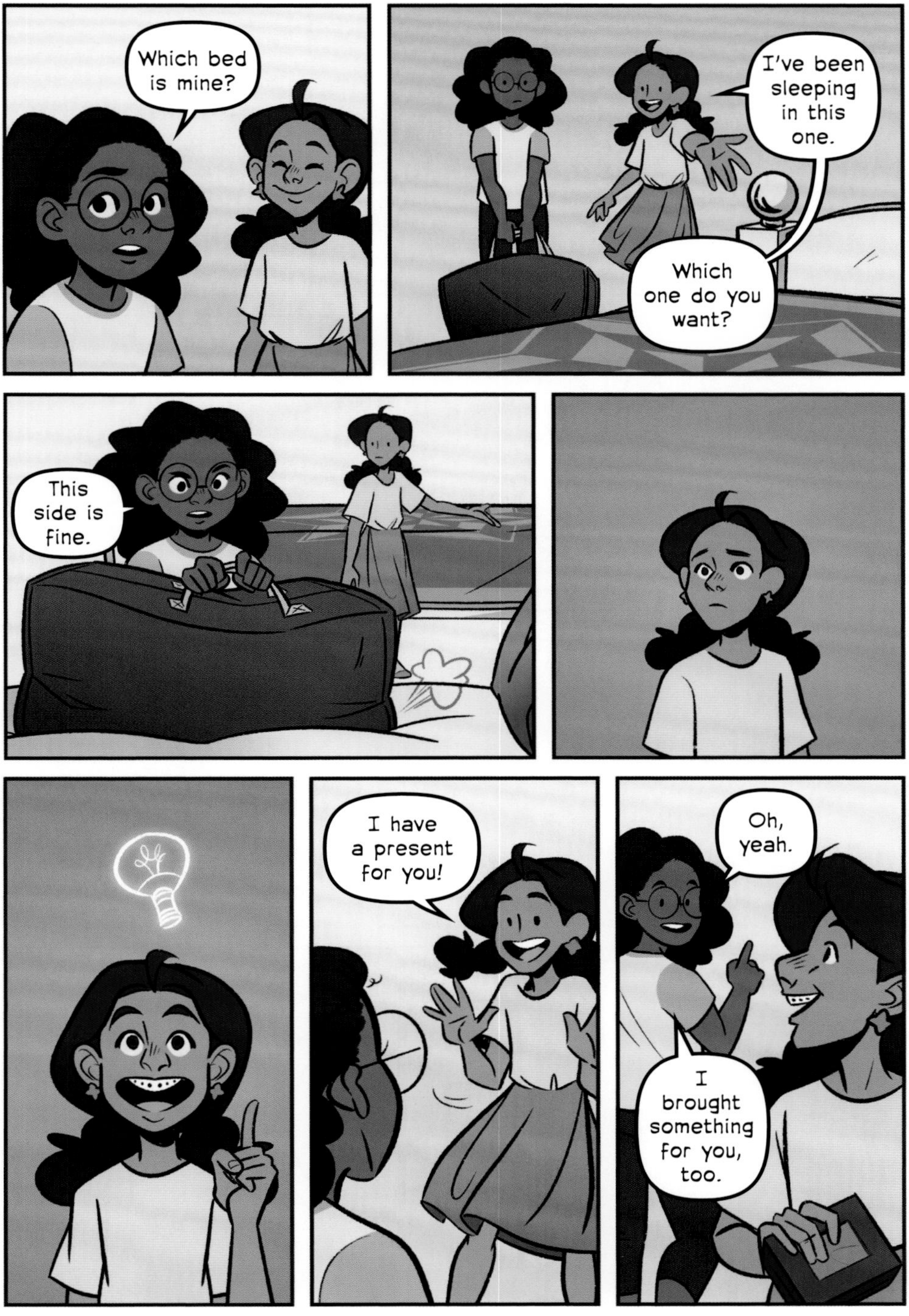
Which bed is mine?
I've been sleeping in this one.
Which one do you want?
This side is fine.
I have a present for you!
Oh, yeah.
I brought something for you, too.

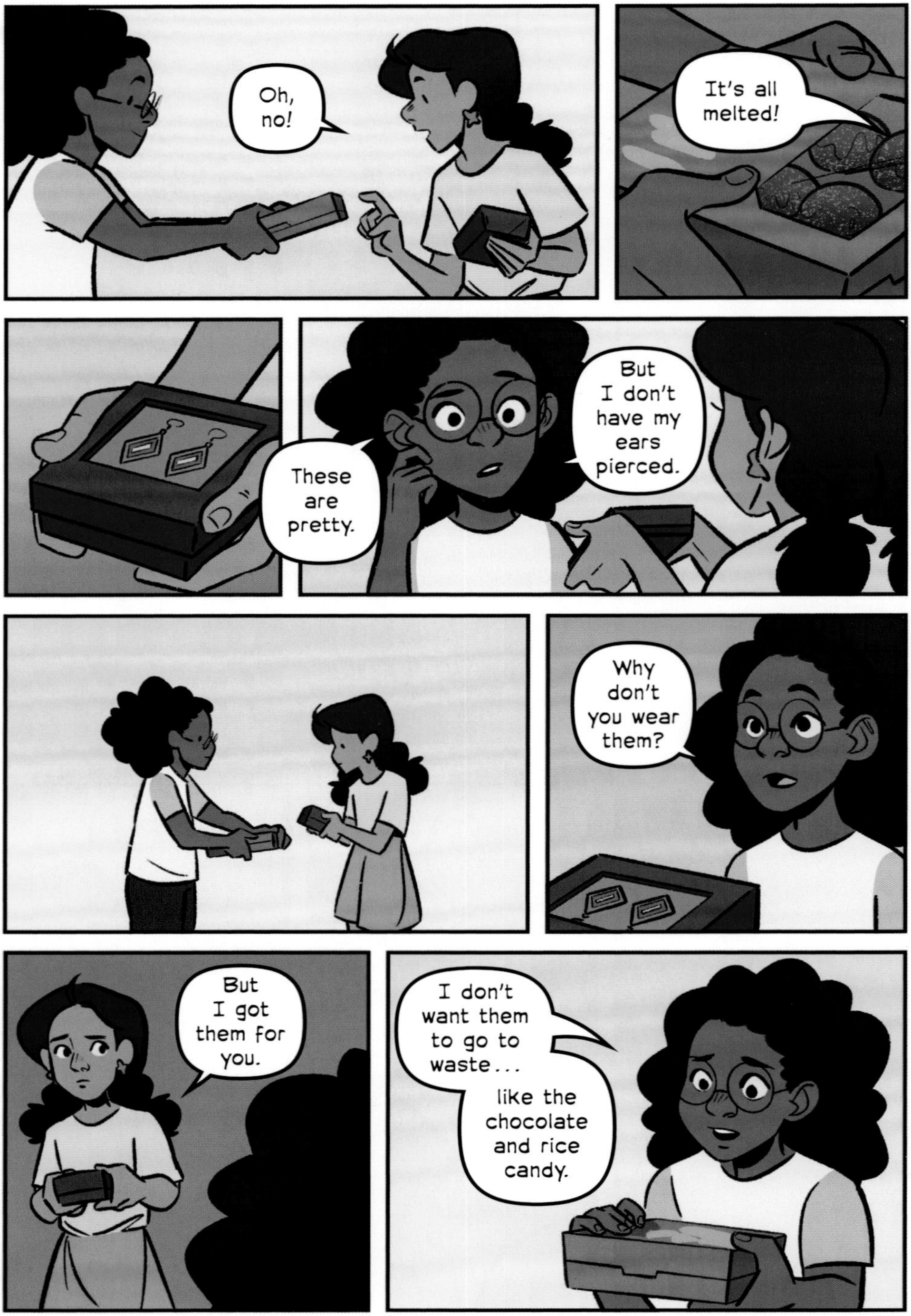
Oh, no!
It's all melted!
These are pretty.
But I don't have my ears pierced.
Why don't you wear them?
But I got them for you.
I don't want them to go to waste...
like the chocolate and rice candy.

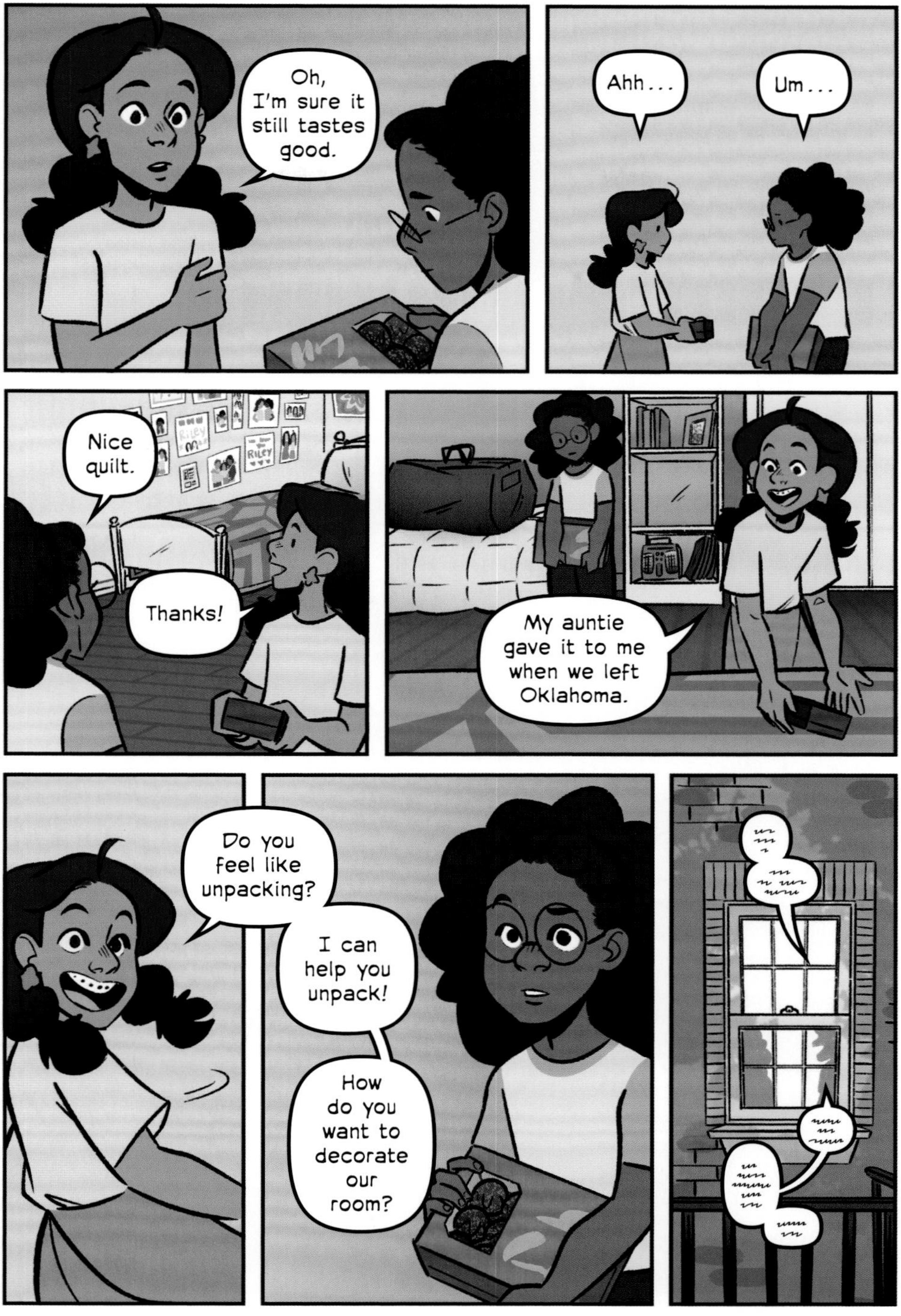
Oh, I'm sure it still tastes good.
Ahh...
Um...
Nice quilt.
Thanks!
My auntie gave it to me when we left Oklahoma.
Do you feel like unpacking?
I can help you unpack!
How do you want to decorate our room?

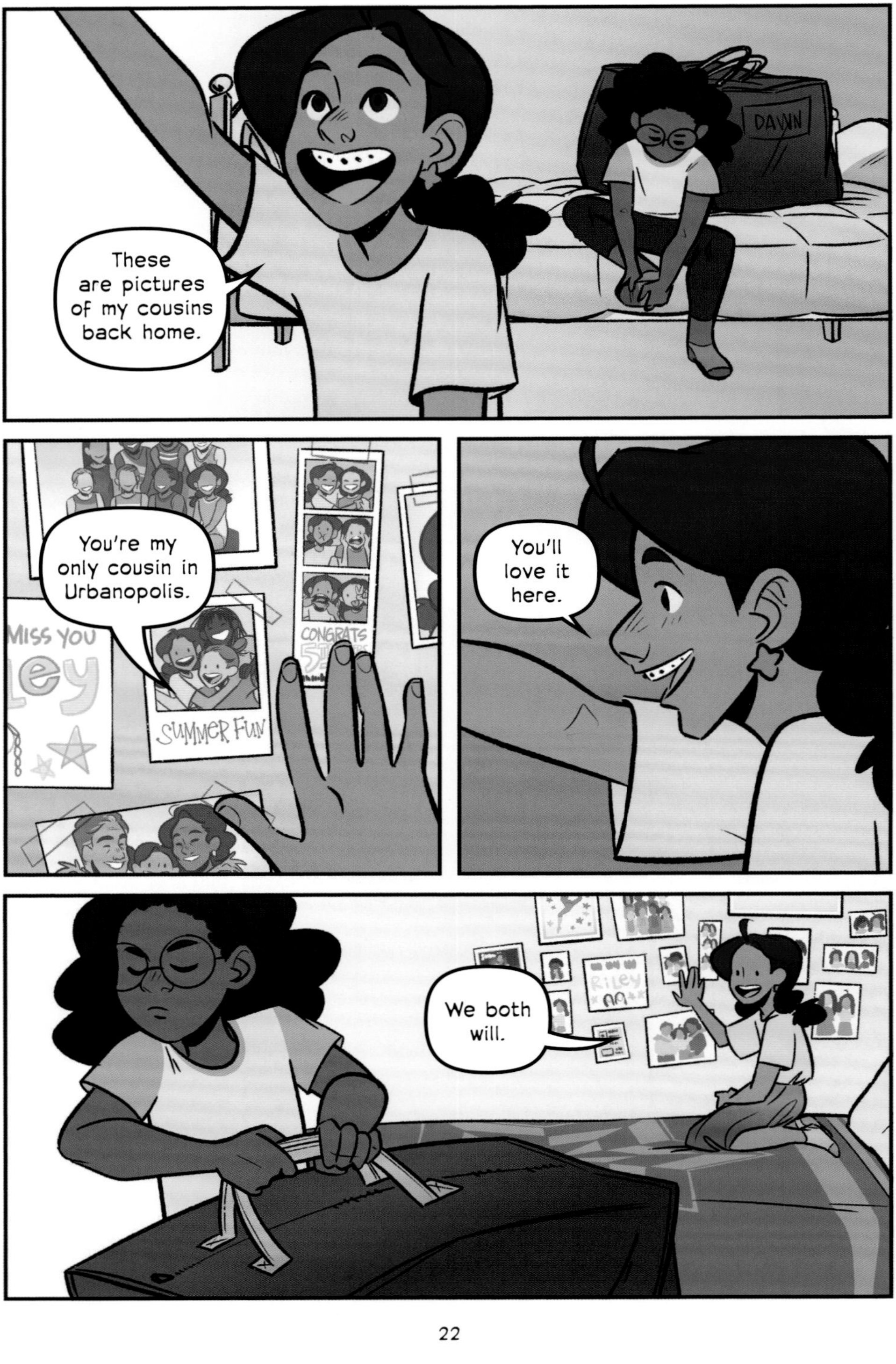
DAWN
These are pictures of my cousins back home.
You're my only cousin in Urbanopolis.
MISS YOU
SUMMER FUN
CONGRATS
You'll love it here.
Riley
We both will.

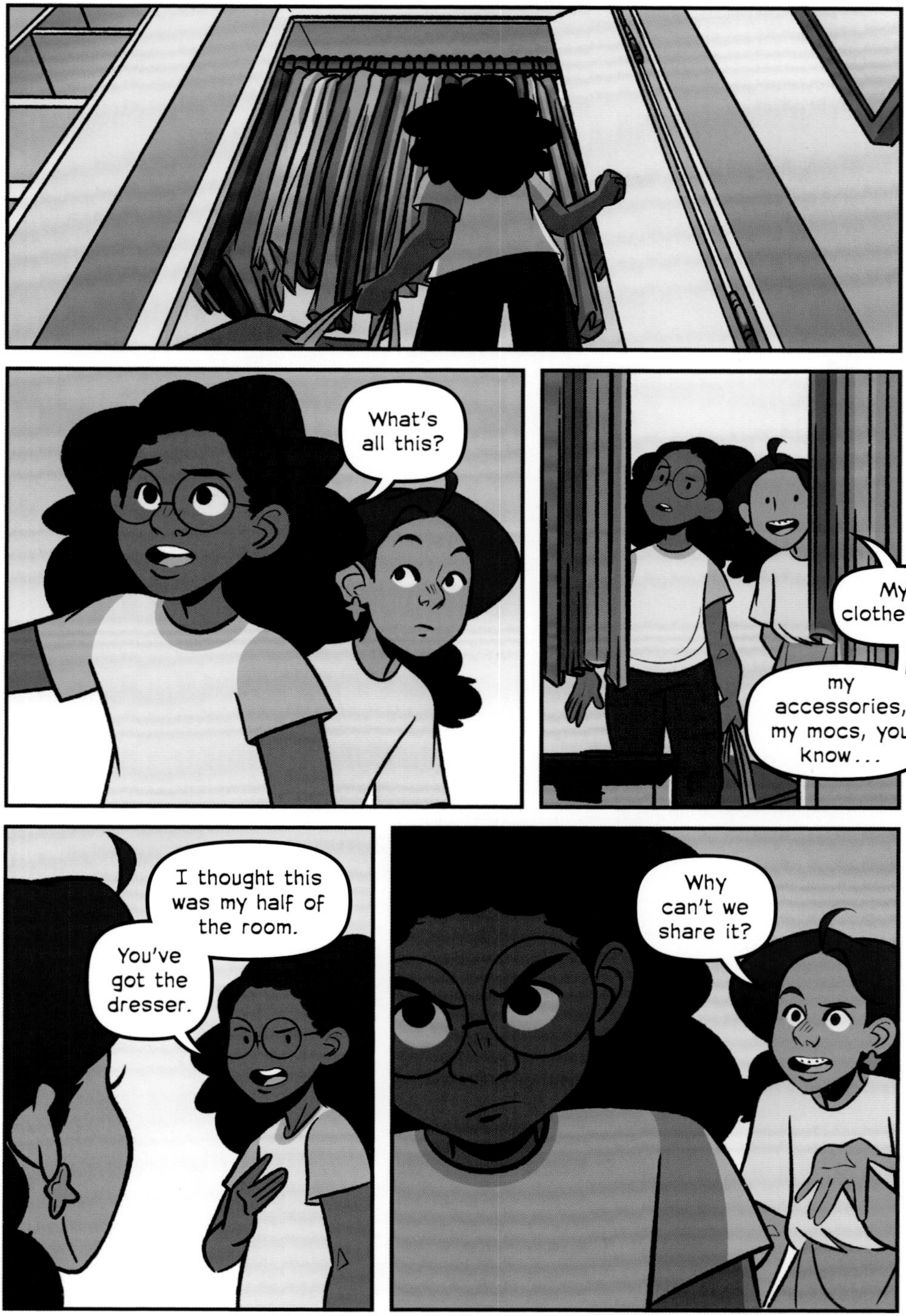
What's all this?
My clothes...
my accessories, my mocs, you know...
I thought this was my half of the room.
You've got the dresser.
Why can't we share it?

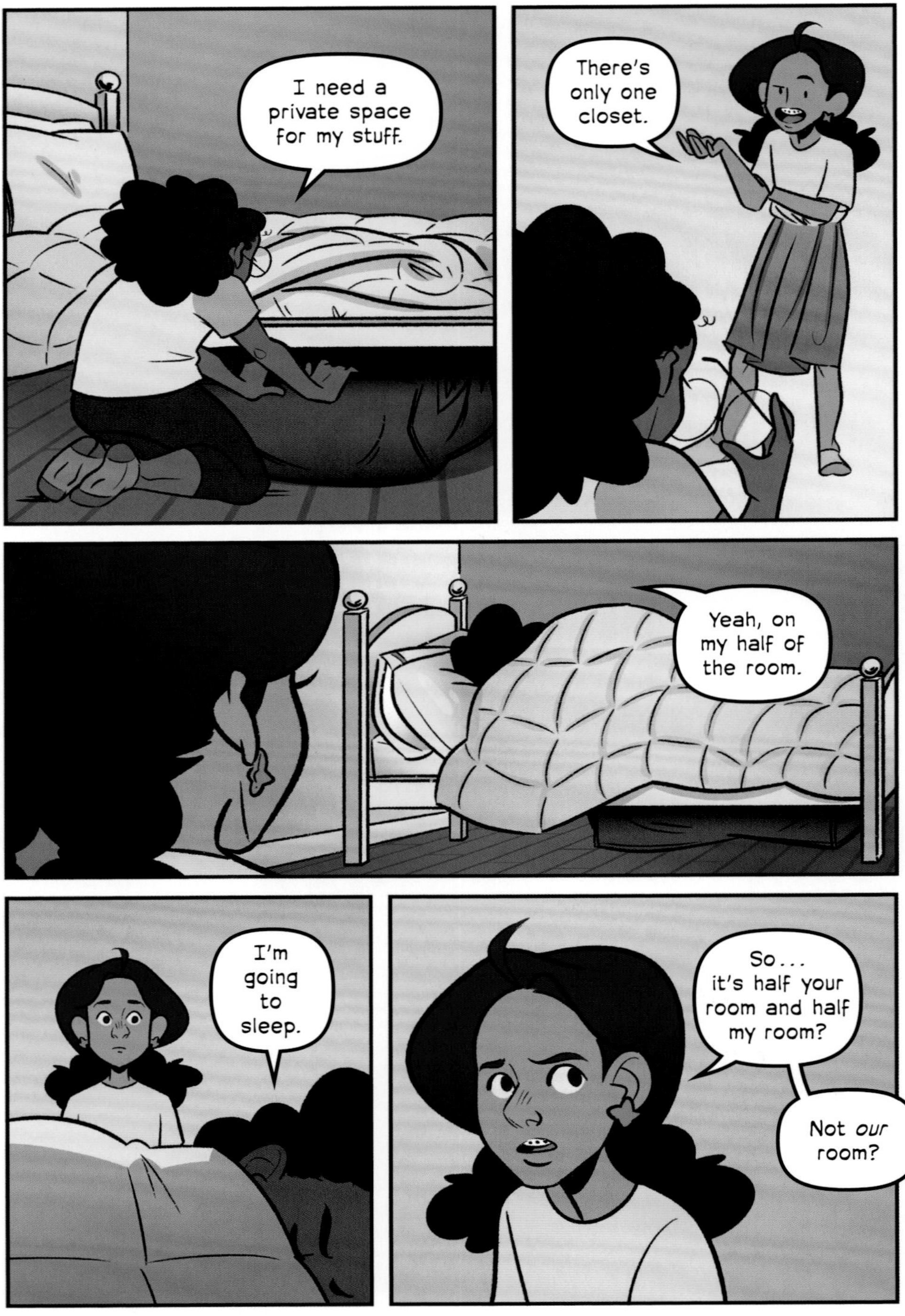
I need a private space for my stuff.
There's only one closet.
Yeah, on my half of the room.
I'm going to sleep.
So... it's half your room and half my room?
Not *our* room?

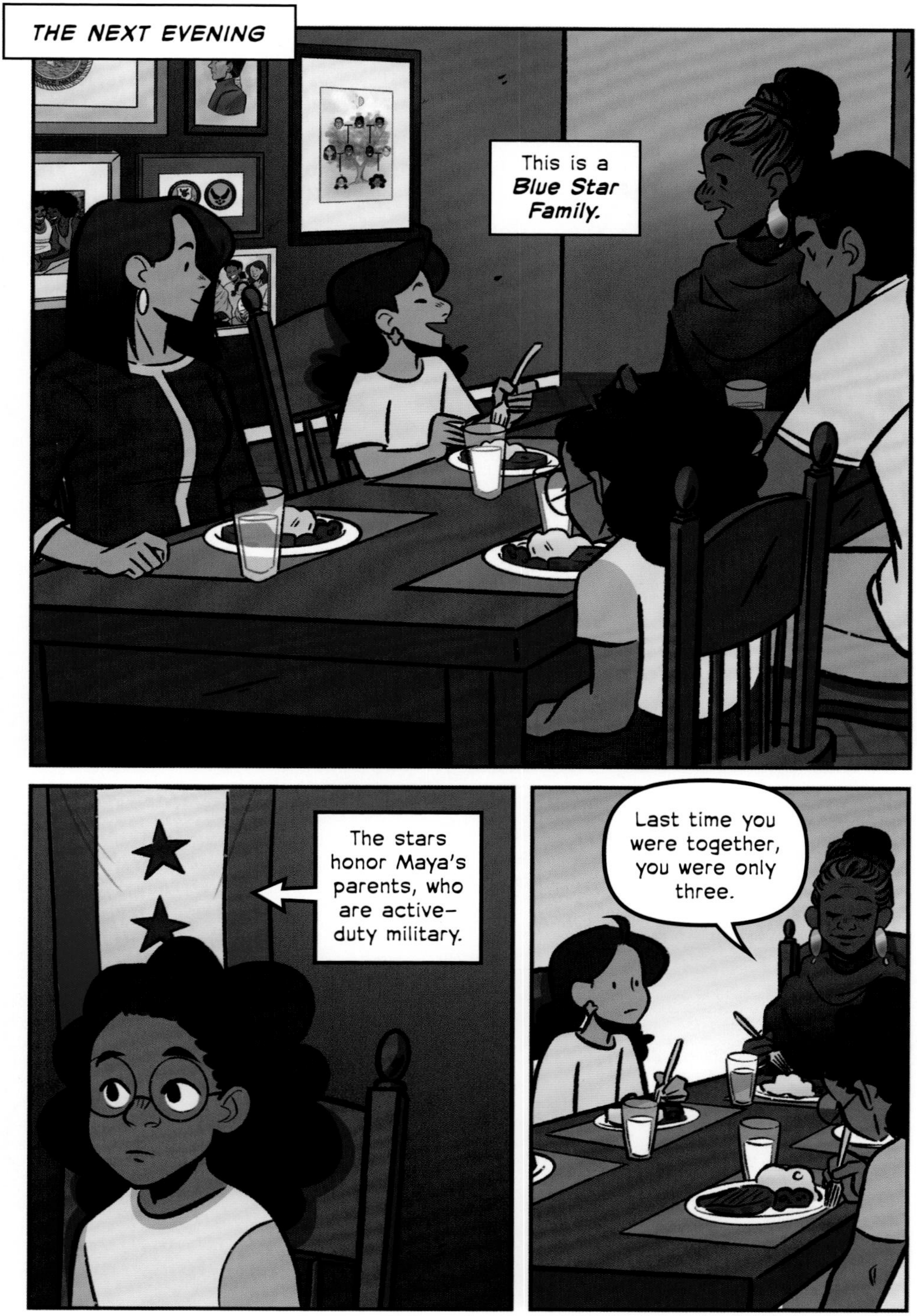
THE NEXT EVENING
This is a Blue Star Family.
The stars honor Maya's parents, who are active-duty military.
Last time you were together, you were only three.

Y'all just loved each other.
Remember?
No.
I guess it's time to make some new memories.
Yeah.

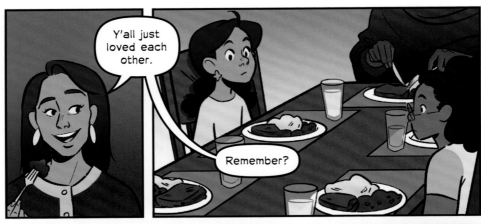

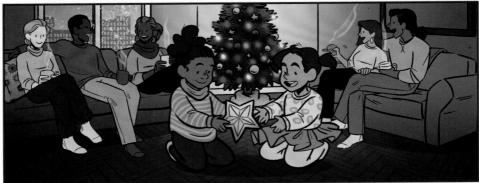

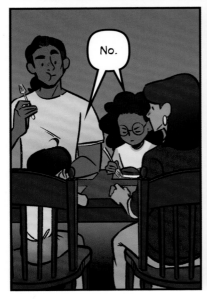

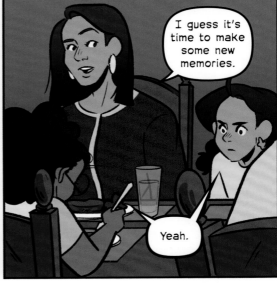

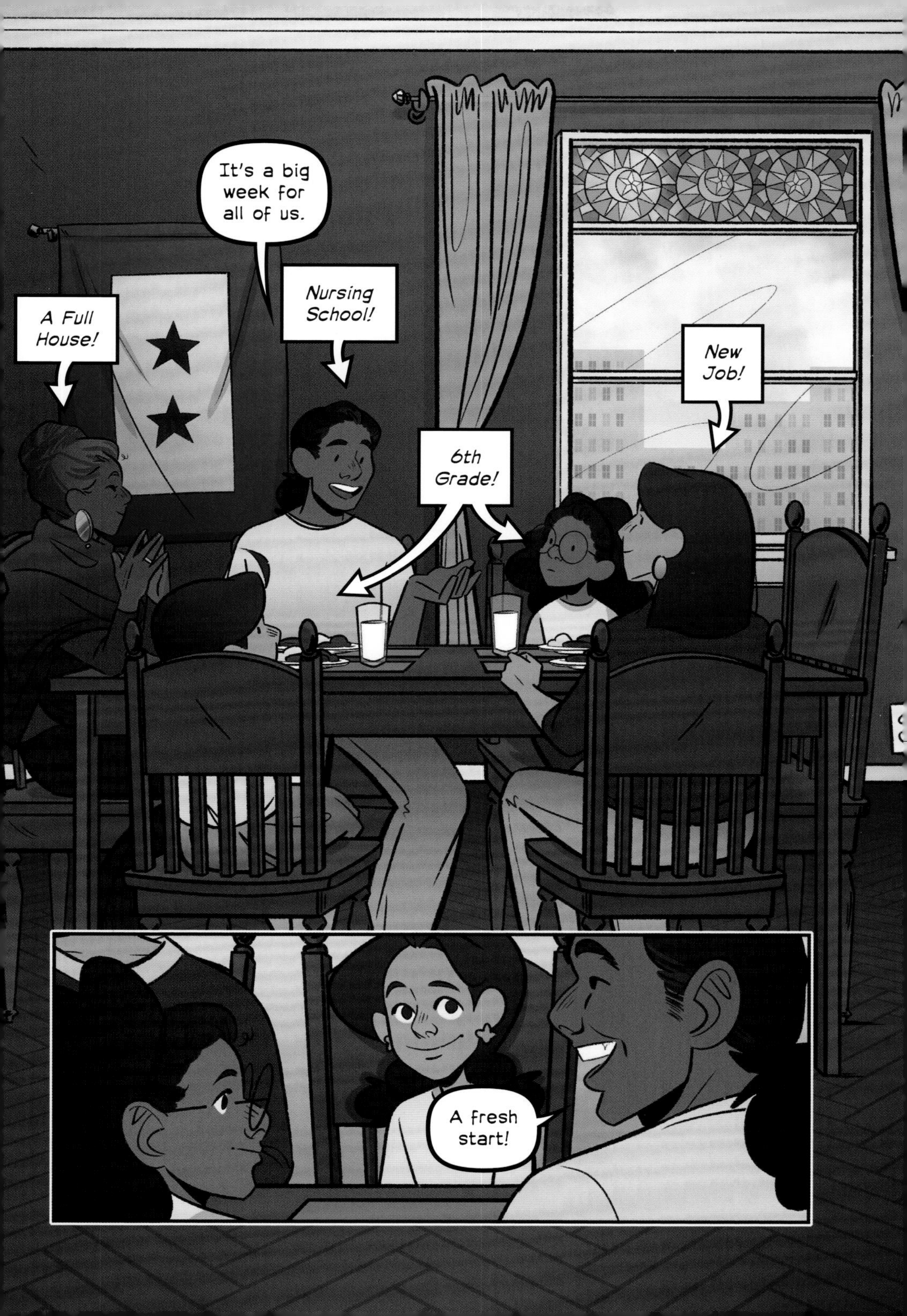
It's a big week for all of us.
A Full House!
Nursing School!
6th Grade!
New Job!
A fresh start!

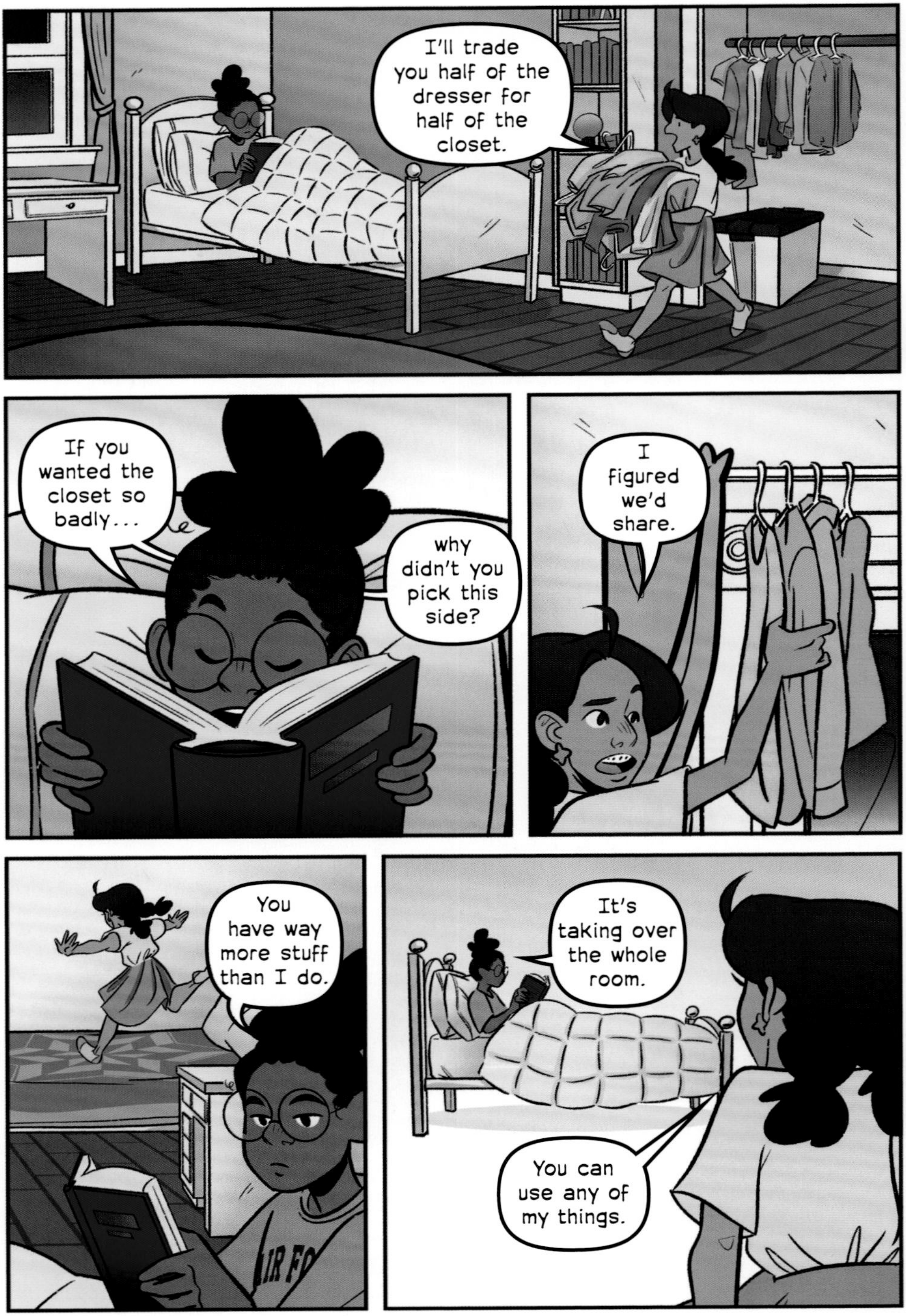
I'll trade you half of the dresser for half of the closet.
If you wanted the closet so badly...
why didn't you pick this side?
I figured we'd share.
You have way more stuff than I do.
It's taking over the whole room.
You can use any of my things.

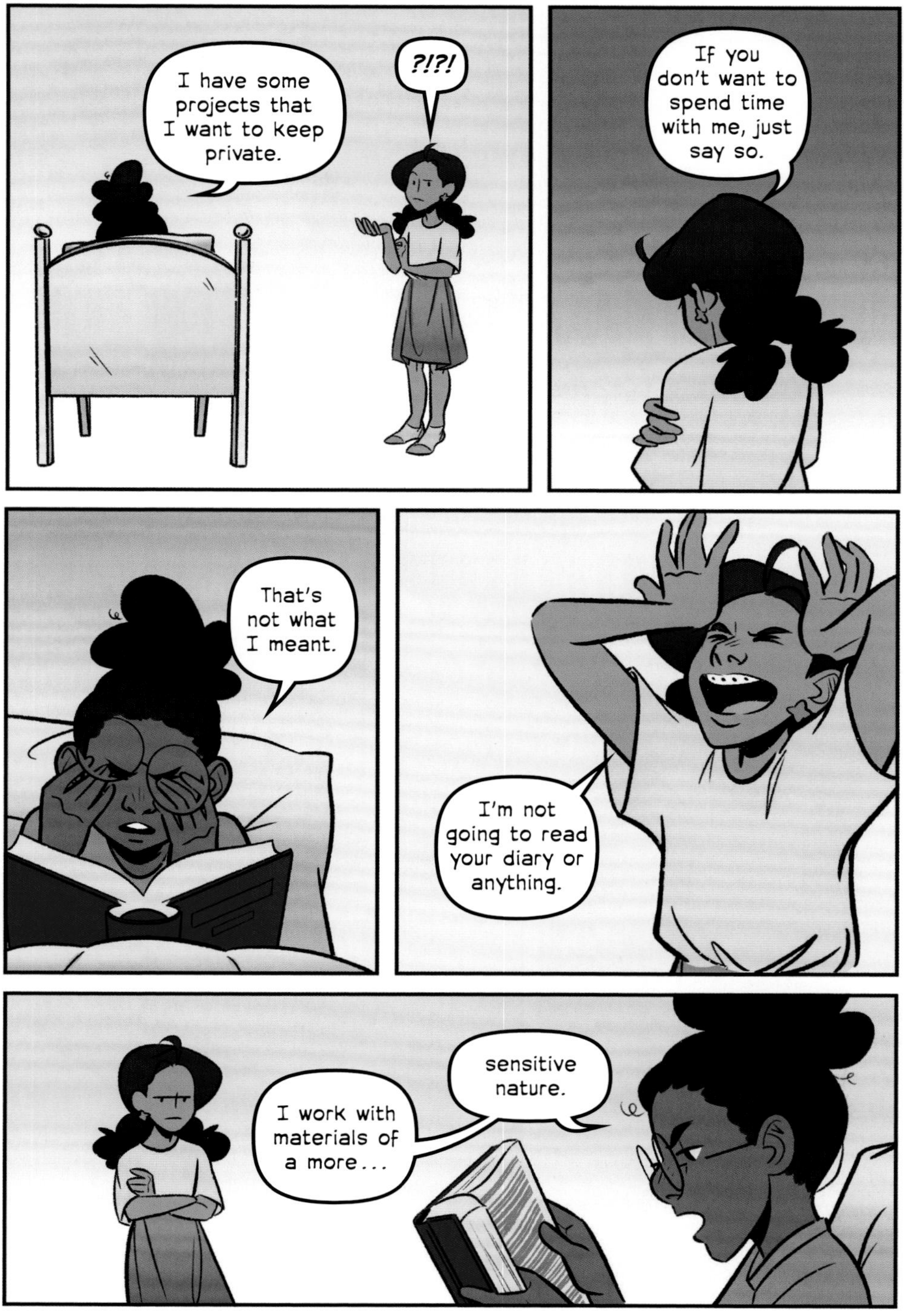
I have some projects that I want to keep private.
?!?!
If you don't want to spend time with me, just say so.
That's not what I meant.
I'm not going to read your diary or anything.
I work with materials of a more...
sensitive nature.

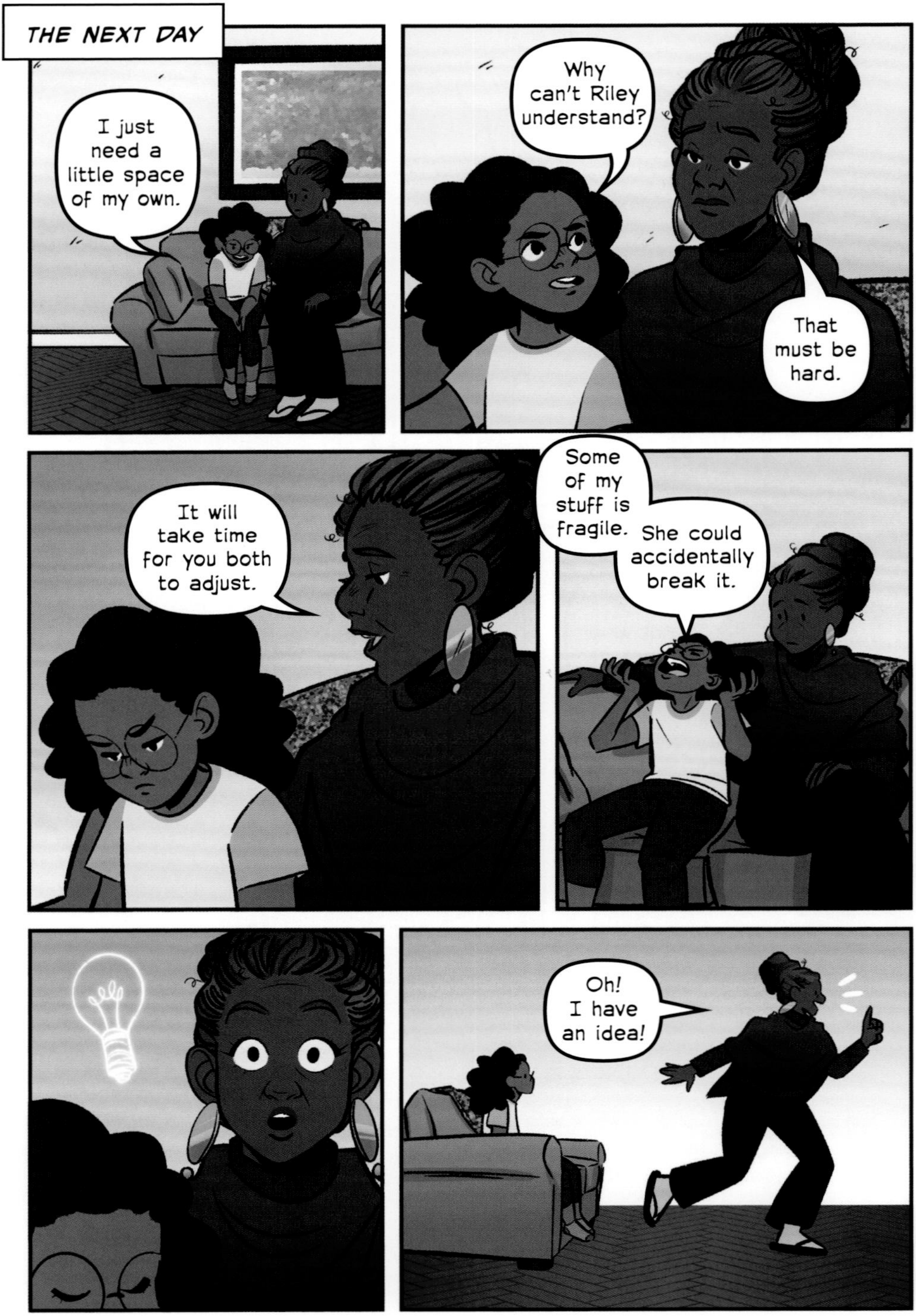
THE NEXT DAY
I just need a little space of my own.
Why can't Riley understand?
That must be hard.
It will take time for you both to adjust.
Some of my stuff is fragile.
She could accidentally break it.
Oh! I have an idea!

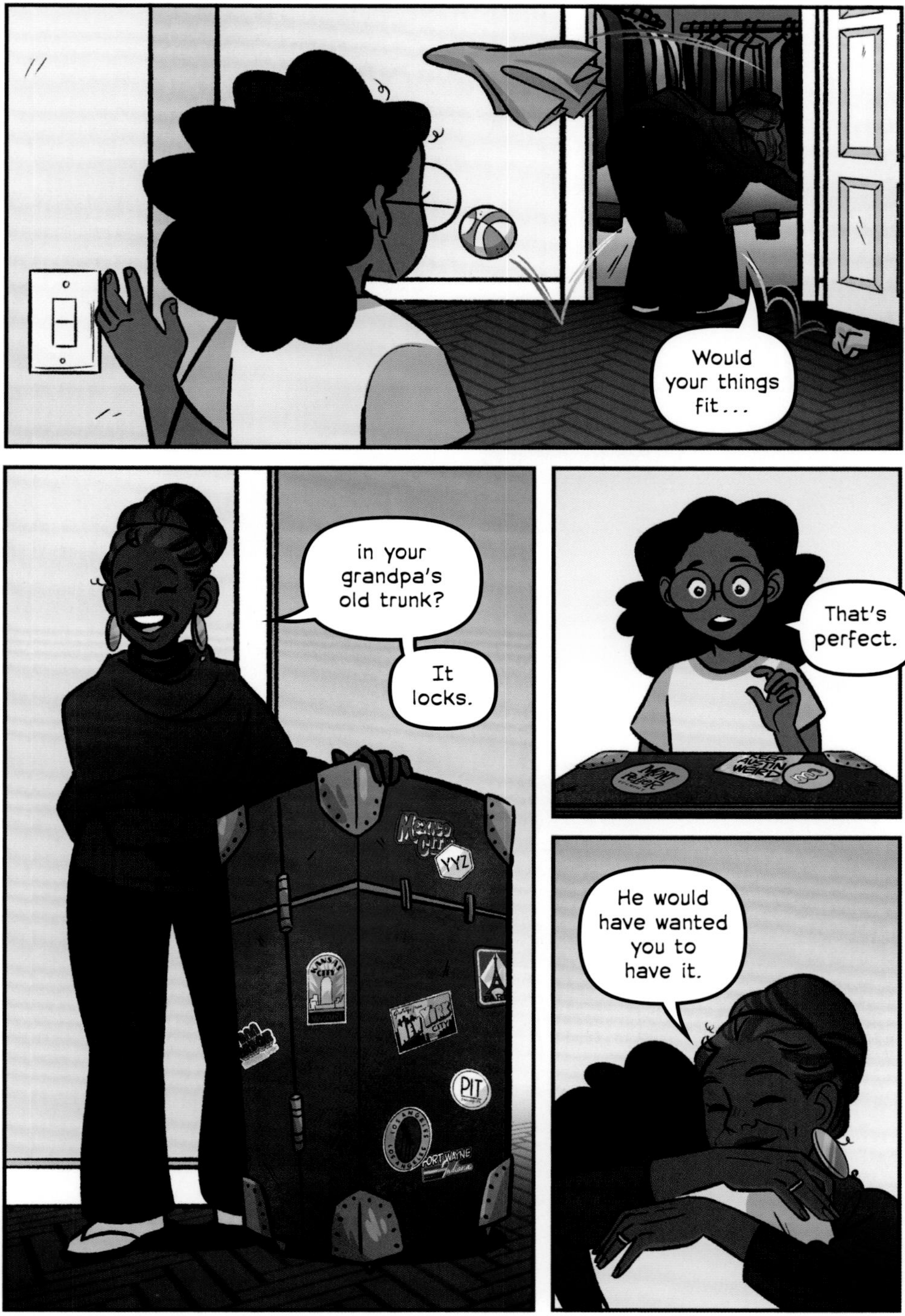
Would your things fit...
in your grandpa's old trunk?
It locks.
That's perfect.
He would have wanted you to have it.

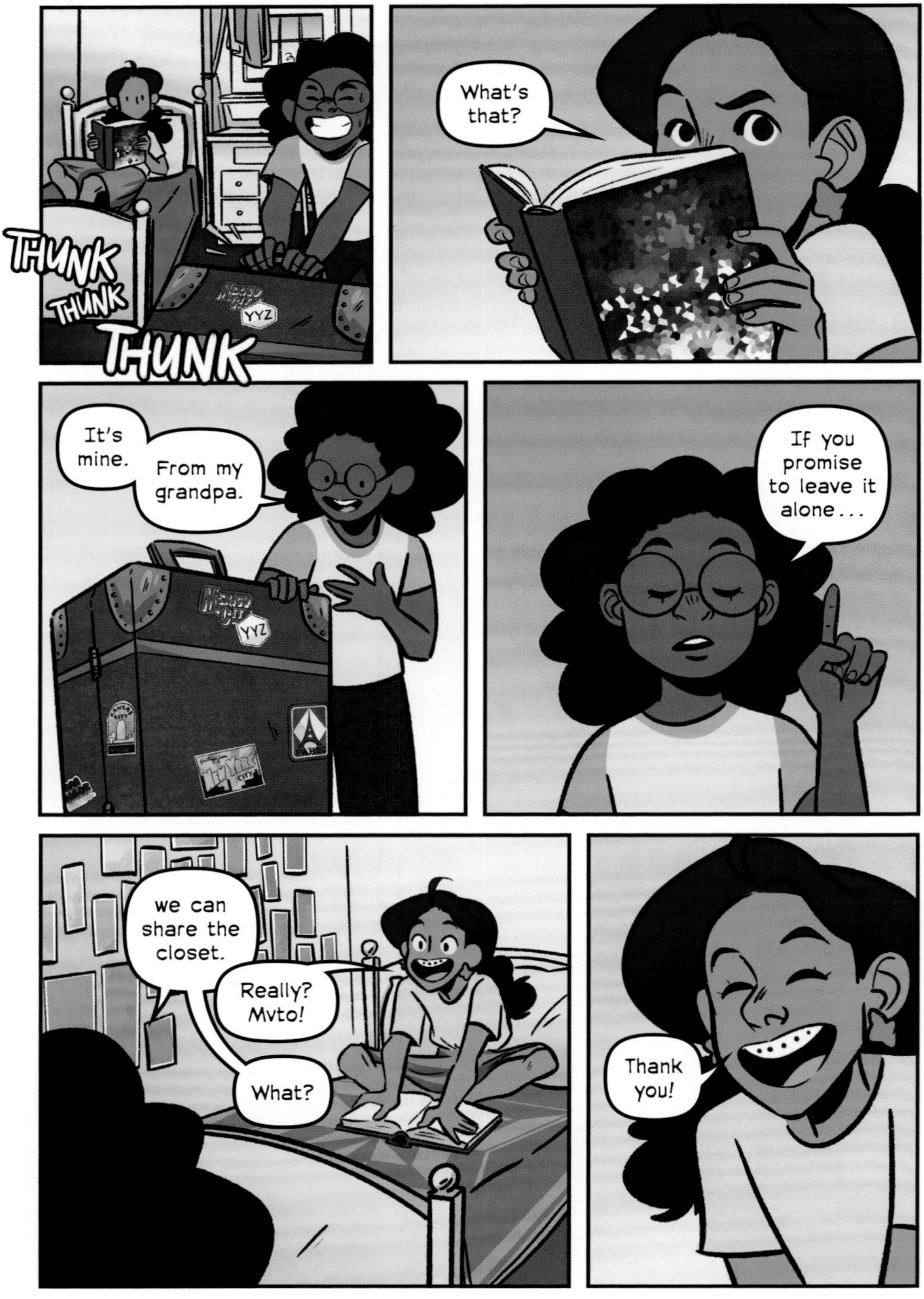
THUNK
THUNK
THUNK
What's that?
It's mine.
From my grandpa.
If you promise to leave it alone...
we can share the closet.
Really? Mvto!
What?
Thank you!

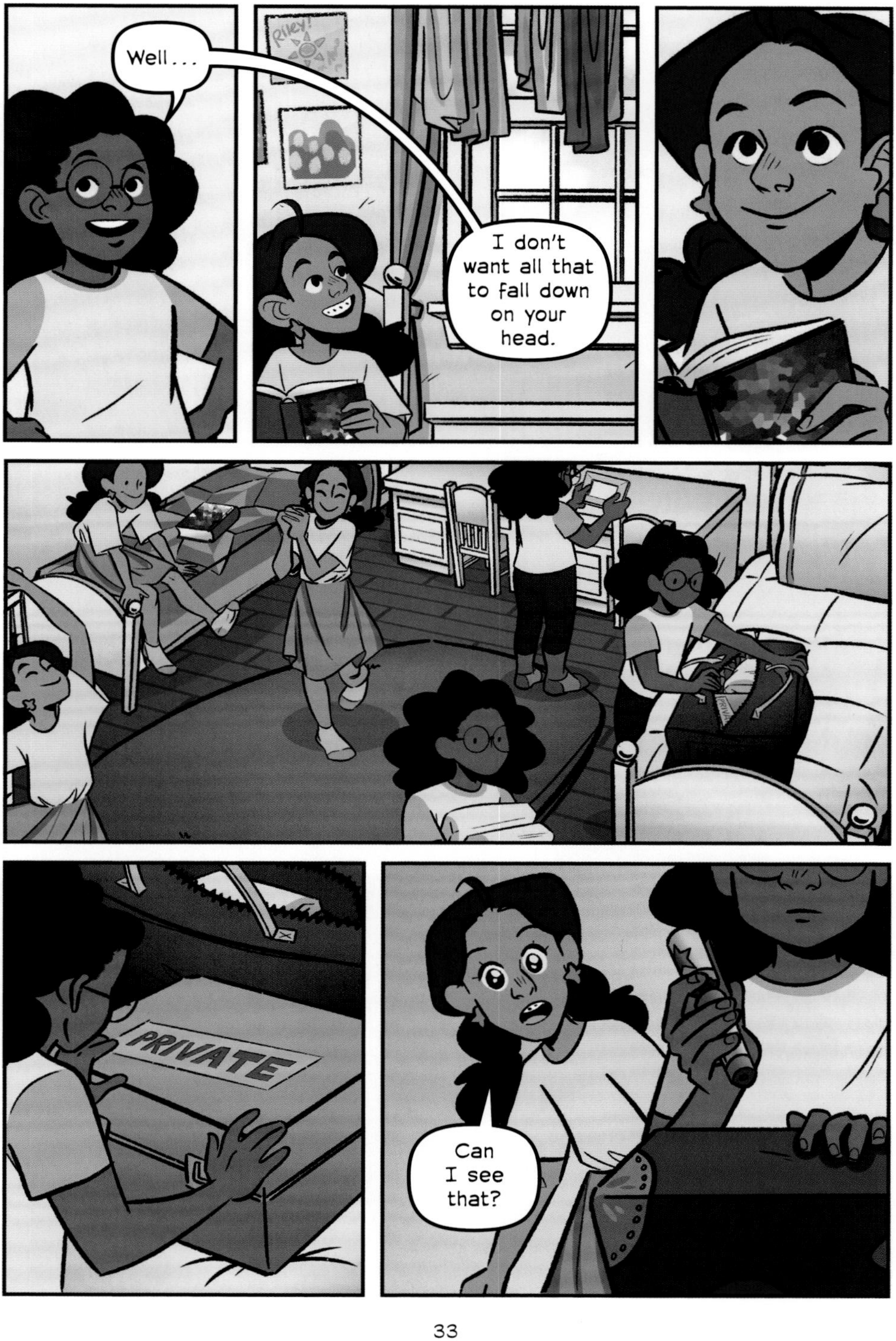
Well . . .
I don't want all that to fall down on your head.
Riley!
PRIVATE
Can I see that?

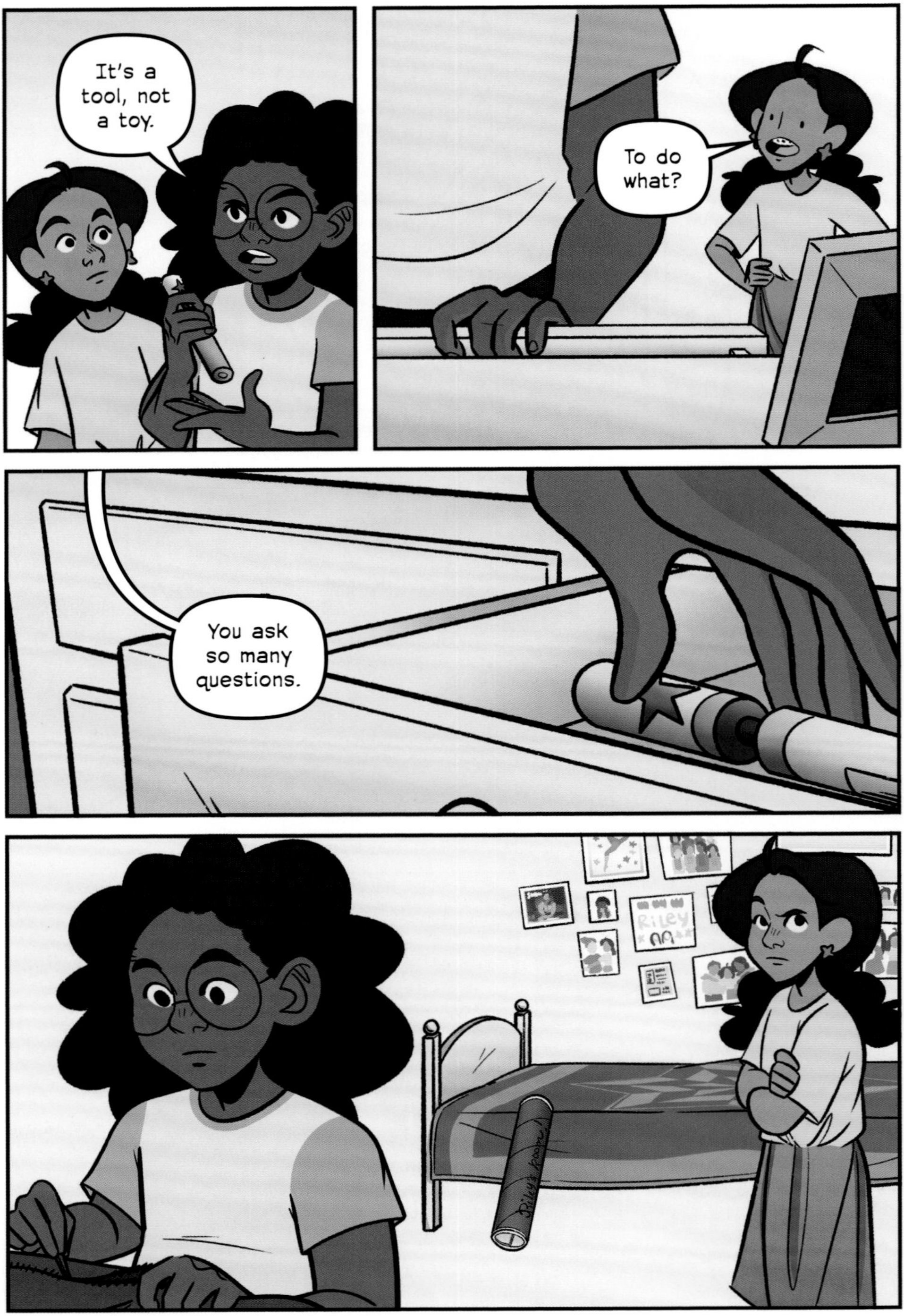
It's a tool, not a toy.
To do what?
You ask so many questions.
Riley

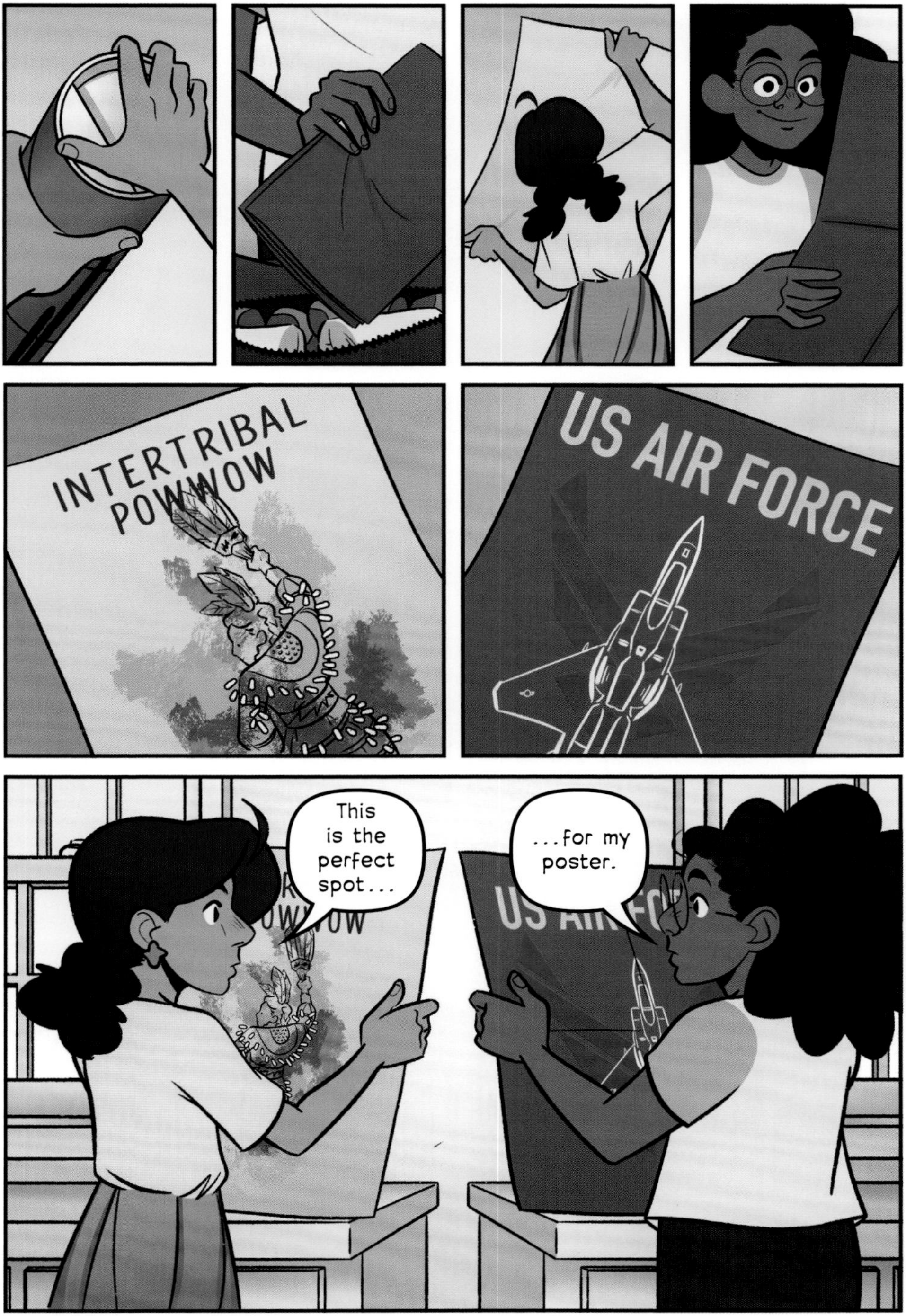
INTERTRIBAL POWWOW
US AIR FORCE
This is the perfect spot...
...for my poster.

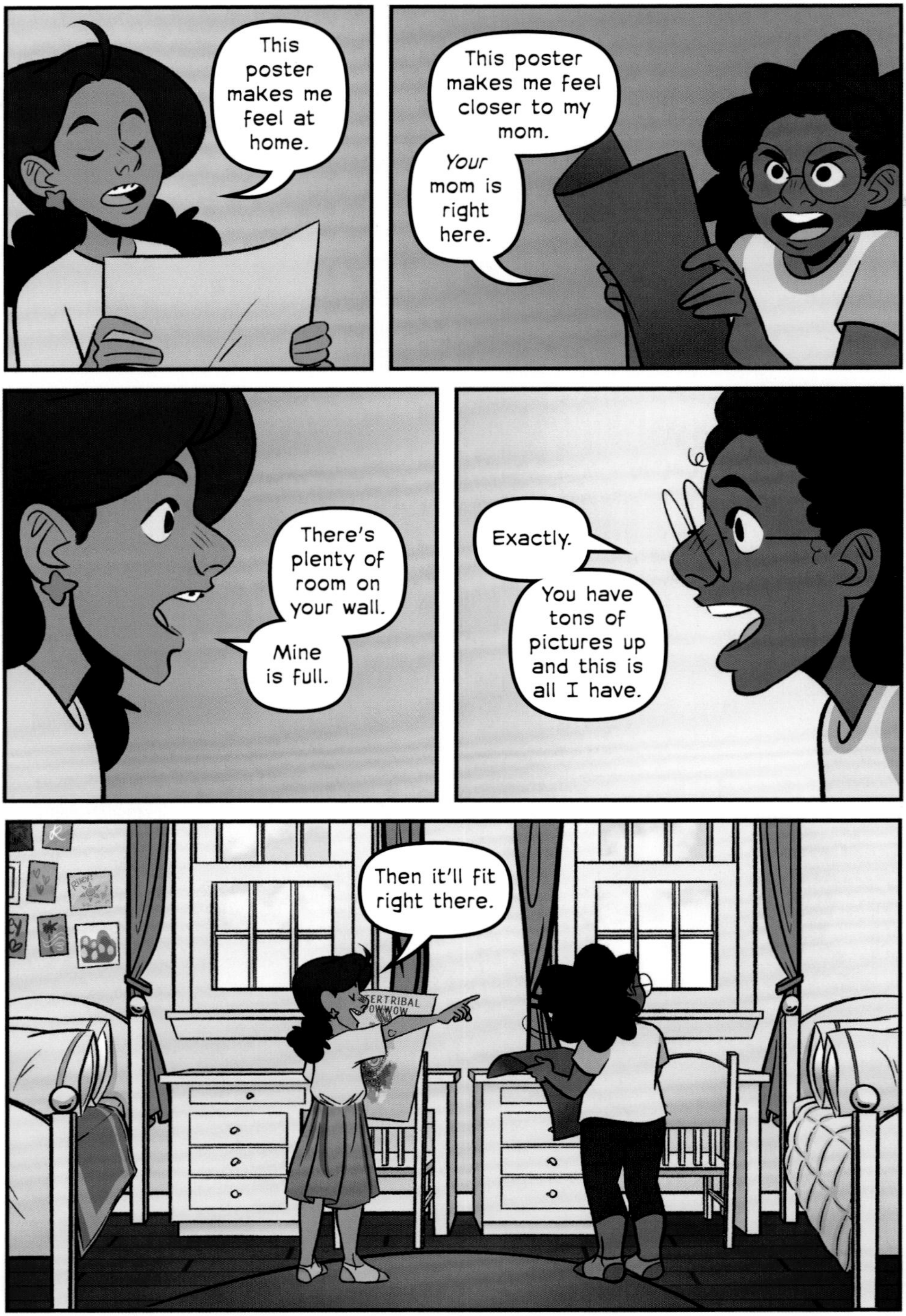
This poster makes me feel at home.
This poster makes me feel closer to my mom.
Your mom is right here.
There's plenty of room on your wall.
Mine is full.
Exactly.
You have tons of pictures up and this is all I have.
Then it'll fit right there.

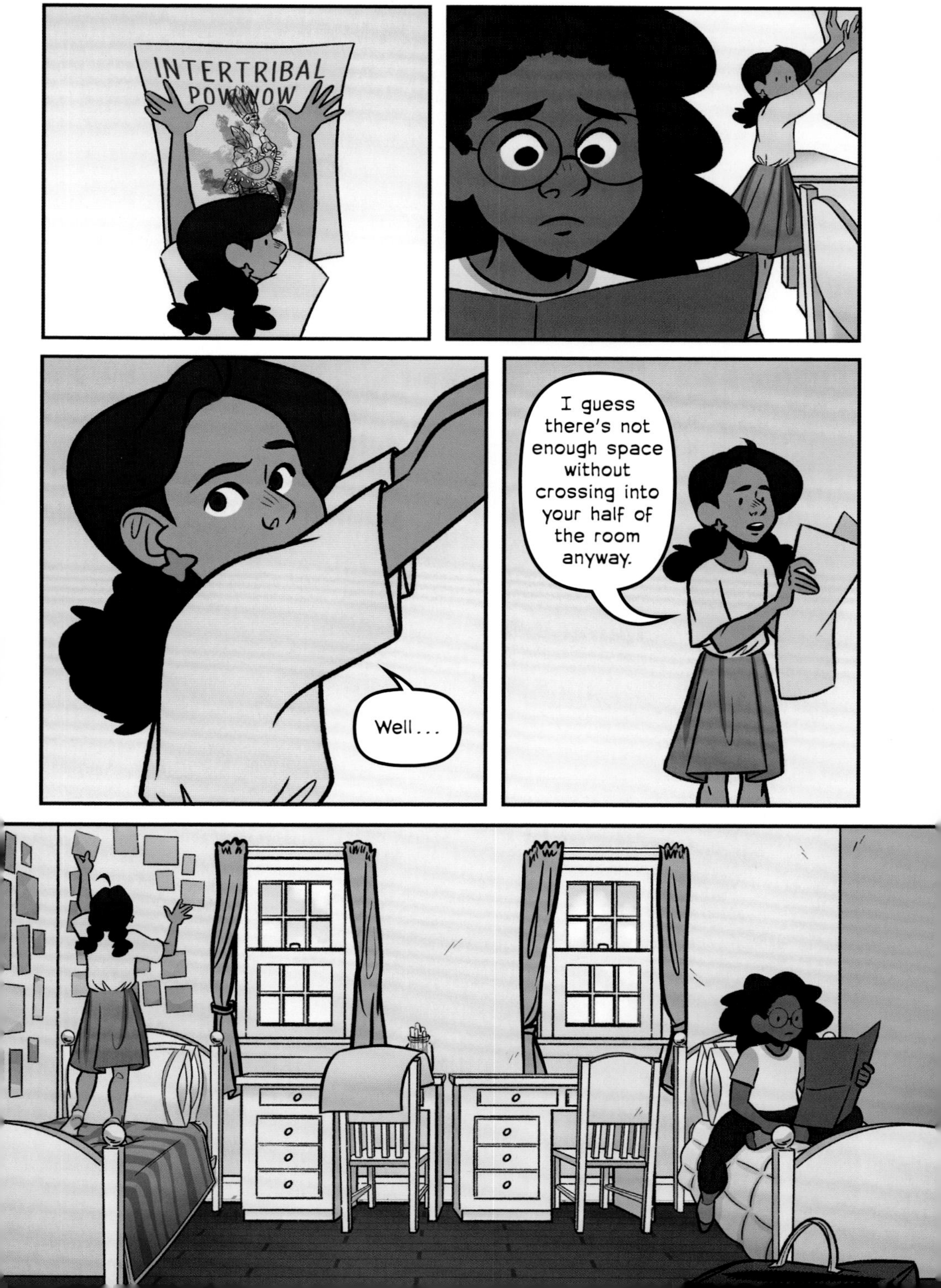
INTERTRIBAL POWWOW
Well . . .
I guess there's not enough space without crossing into your half of the room anyway.

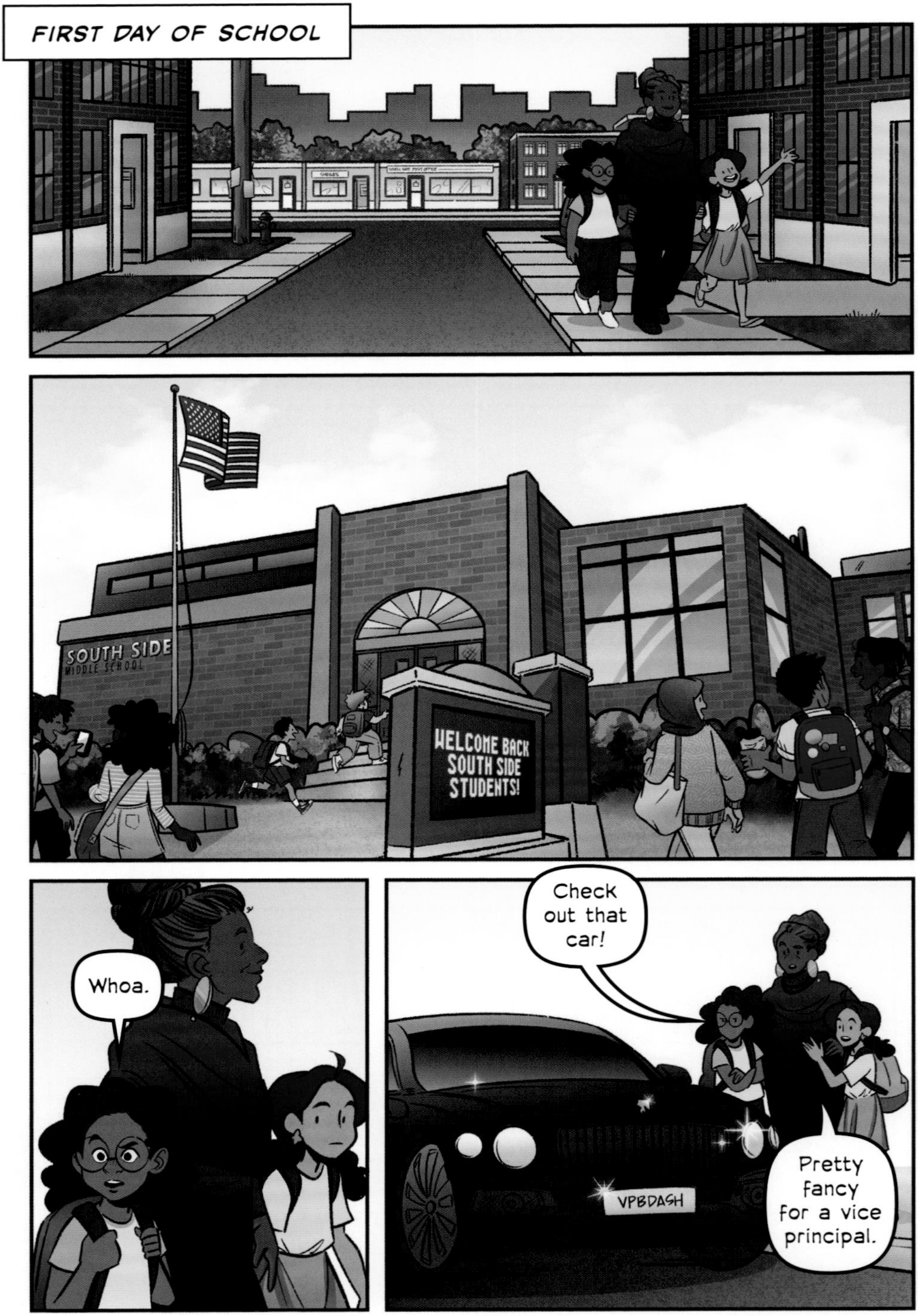
FIRST DAY OF SCHOOL
SOUTH SIDE MIDDLE SCHOOL
WELCOME BACK SOUTH SIDE STUDENTS!
Whoa.
Check out that car!
VPBDASH
Pretty fancy for a vice principal.

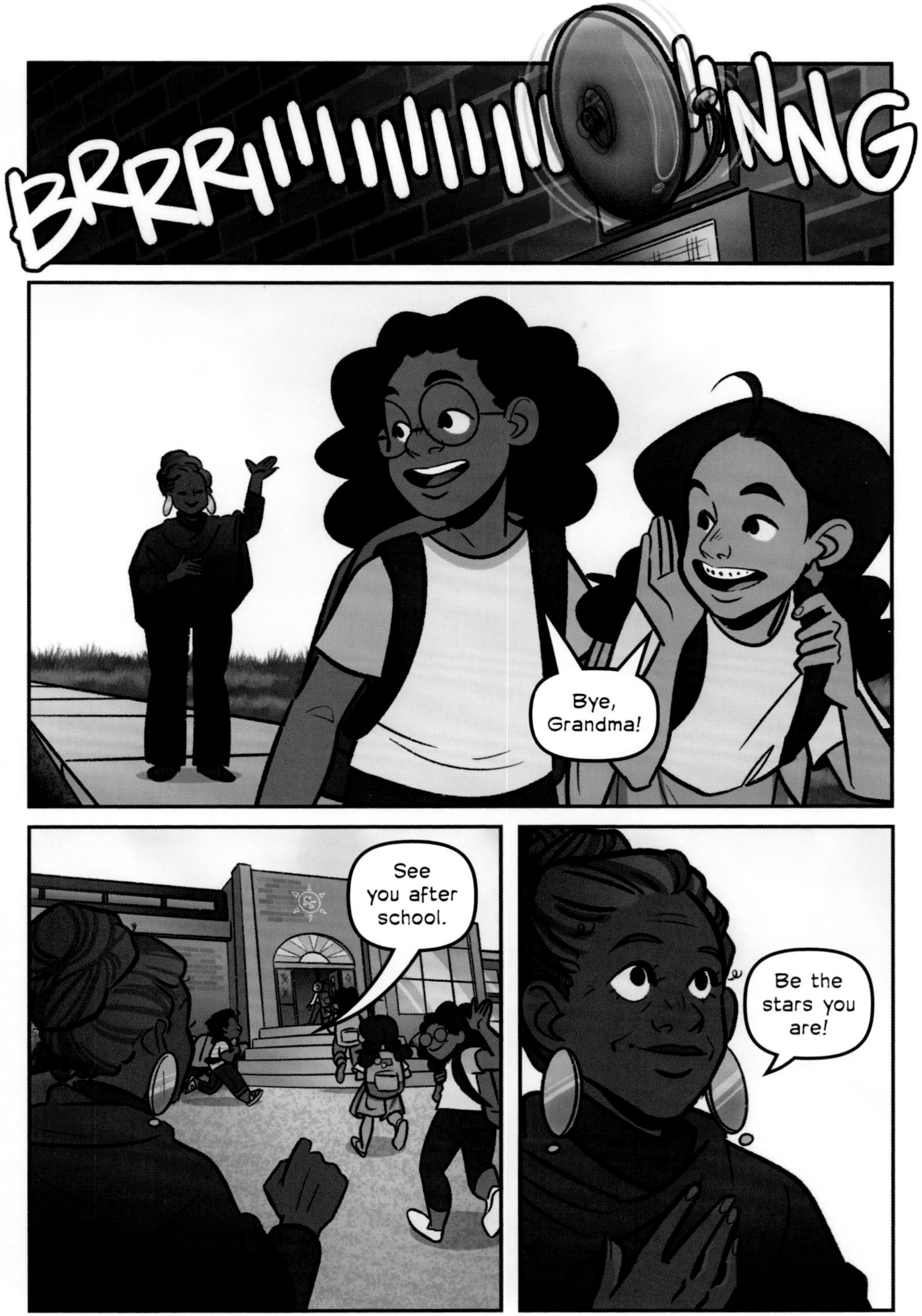
BRRRIIIIIIIIIIIIIIINNG
Bye, Grandma!
See you after school.
Be the stars you are!

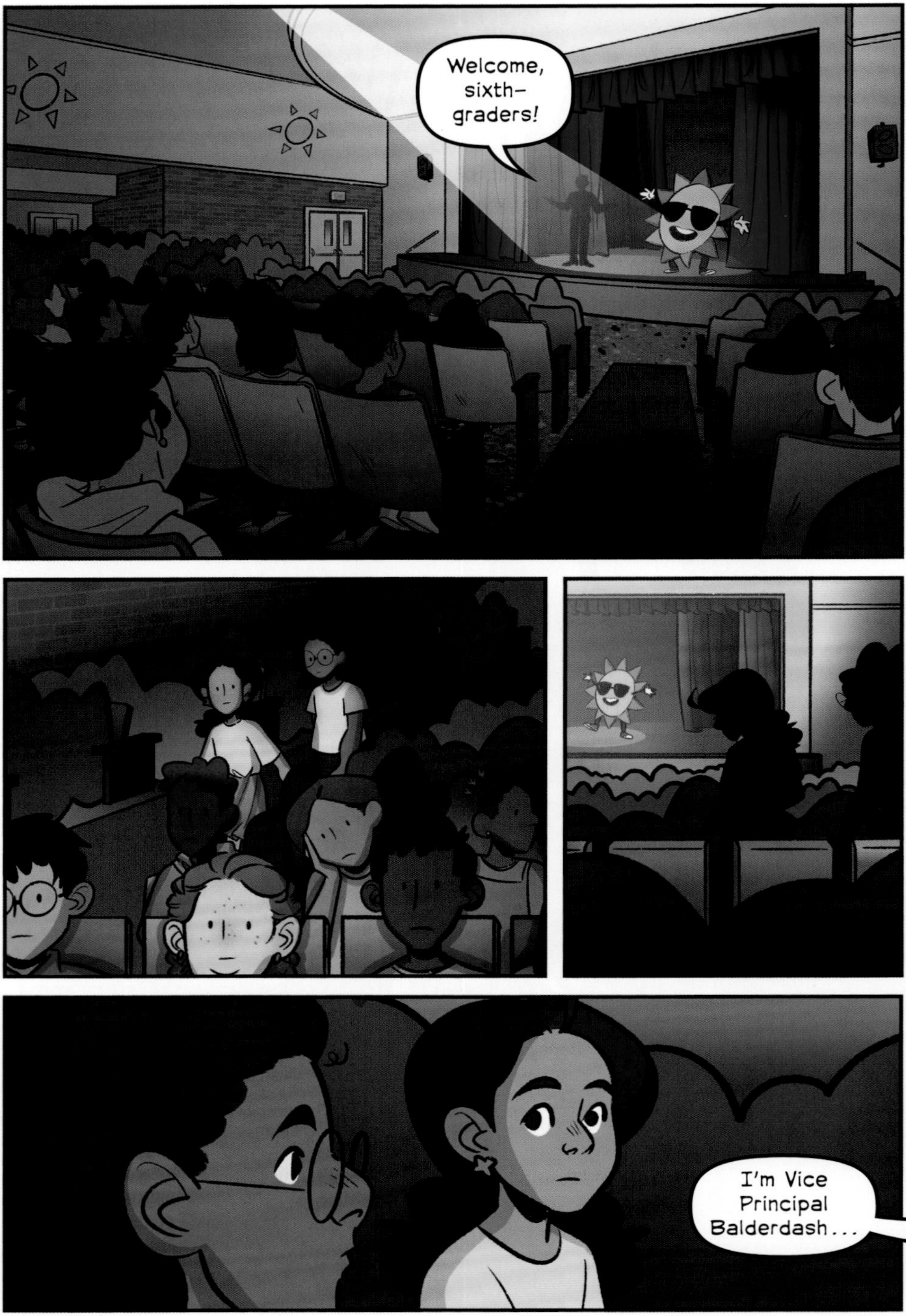
Welcome, sixth-graders!
I'm Vice Principal Balderdash...

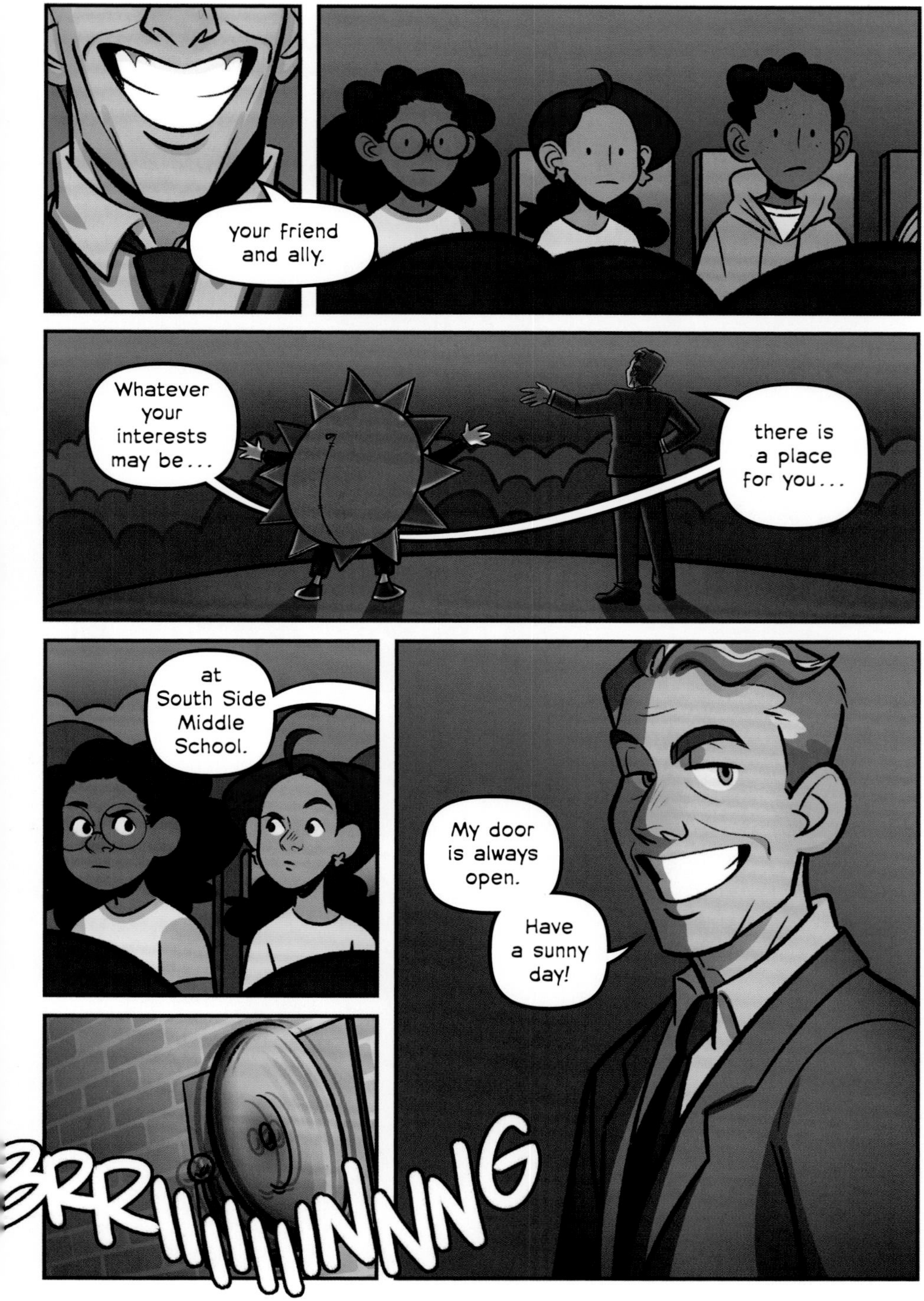
your friend and ally.
Whatever your interests may be...
there is a place for you...
at South Side Middle School.
My door is always open.
Have a sunny day!
BRRIIIIIIINNNNG

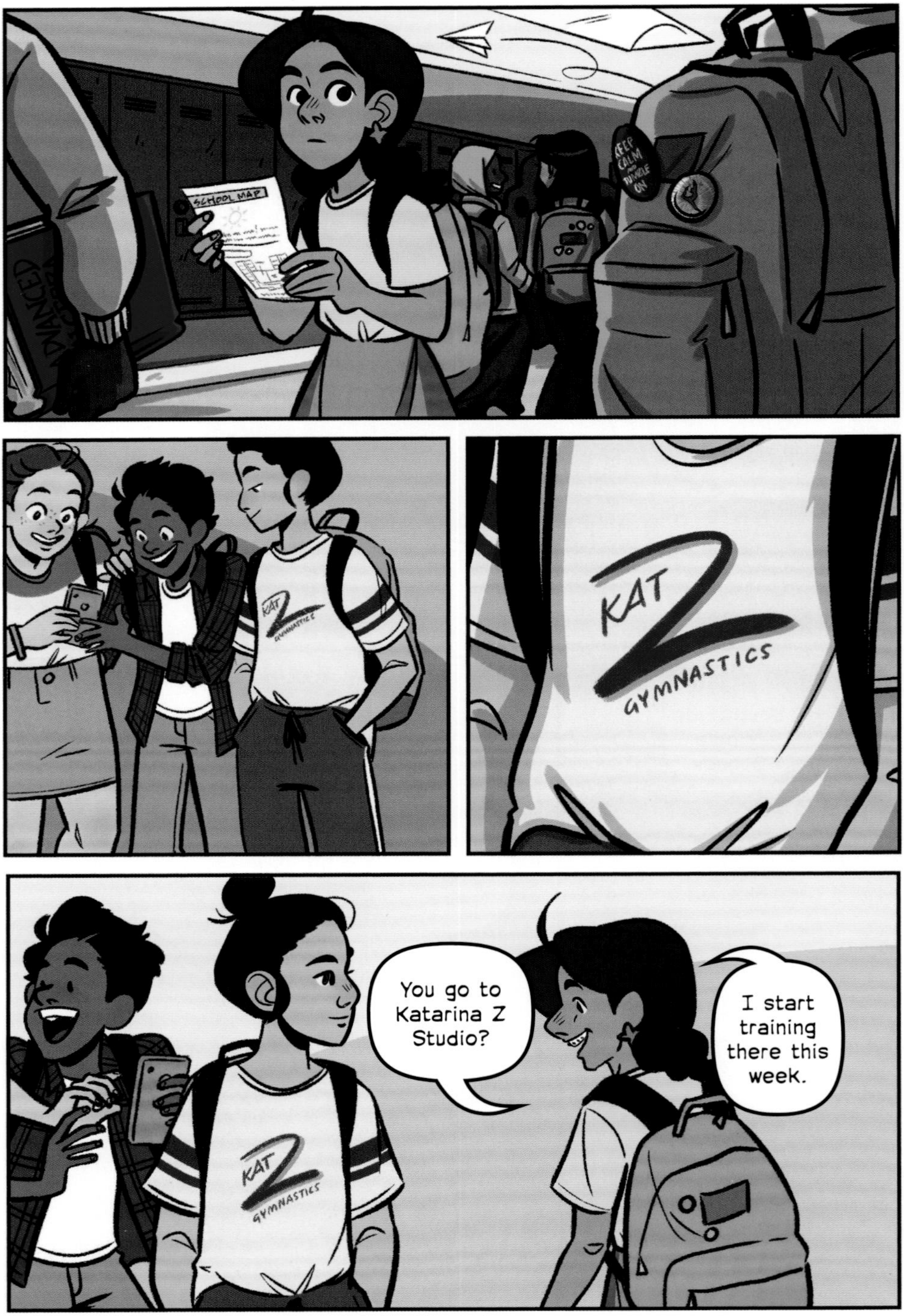
SCHOOL MAP
KAT Z GYMNASTICS
You go to Katarina Z Studio?
I start training there this week.

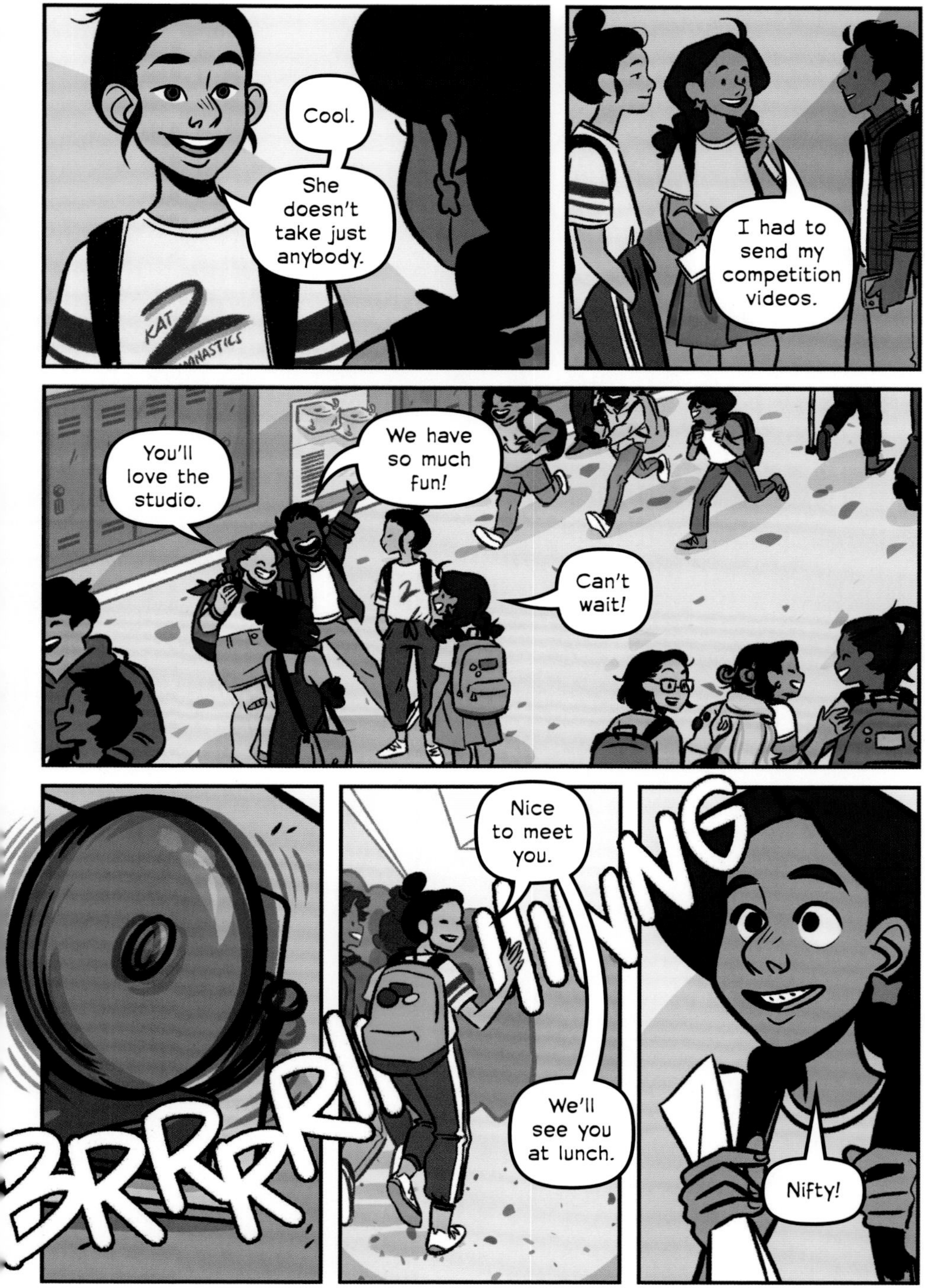
KAT Z GYMNASTICS
Cool.
She doesn't take just anybody.
I had to send my competition videos.
You'll love the studio.
We have so much fun!
Can't wait!
Nice to meet you.
BRRRRIIIIIIIING
We'll see you at lunch.
Nifty!

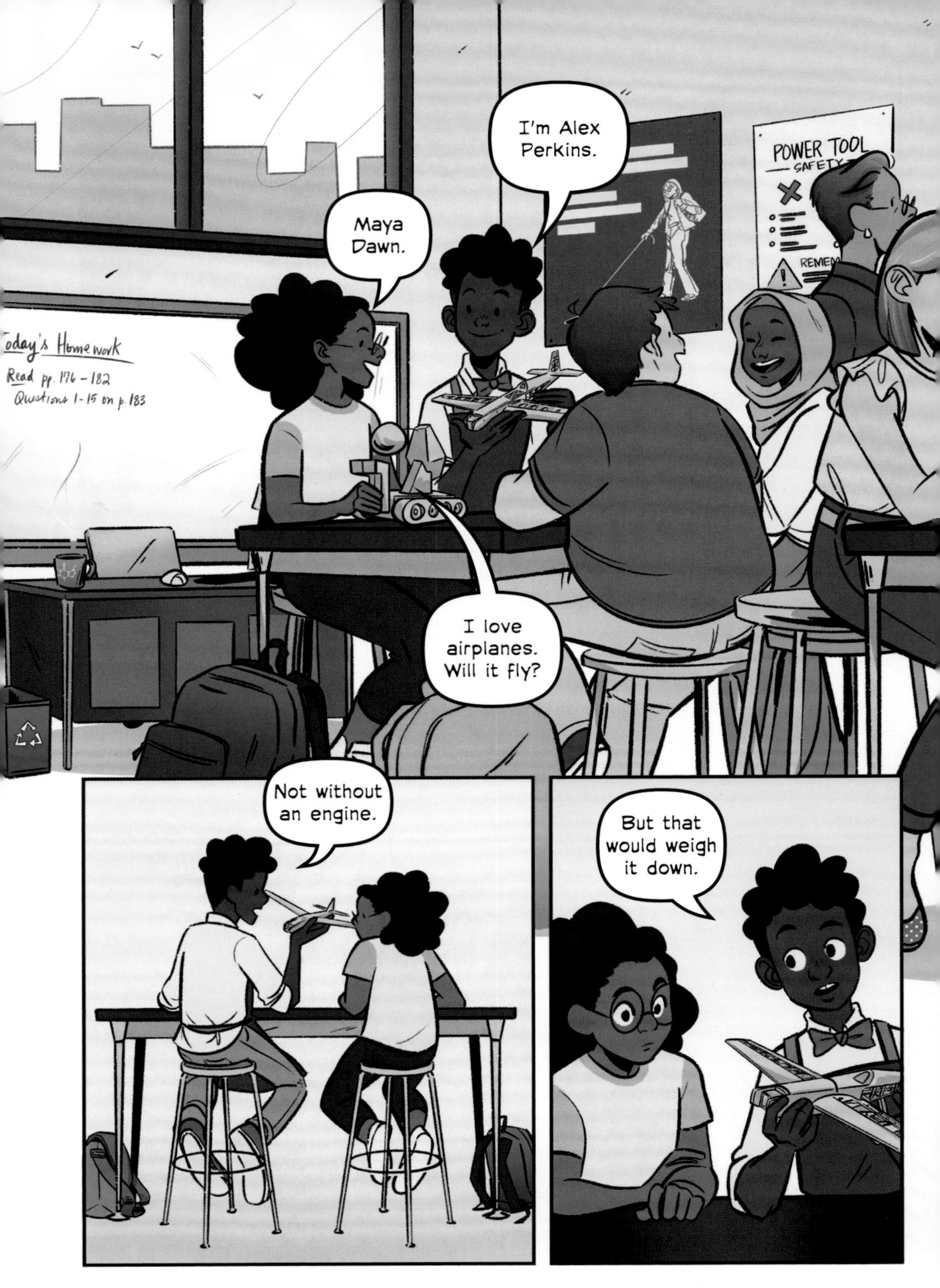
Today's Homework
Read pp. 176 – 182
Questions 1-15 on p. 183
POWER TOOL
SAFETY
I'm Alex Perkins.
Maya Dawn.
I love airplanes. Will it fly?
Not without an engine.
But that would weigh it down.

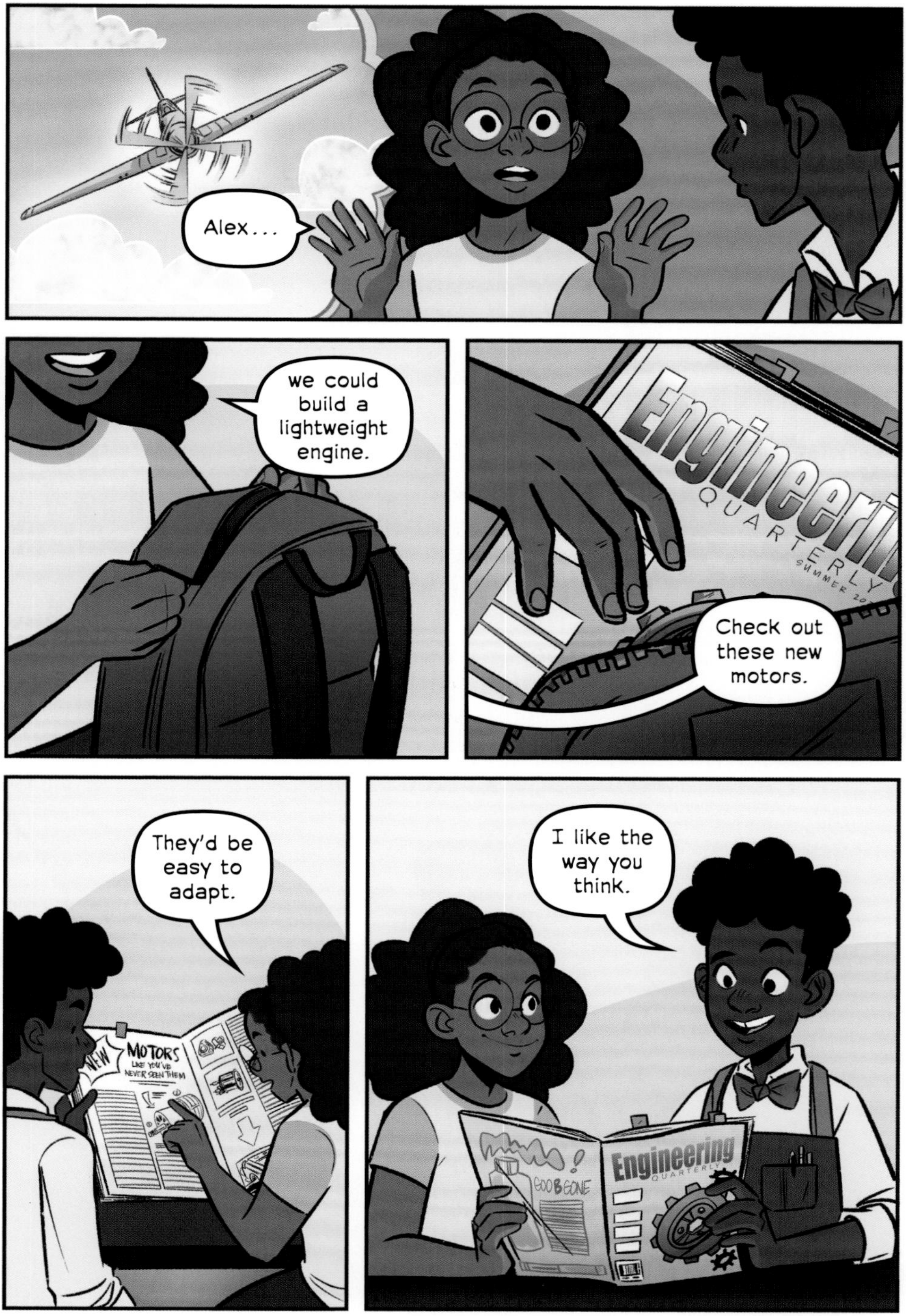
Alex...
we could build a lightweight engine.
Engineering QUARTERLY
Check out these new motors.
They'd be easy to adapt.
NEW
MOTORS LIKE YOU'VE NEVER SEEN THEM
I like the way you think.
Engineering QUARTERLY
GOO B GONE

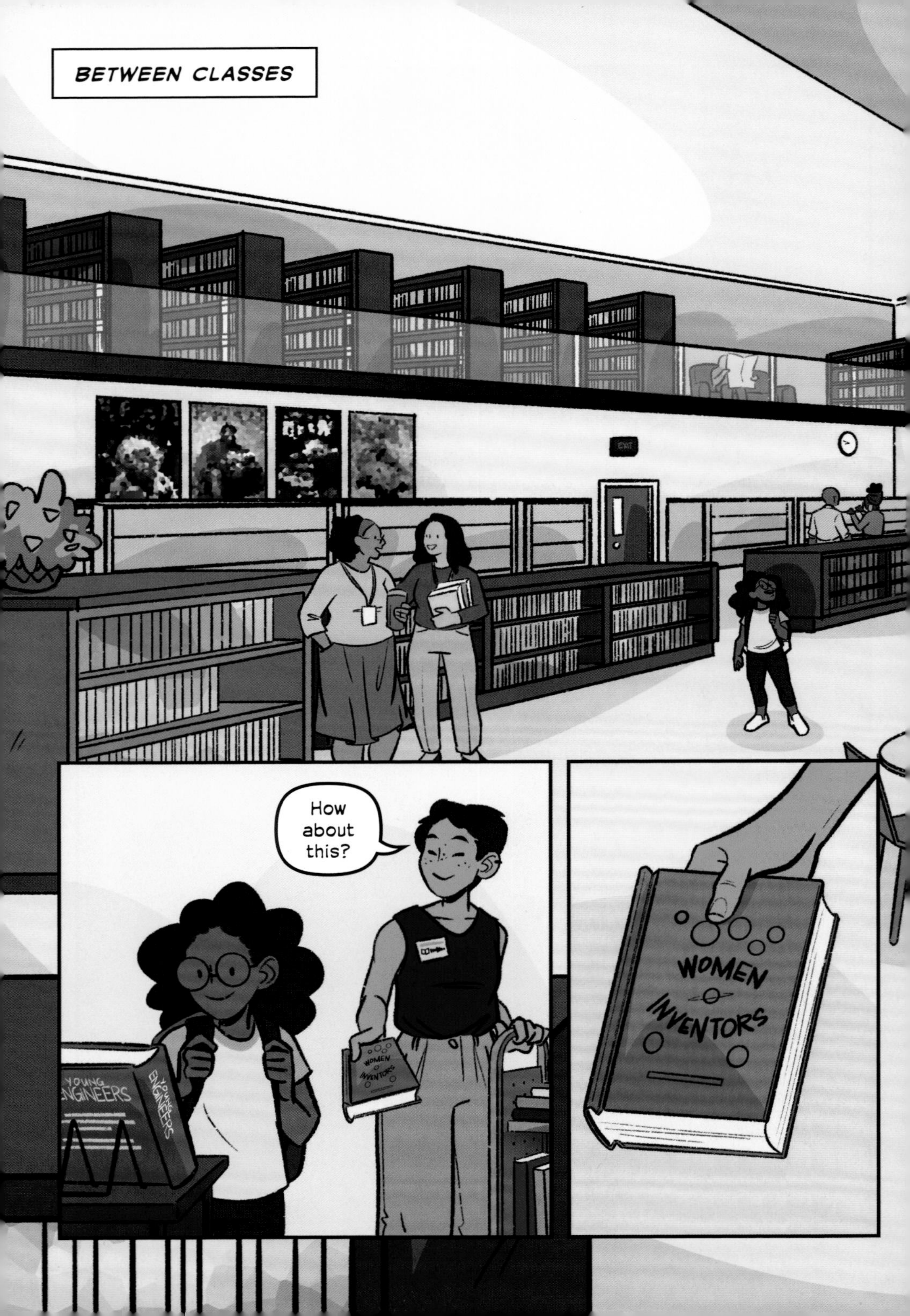
BETWEEN CLASSES
How about this?
YOUNG ENGINEERS
WOMEN INVENTORS

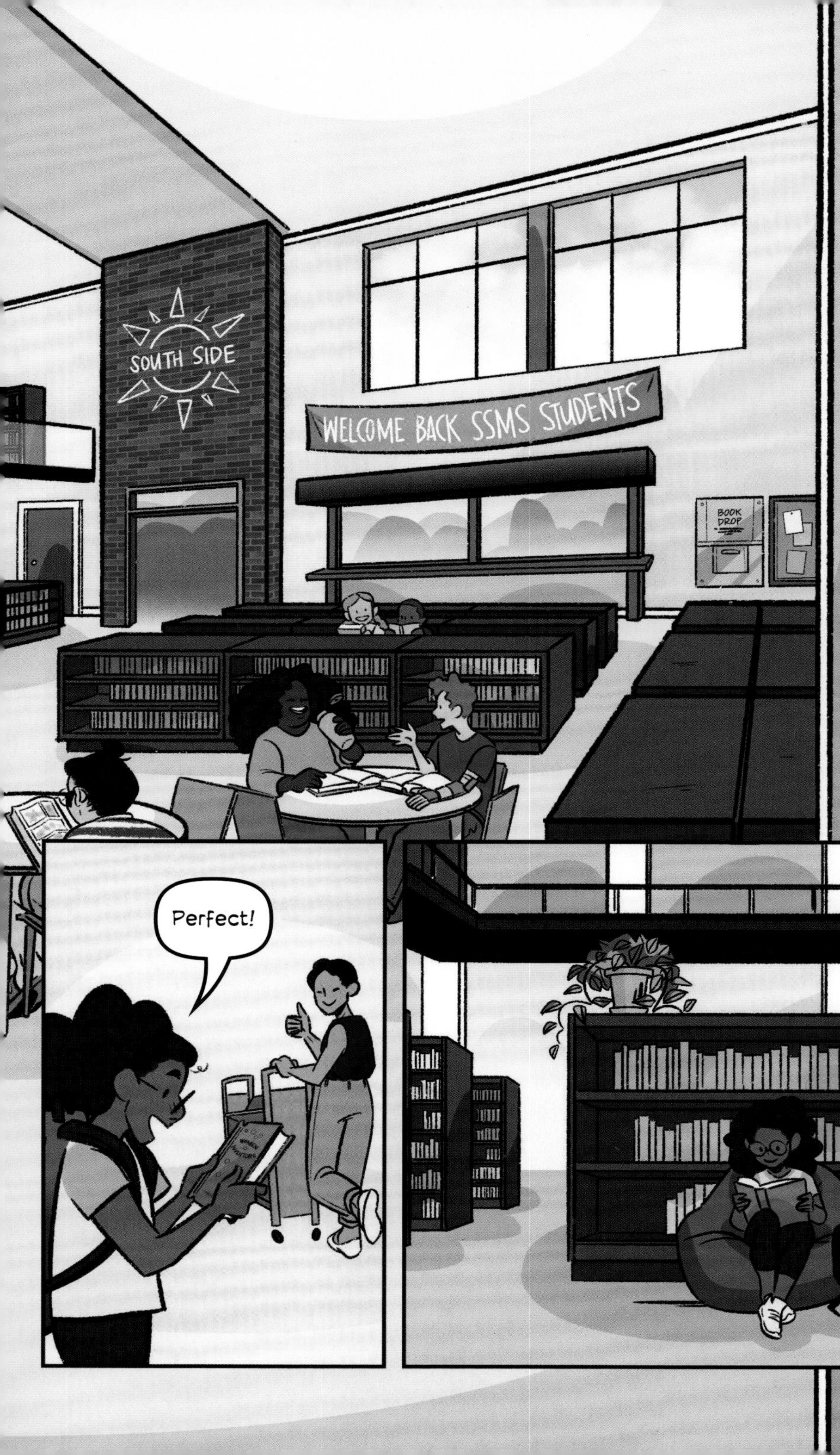
SOUTH SIDE
WELCOME BACK SSMS STUDENTS
BOOK DROP
Perfect!

SOUT
Hmf.

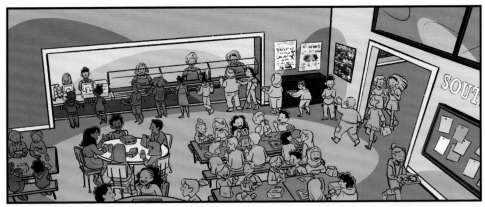

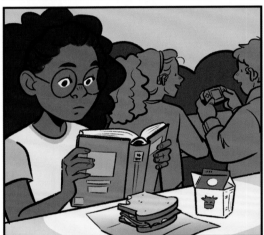

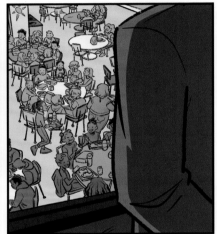

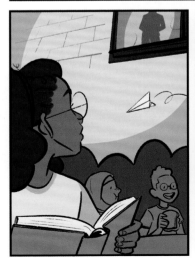

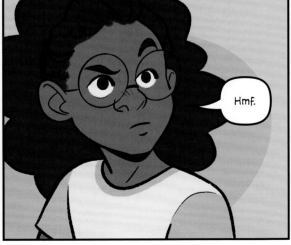

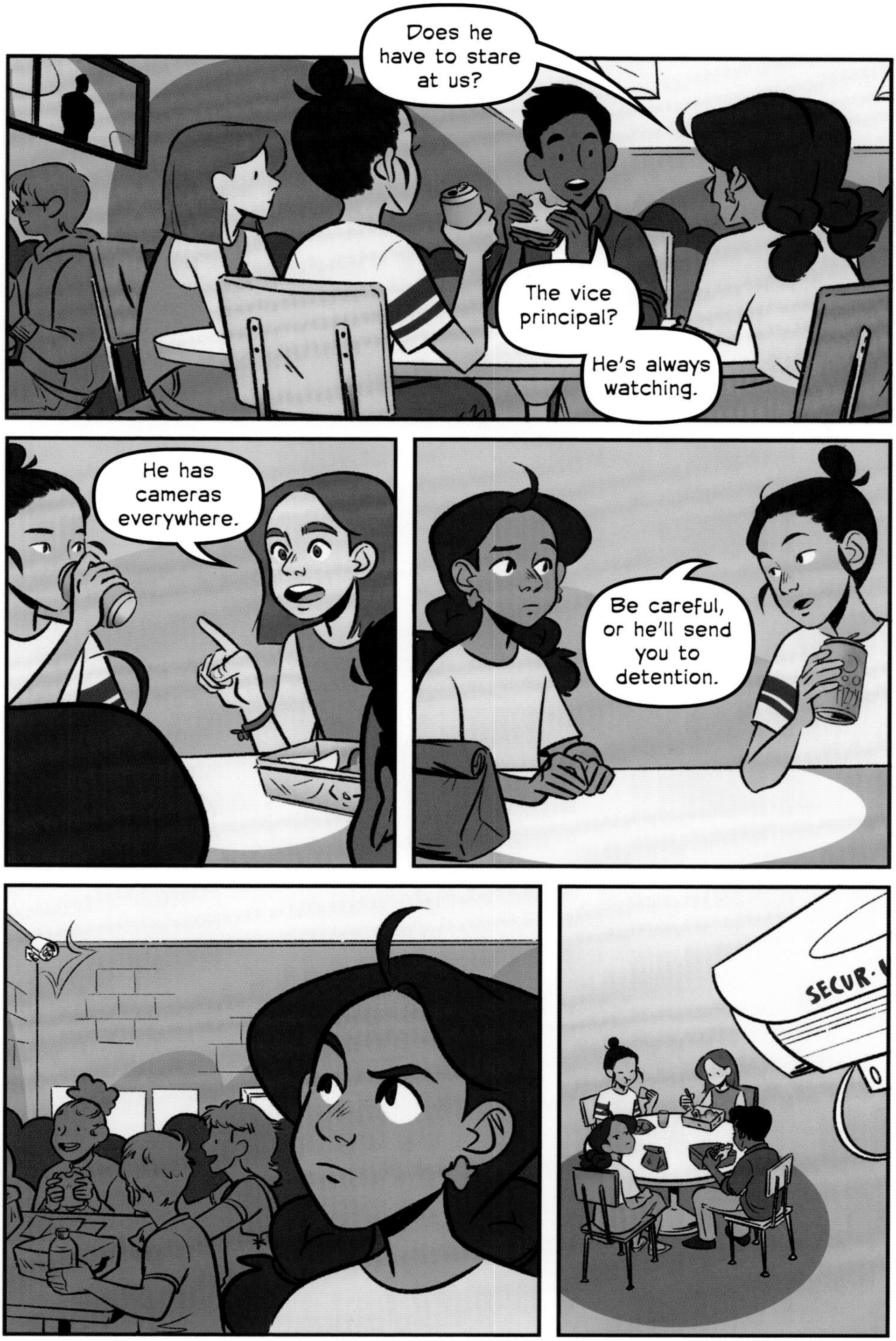
Does he have to stare at us?
The vice principal?
He's always watching.
He has cameras everywhere.
Be careful, or he'll send you to detention.
FIZZY
SECUR-

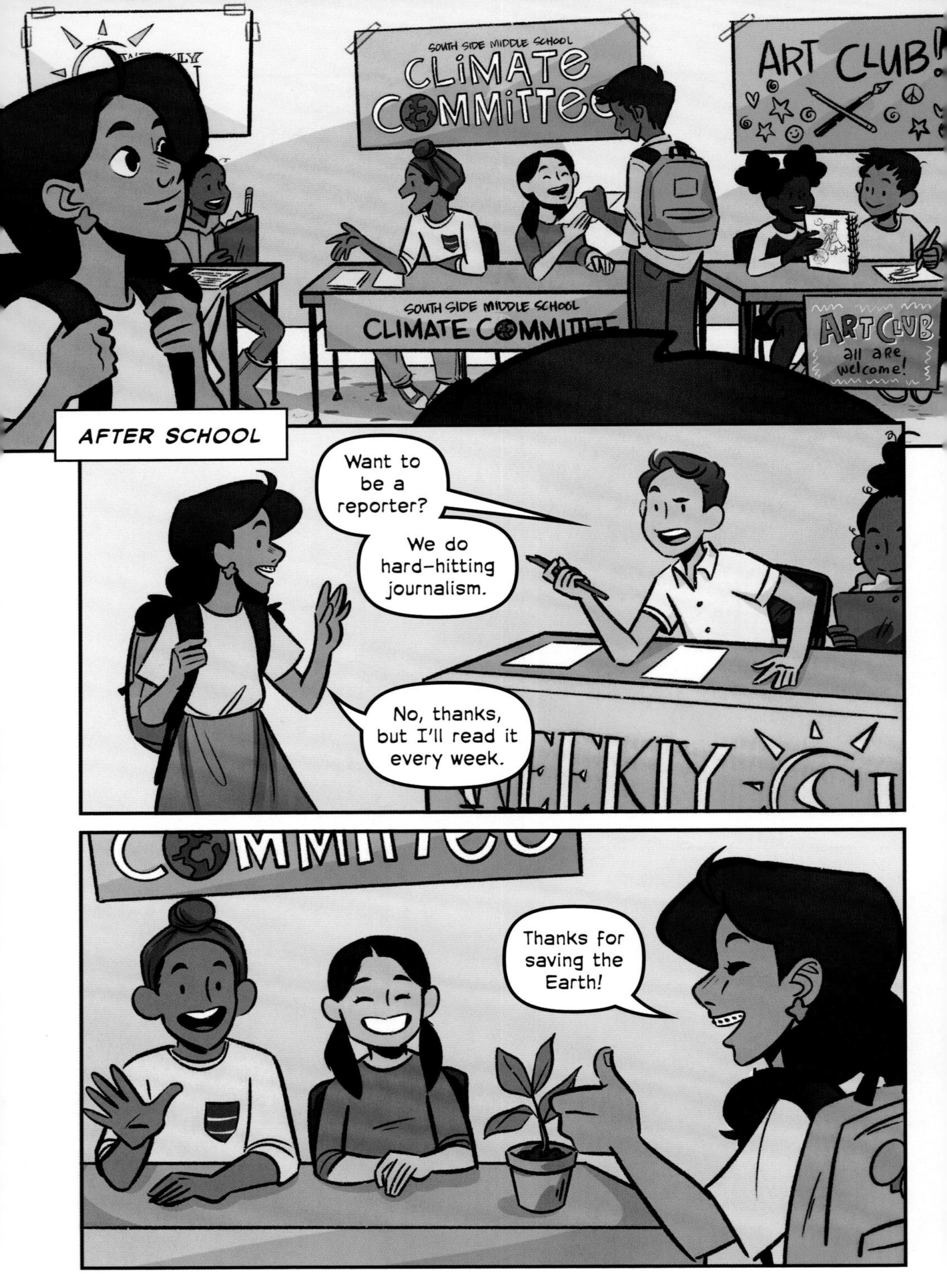
SOUTH SIDE MIDDLE SCHOOL
CLIMATE COMMITTE
ART CLUB!
SOUTH SIDE MIDDLE SCHOOL
CLIMATE COMMI
ART CLUB all are welcome!
AFTER SCHOOL
Want to be a reporter?
We do hard-hitting journalism.
No, thanks, but I'll read it every week.
Thanks for saving the Earth!

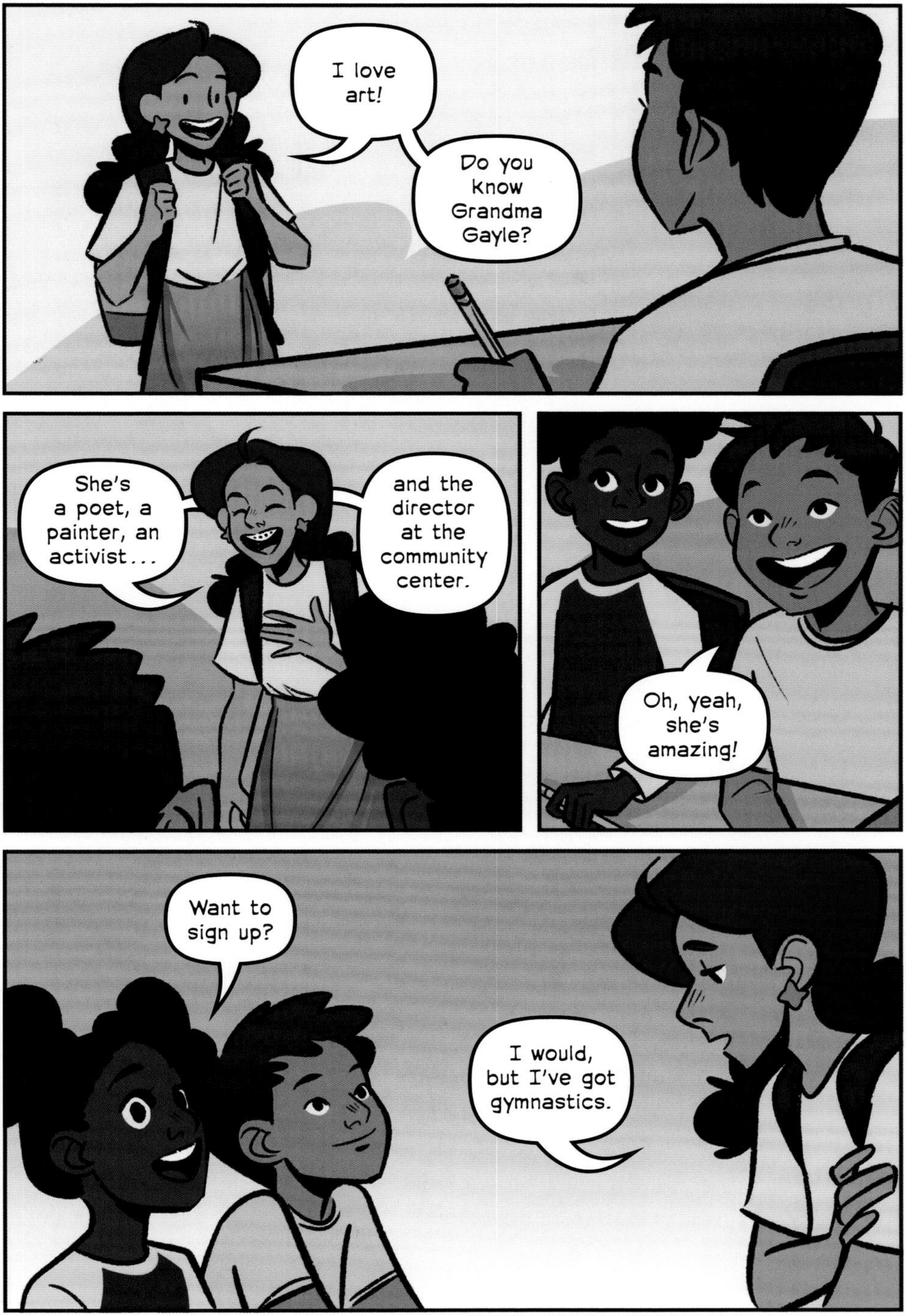
I love art!
Do you know Grandma Gayle?
She's a poet, a painter, an activist...
and the director at the community center.
Oh, yeah, she's amazing!
Want to sign up?
I would, but I've got gymnastics.

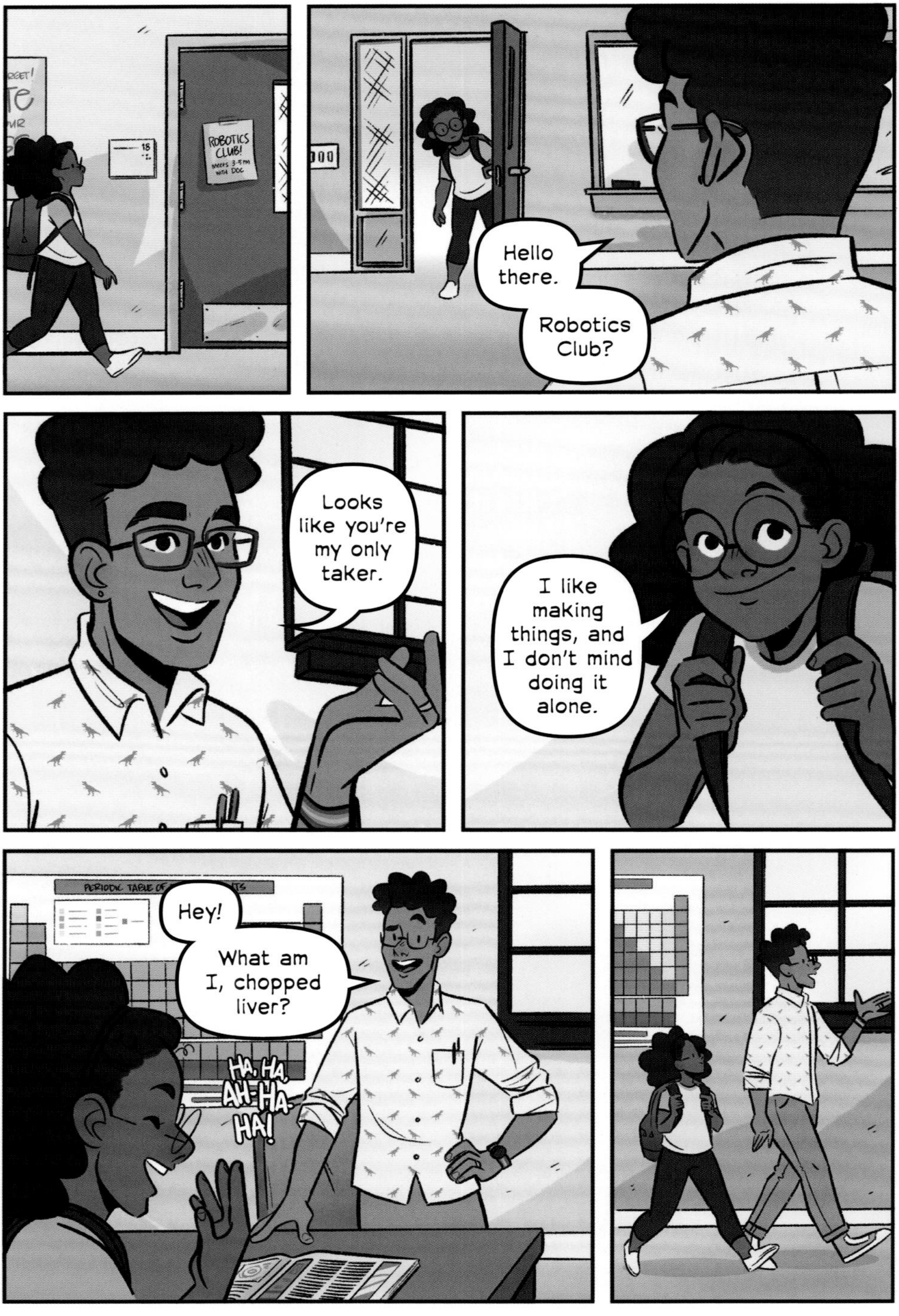
ROBOTICS CLUB!
MEETS 3-5PM WITH DOC
Hello there.
Robotics Club?
Looks like you're my only taker.
I like making things, and I don't mind doing it alone.
Hey!
What am I, chopped liver?
HA, HA, AH-HA-HA!

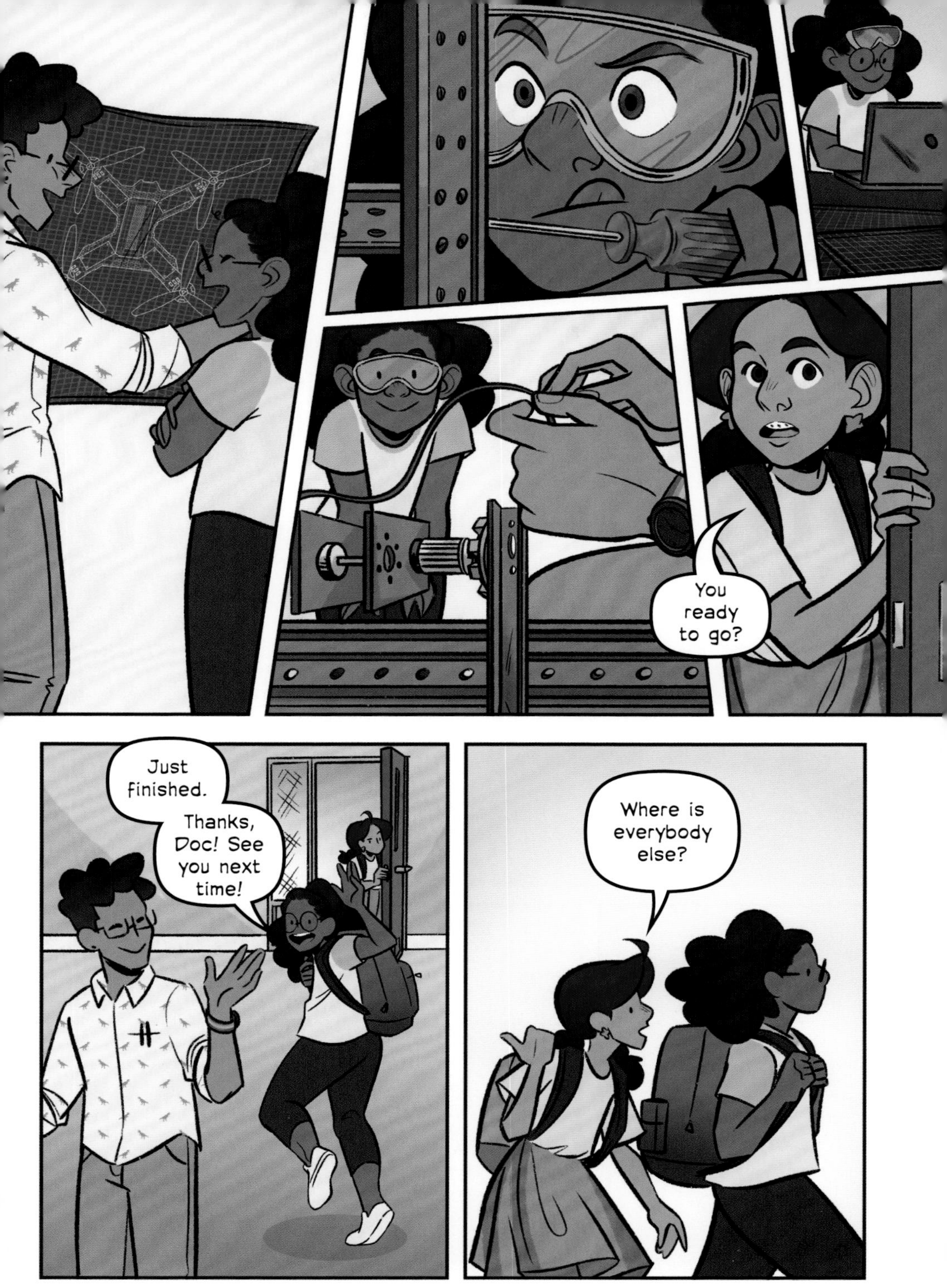
You ready to go?
Just finished.
Thanks, Doc! See you next time!
Where is everybody else?

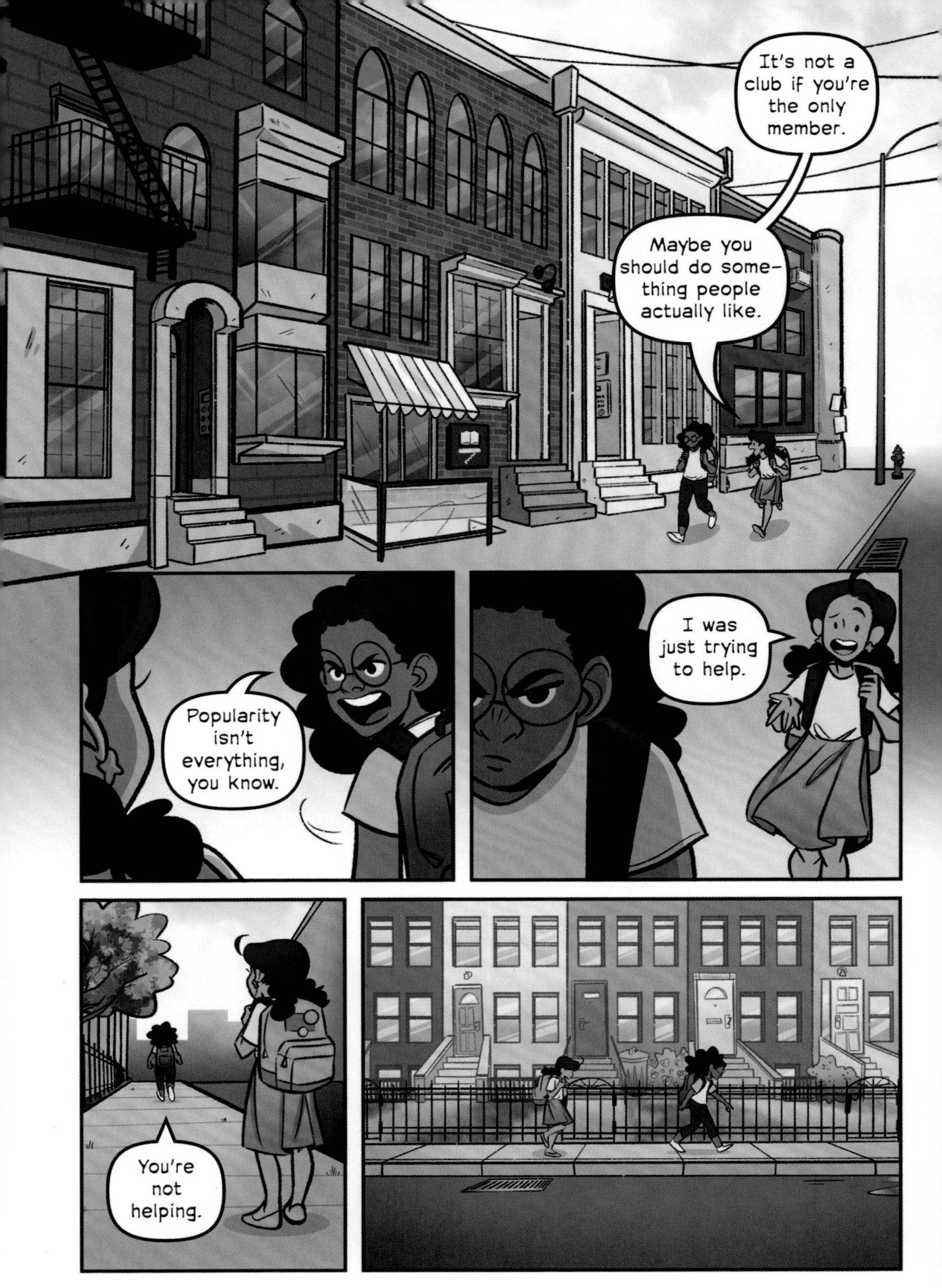
It's not a club if you're the only member.
Maybe you should do some-thing people actually like.
Popularity isn't everything, you know.
I was just trying to help.
You're not helping.

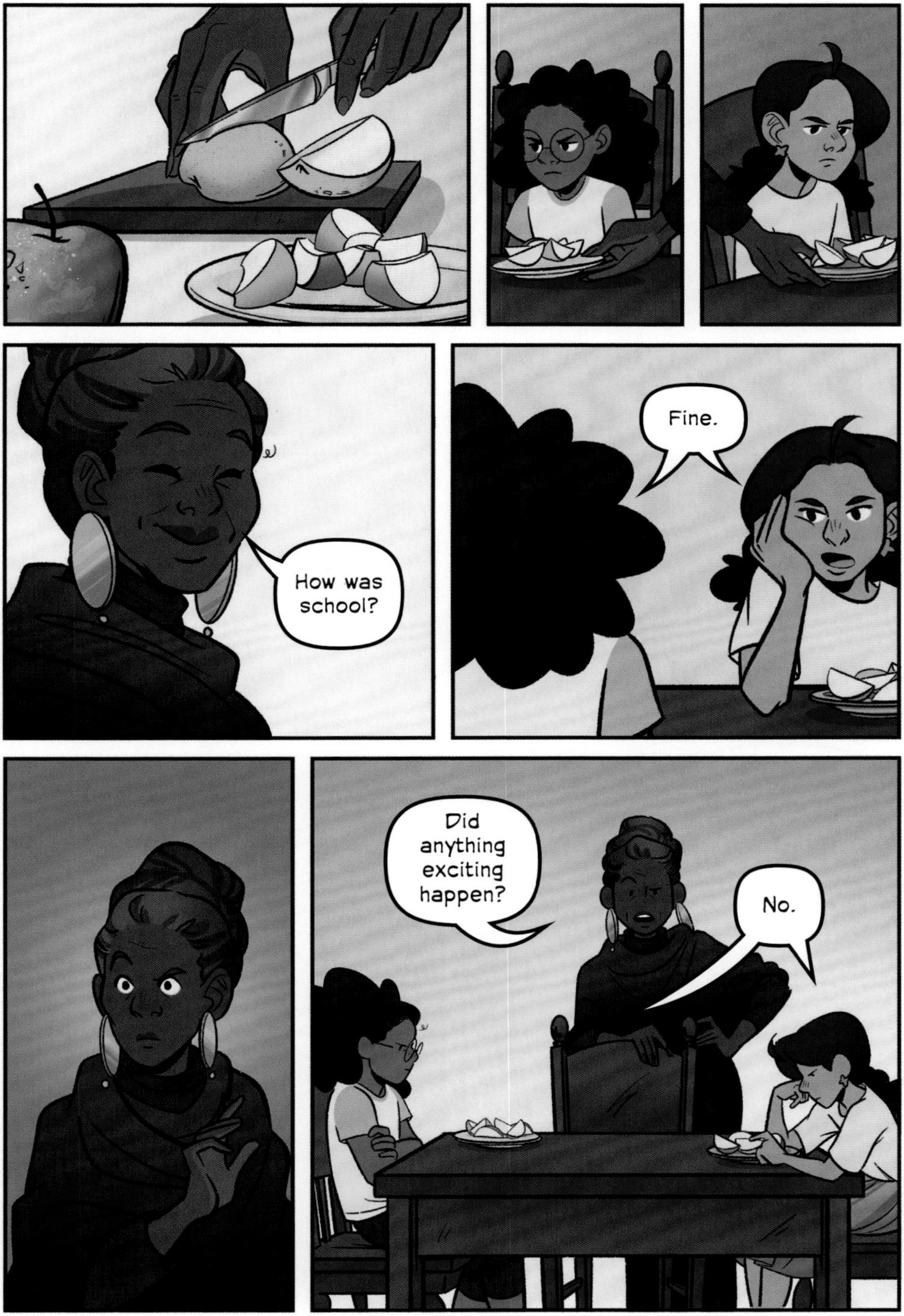
How was school?
Fine.
Did anything exciting happen?
No.

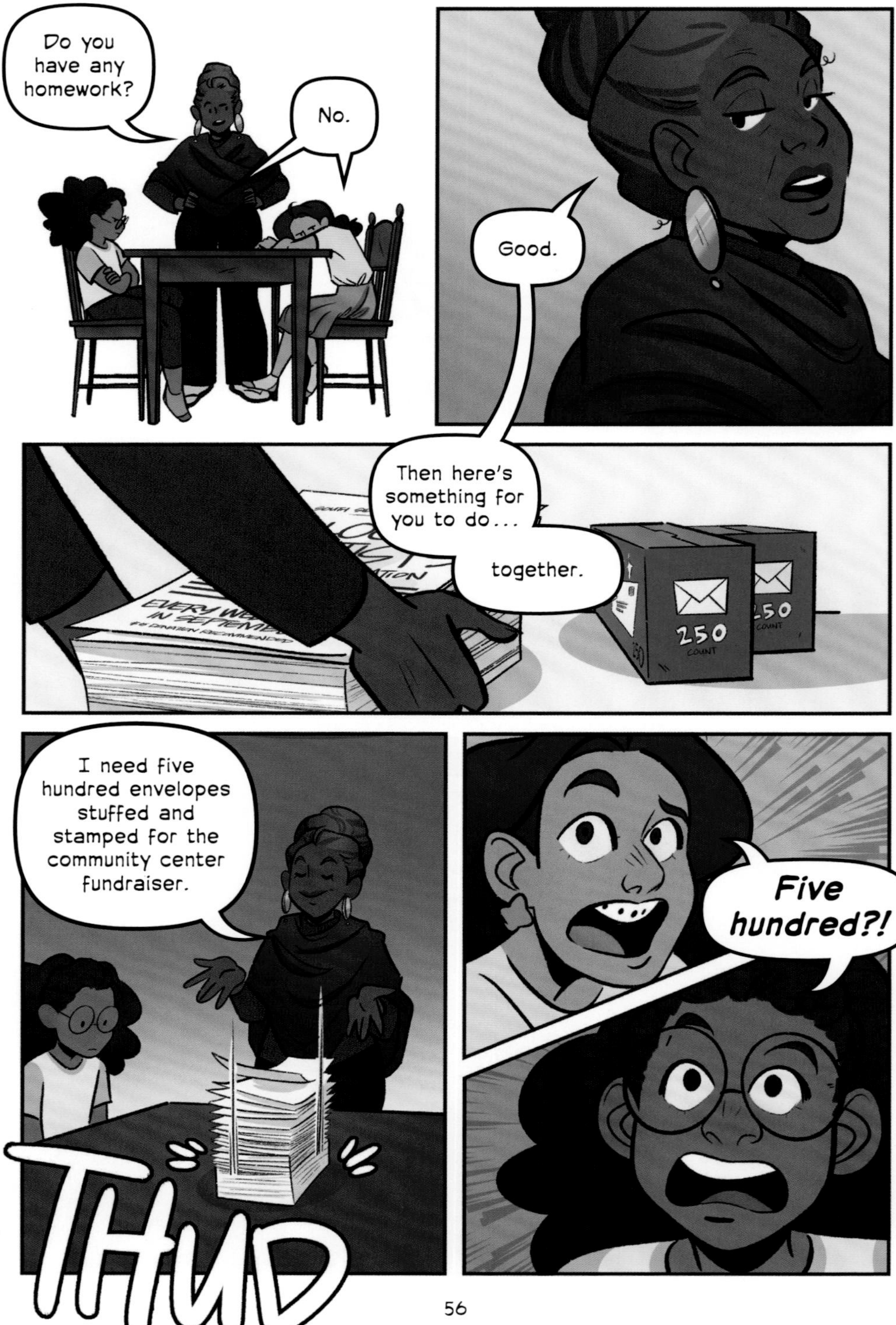
Do you have any homework?
No.
Good.
Then here's something for you to do...
together.
250 COUNT
I need five hundred envelopes stuffed and stamped for the community center fundraiser.
THUD
Five hundred?!

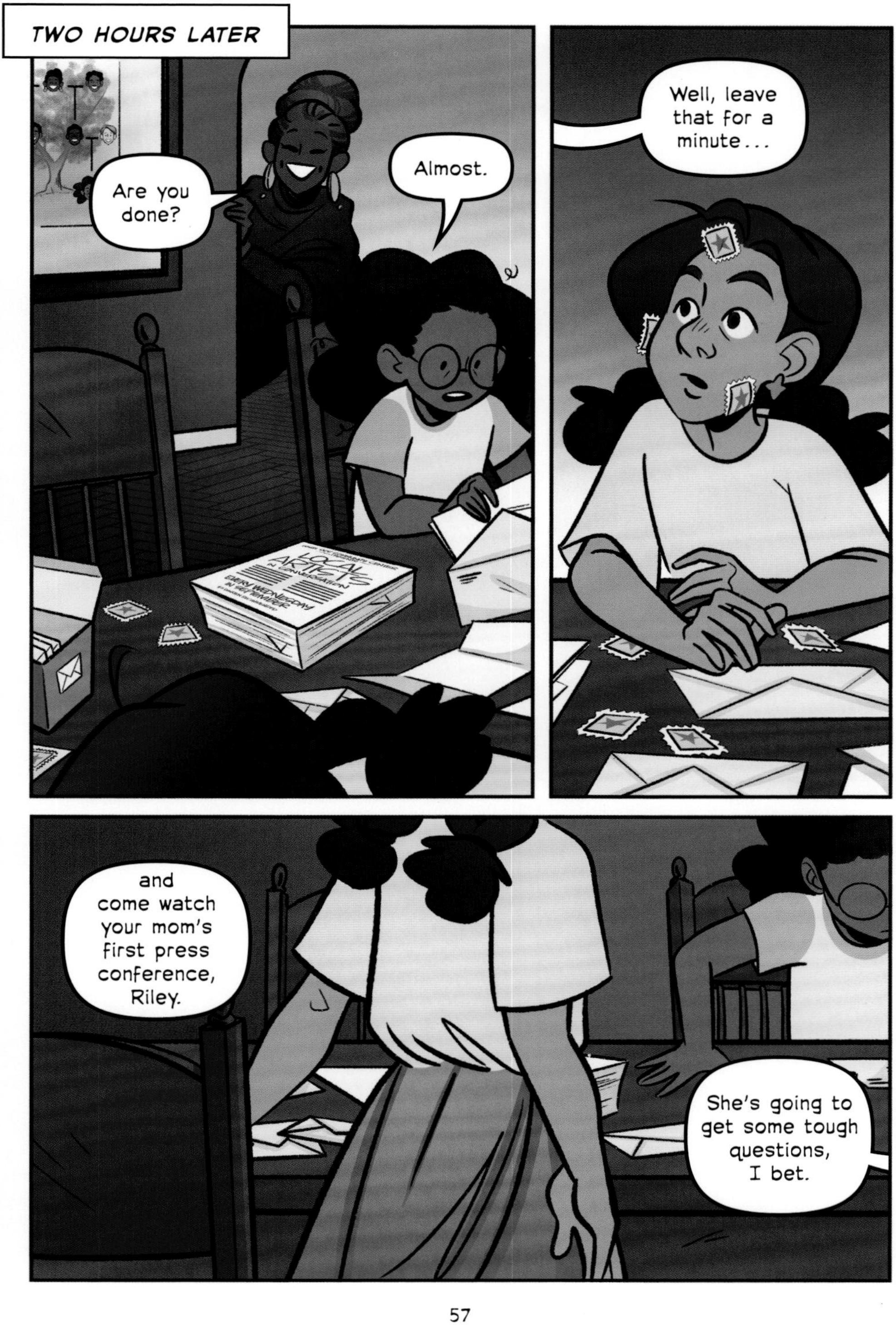
TWO HOURS LATER
Are you done?
Almost.
LOCAL ARTISTS
IN CONVERSATION
EVERY WEDNESDAY IN SEPTEMBER
Well, leave that for a minute...
and come watch your mom's first press conference, Riley.
She's going to get some tough questions, I bet.

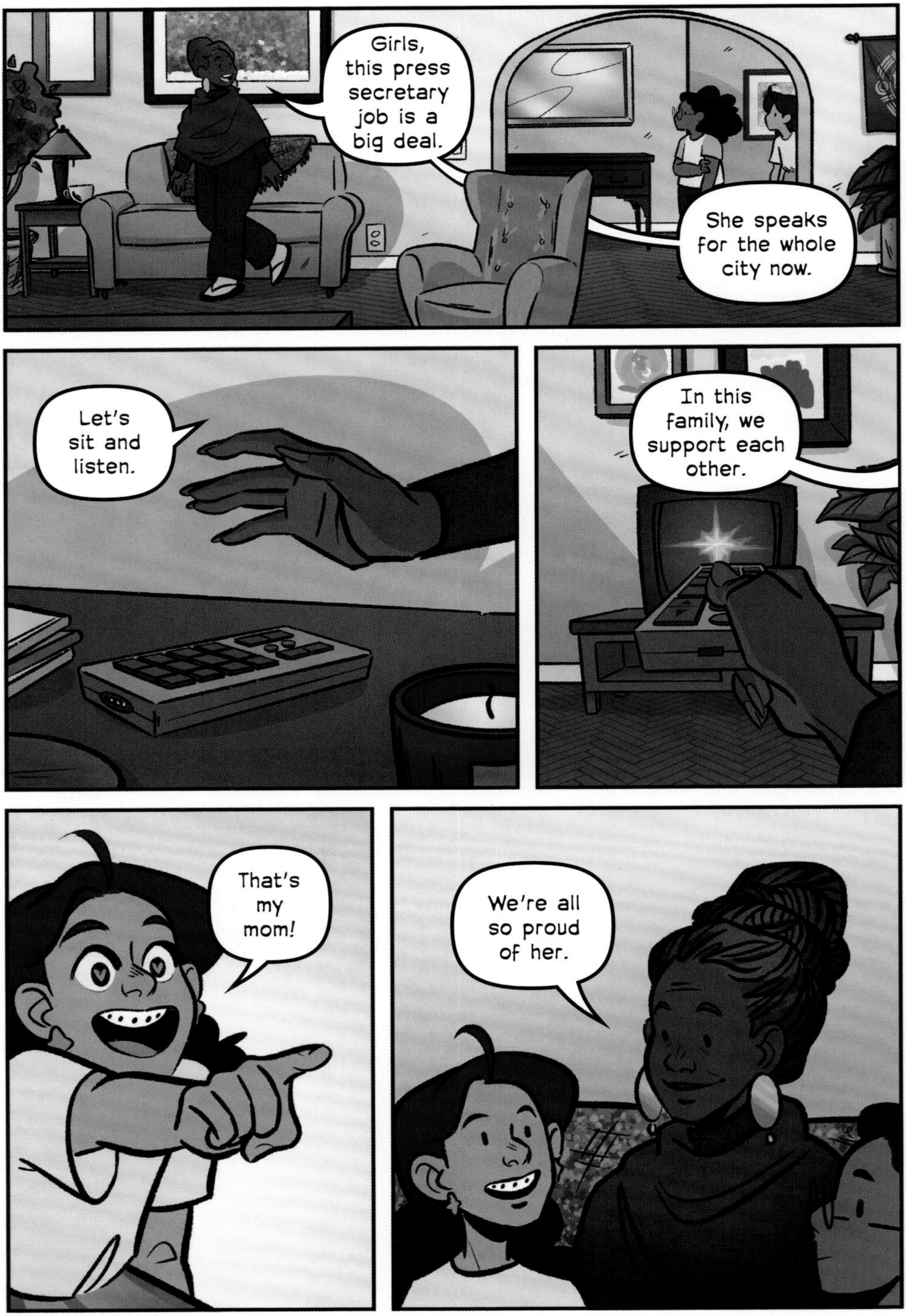
Girls, this press secretary job is a big deal.
She speaks for the whole city now.
Let's sit and listen.
In this family, we support each other.
That's my mom!
We're all so proud of her.

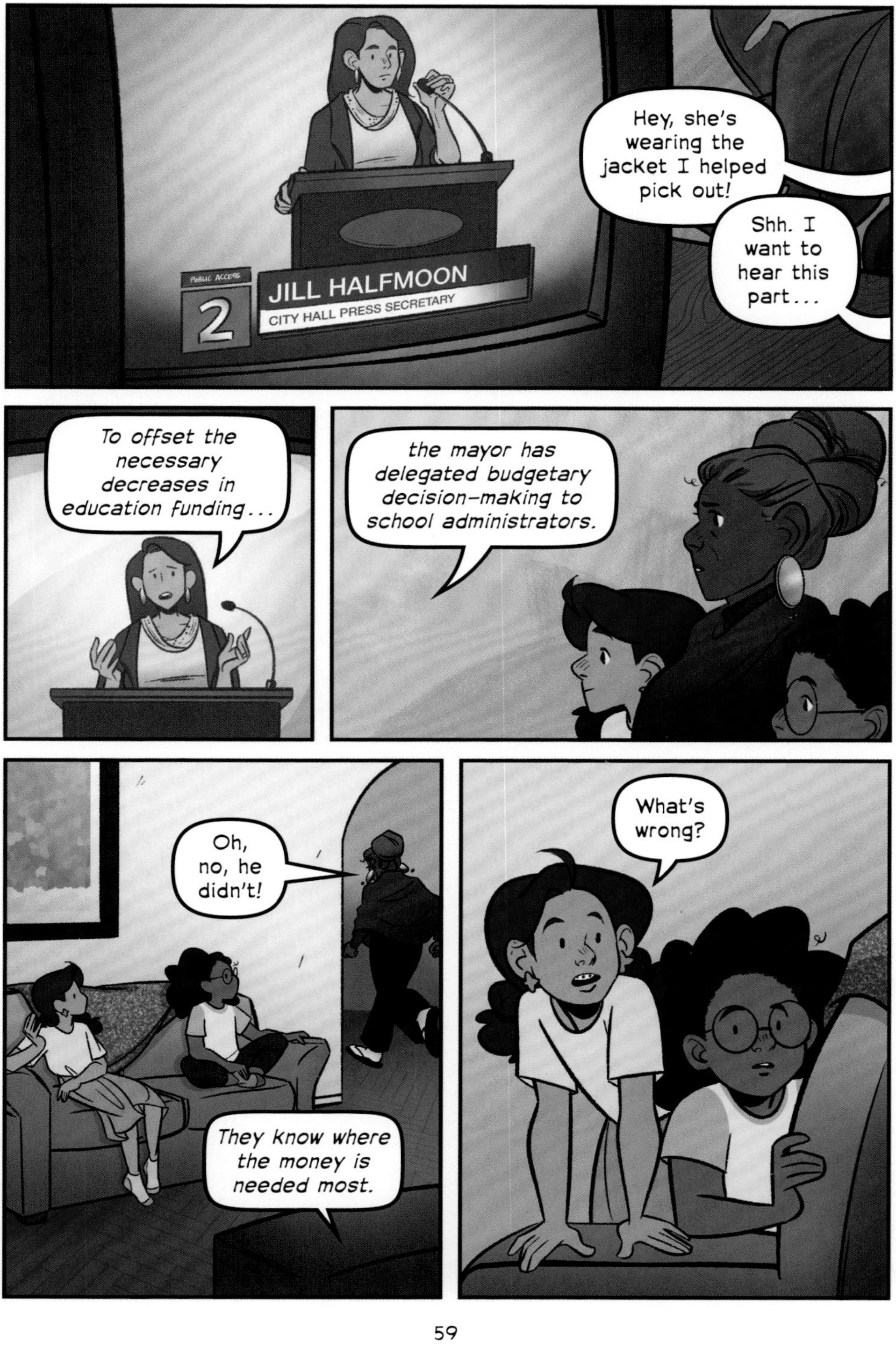
PUBLIC ACCESS
2
JILL HALFMOON
CITY HALL PRESS SECRETARY
Hey, she's wearing the jacket I helped pick out!
Shh. I want to hear this part...
To offset the necessary decreases in education funding...
the mayor has delegated budgetary decision-making to school administrators.
Oh, no, he didn't!
They know where the money is needed most.
What's wrong?

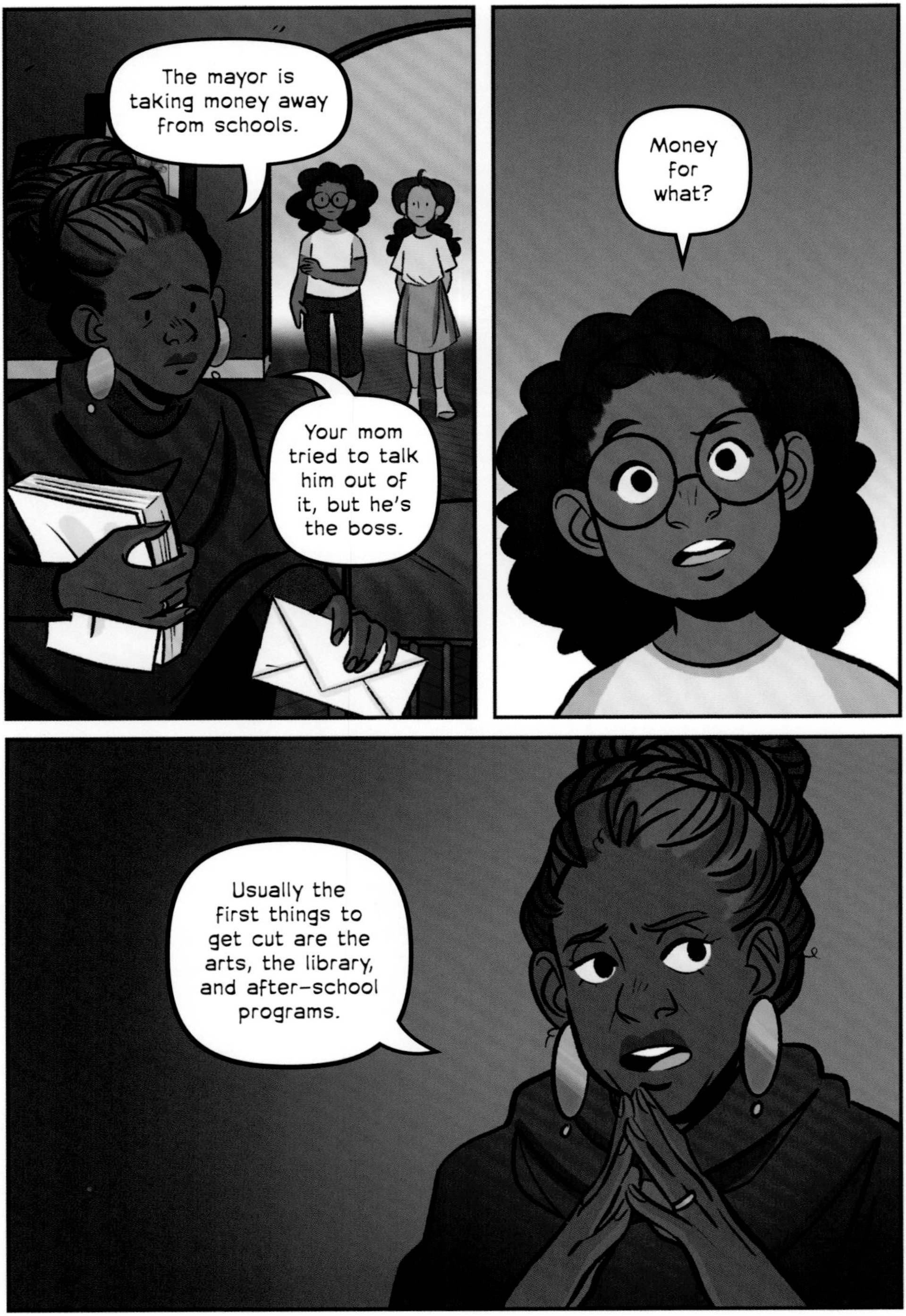
The mayor is taking money away from schools.
Your mom tried to talk him out of it, but he's the boss.
Money for what?
Usually the first things to get cut are the arts, the library, and after-school programs.

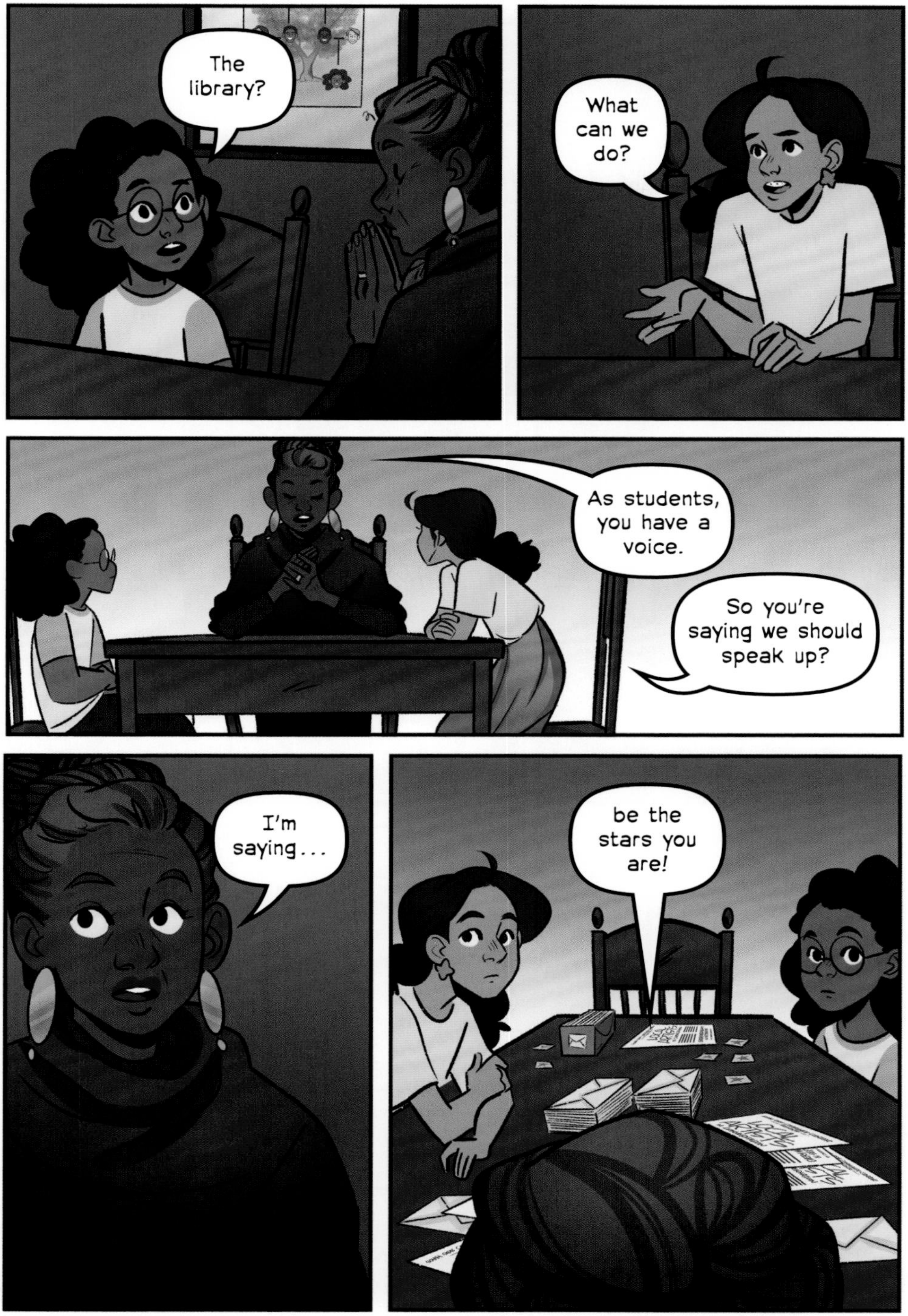
The library?
What can we do?
As students, you have a voice.
So you're saying we should speak up?
I'm saying...
be the stars you are!

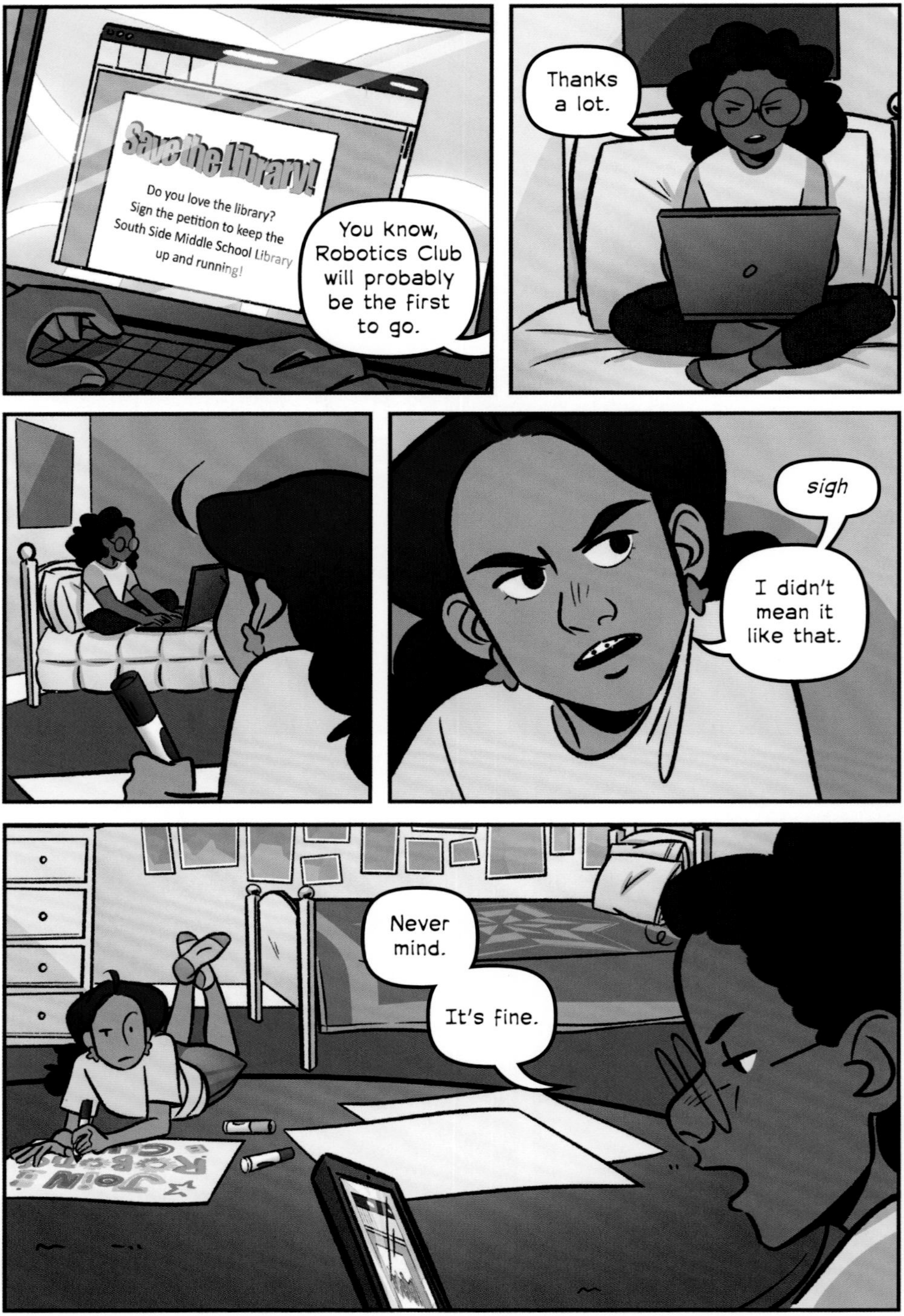
Save the Library!
Do you love the library? Sign the petition to keep the South Side Middle School Library up and running!
You know, Robotics Club will probably be the first to go.
Thanks a lot.
sigh
I didn't mean it like that.
Never mind.
It's fine.
Join Robotics Club

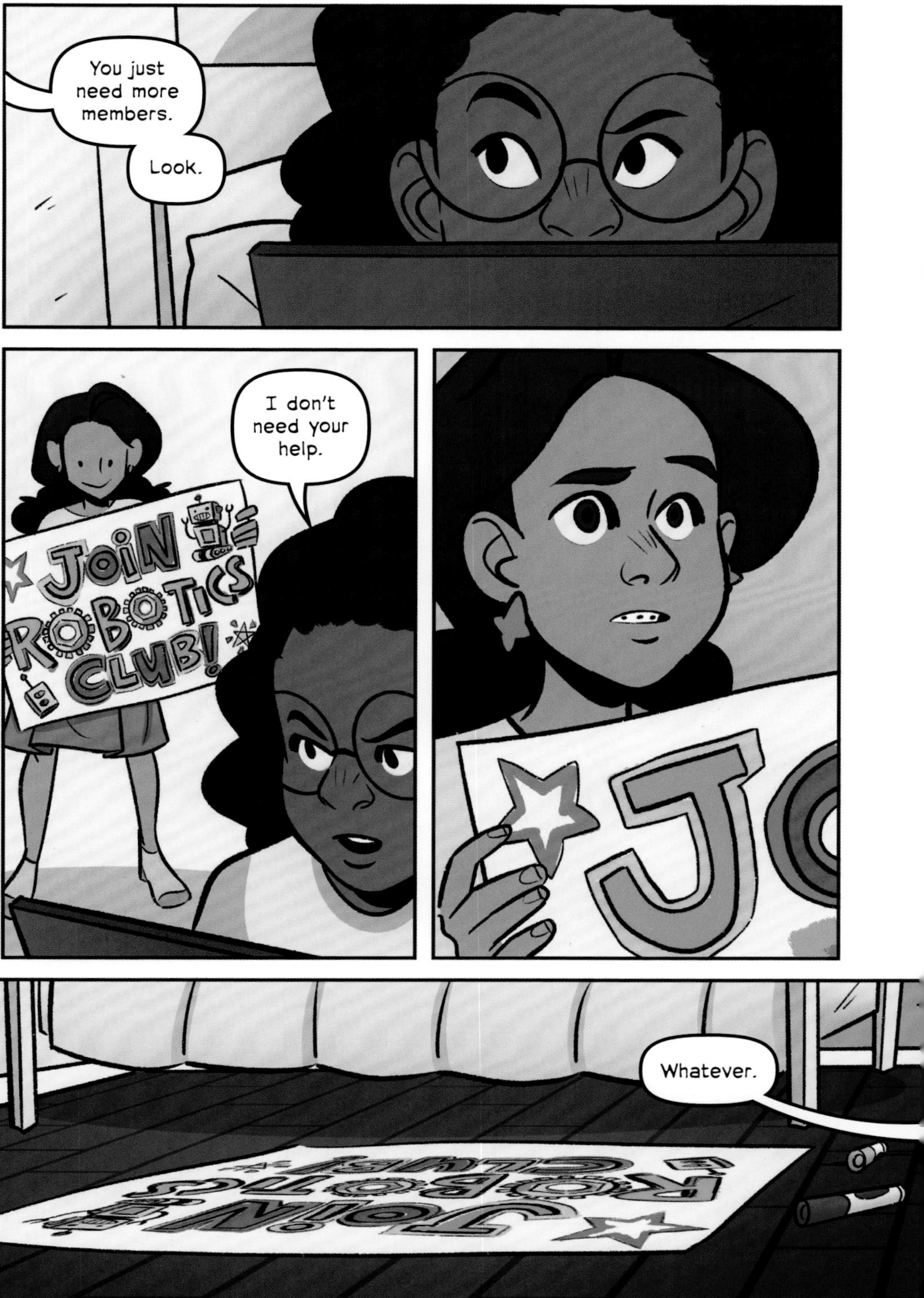
You just need more members.
Look.
I don't need your help.
JOIN ROBOTICS CLUB!
Whatever.

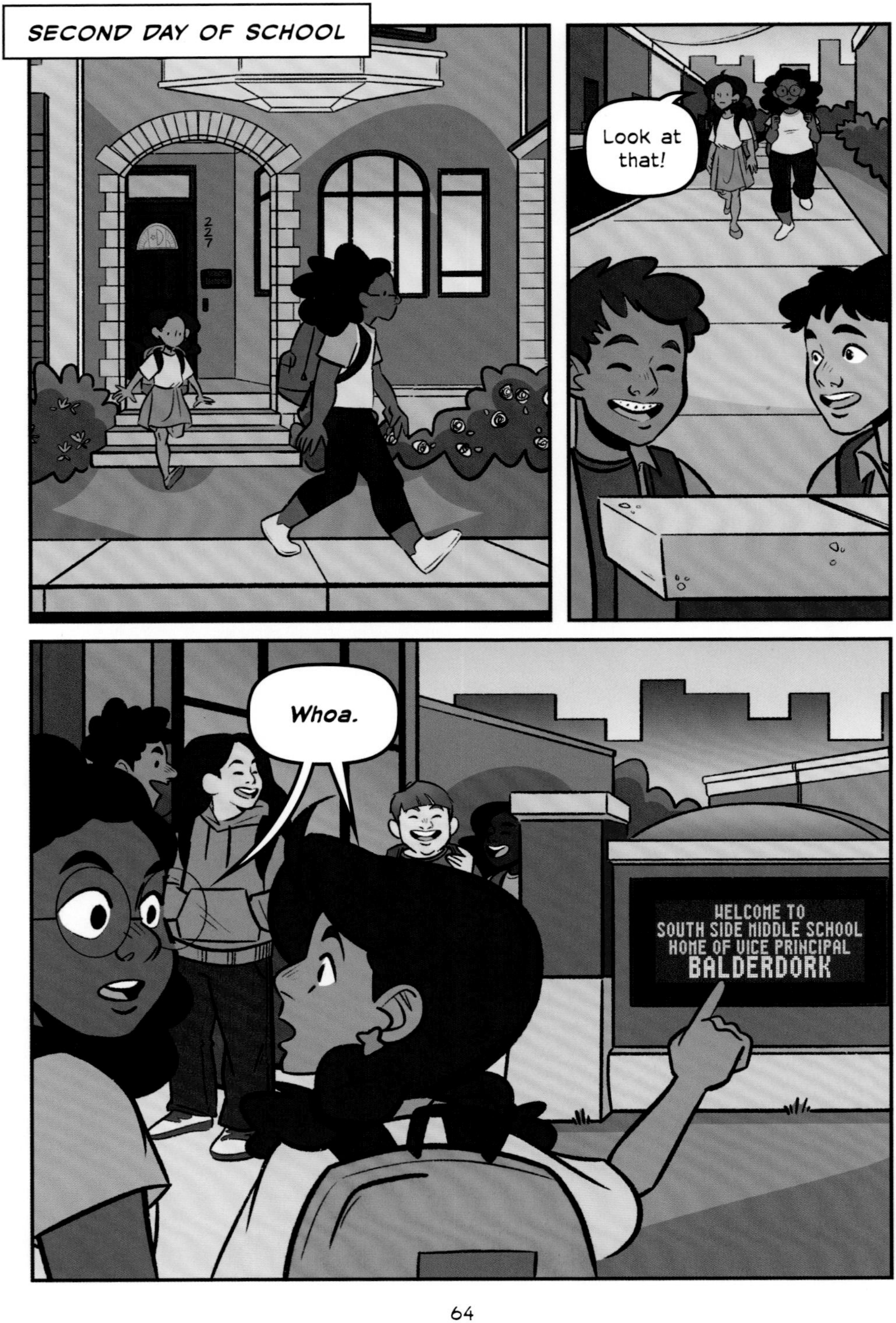
SECOND DAY OF SCHOOL
227
Look at that!
Whoa.
WELCOME TO
SOUTH SIDE MIDDLE SCHOOL
HOME OF VICE PRINCIPAL
BALDERDORK

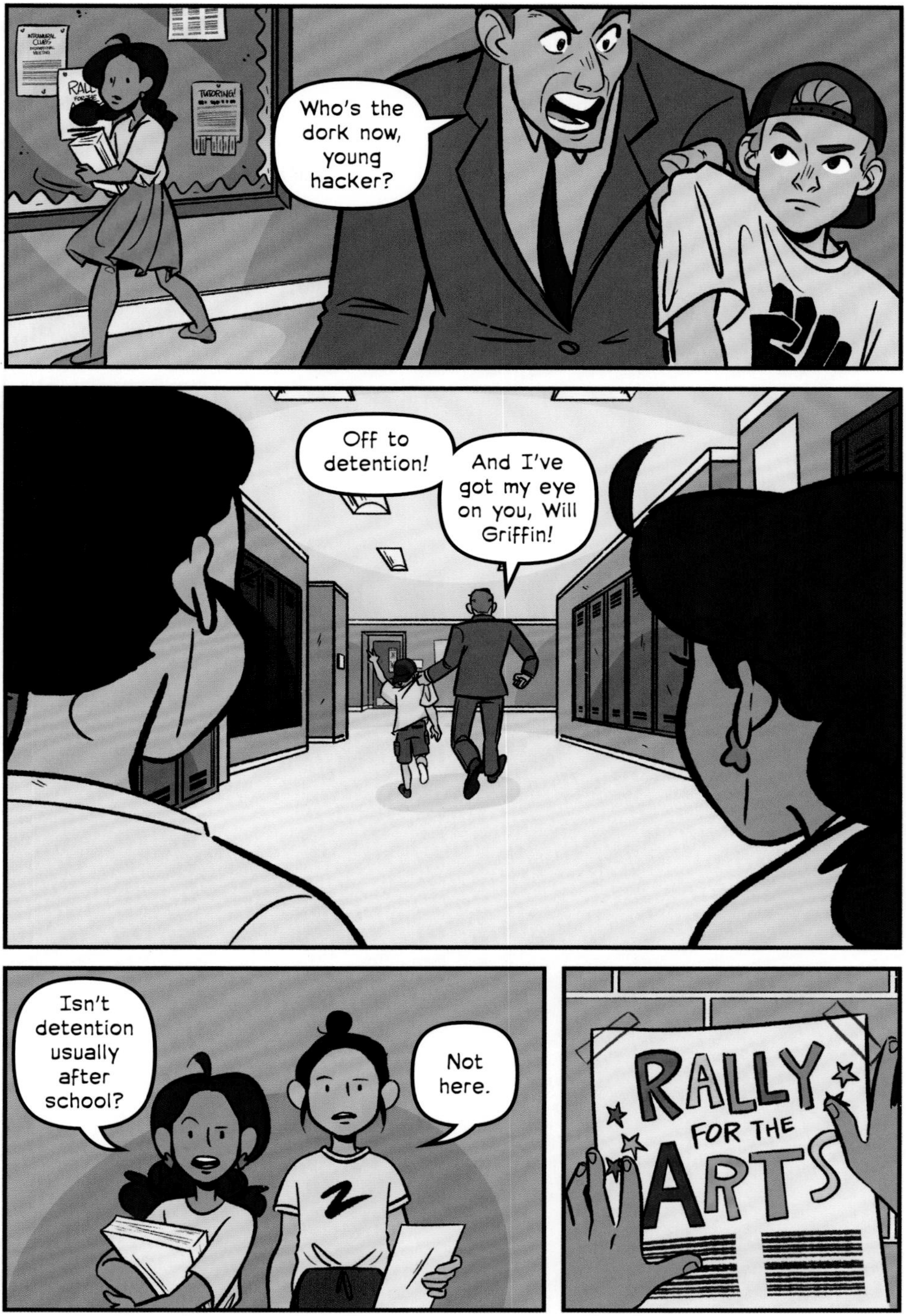
TUTORING!
Who's the dork now, young hacker?
Off to detention!
And I've got my eye on you, Will Griffin!
Isn't detention usually after school?
Not here.
RALLY FOR THE ARTS

It's all detention all the time at SSMS.
Balderdash is scary strict.
IN-SCHOOL DETENTION BLOCK 3
Detention is full!
Make room for one more.

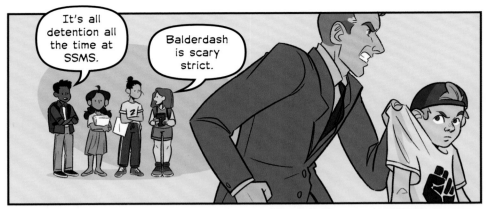

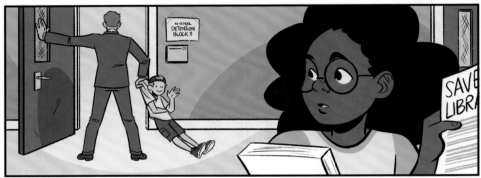

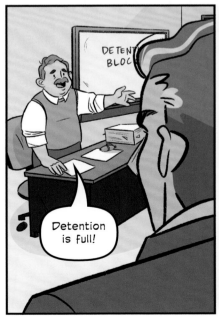

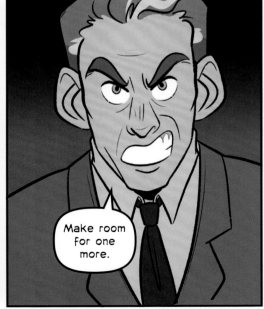

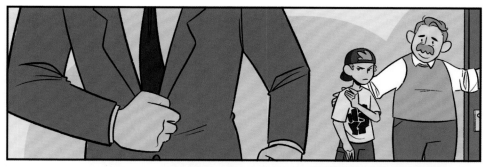

No unauthorized posters!

Pesky kids!

Send them all to detention!

If only there was more room...

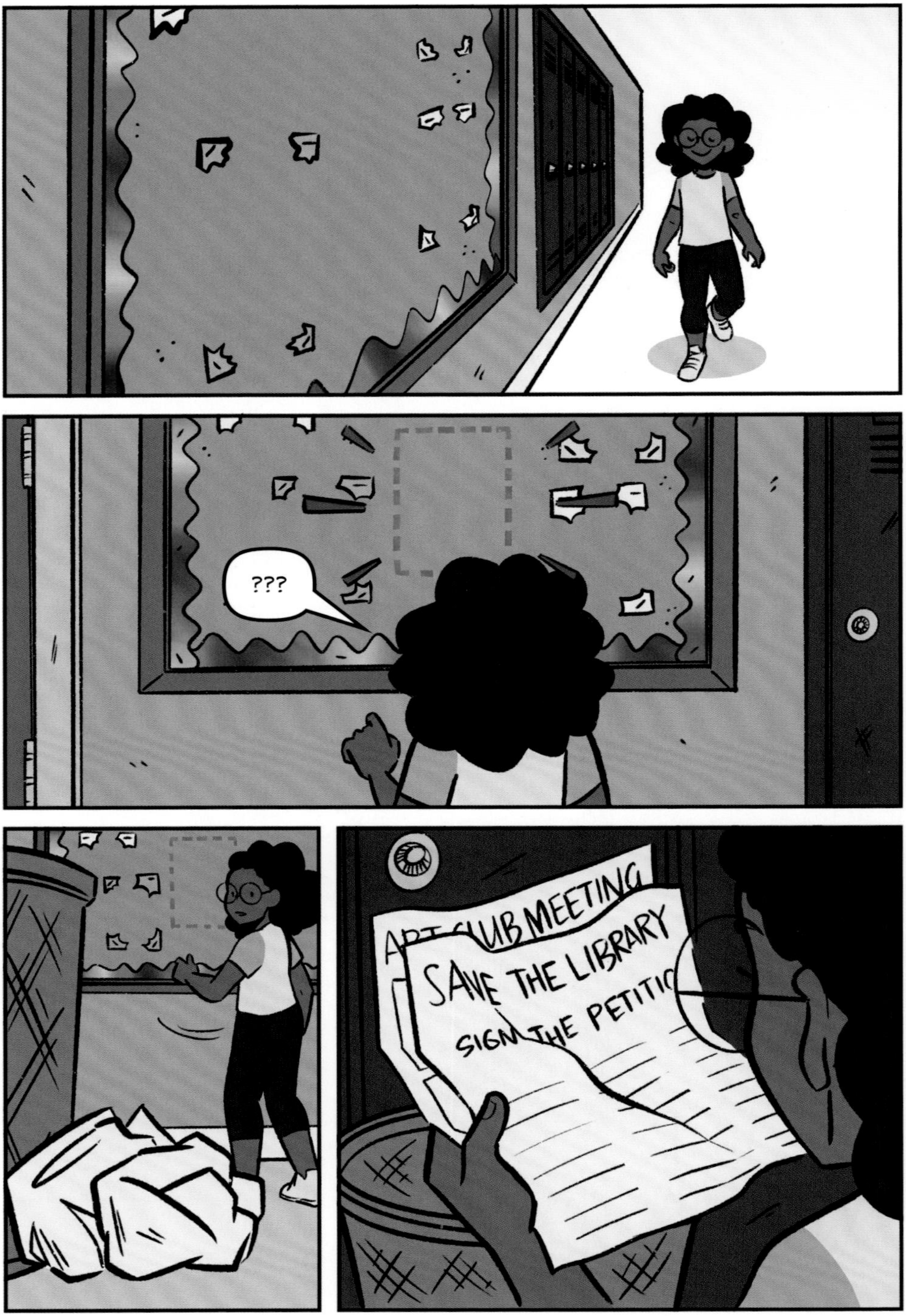
???
ART CLUB MEETING
SAVE THE LIBRARY
SIGN THE PETITIO

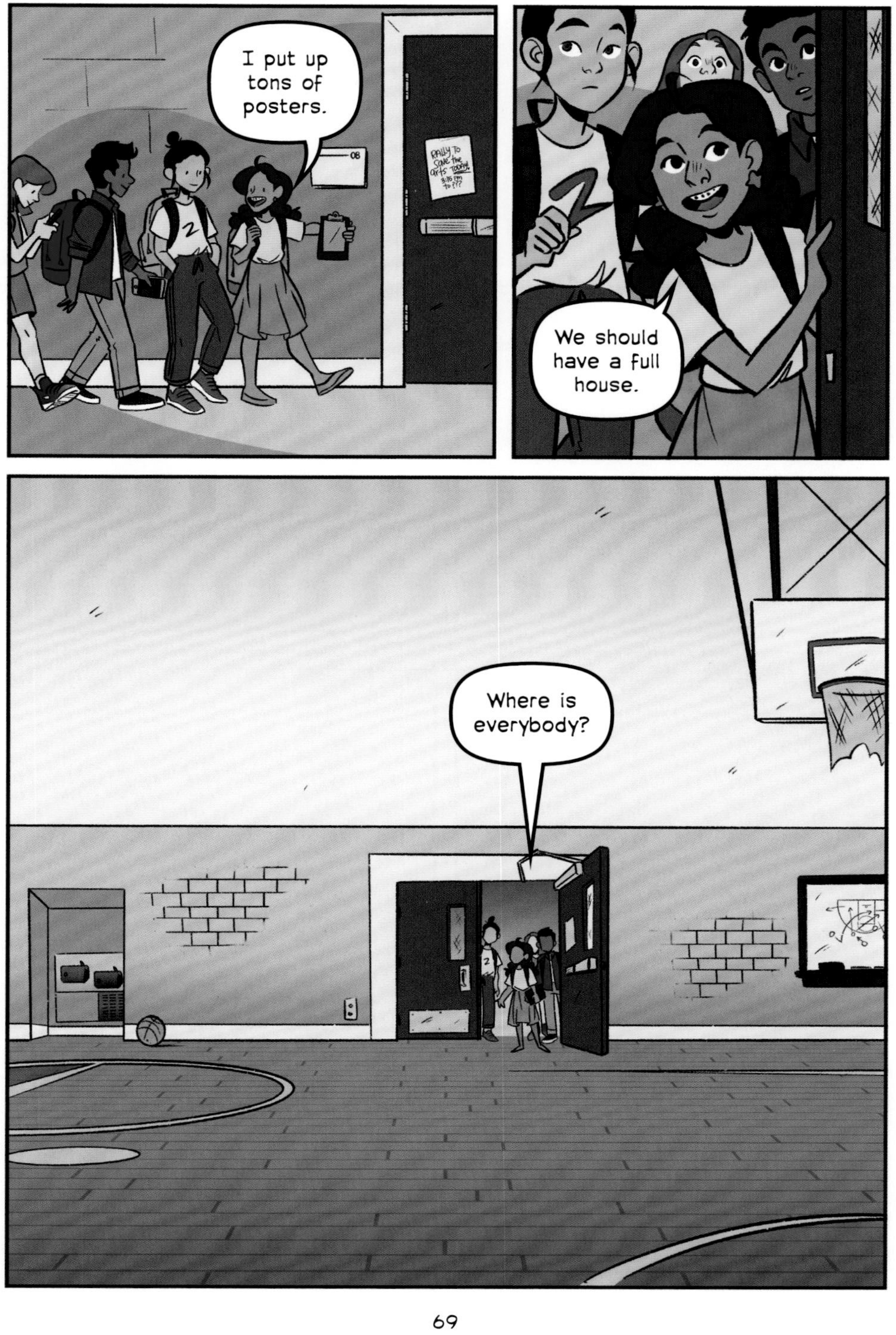
08
RALLY TO Save the arts TODAY! 3:15 PM to ???
I put up tons of posters.
We should have a full house.
Where is everybody?

THE WEEKEND

BZZZZZZZ!

BUZZZ

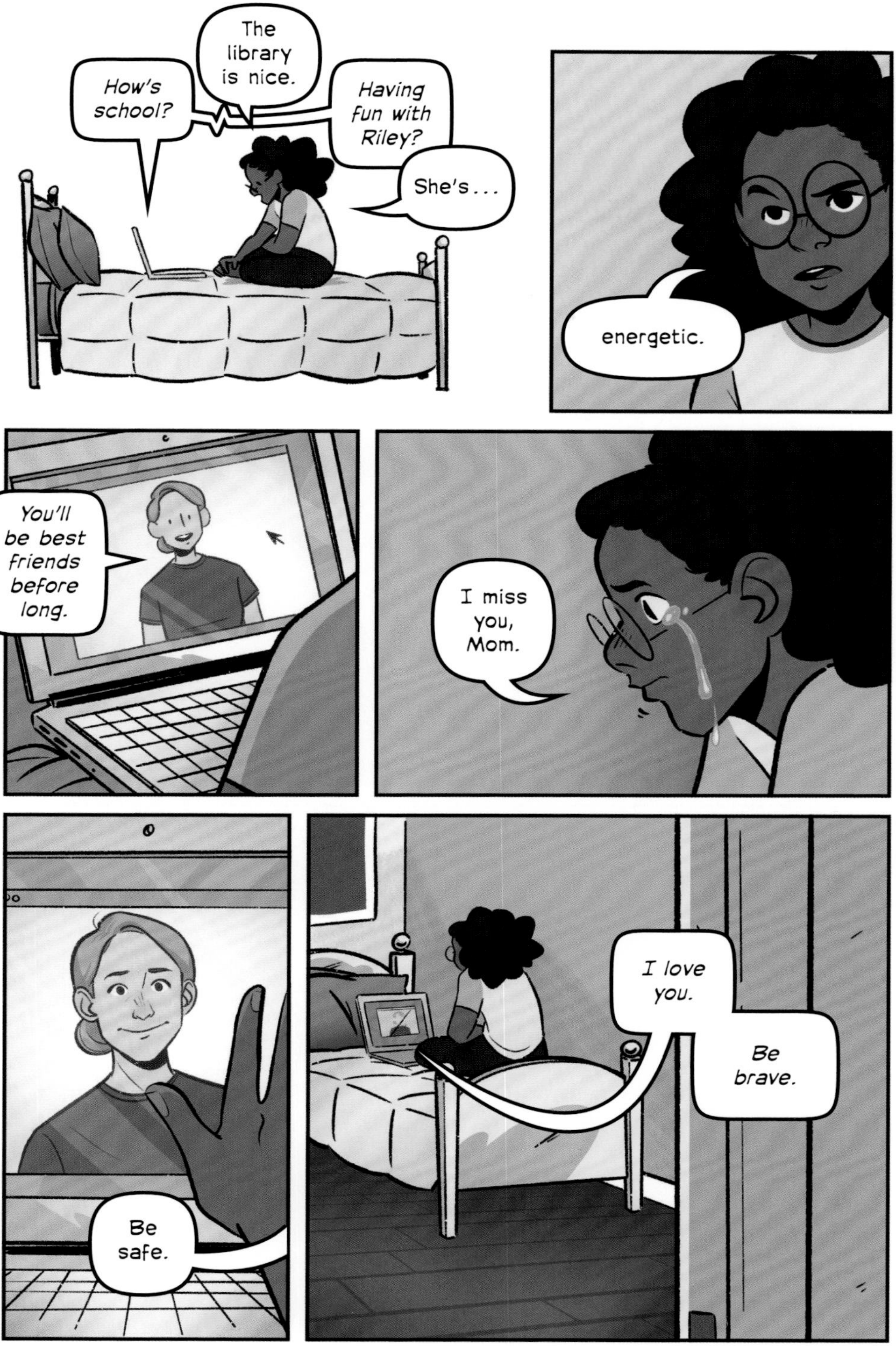
How's school?
The library is nice.
Having fun with Riley?
She's...
energetic.
You'll be best friends before long.
I miss you, Mom.
I love you.
Be brave.
Be safe.

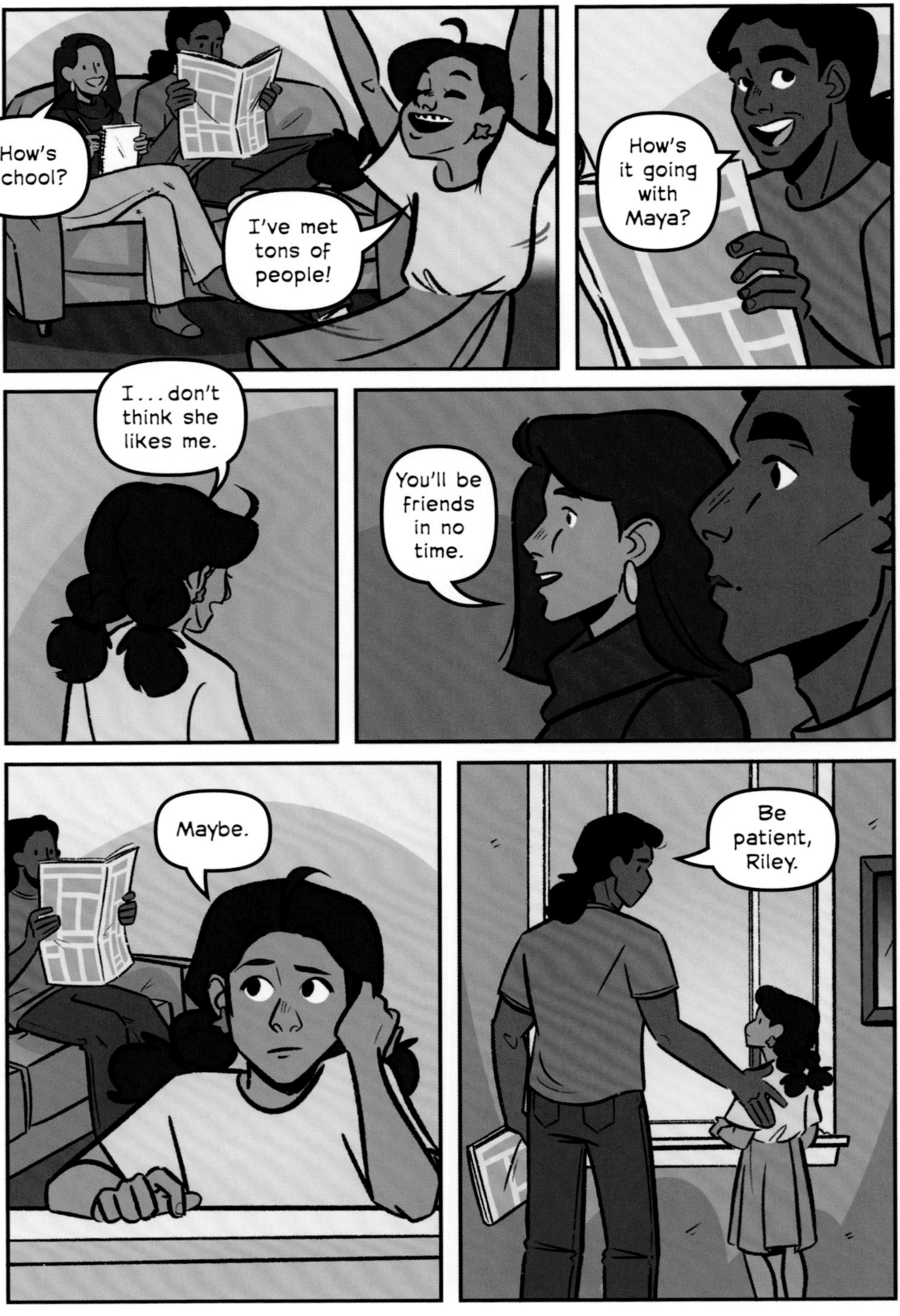
How's school?
I've met tons of people!
How's it going with Maya?
I...don't think she likes me.
You'll be friends in no time.
Maybe.
Be patient, Riley.

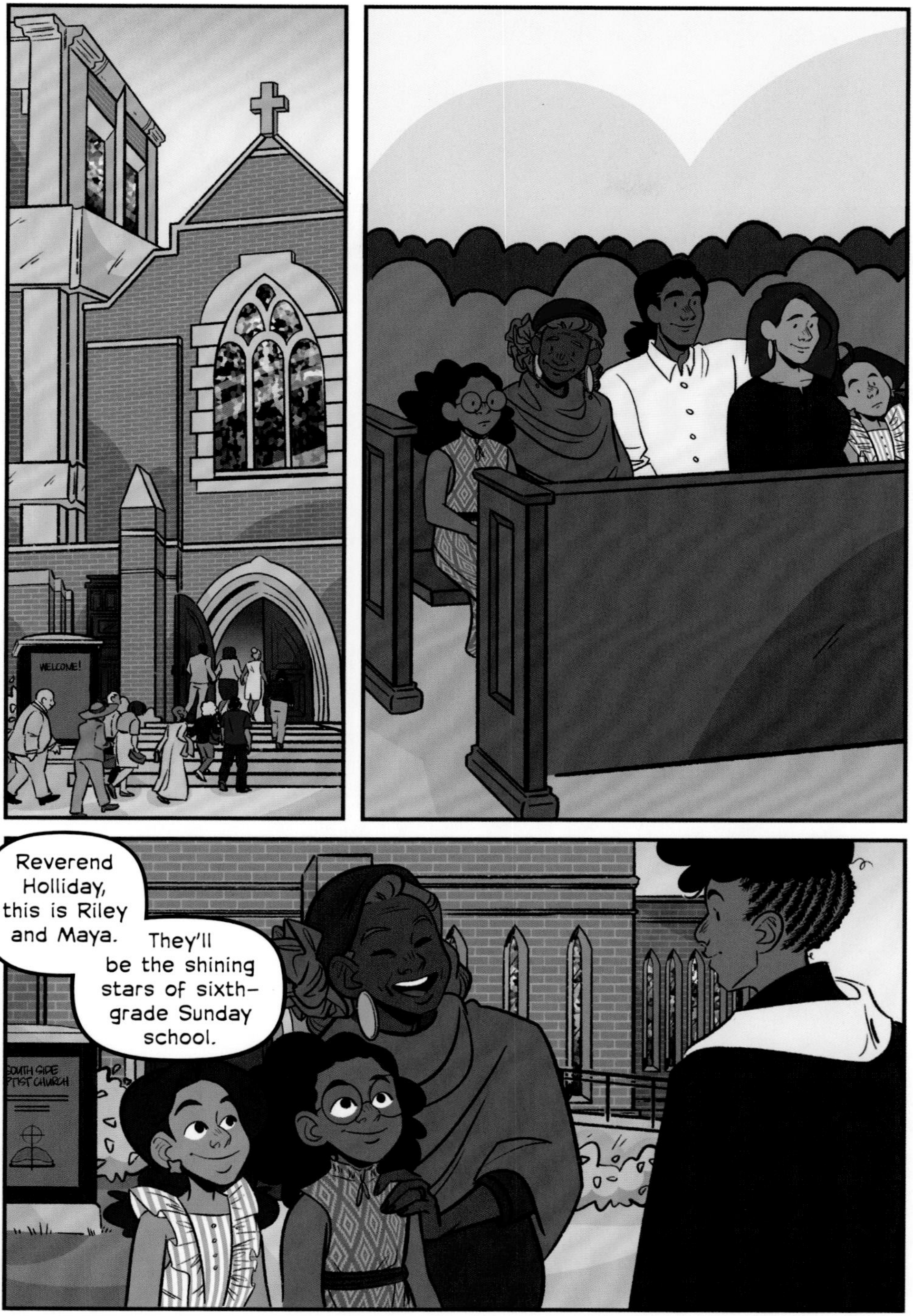
WELCOME!
Reverend Holliday, this is Riley and Maya.
They'll be the shining stars of sixth-grade Sunday school.

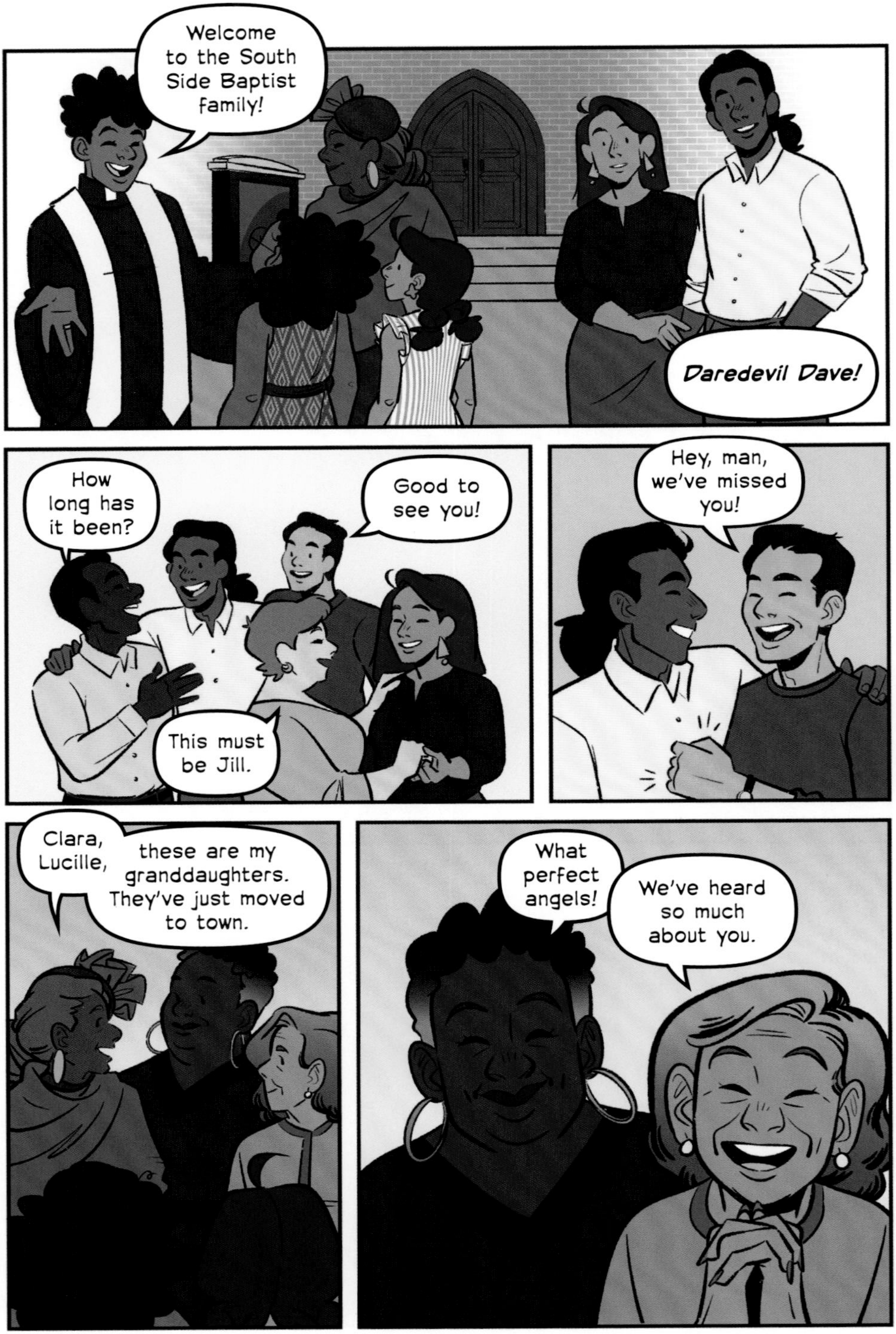
Welcome to the South Side Baptist family!
Daredevil Dave!
How long has it been?
Good to see you!
This must be Jill.
Hey, man, we've missed you!
Clara, Lucille,
these are my granddaughters. They've just moved to town.
What perfect angels!
We've heard so much about you.

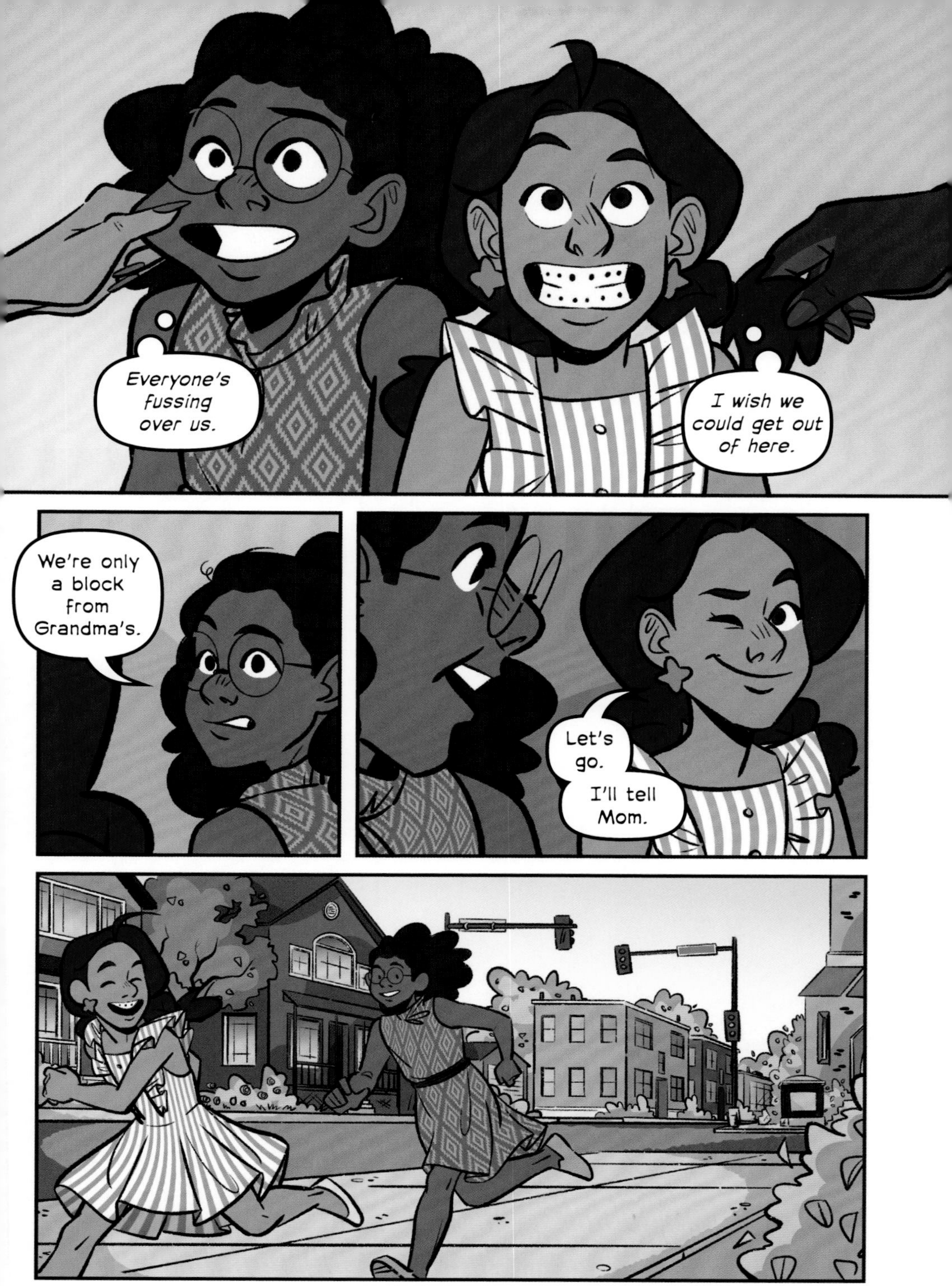
Everyone's fussing over us.
I wish we could get out of here.
We're only a block from Grandma's.
Let's go.
I'll tell Mom.

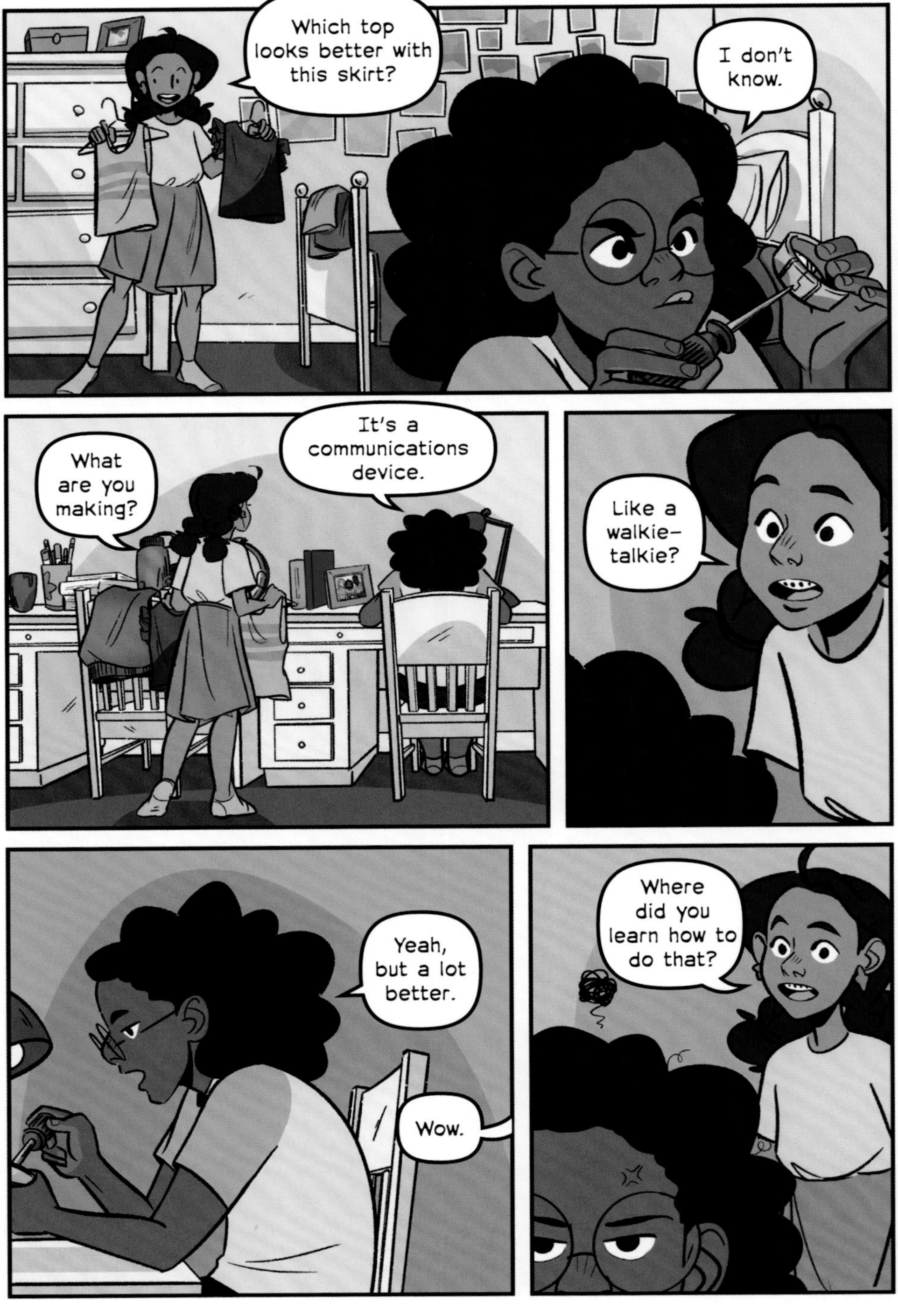
Which top looks better with this skirt?
I don't know.
What are you making?
It's a communications device.
Like a walkie-talkie?
Yeah, but a lot better.
Wow.
Where did you learn how to do that?

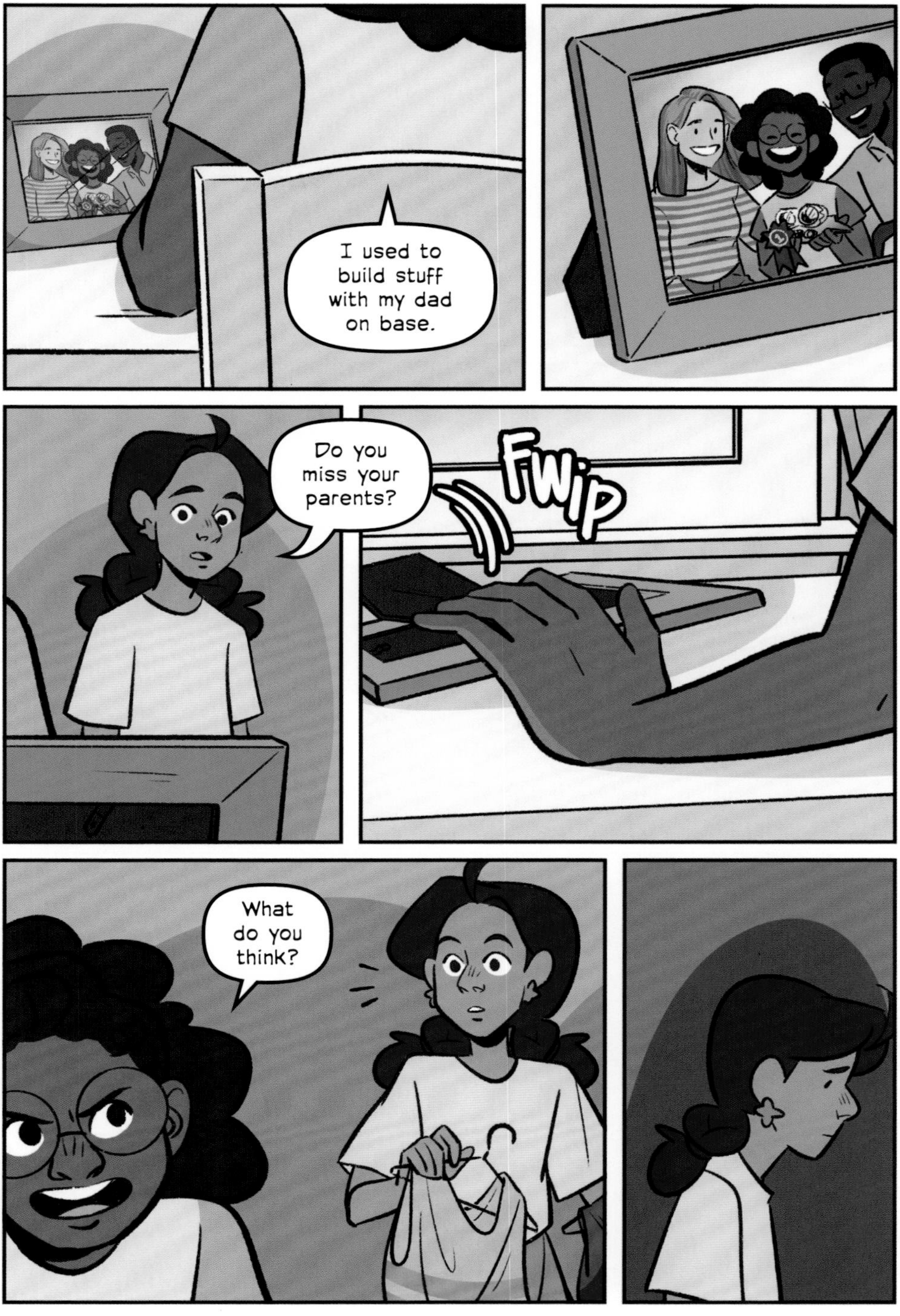
I used to build stuff with my dad on base.
Do you miss your parents?
FWIP
What do you think?

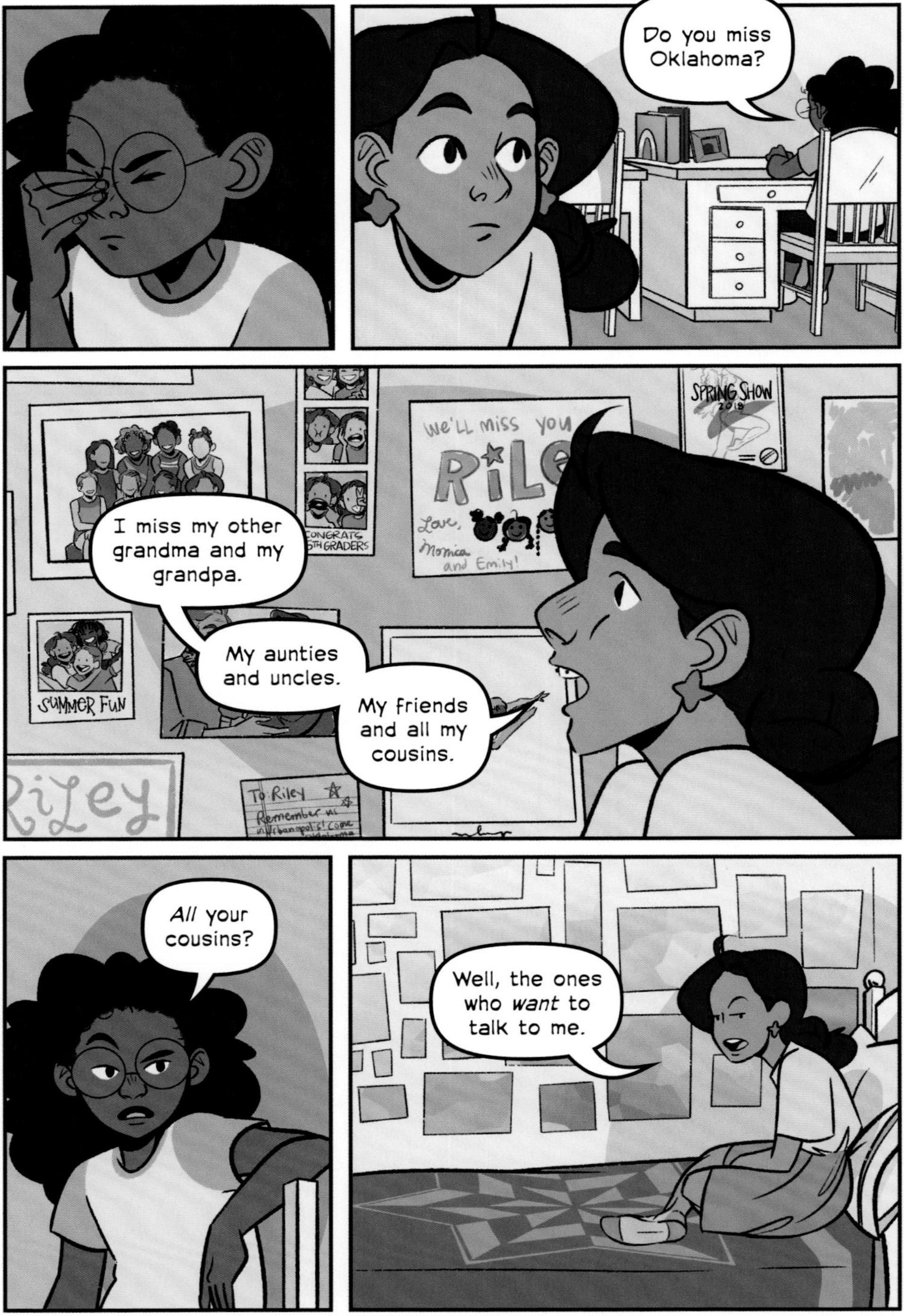
Do you miss Oklahoma?
SPRING SHOW
WE'LL MISS YOU
Love,
and Emily!
CONGRATS 5TH GRADERS
I miss my other grandma and my grandpa.
My aunties and uncles.
SUMMER FUN
My friends and all my cousins.
RiLey
To Riley
All your cousins?
Well, the ones who *want* to talk to me.

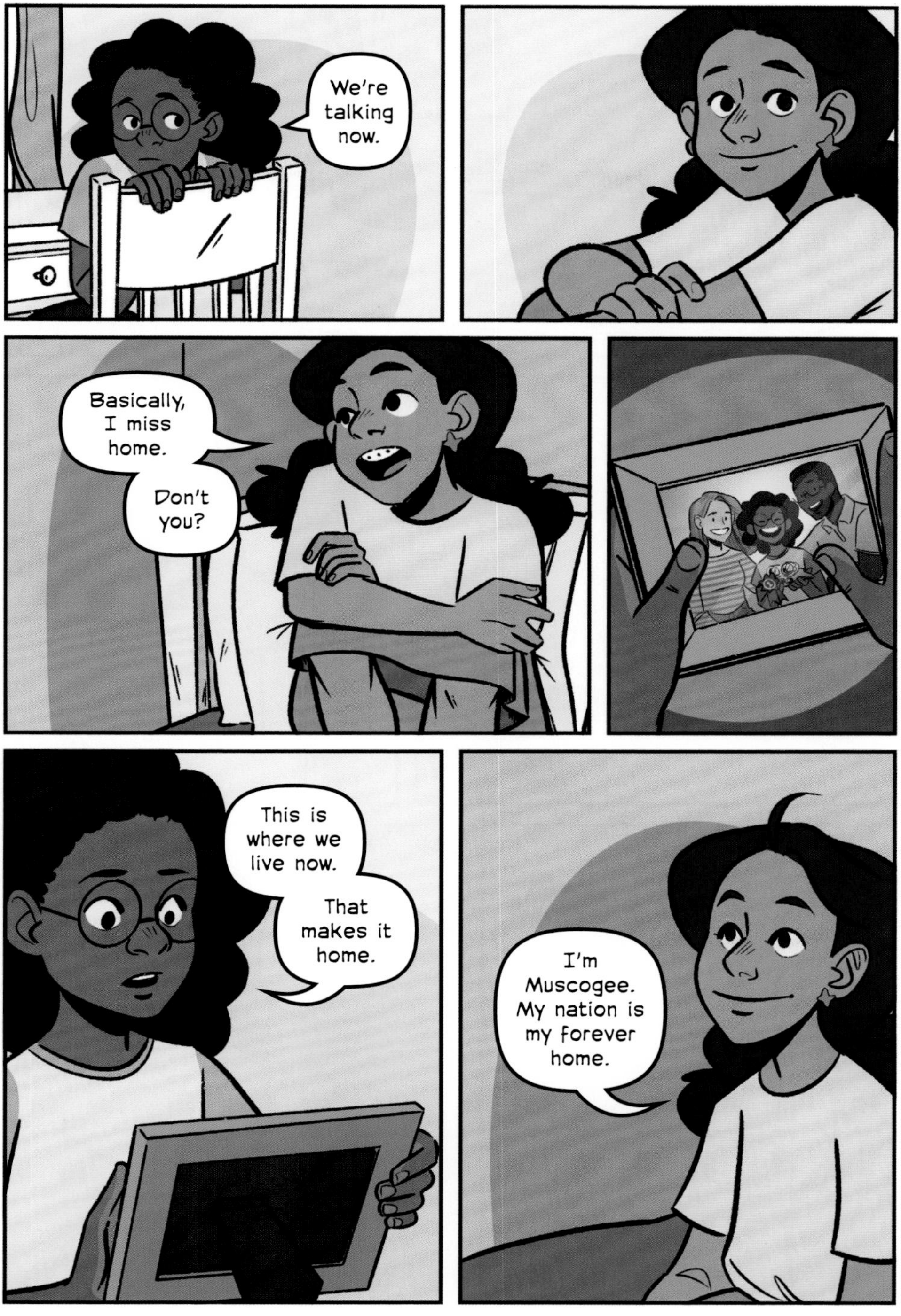
We're talking now.
Basically, I miss home.
Don't you?
This is where we live now.
That makes it home.
I'm Muscogee. My nation is my forever home.

I can't imagine what that feels like.
ADVANCED ENGINEERING
I never thought I'd be an urban Native.
And now I'm an *Urbanopolis* Native.
I never thought I'd live in one place.
We'll have to make the best of it.

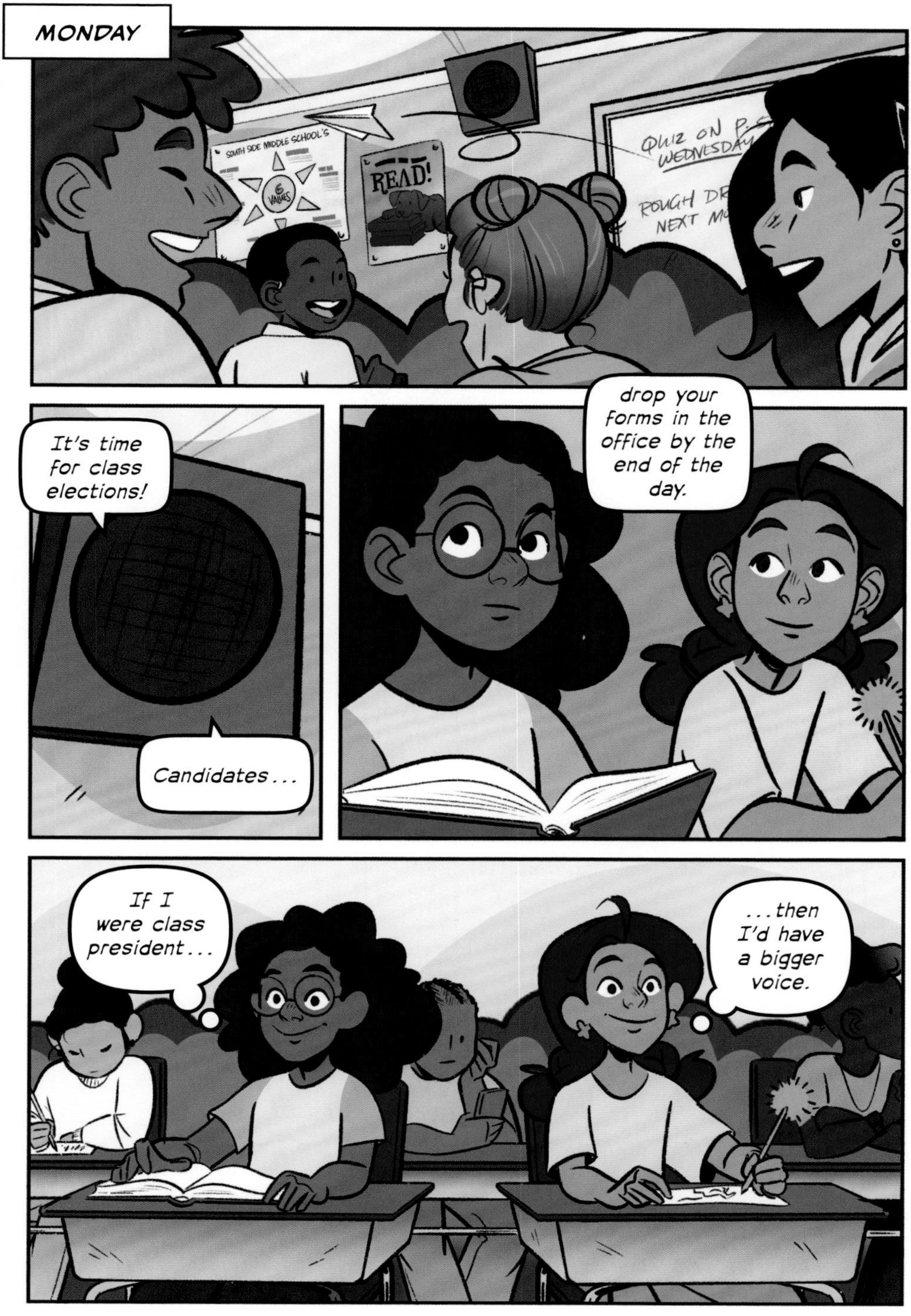
MONDAY
SOUTH SIDE MIDDLE SCHOOL'S
6 VALUES
READ!
QUIZ ON P.
WEDNESDAY
ROUGH DR
NEXT M
It's time for class elections!
Candidates . . .
drop your forms in the office by the end of the day.
If I were class president . . .
. . . then I'd have a bigger voice.

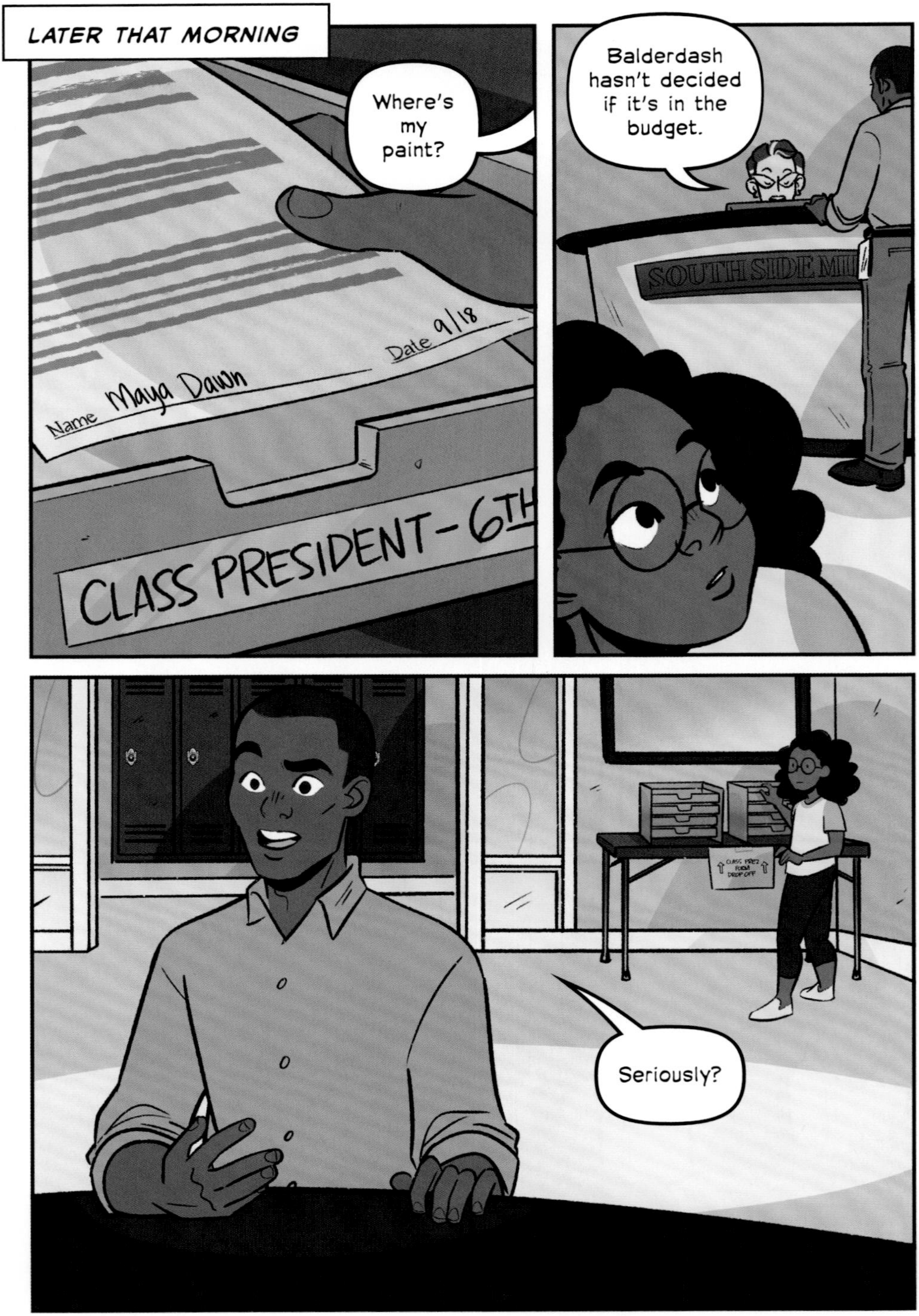
LATER THAT MORNING
Where's my paint?
Date 9/18
Name Maya Dawn
CLASS PRESIDENT-6TH
Balderdash hasn't decided if it's in the budget.
SOUTH SIDE MI
Seriously?

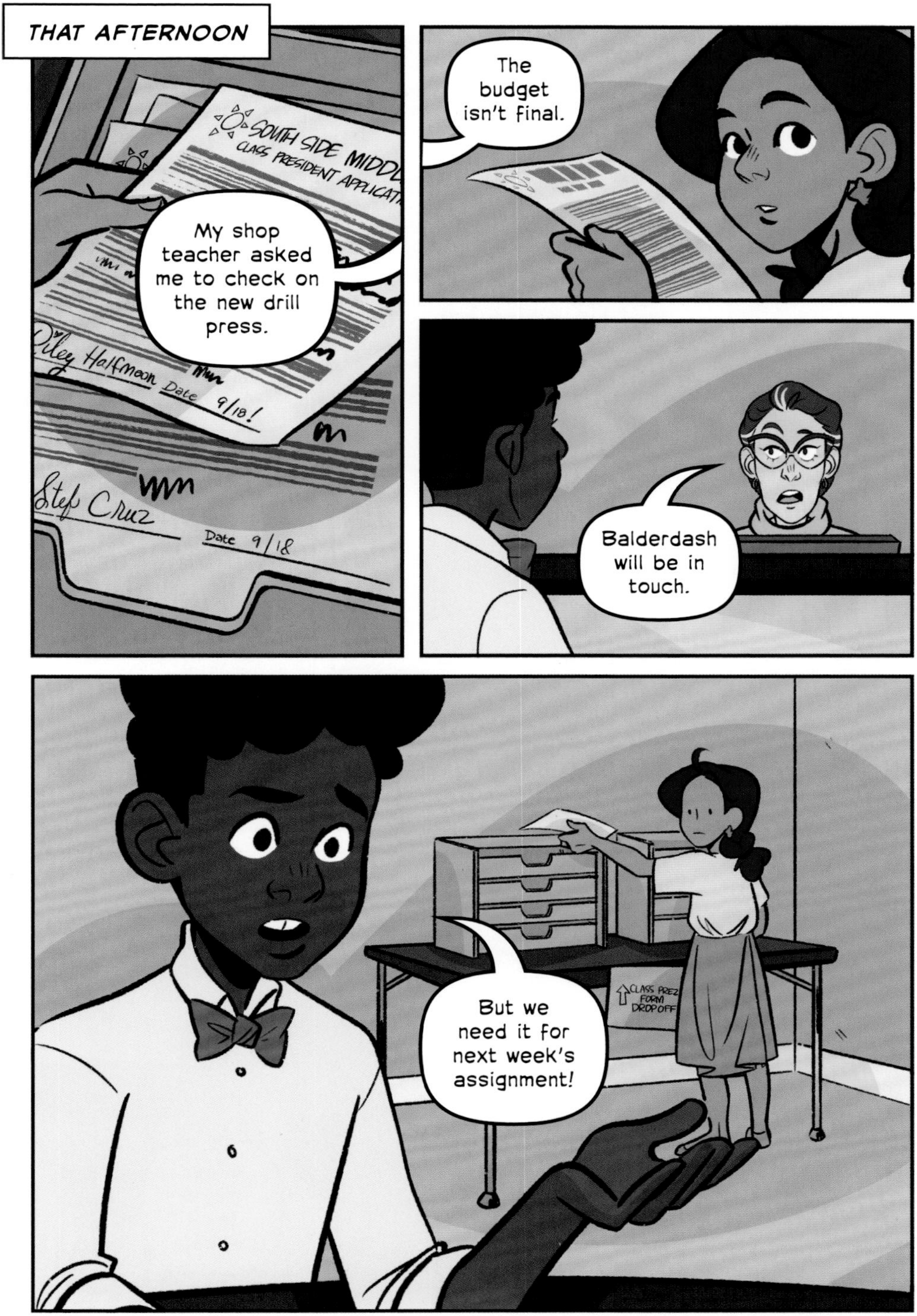
THAT AFTERNOON
My shop teacher asked me to check on the new drill press.
Stef Cruz
Date 9/18
The budget isn't final.
Balderdash will be in touch.
But we need it for next week's assignment!
CLASS PREZ FORM DROPOFF

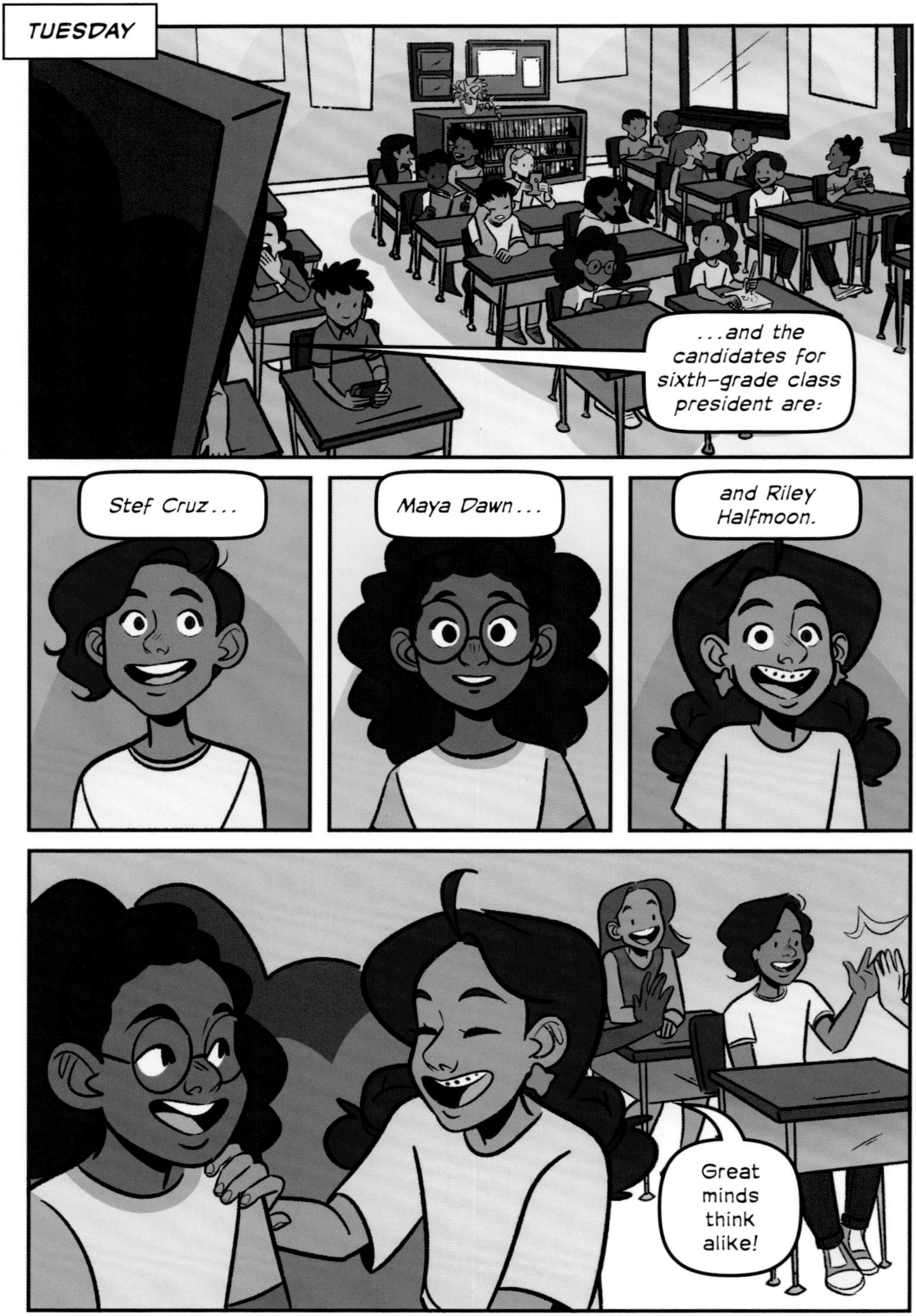
TUESDAY
...and the candidates for sixth-grade class president are:
Stef Cruz...
Maya Dawn...
and Riley Halfmoon.
Great minds think alike!

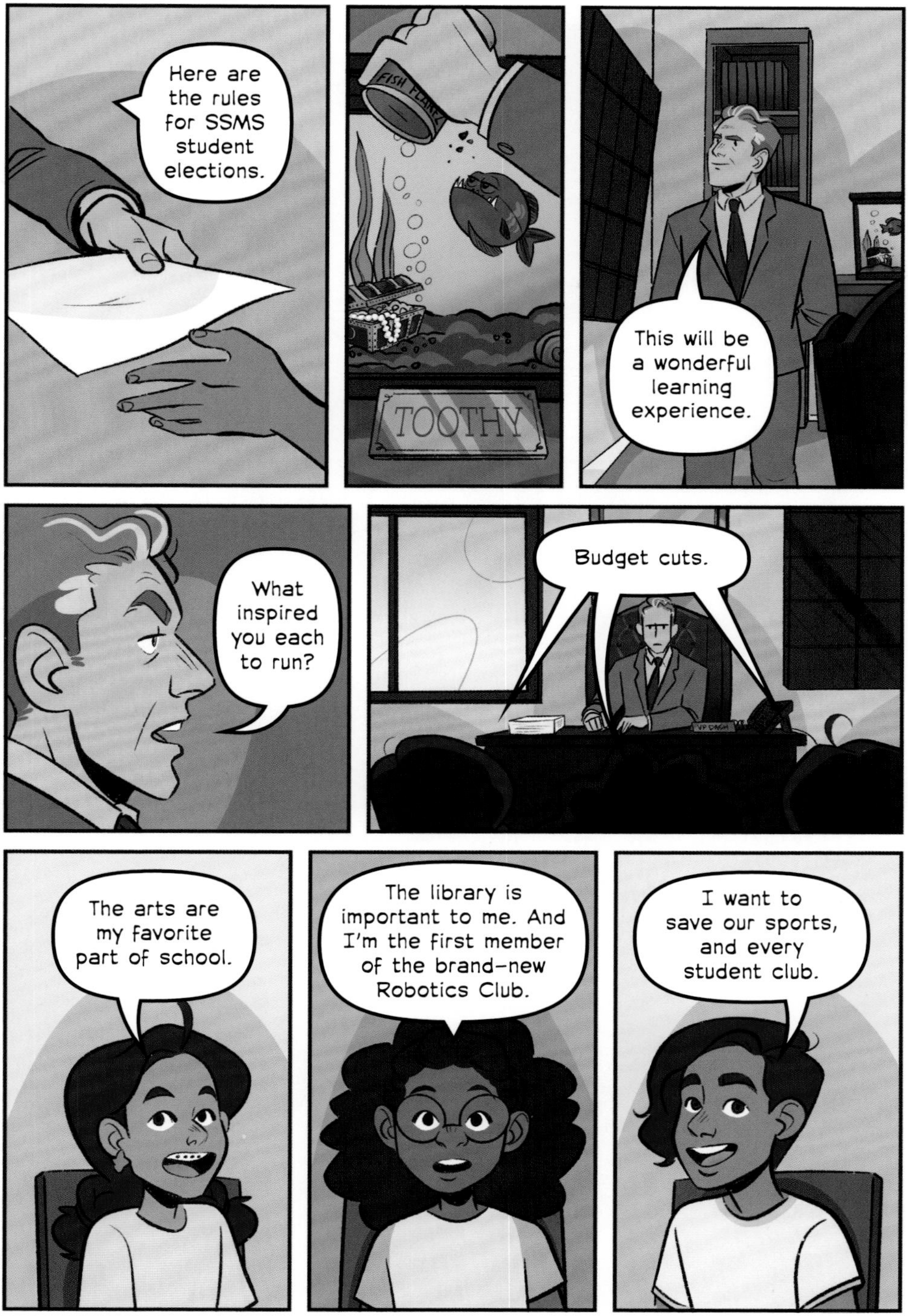
Here are the rules for SSMS student elections.
FISH FLAKES
TOOTHY
This will be a wonderful learning experience.
What inspired you each to run?
Budget cuts.
VP DASH
The arts are my favorite part of school.
The library is important to me. And I'm the first member of the brand-new Robotics Club.
I want to save our sports, and every student club.

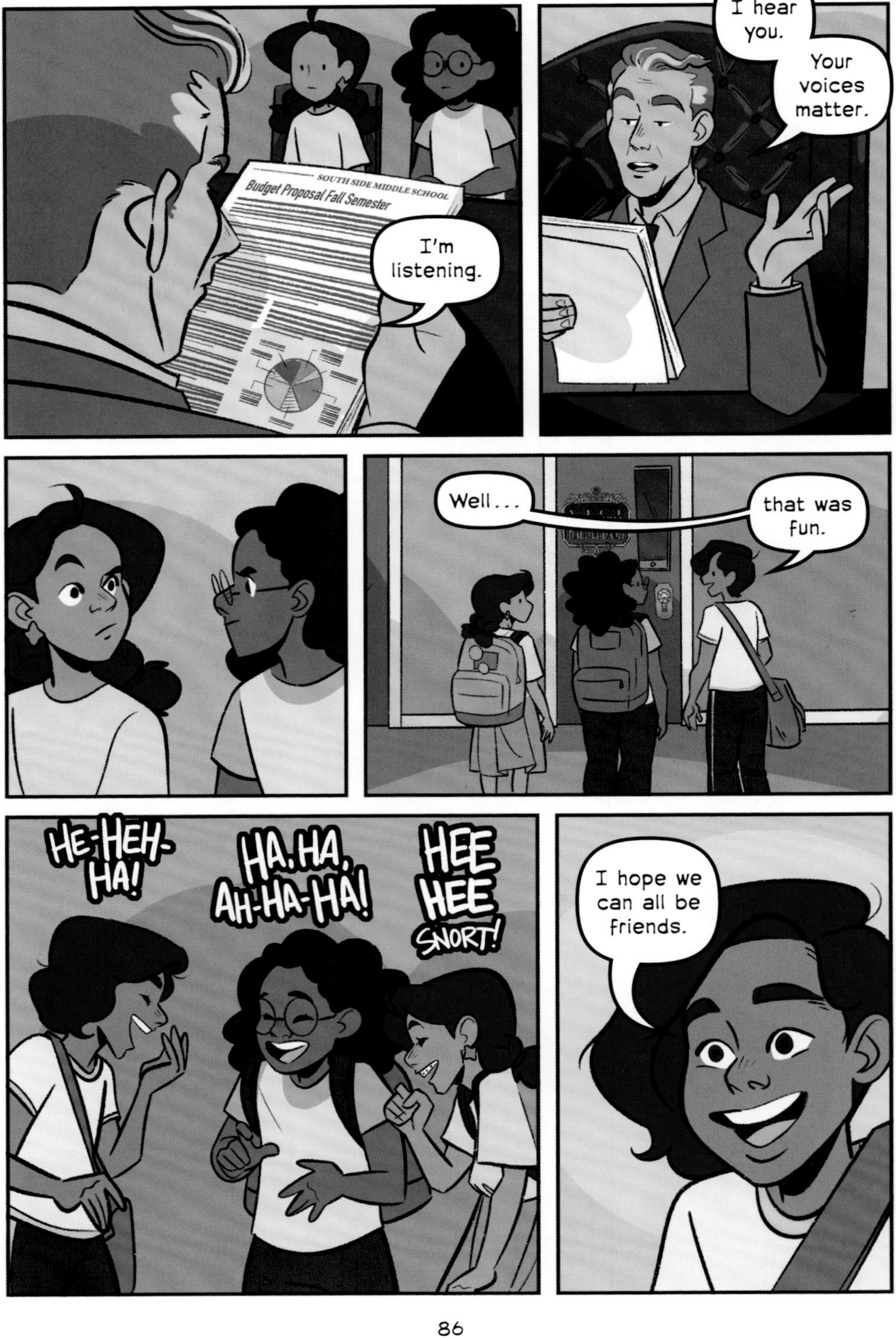
SOUTH SIDE MIDDLE SCHOOL
Budget Proposal Fall Semester
I'm listening.
I hear you.
Your voices matter.
Well...
that was fun.
HE-HEH-HA!
HA, HA, AH-HA-HA!
HEE HEE SNORT!
I hope we can all be friends.

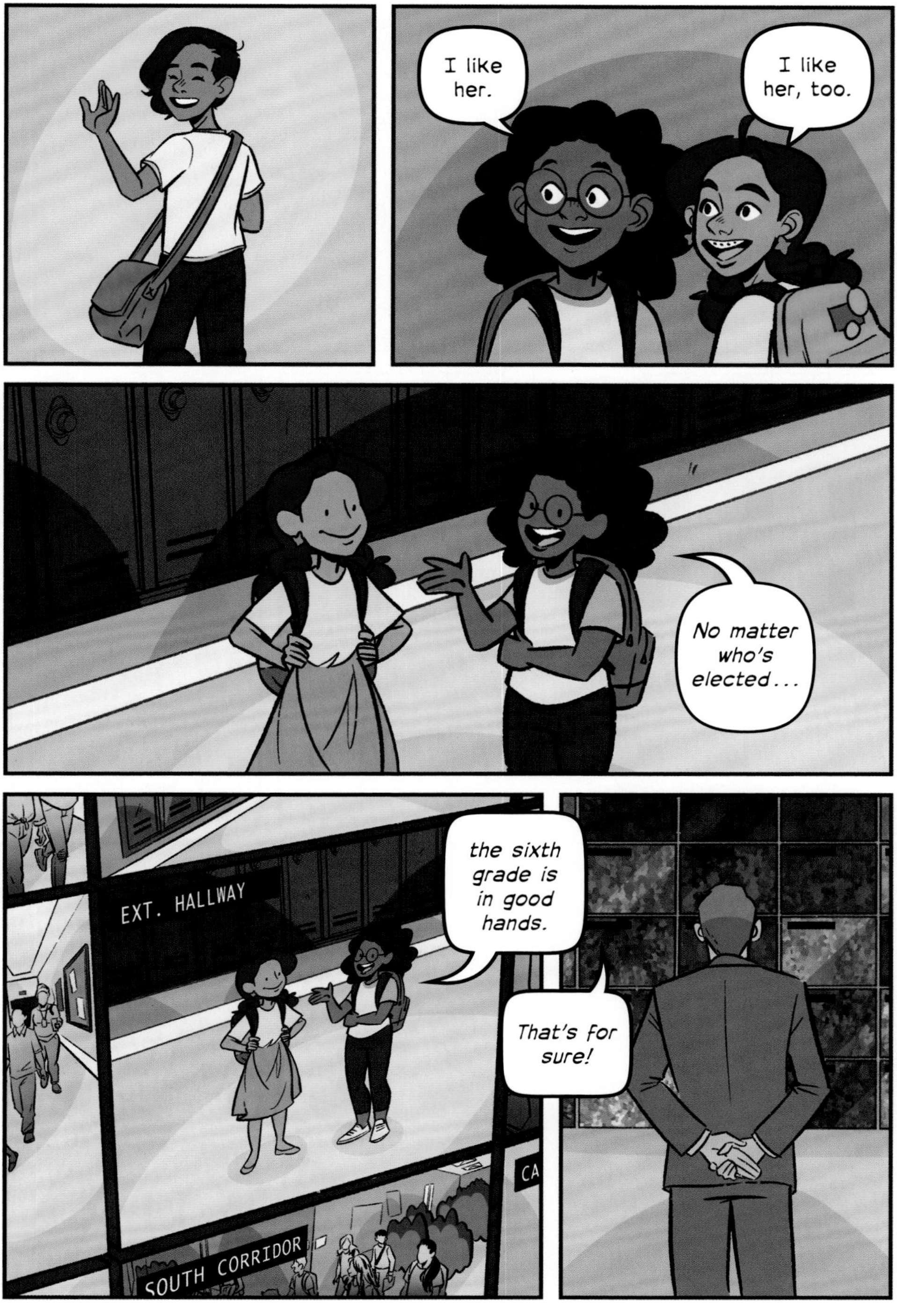
I like her.
I like her, too.
No matter who's elected...
EXT. HALLWAY
the sixth grade is in good hands.
That's for sure!
SOUTH CORRIDOR

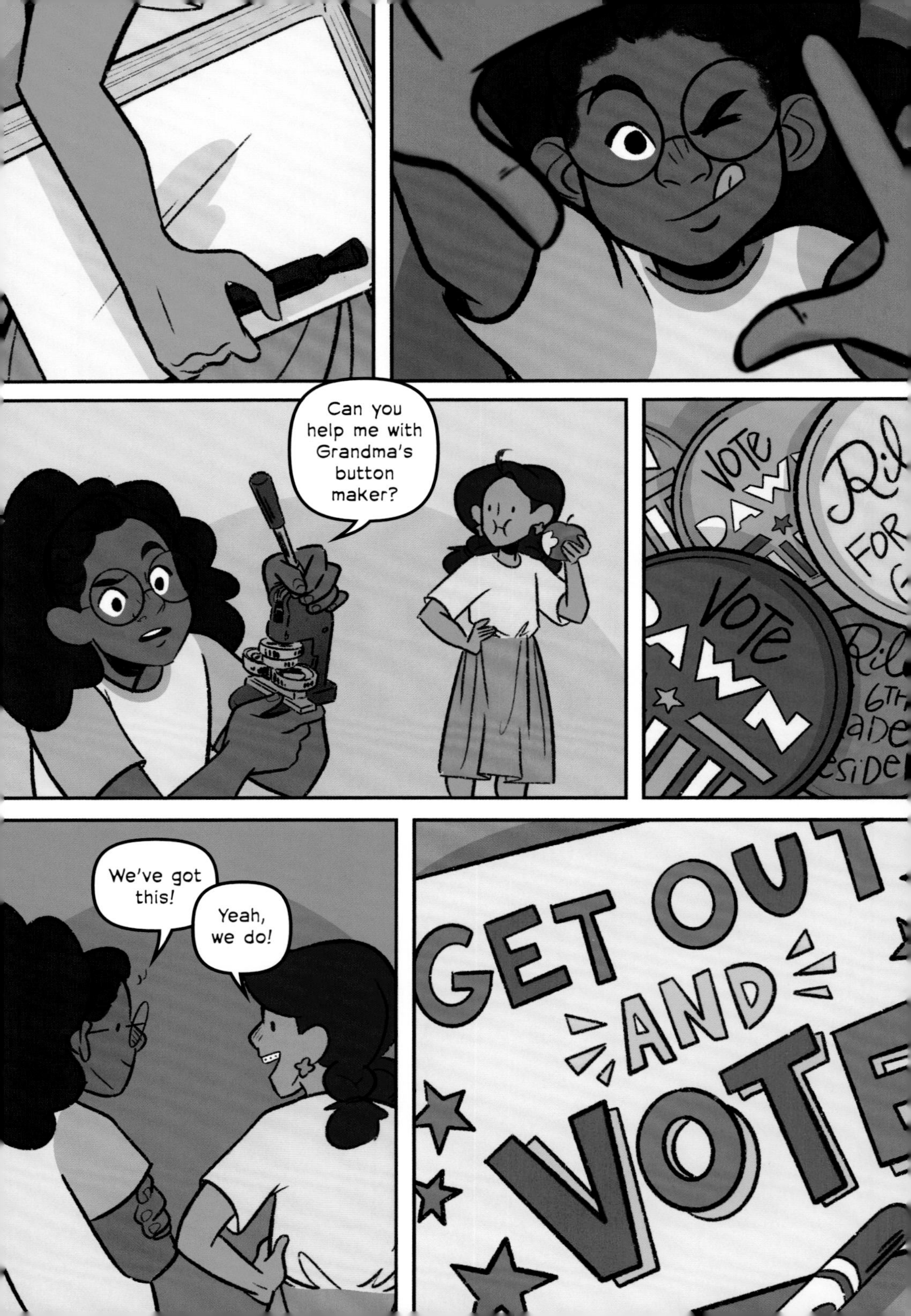
Can you help me with Grandma's button maker?
VOTE
VOTE
We've got this!
Yeah, we do!
GET OUT AND VOTE

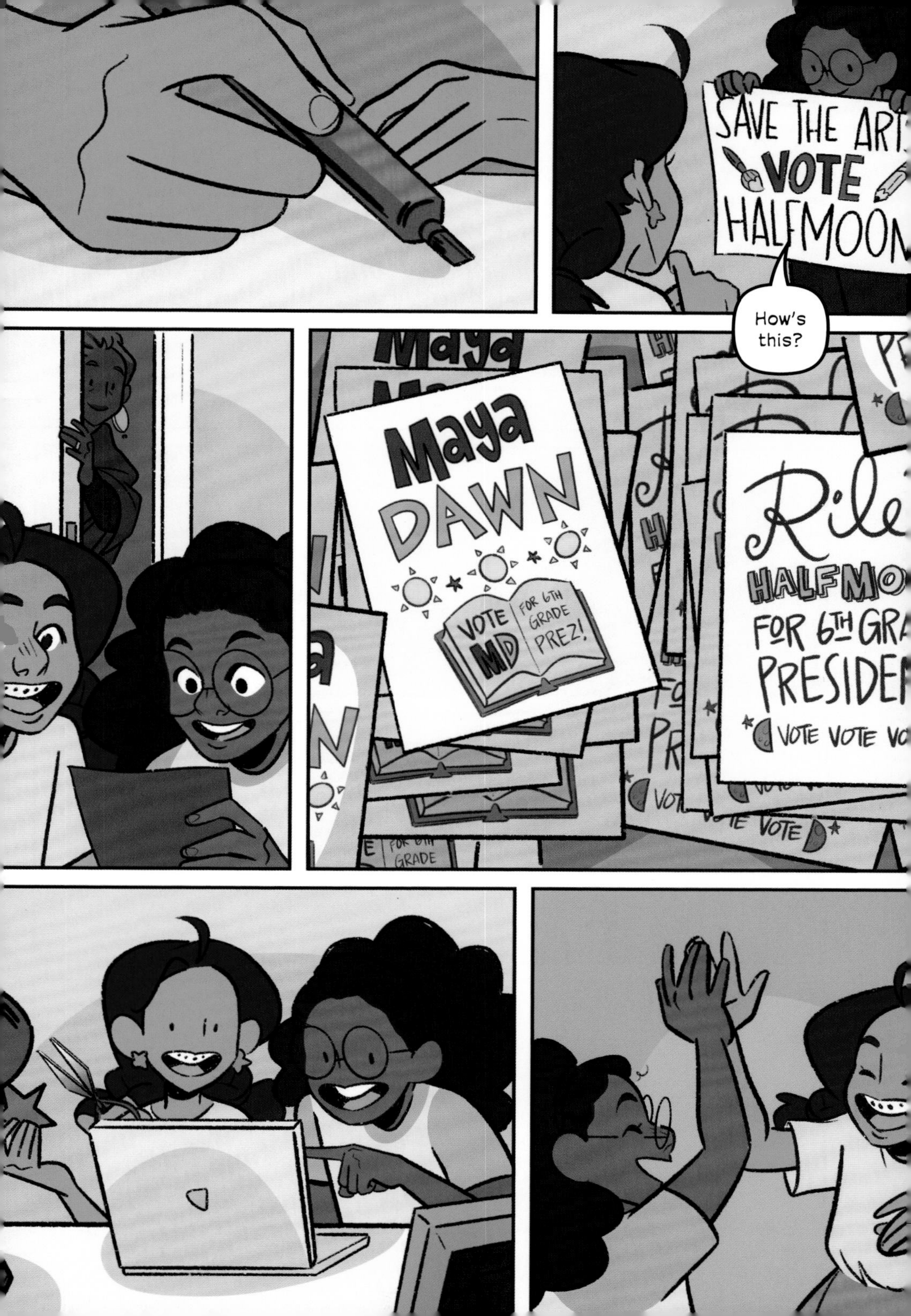

SAVE THE ARTS
VOTE
HALFMOON
How's this?
Maya DAWN
VOTE MD
FOR 6TH GRADE PREZ!
HALFMO
FOR 6TH GRA
PRESIDE
VOTE VOTE VO

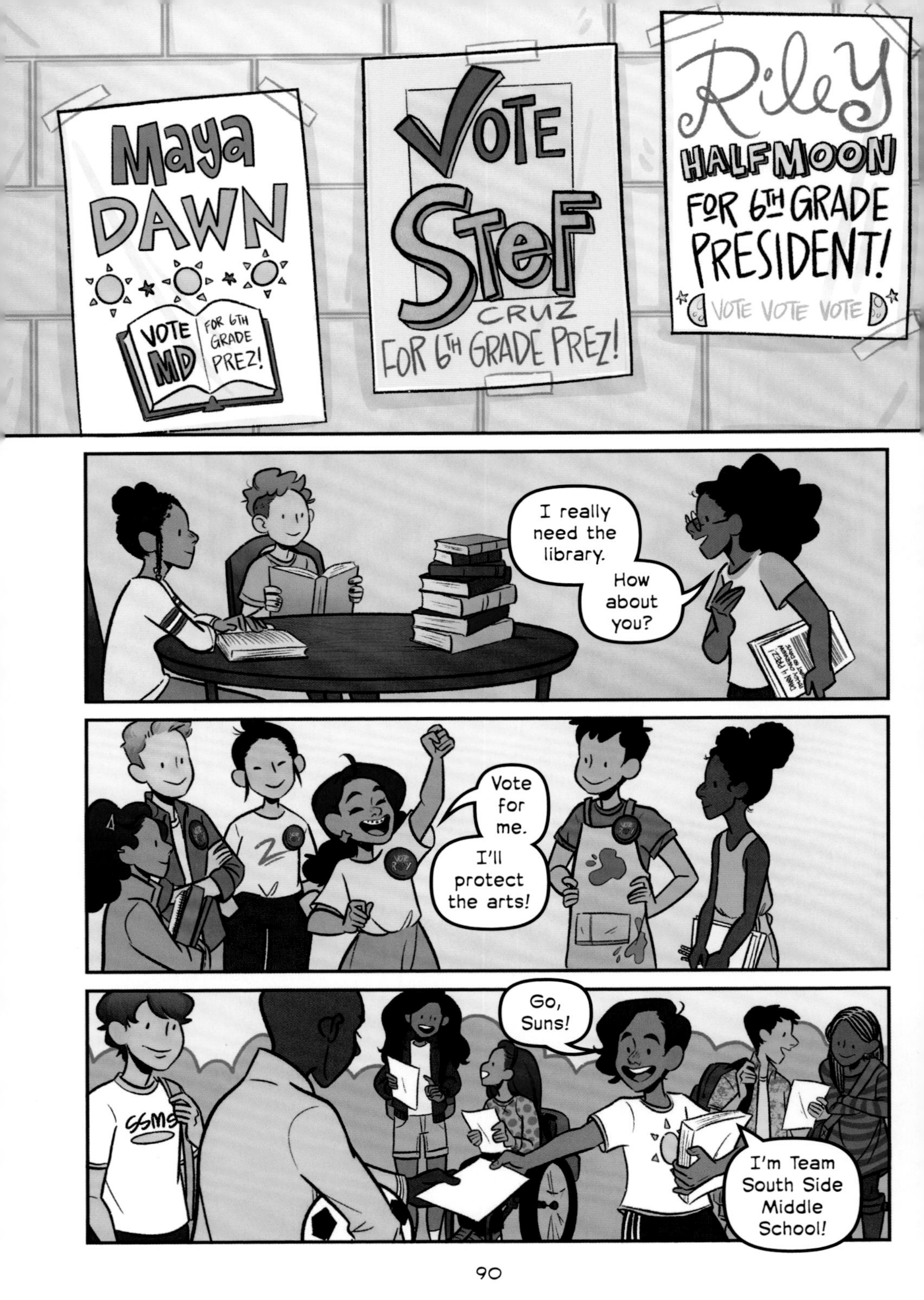
Maya DAWN
VOTE MD
FOR 6TH GRADE PREZ!
VOTE Stef CRUZ
FOR 6TH GRADE PREZ!
Riley HALFMOON
FOR 6TH GRADE PRESIDENT!
VOTE VOTE VOTE
I really need the library.
How about you?
Vote for me.
I'll protect the arts!
Go, Suns!
I'm Team South Side Middle School!
SSMS

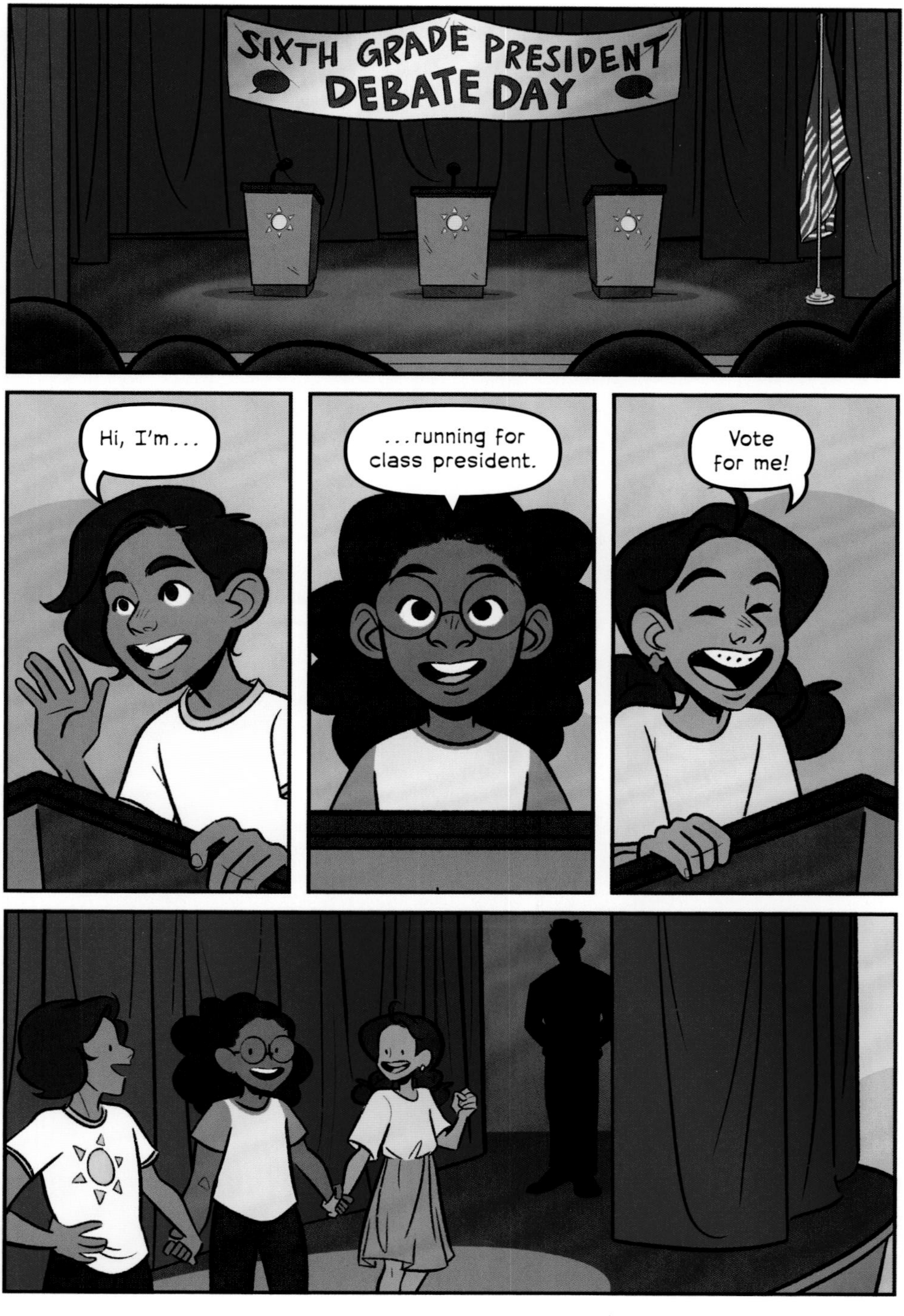
SIXTH GRADE PRESIDENT
DEBATE DAY
Hi, I'm...
...running for class president.
Vote for me!

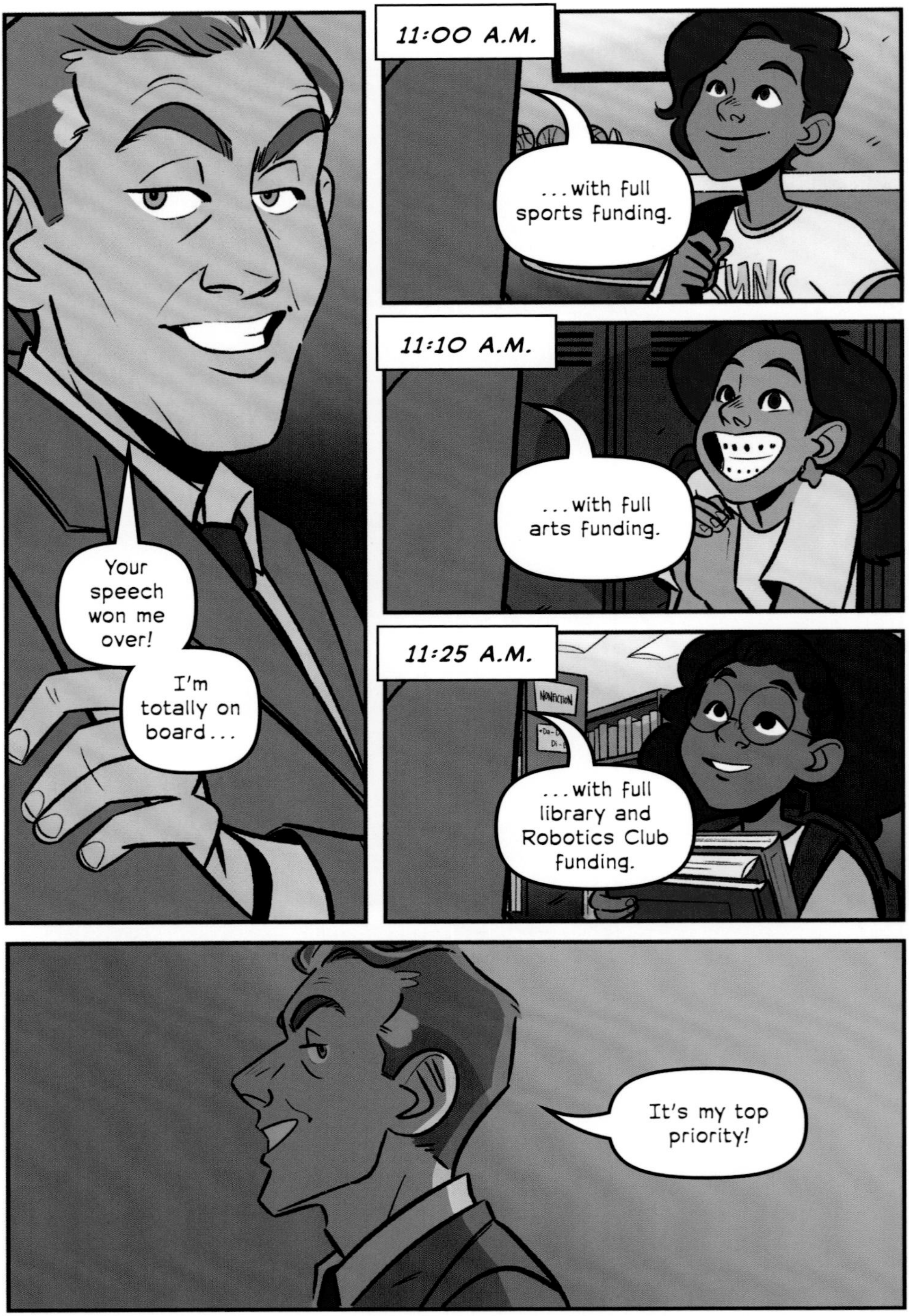

Your speech won me over!
I'm totally on board...
11:00 A.M.
...with full sports funding.
11:10 A.M.
...with full arts funding.
11:25 A.M.
...with full library and Robotics Club funding.
It's my top priority!

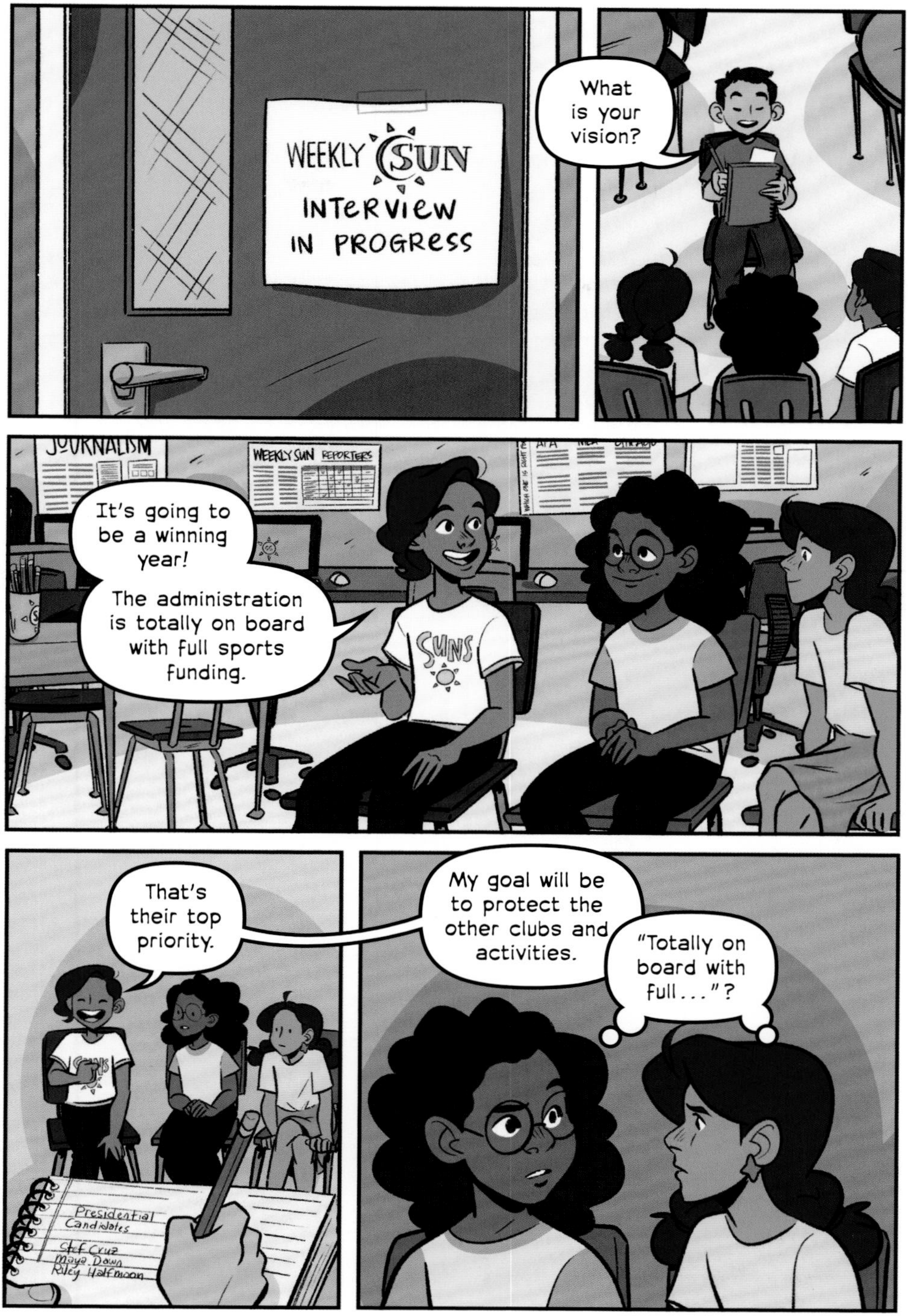
WEEKLY SUN
INTERVIEW IN PROGRESS
What is your vision?
JOURNALISM
WEEKLY SUN REPORTERS
It's going to be a winning year!
The administration is totally on board with full sports funding.
That's their top priority.
My goal will be to protect the other clubs and activities.
"Totally on board with full . . ."?
Presidential Candidates
Stef Cruz
Maya Down
Riley Halfmoon

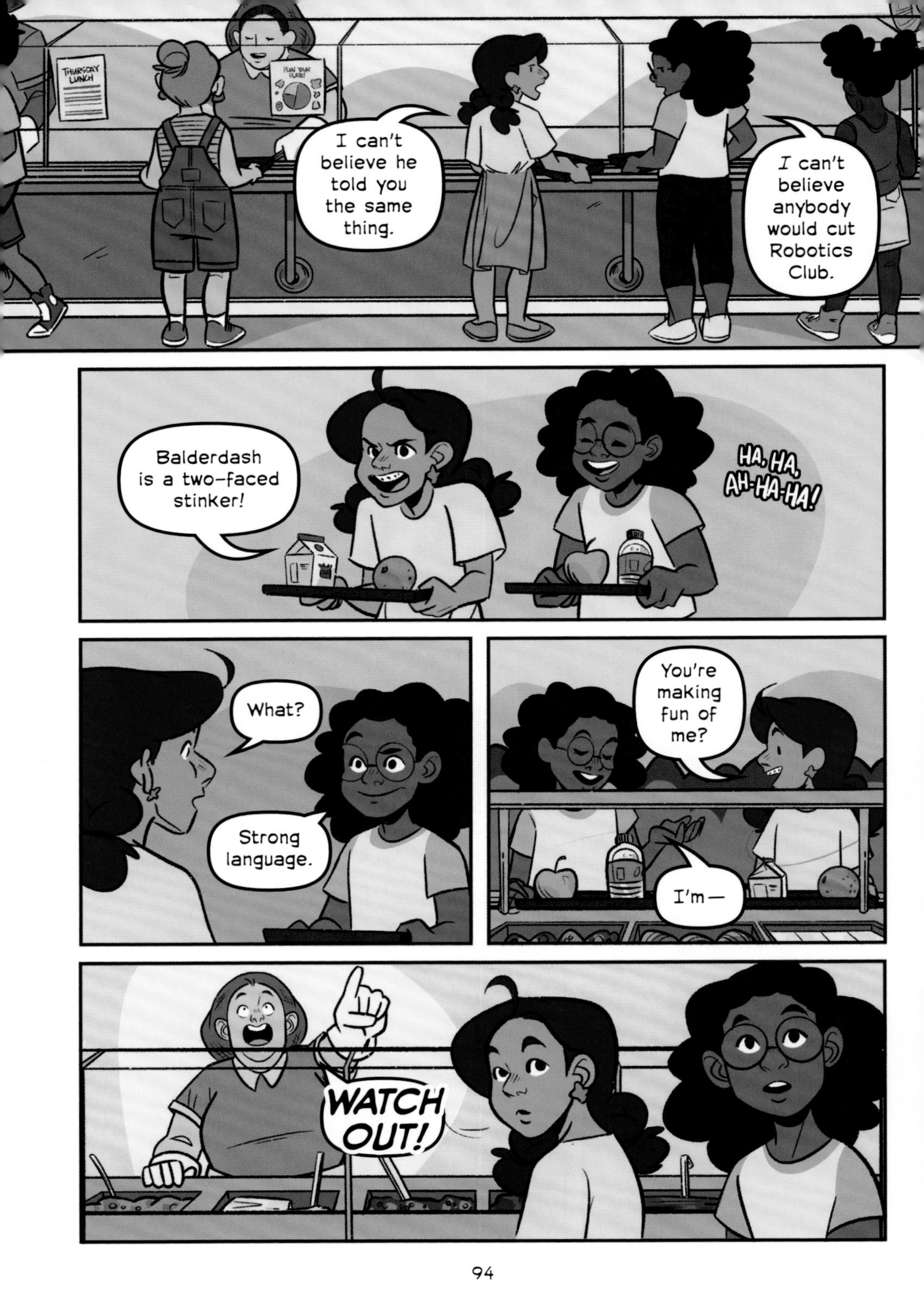

I can't believe he told you the same thing.
I can't believe anybody would cut Robotics Club.
Balderdash is a two-faced stinker!
HA, HA, AH-HA-HA!
What?
Strong language.
You're making fun of me?
I'm—
WATCH OUT!

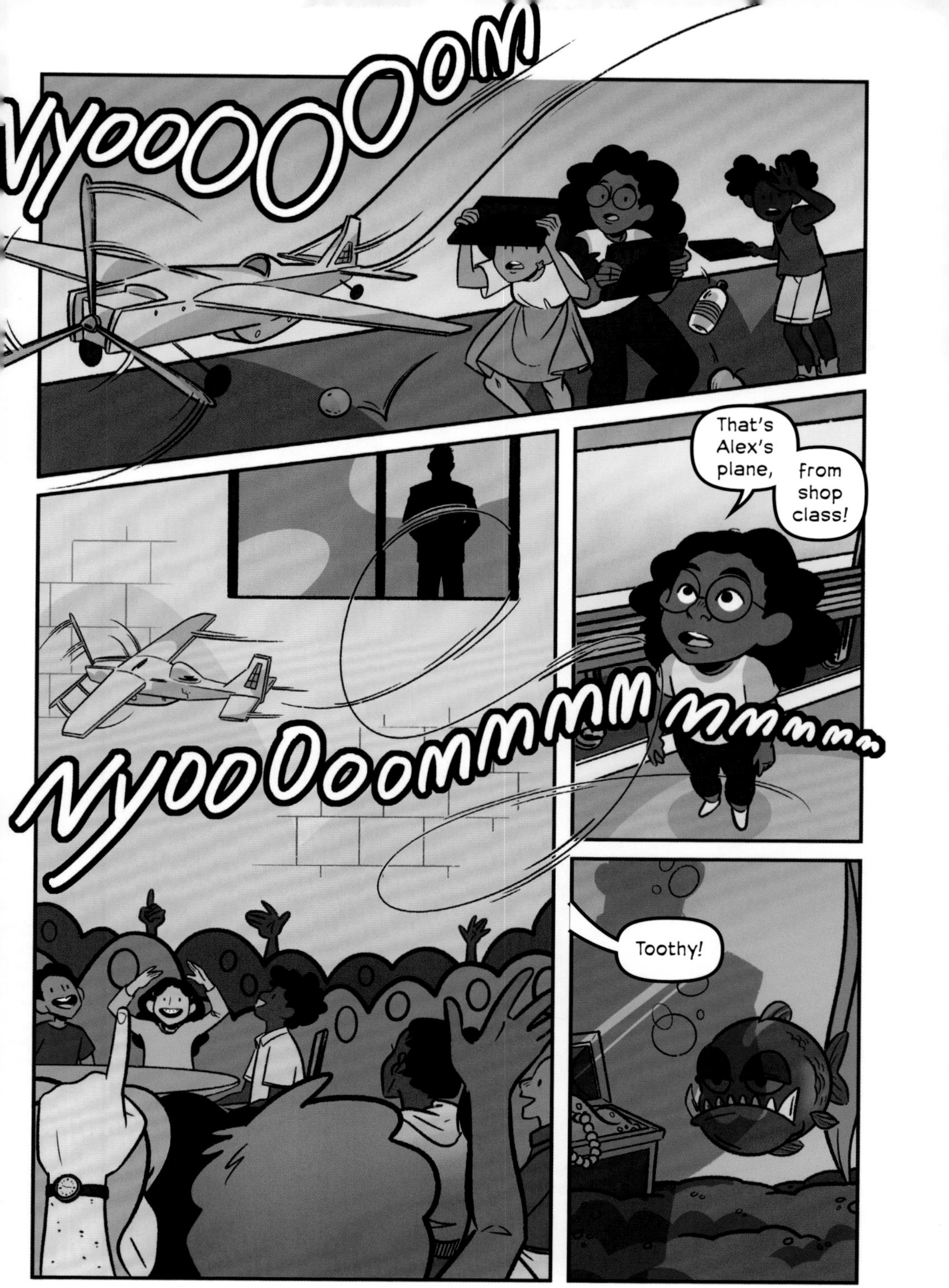

VYOOOOOOOM
That's Alex's plane,
from shop class!
NYOOOOOOMMMMMMMMM
Toothy!

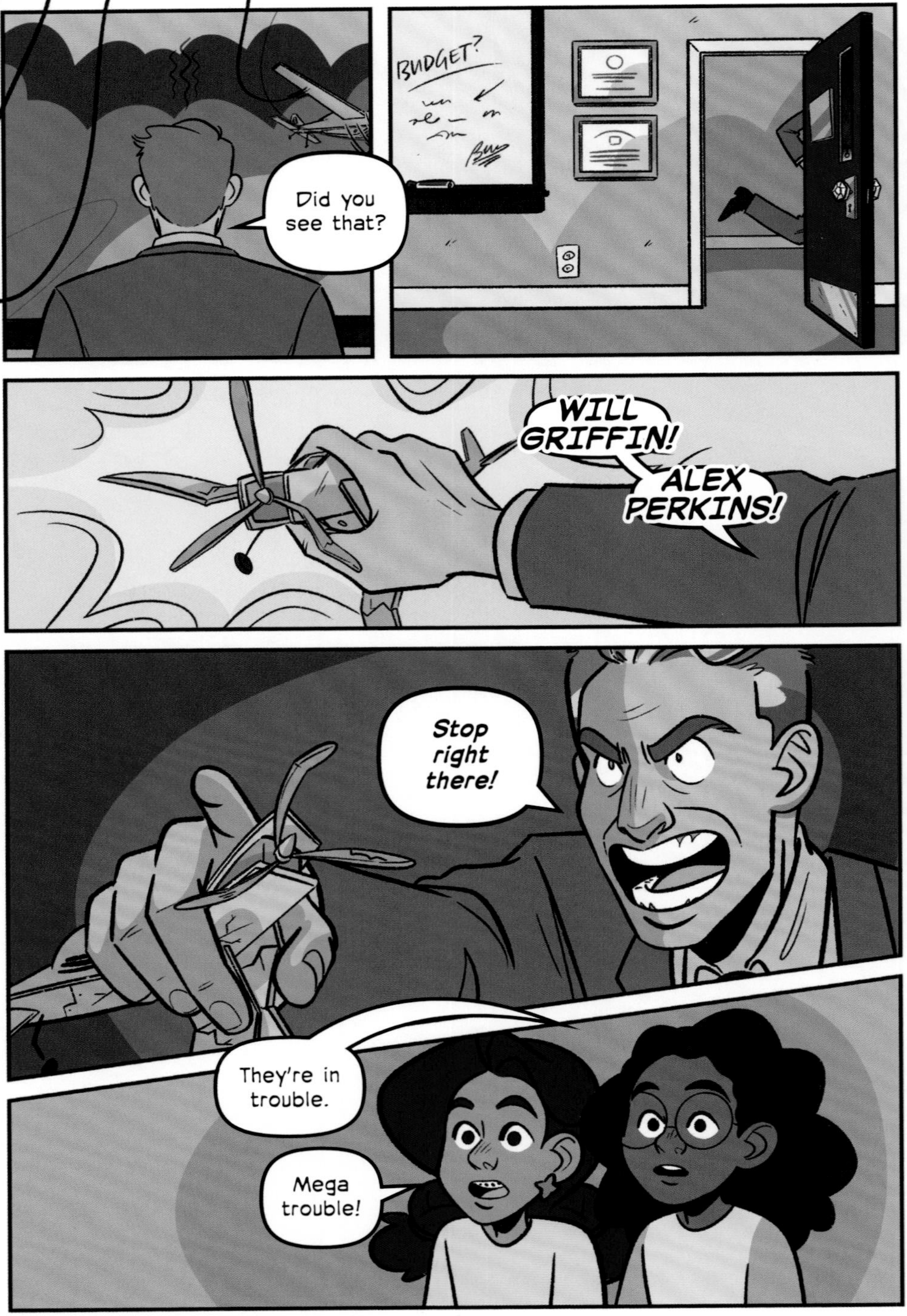
BUDGET?
Did you see that?
WILL GRIFFIN!
ALEX PERKINS!
Stop right there!
They're in trouble.
Mega trouble!

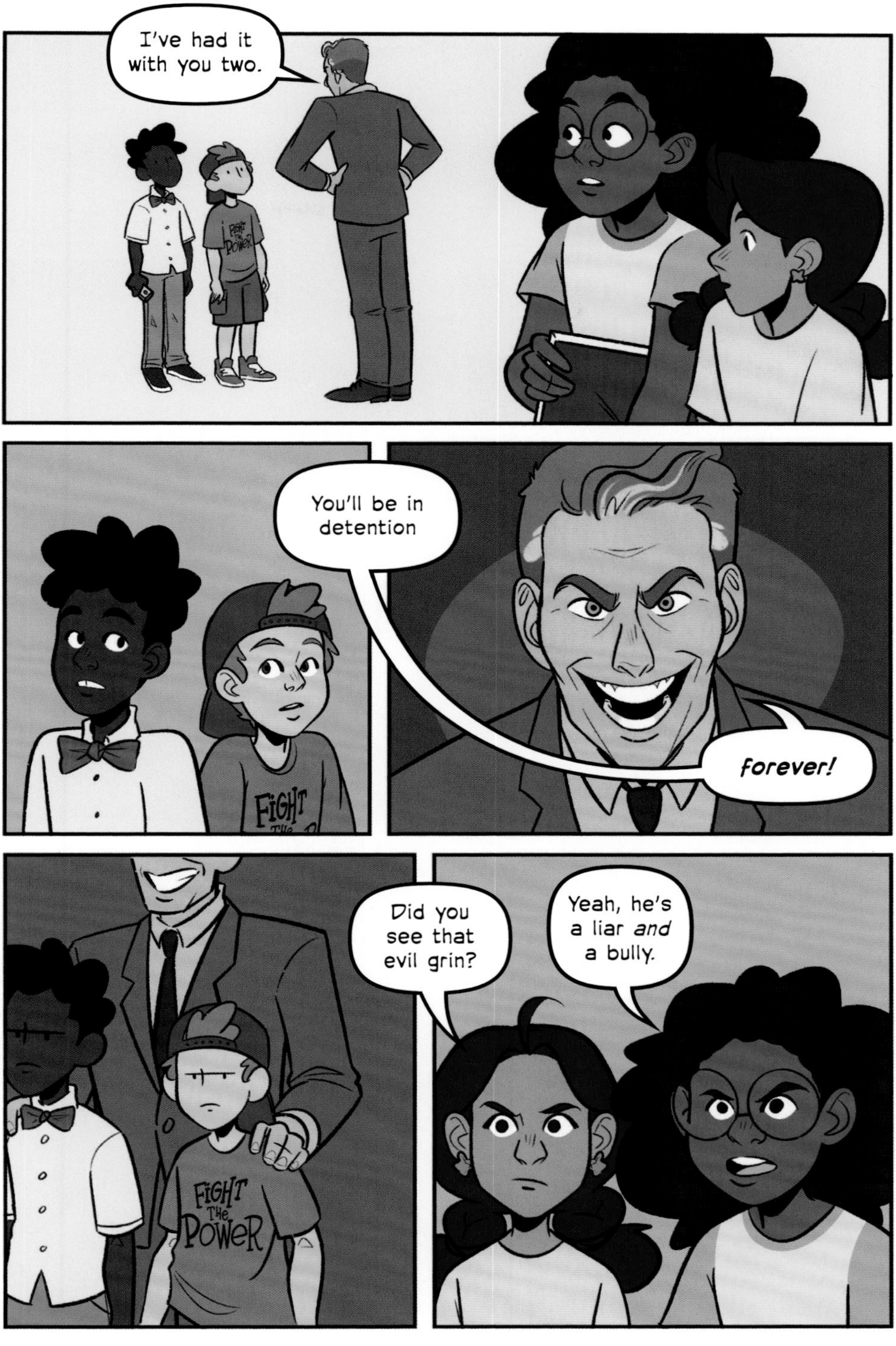
I've had it with you two.
You'll be in detention
forever!
FIGHT THE POWER
Did you see that evil grin?
Yeah, he's a liar *and* a bully.
FIGHT THE POWER

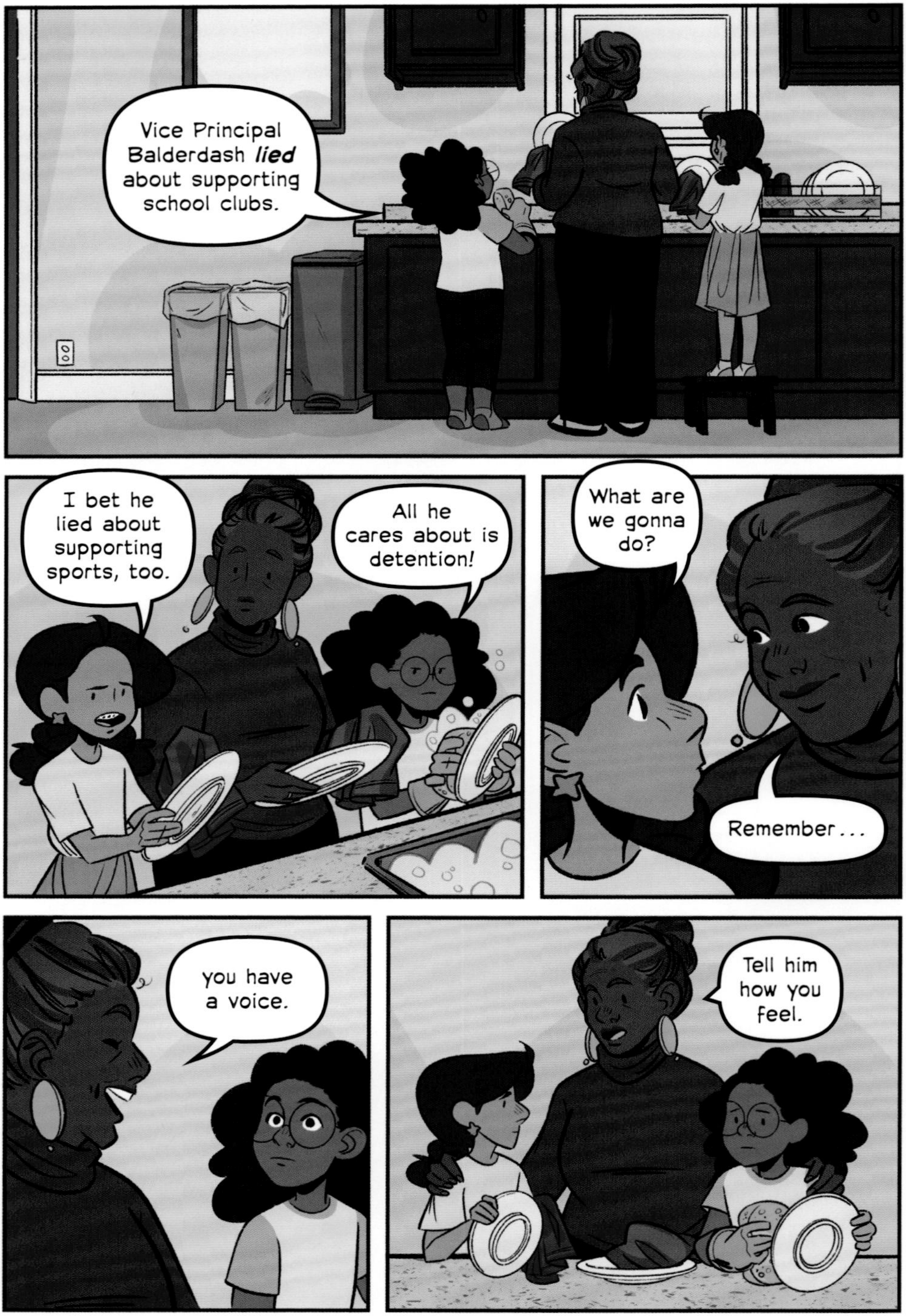

Vice Principal Balderdash ***lied*** about supporting school clubs.
I bet he lied about supporting sports, too.
All he cares about is detention!
What are we gonna do?
Remember . . .
you have a voice.
Tell him how you feel.

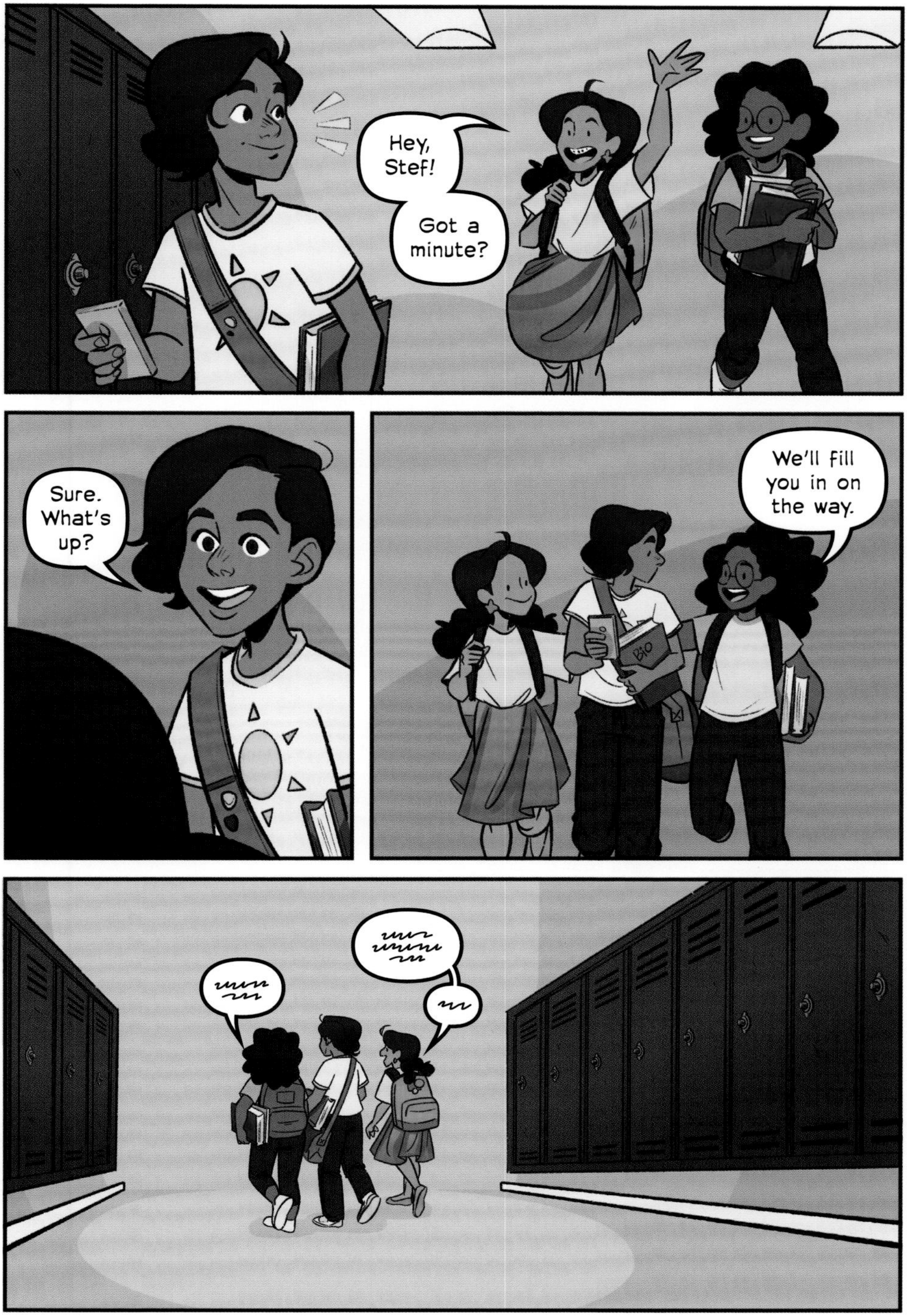
Hey, Stef!
Got a minute?
Sure. What's up?
We'll fill you in on the way.

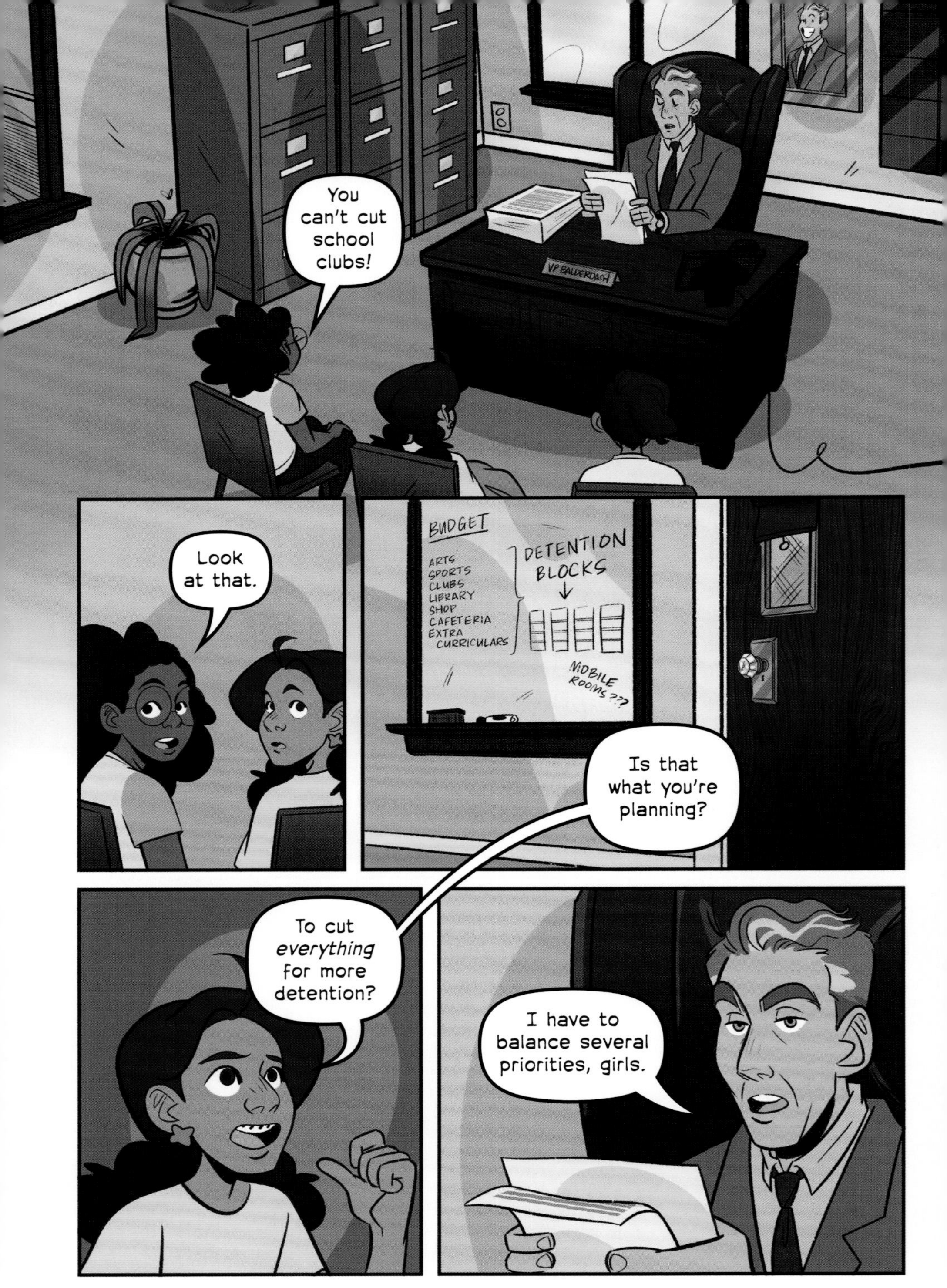
You can't cut school clubs!
VP BALDERDASH
Look at that.
BUDGET
ARTS
SPORTS
CLUBS
LIBRARY
SHOP
CAFETERIA
EXTRA CURRICULARS
DETENTION BLOCKS
MOBILE ROOMS???
Is that what you're planning?
To cut *everything* for more detention?
I have to balance several priorities, girls.

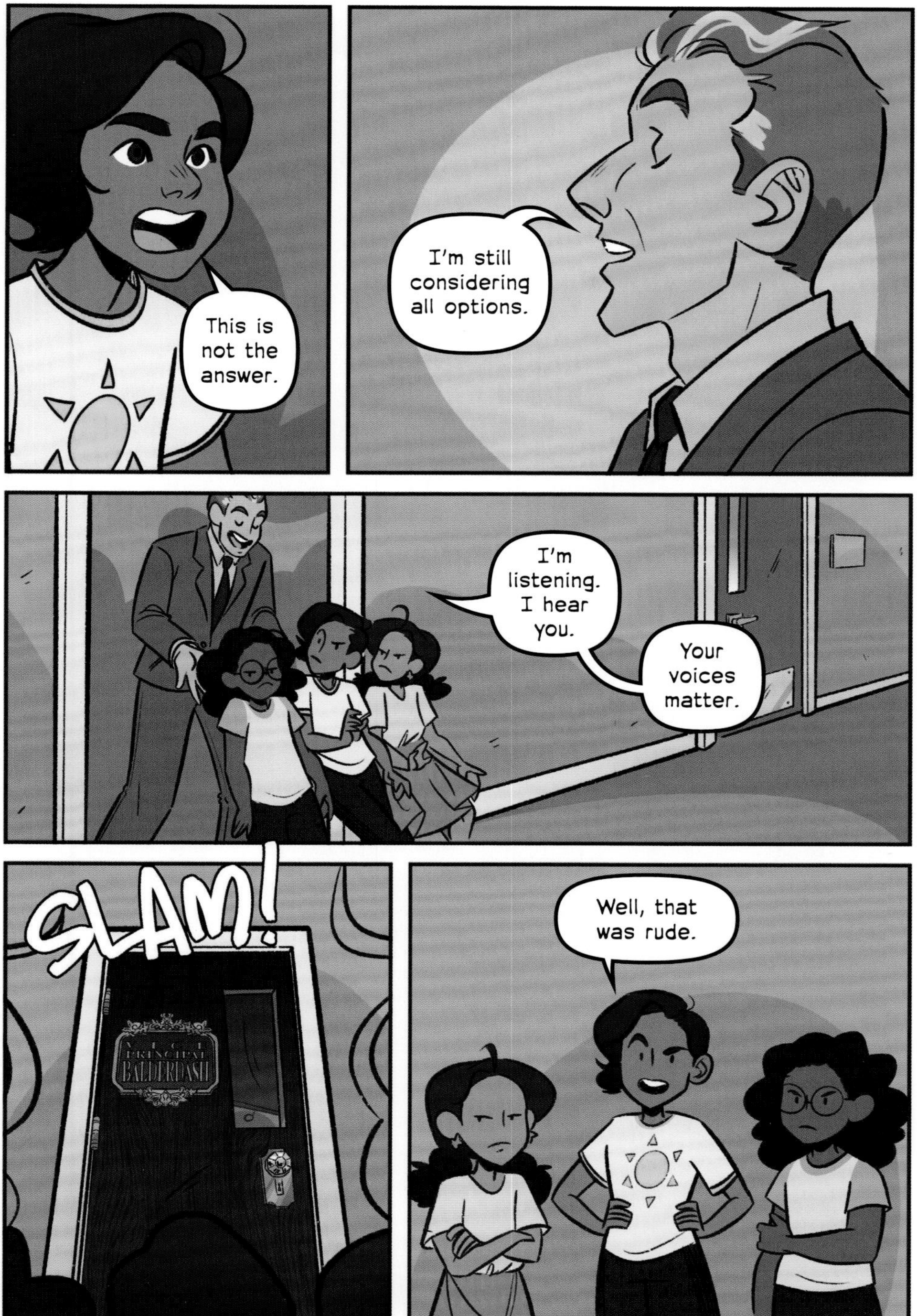
This is not the answer.
I'm still considering all options.
I'm listening. I hear you.
Your voices matter.
SLAM!
VICE PRINCIPAL BALDERDASH
Well, that was rude.

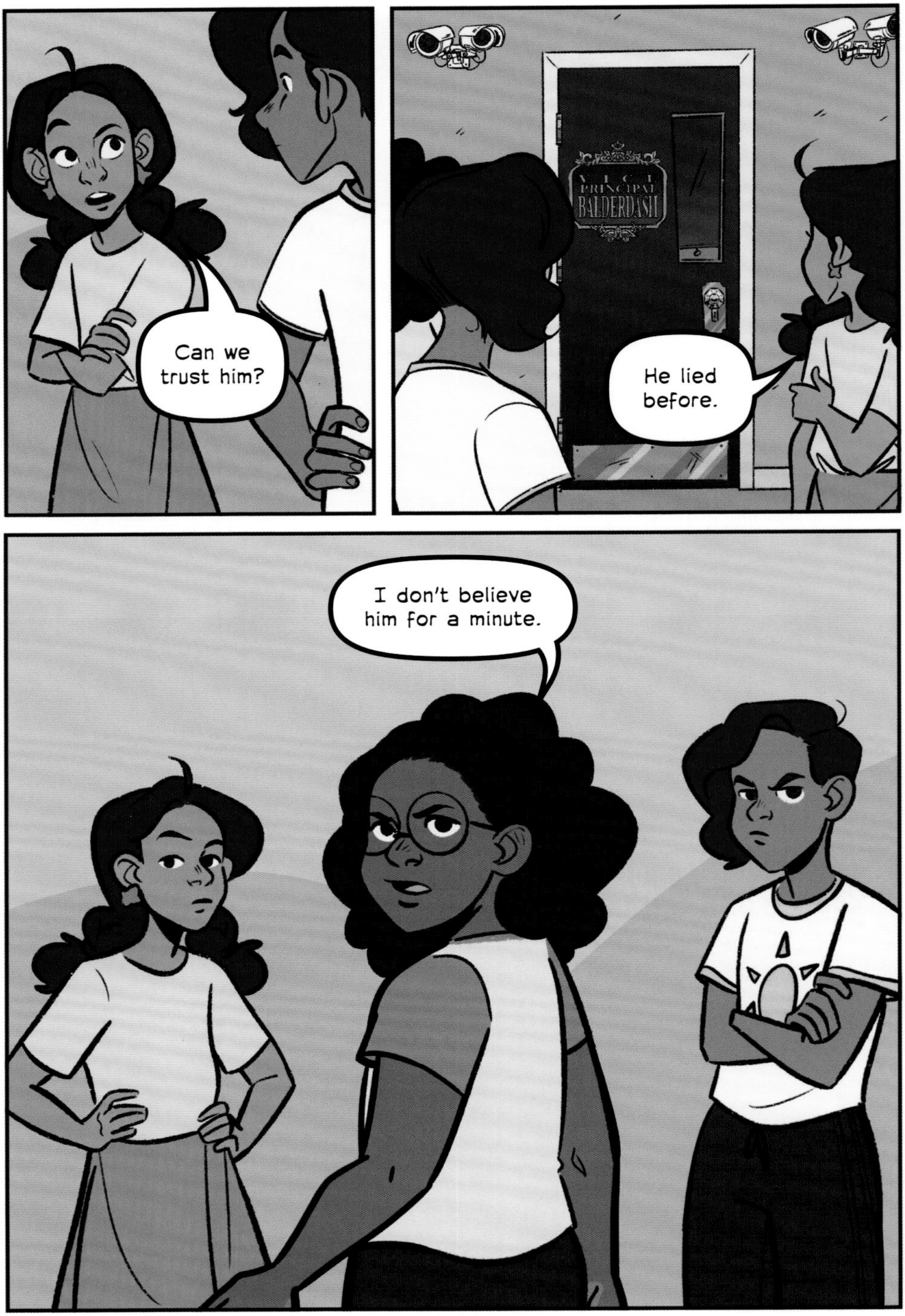
Can we trust him?
VICE PRINCIPAL BALDERDASH
He lied before.
I don't believe him for a minute.

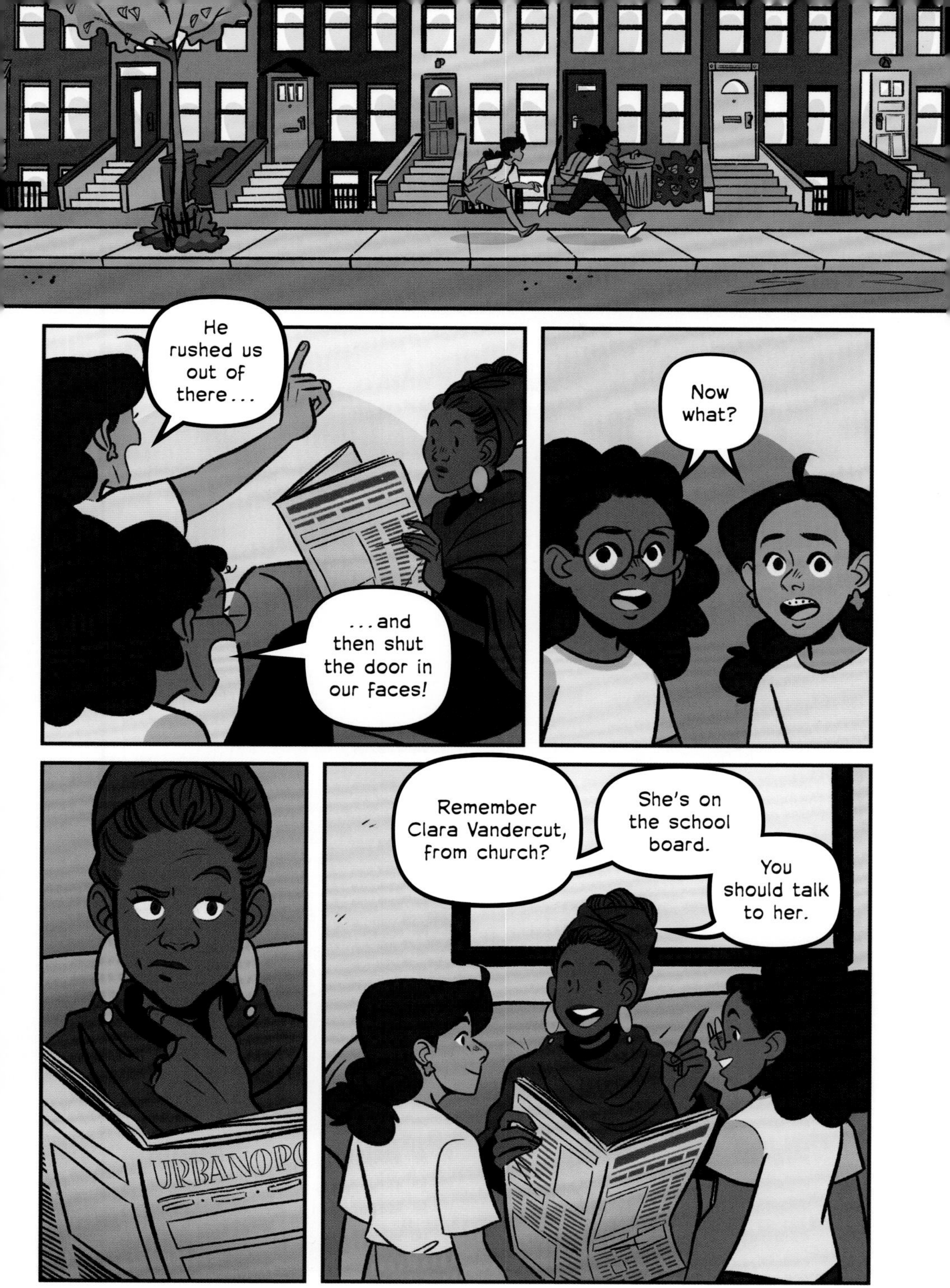
He rushed us out of there...
...and then shut the door in our faces!
Now what?
URBANOPO
Remember Clara Vandercut, from church?
She's on the school board.
You should talk to her.

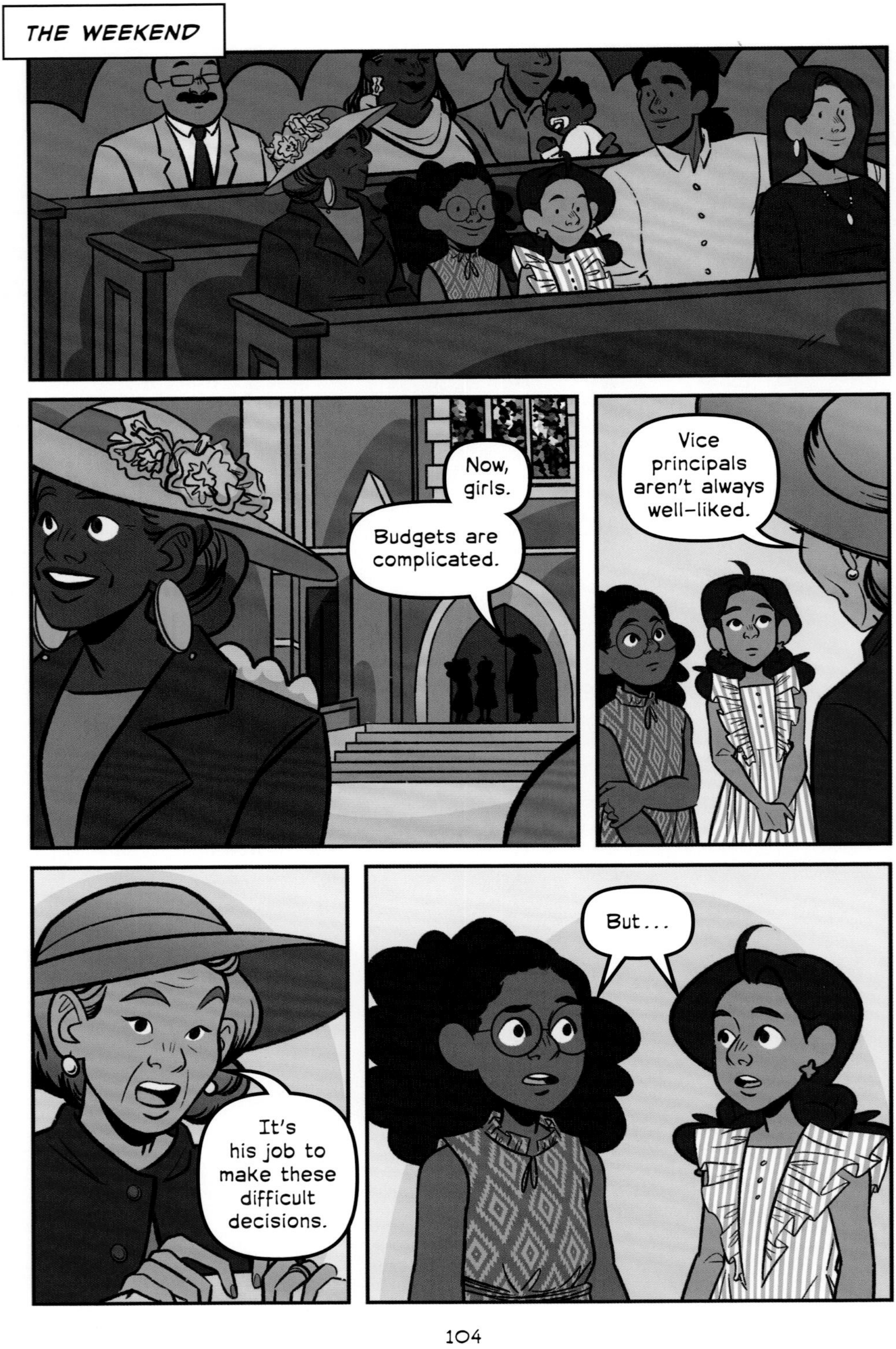
THE WEEKEND
Now, girls.
Budgets are complicated.
Vice principals aren't always well-liked.
It's his job to make these difficult decisions.
But...

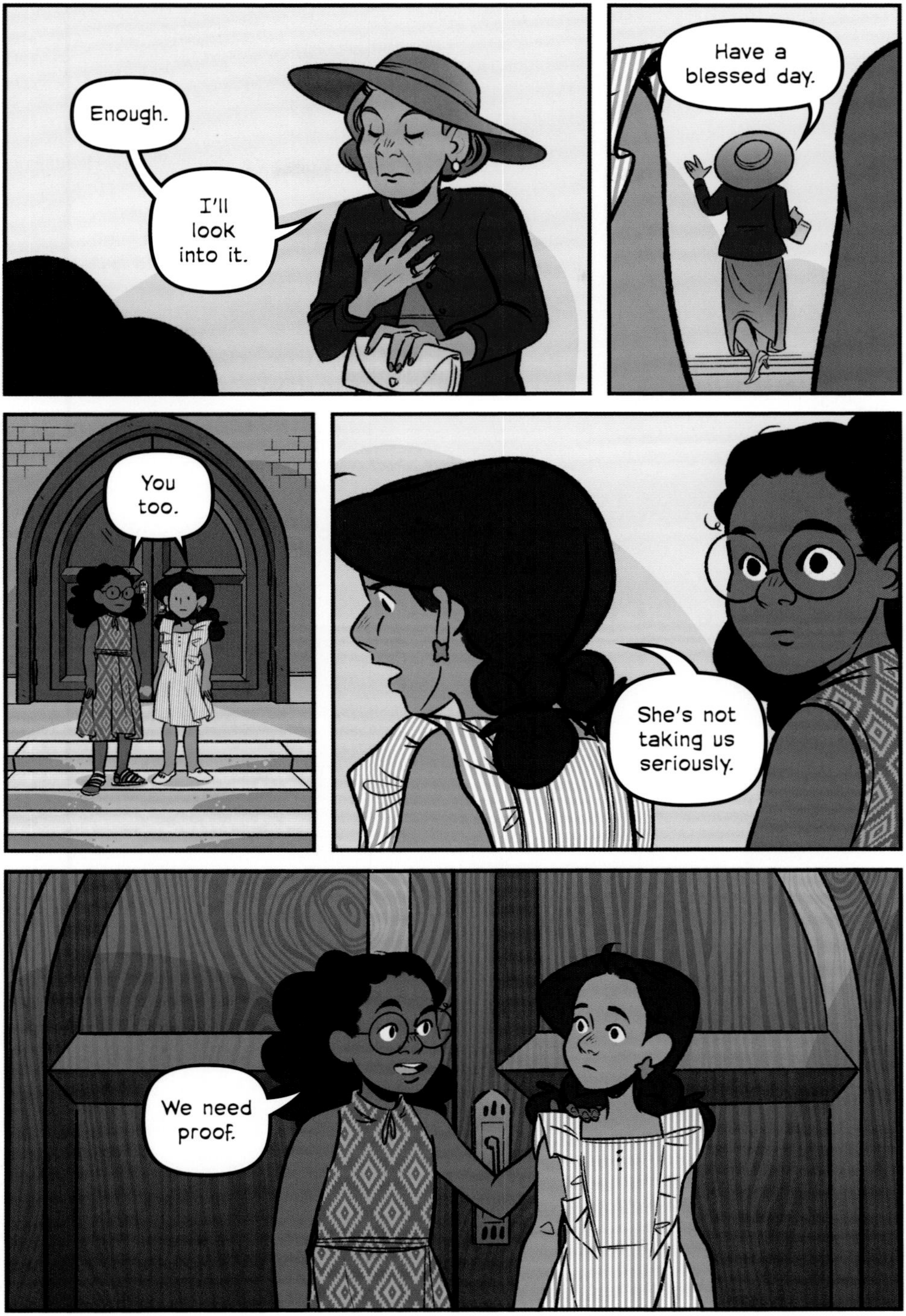

Enough.
I'll look into it.
Have a blessed day.
You too.
She's not taking us seriously.
We need proof.

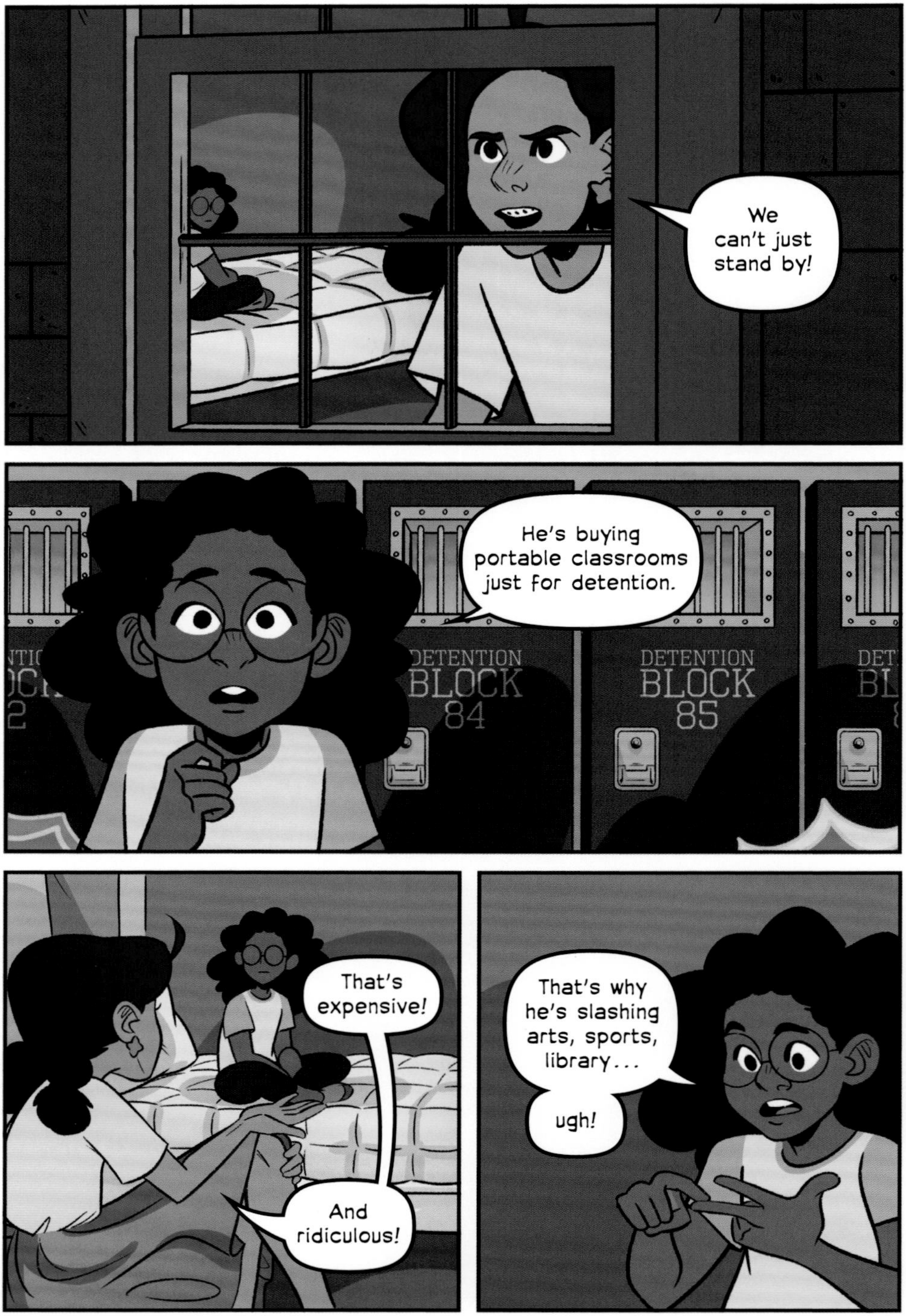
We can't just stand by!
He's buying portable classrooms just for detention.
DETENTION BLOCK 84
DETENTION BLOCK 85
That's expensive!
And ridiculous!
That's why he's slashing arts, sports, library...
ugh!

You forgot Robotics Club.

I would never.

By the time everyone realizes what he's up to, it will be too late.

There must be more evidence in his office.

We have to get in there and find it.

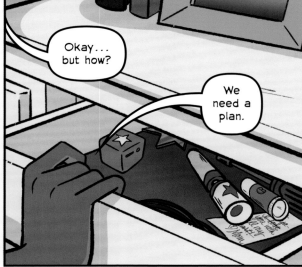

Okay... but how?

We need a plan.

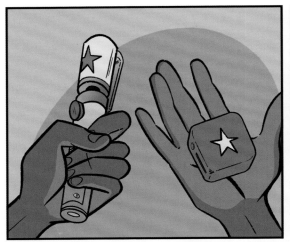

You put blue stars on everything?

Because my parents are military.

I *love* blue stars.

I love your quilt.

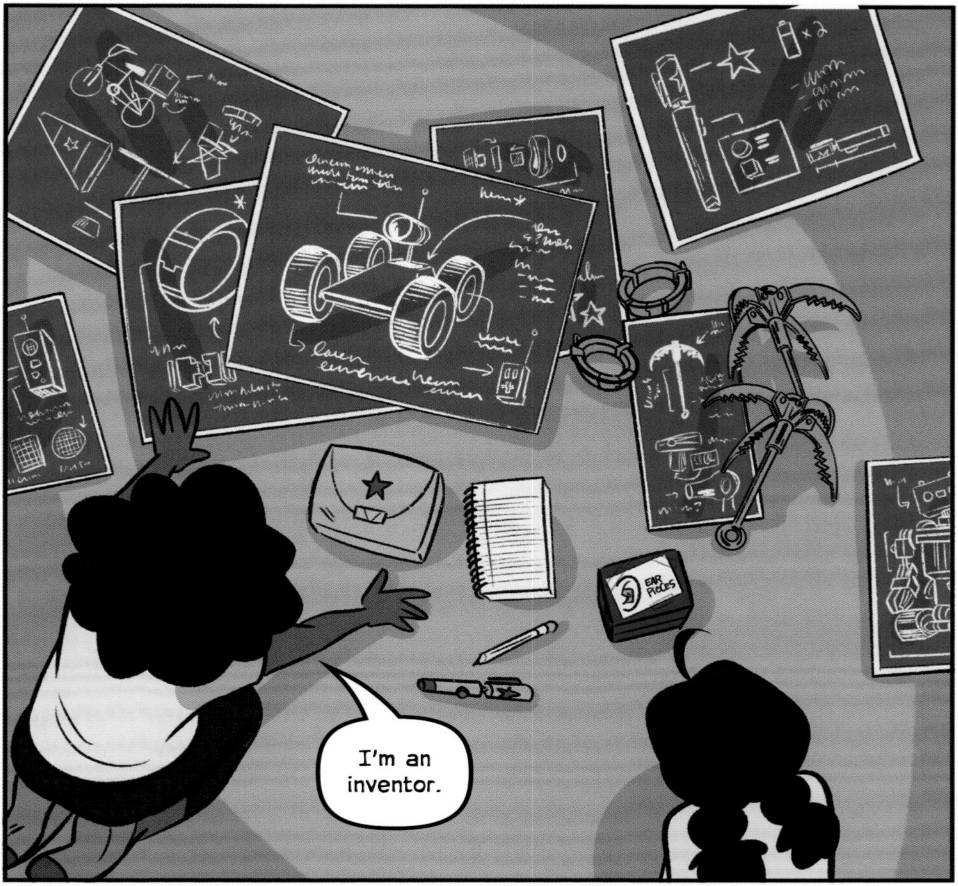
EAR PIECES
I'm an inventor.

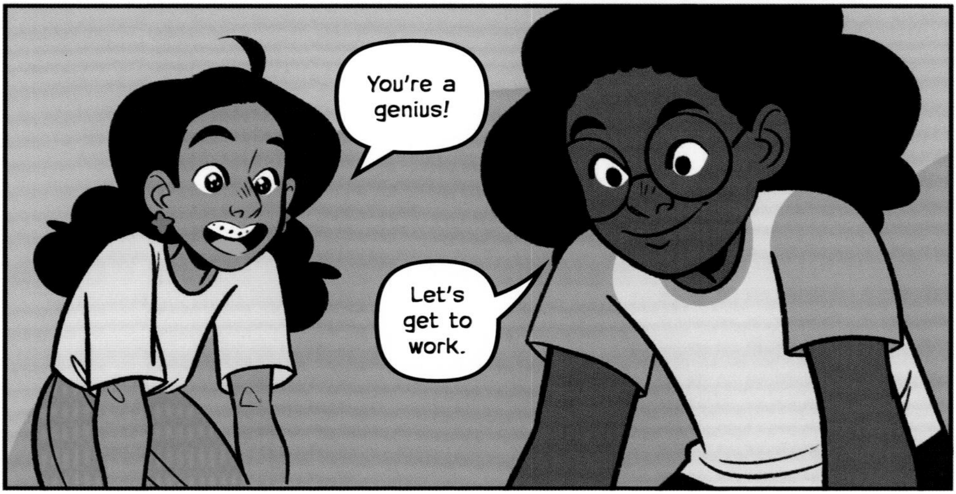
You're a genius!
Let's get to work.

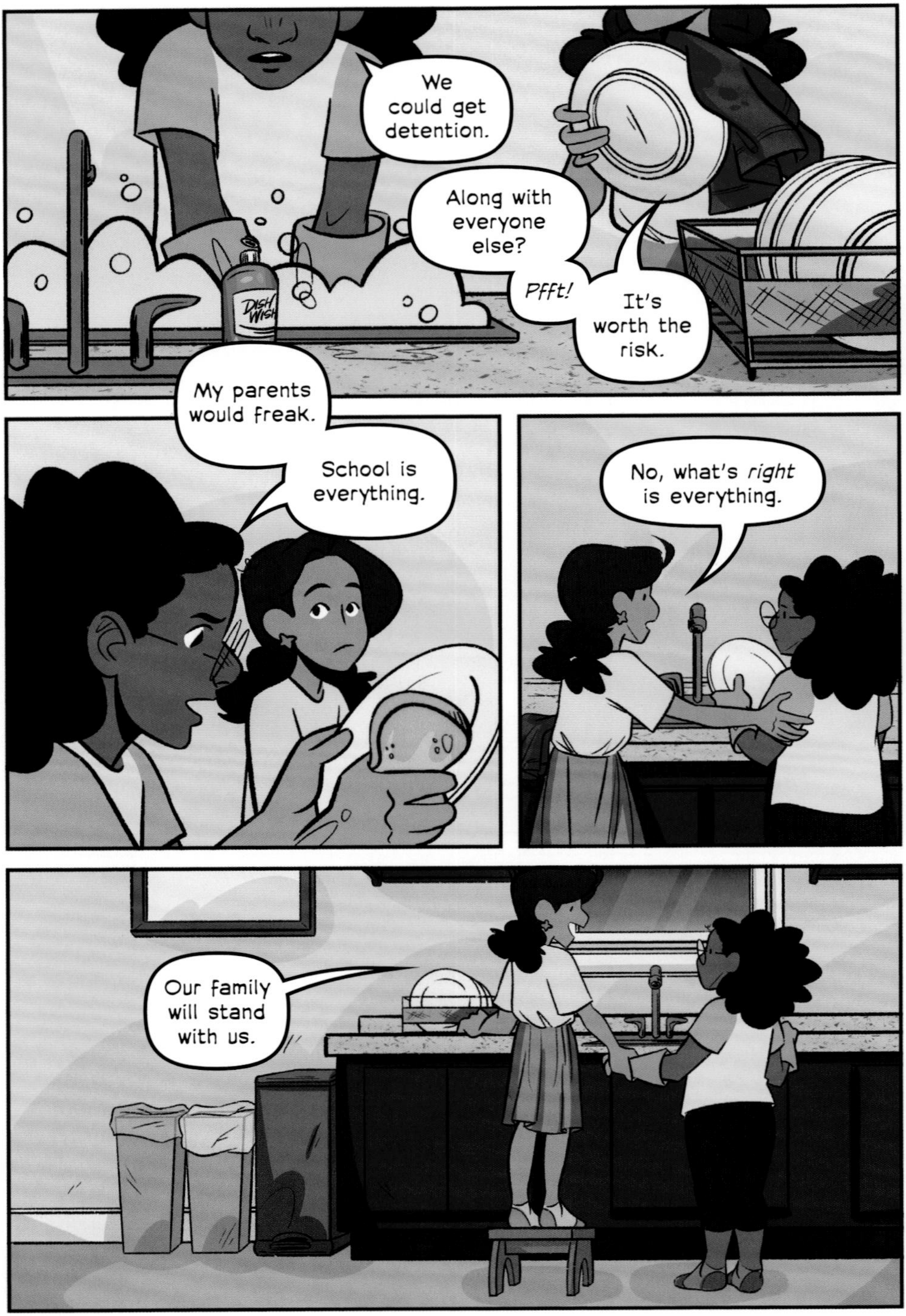
We could get detention.
Along with everyone else?
Pfft!
It's worth the risk.
My parents would freak.
School is everything.
No, what's *right* is everything.
Our family will stand with us.
DISH WISH

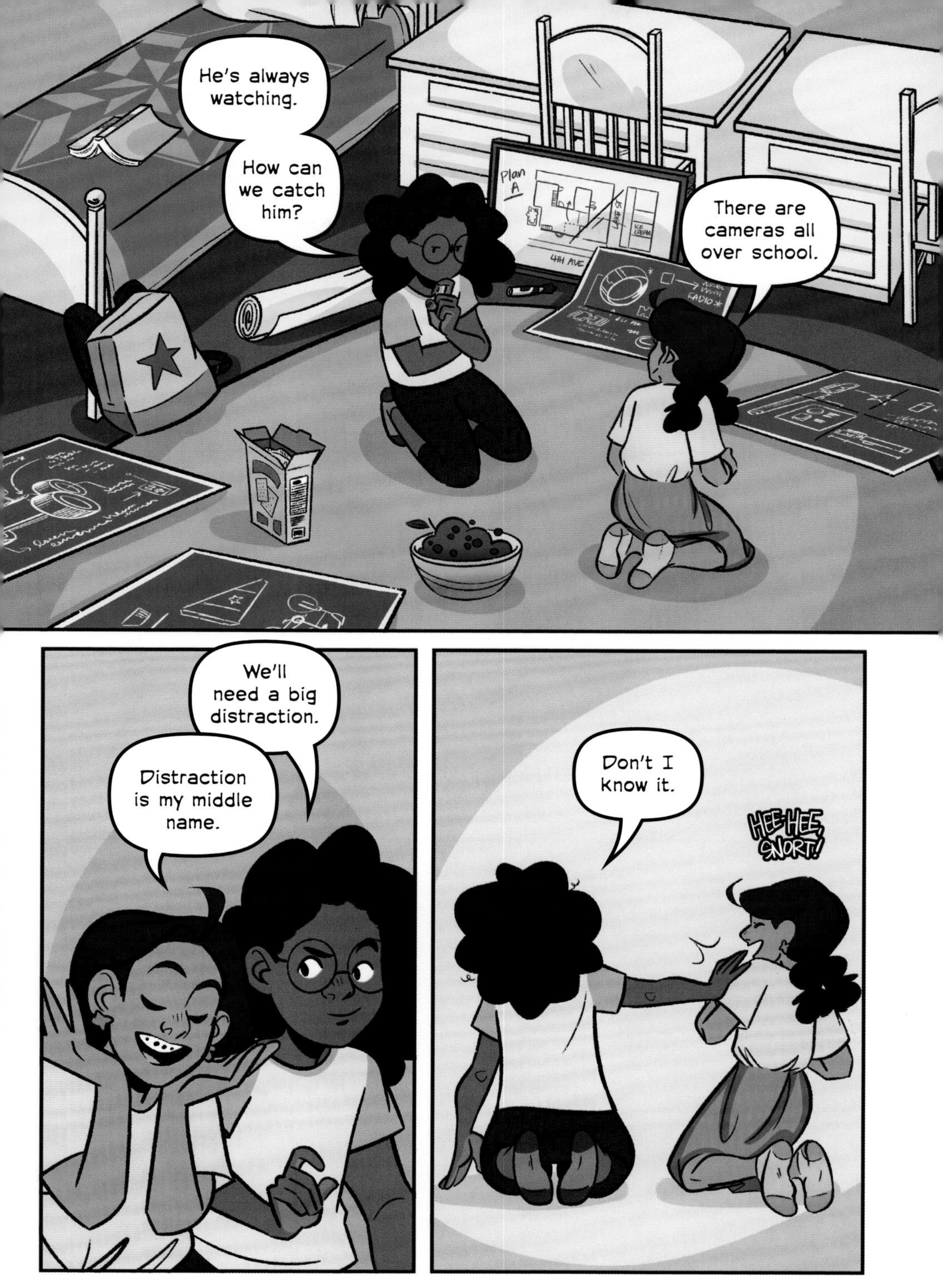
He's always watching.
How can we catch him?
Plan A
4TH AVE
There are cameras all over school.
We'll need a big distraction.
Distraction is my middle name.
Don't I know it.
HEE-HEE, SNORT!

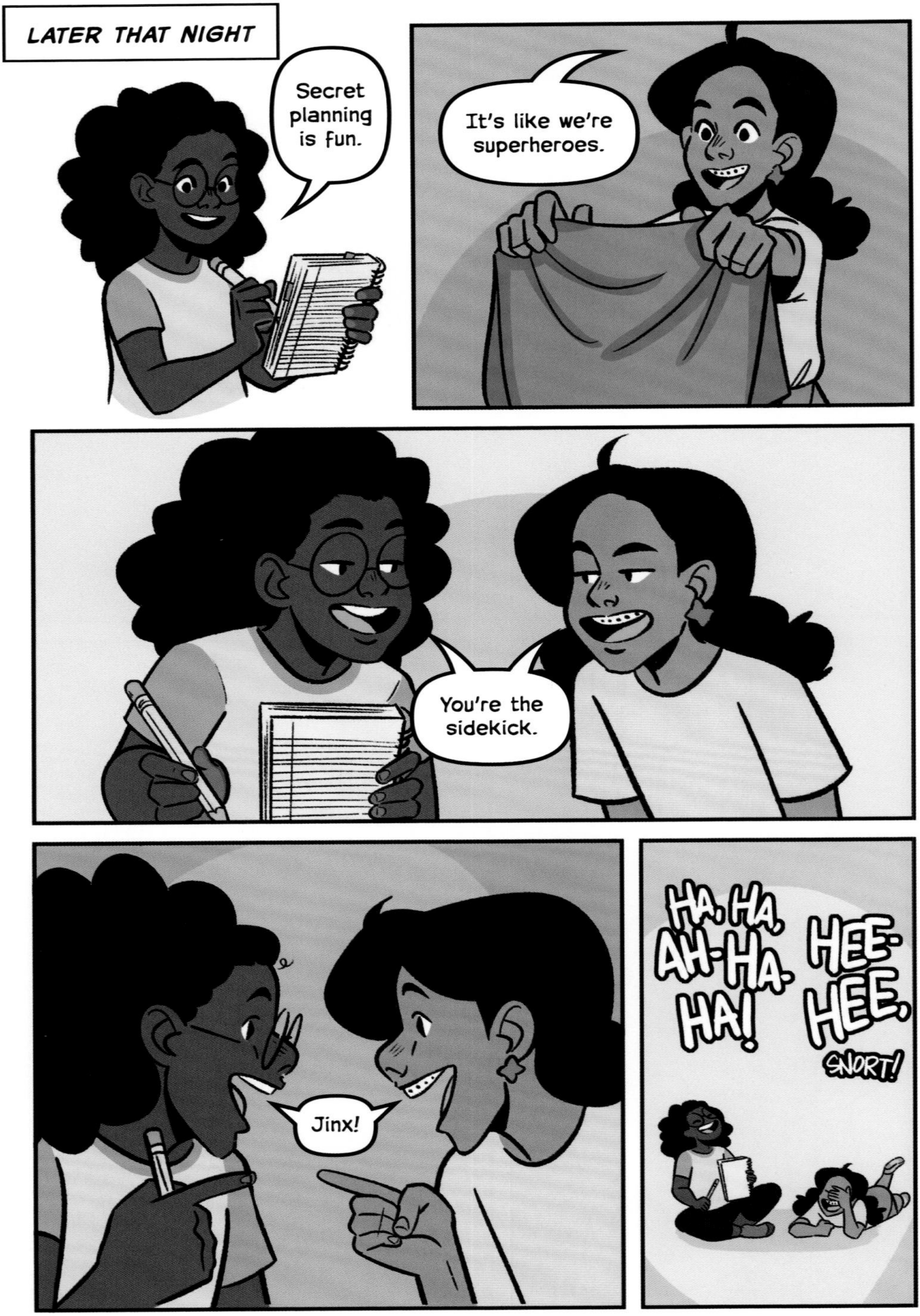
LATER THAT NIGHT
Secret planning is fun.
It's like we're superheroes.
You're the sidekick.
Jinx!
HA, HA, AH-HA, HA!
HEE-HEE, HEE,
SNORT!

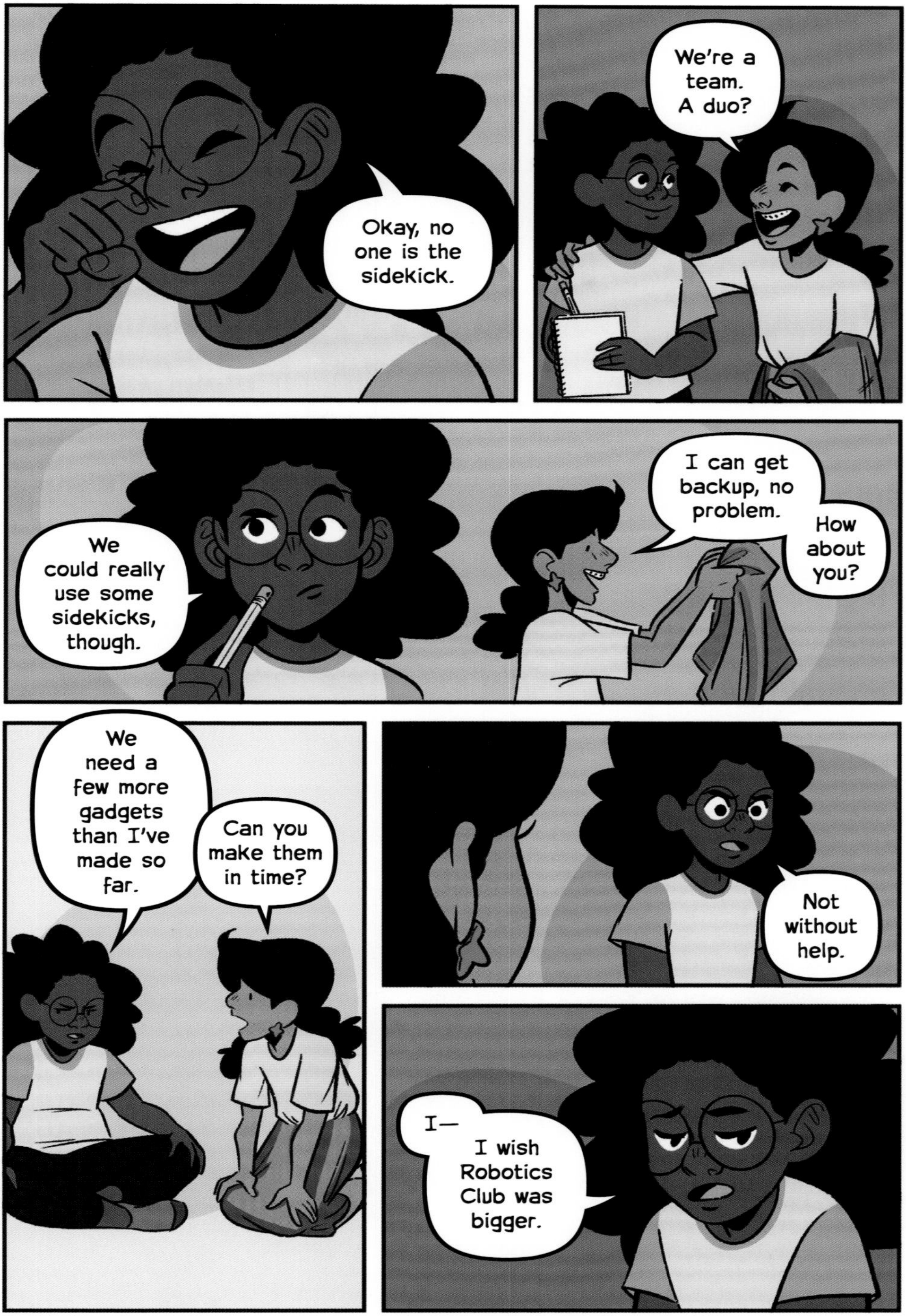
Okay, no one is the sidekick.
We're a team. A duo?
We could really use some sidekicks, though.
I can get backup, no problem.
How about you?
We need a few more gadgets than I've made so far.
Can you make them in time?
Not without help.
I—
I wish Robotics Club was bigger.

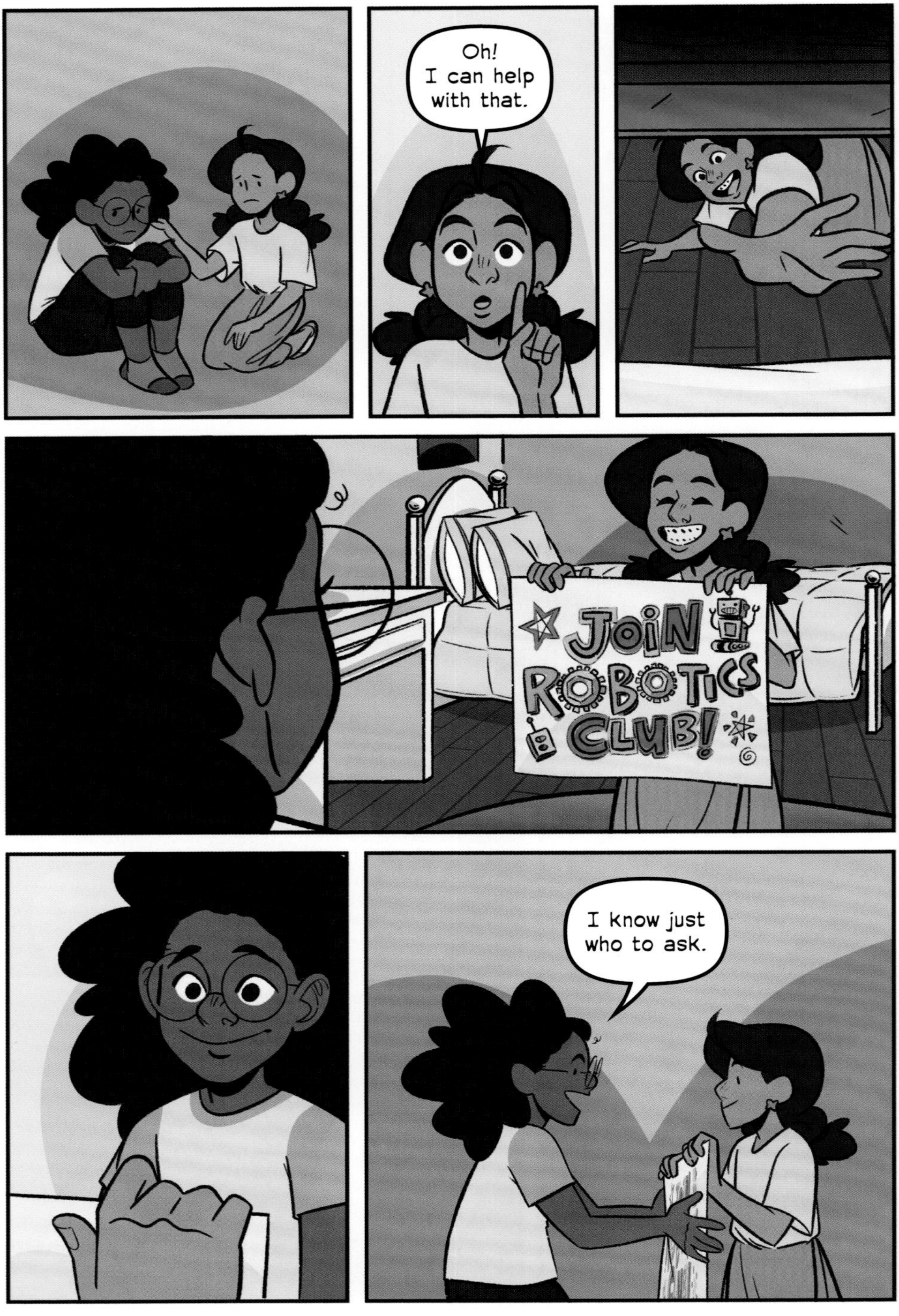
Oh!
I can help
with that.
JOIN
ROBOTICS
CLUB!
I know just
who to ask.

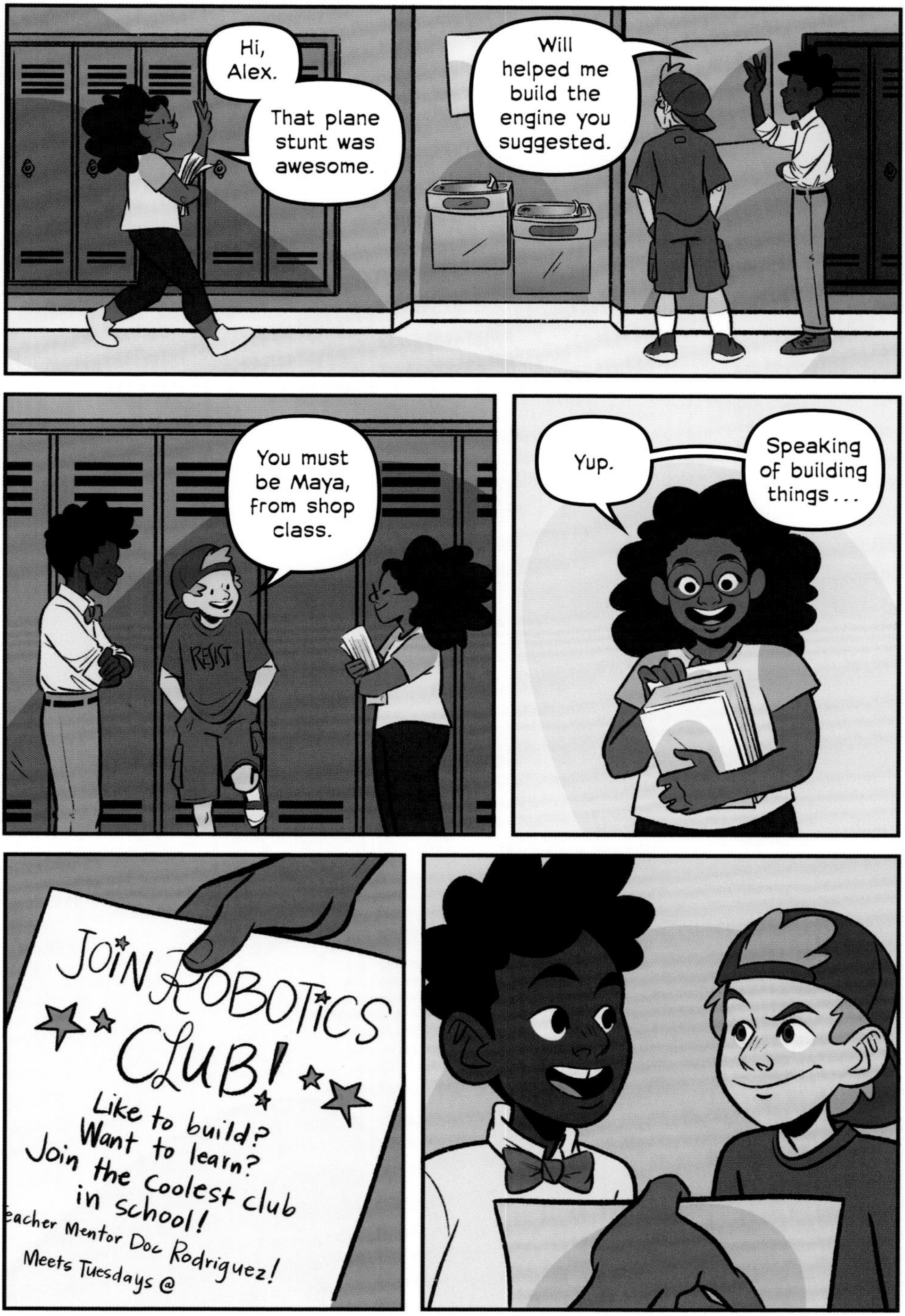

Hi, Alex.
That plane stunt was awesome.
Will helped me build the engine you suggested.
You must be Maya, from shop class.
RESIST
Yup.
Speaking of building things . . .
JOIN ROBOTICS CLUB!
Like to build? Want to learn? Join the coolest club in school!
Teacher Mentor Doc Rodriguez!
Meets Tuesdays @

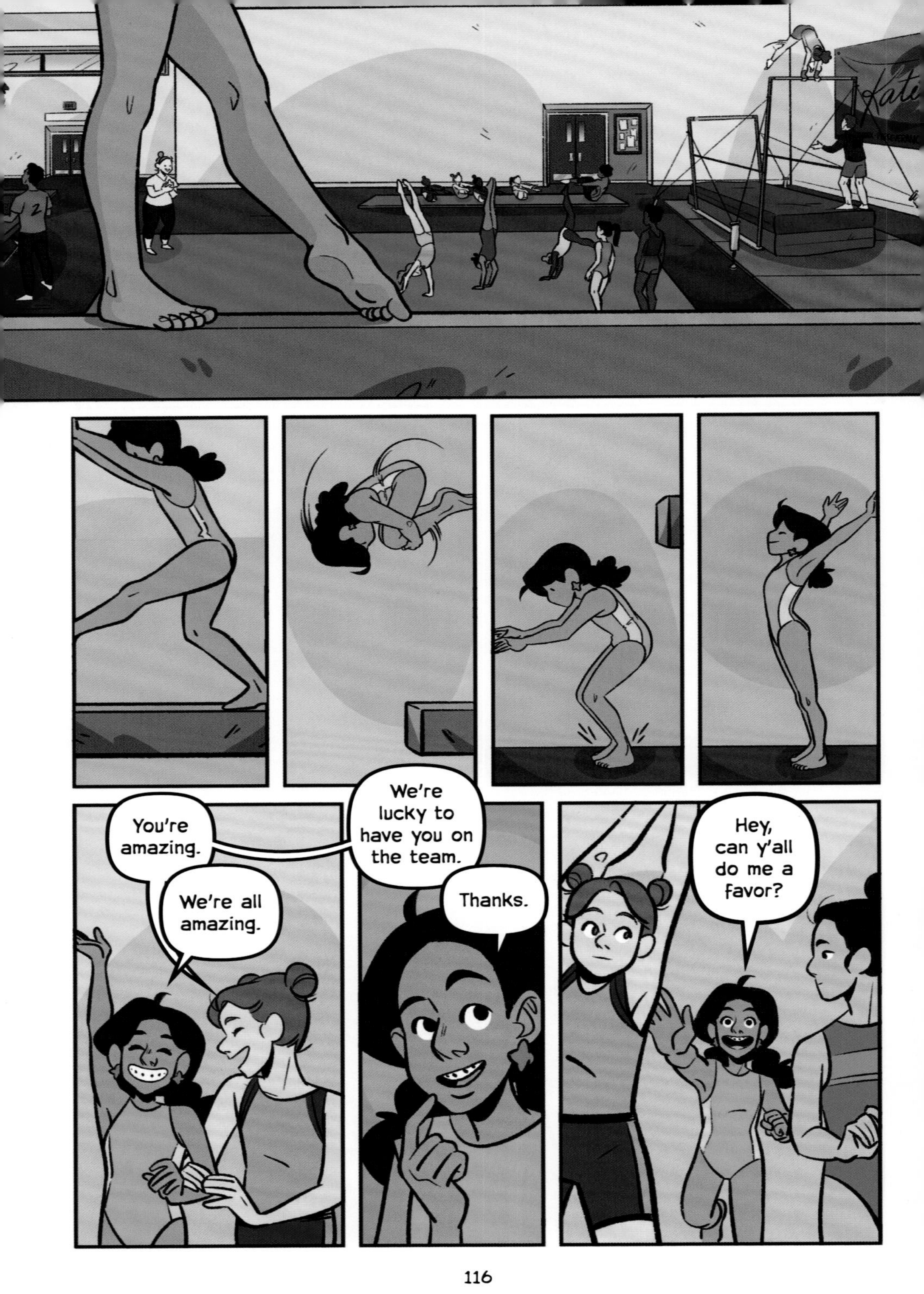
You're amazing.
We're lucky to have you on the team.
We're all amazing.
Thanks.
Hey, can y'all do me a favor?

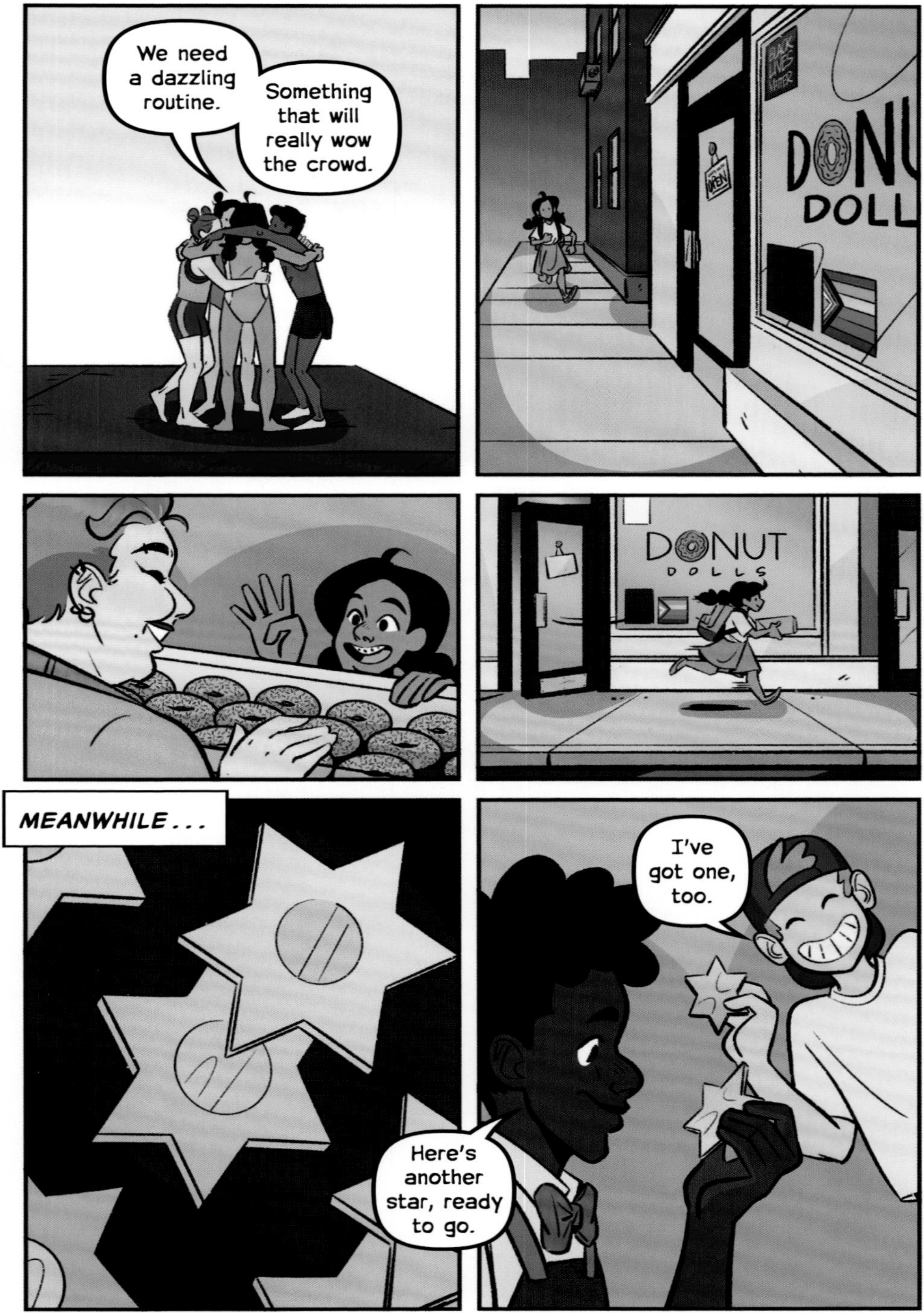
We need a dazzling routine.
Something that will really wow the crowd.
BLACK LIVES MATTER
OPEN
DONU
DOLL
DONUT
DOLLS
MEANWHILE . . .
I've got one, too.
Here's another star, ready to go.

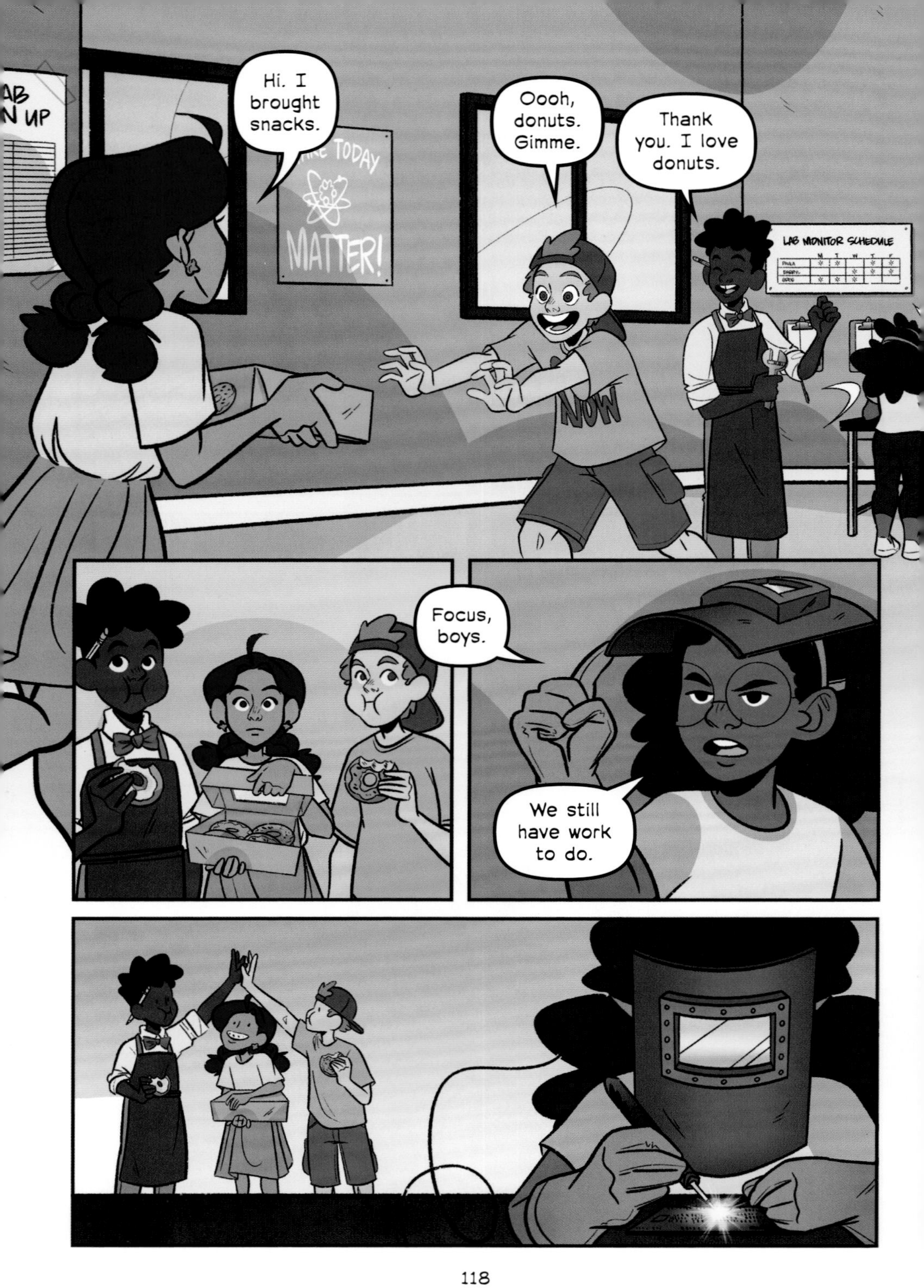
Hi. I brought snacks.
MATTER!
Oooh, donuts. Gimme.
Thank you. I love donuts.
LAB MONITOR SCHEDULE
NOW
Focus, boys.
We still have work to do.

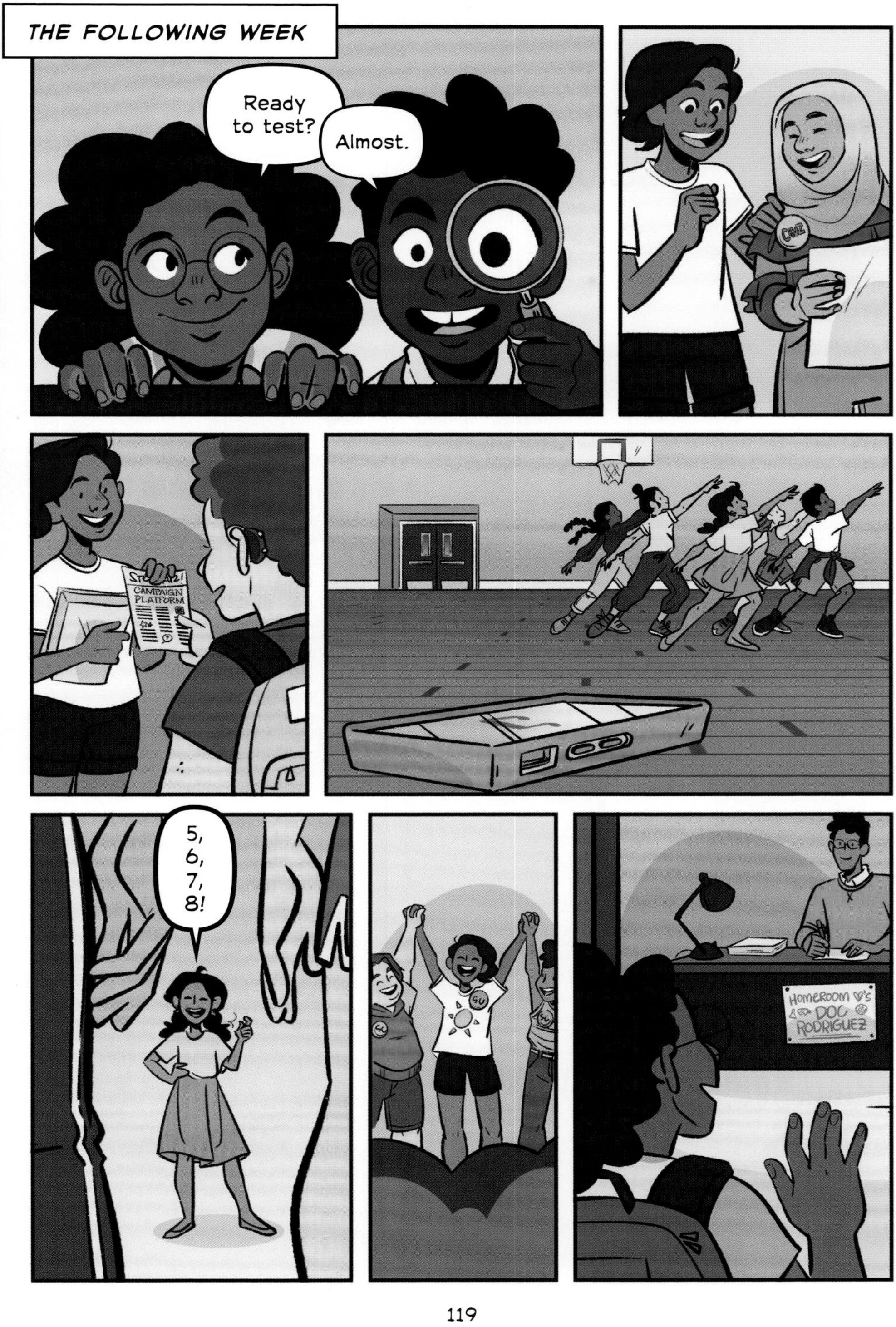
THE FOLLOWING WEEK
Ready to test?
Almost.
CRUZ
CAMPAIGN PLATFORM
5, 6, 7, 8!
Homeroom ♡'s DOC RODRIGUEZ

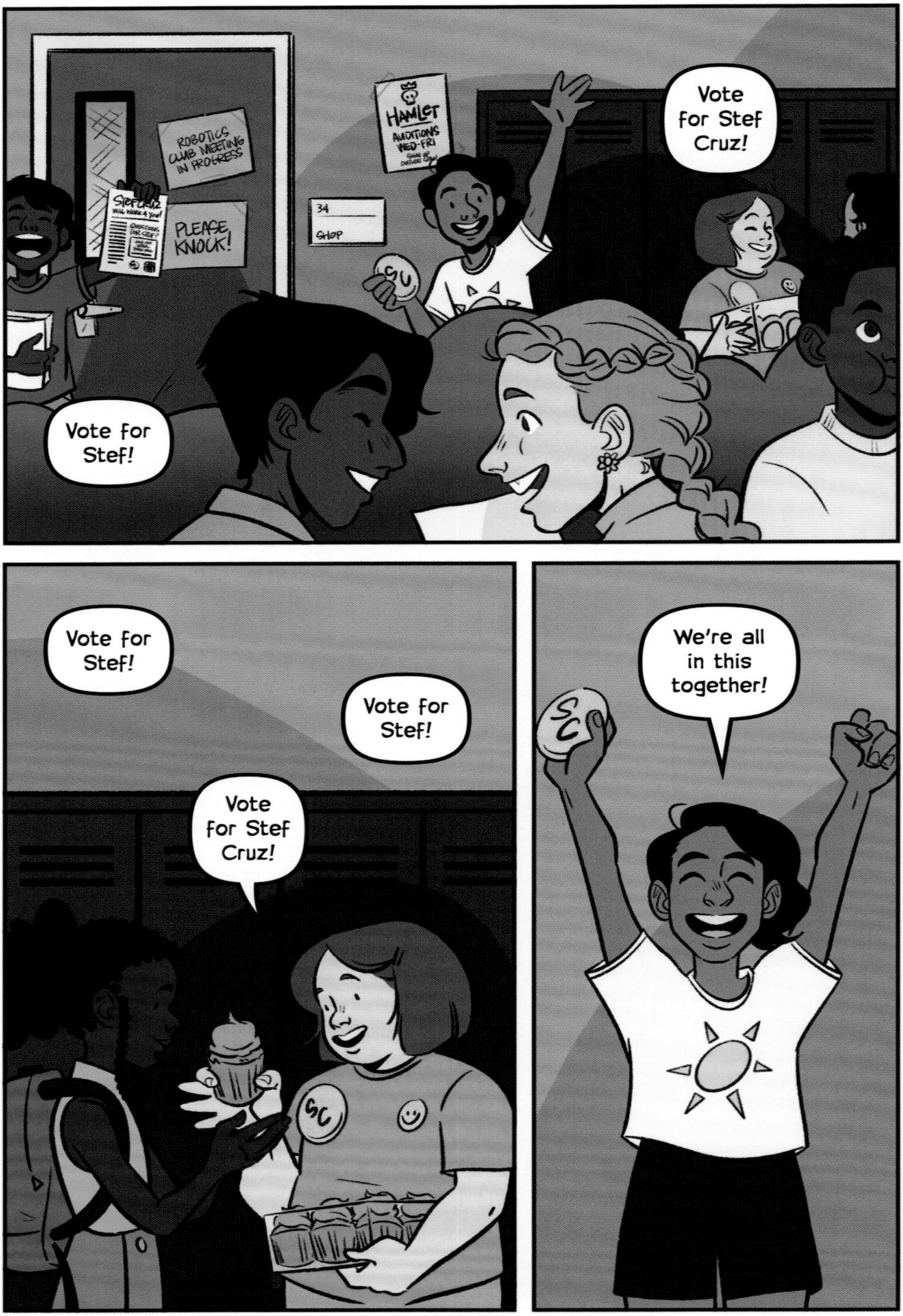
ROBOTICS CLUB MEETING IN PROGRESS
PLEASE KNOCK!
HAMLET AUDITIONS WED-FRI
34
SHOP
Vote for Stef Cruz!
Vote for Stef!
Vote for Stef!
Vote for Stef!
Vote for Stef Cruz!
We're all in this together!

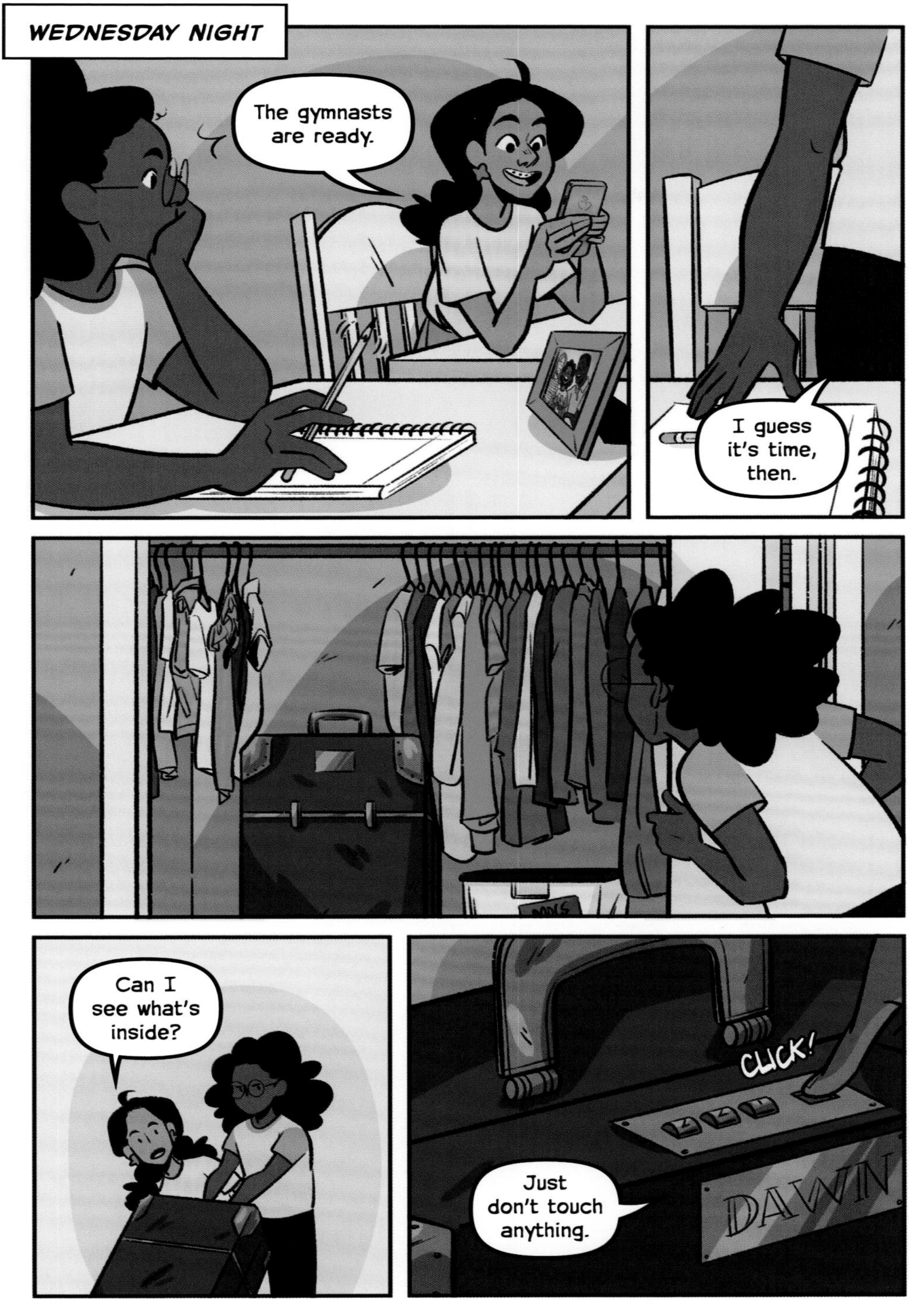
WEDNESDAY NIGHT
The gymnasts are ready.
I guess it's time, then.
Can I see what's inside?
CLICK!
Just don't touch anything.
DAWN

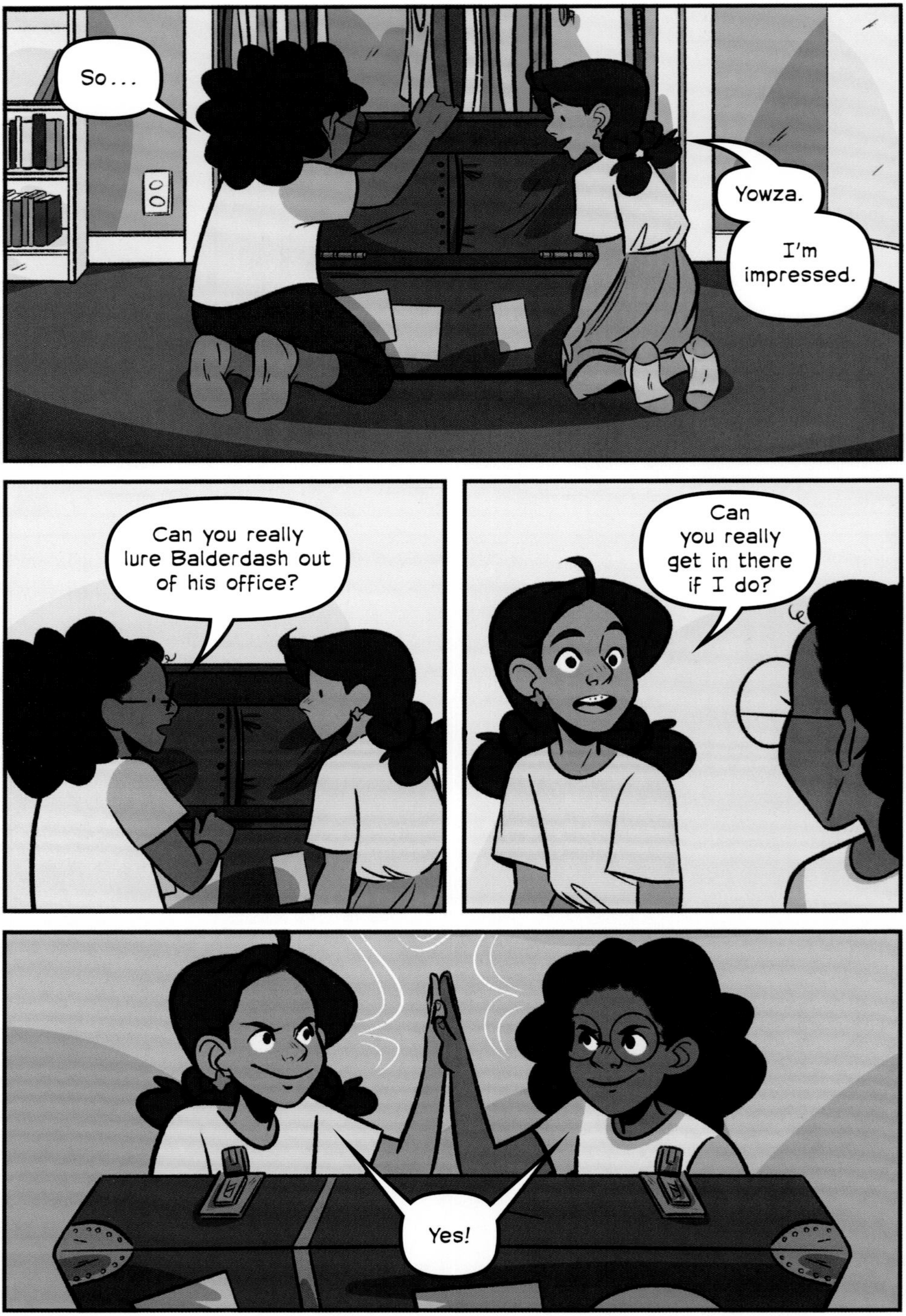
So...
Yowza.
I'm impressed.
Can you really lure Balderdash out of his office?
Can you really get in there if I do?
Yes!

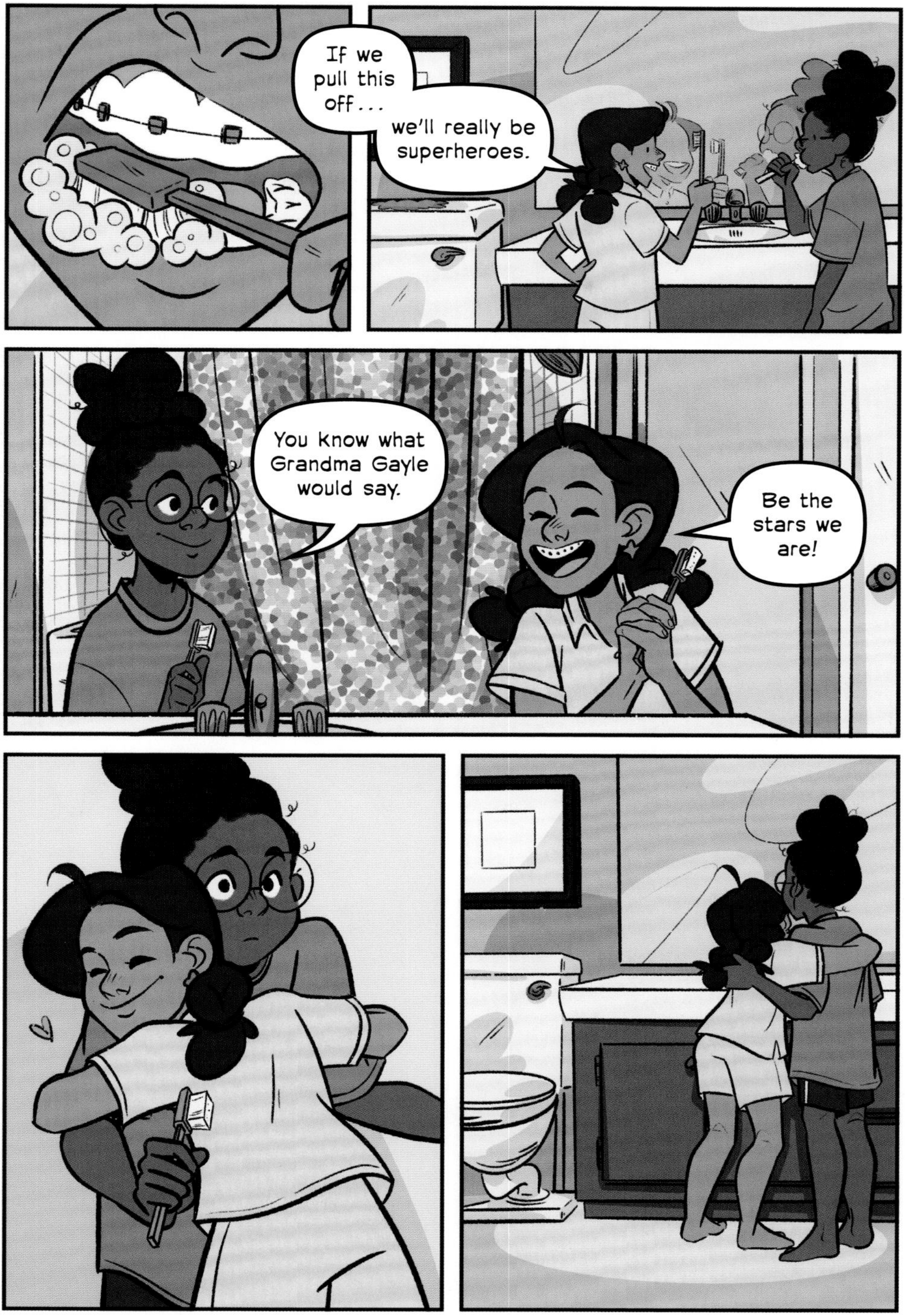

If we pull this off...
we'll really be superheroes.
You know what Grandma Gayle would say.
Be the stars we are!

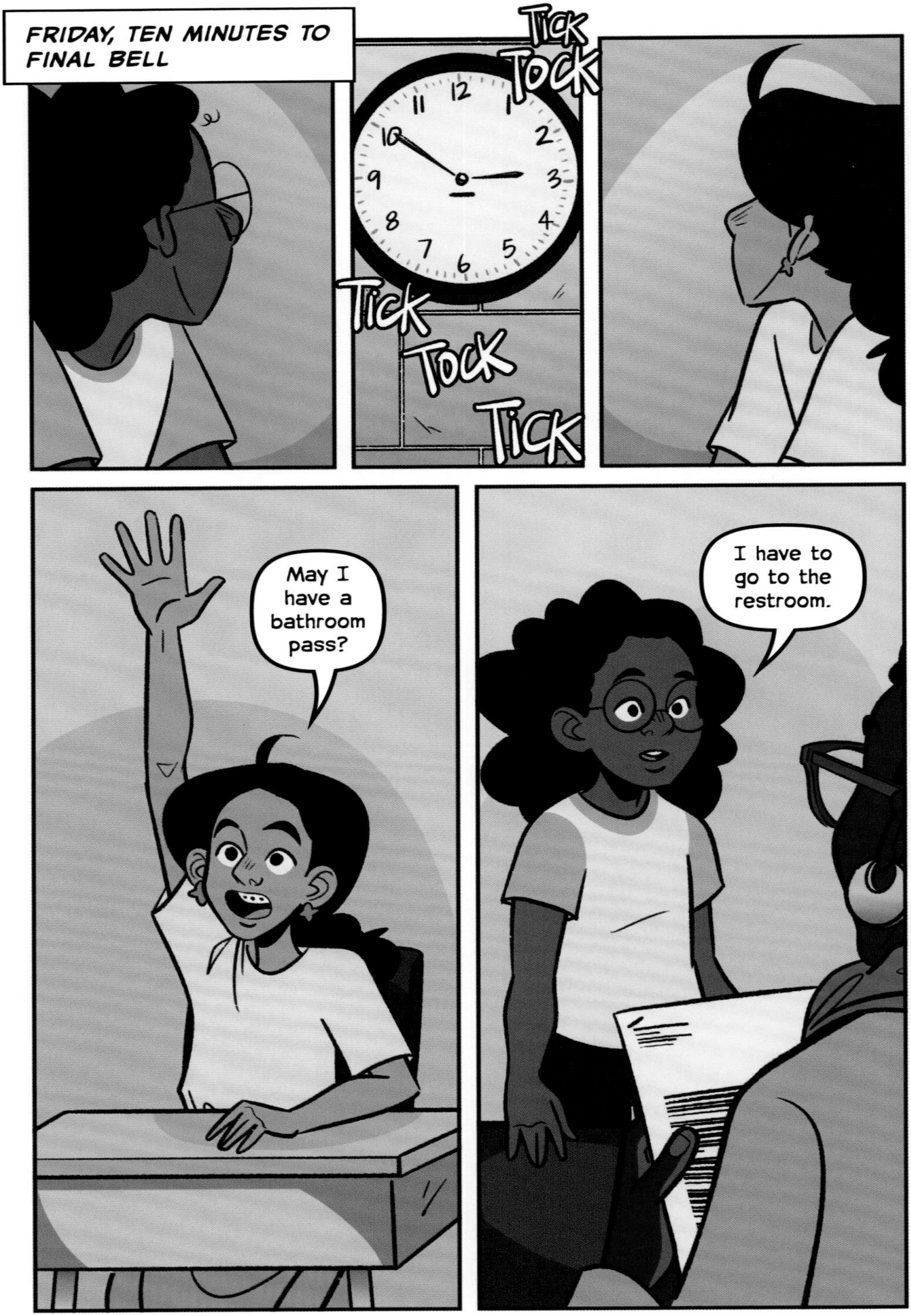
FRIDAY, TEN MINUTES TO FINAL BELL
TICK
TOCK
TICK
TOCK
TICK
May I have a bathroom pass?
I have to go to the restroom.

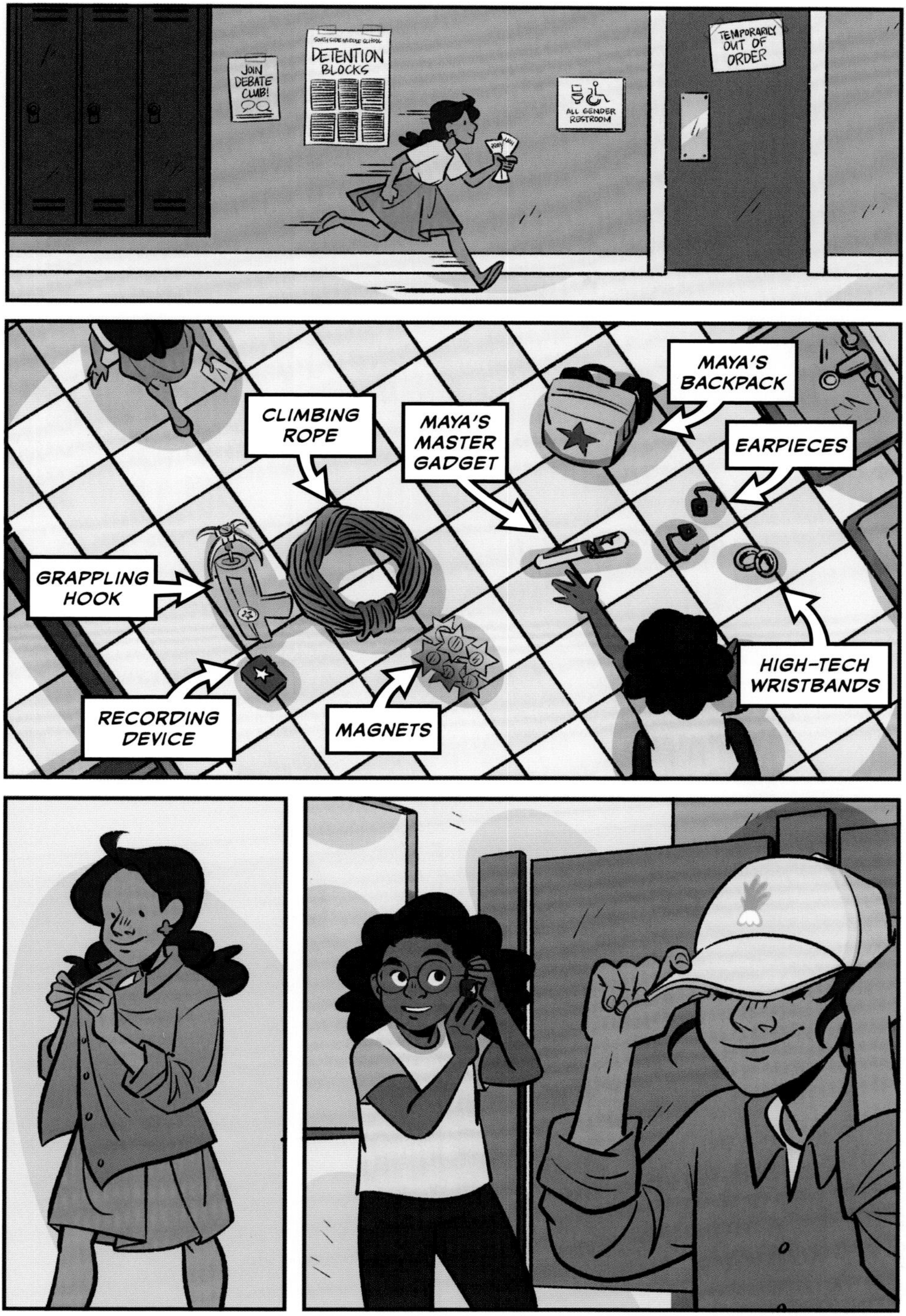
JOIN DEBATE CLUB!
SOUTH SIDE MIDDLE SCHOOL
DETENTION BLOCKS
ALL GENDER RESTROOM
TEMPORARILY OUT OF ORDER
CLIMBING ROPE
MAYA'S MASTER GADGET
MAYA'S BACKPACK
EARPIECES
GRAPPLING HOOK
HIGH-TECH WRISTBANDS
RECORDING DEVICE
MAGNETS

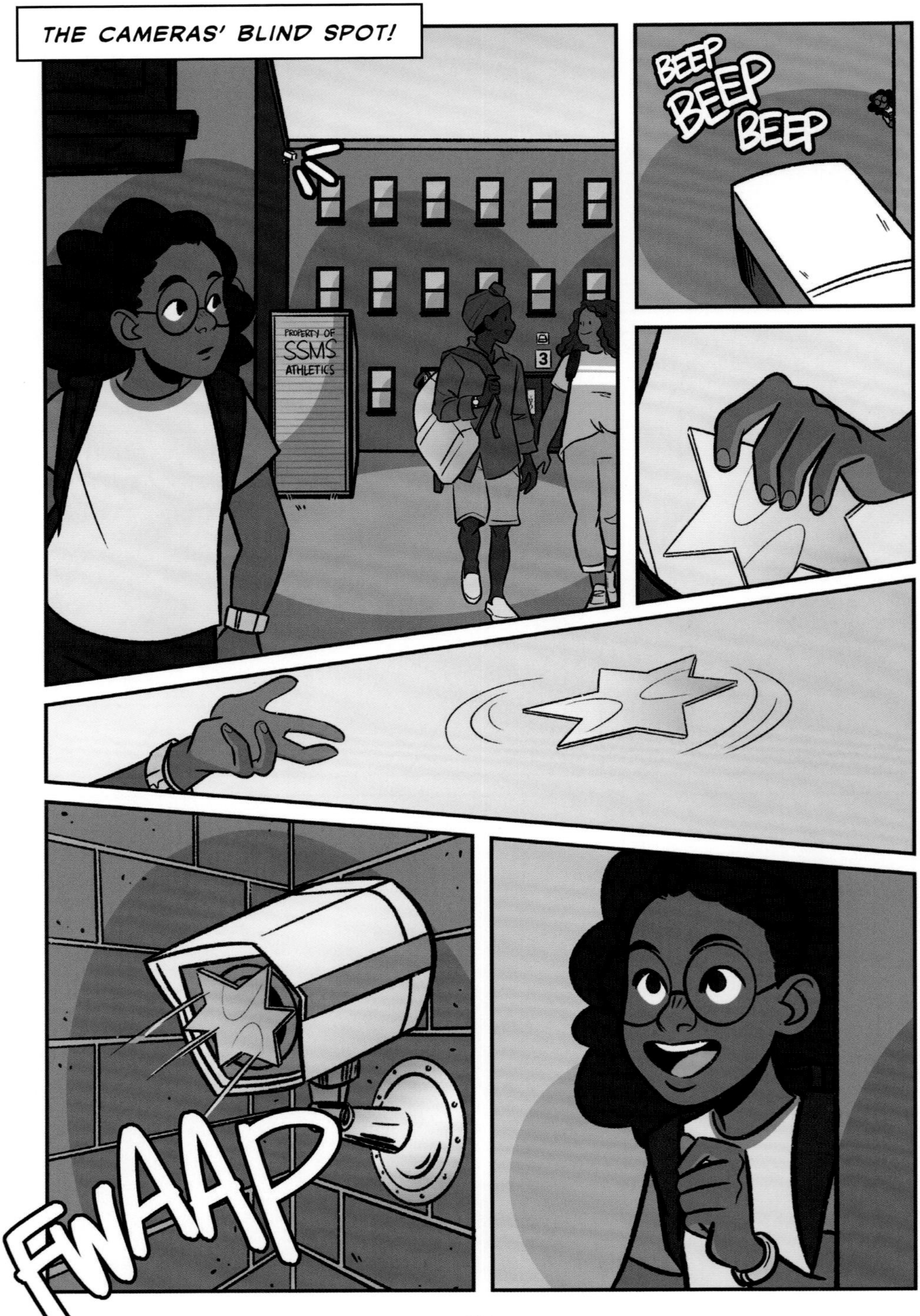
THE CAMERAS' BLIND SPOT!
PROPERTY OF
SSMS
ATHLETICS
3
BEEP
BEEP
BEEP
FWAAP

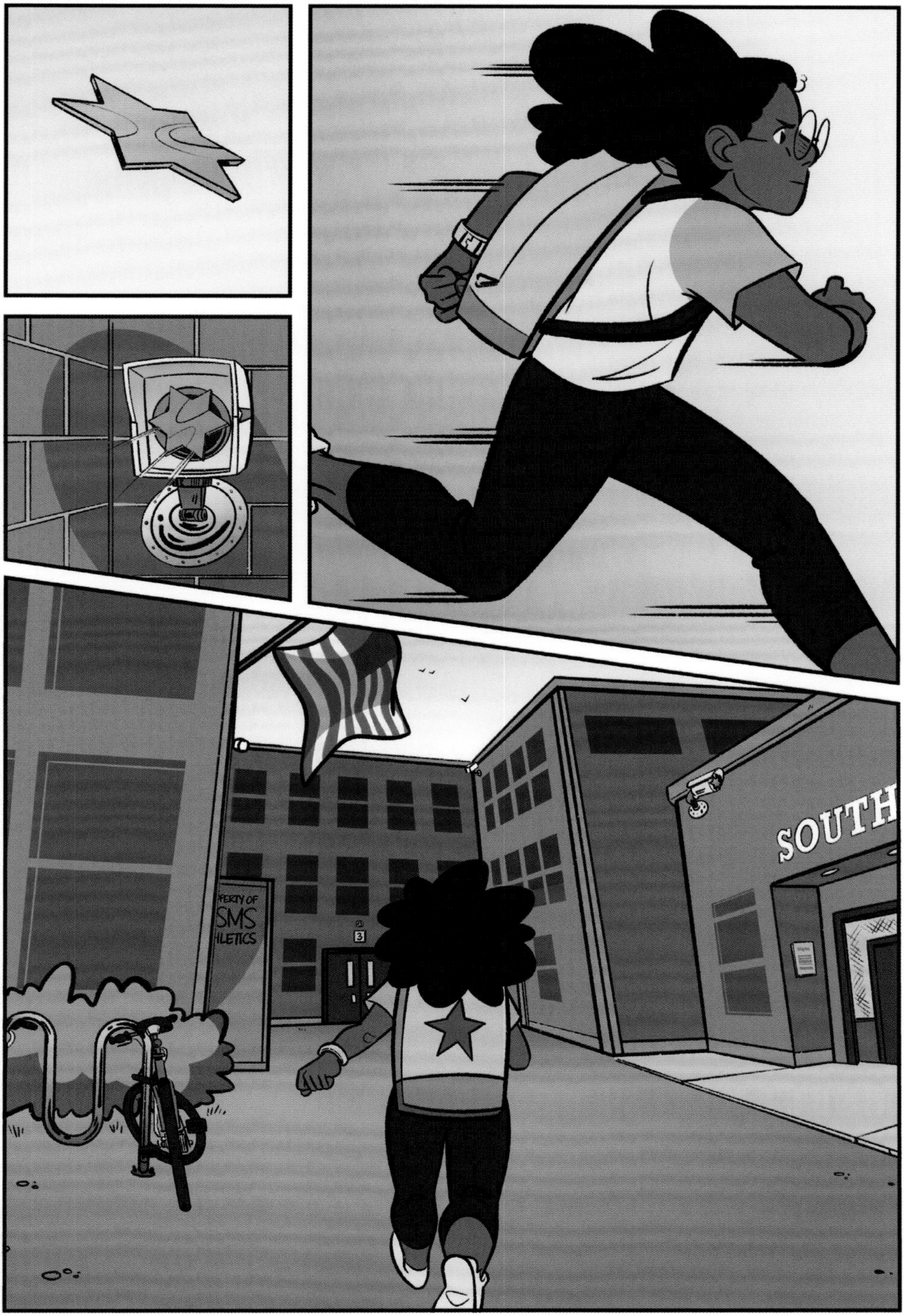
PERTY OF
SMS
HLETICS
3
SOUTH

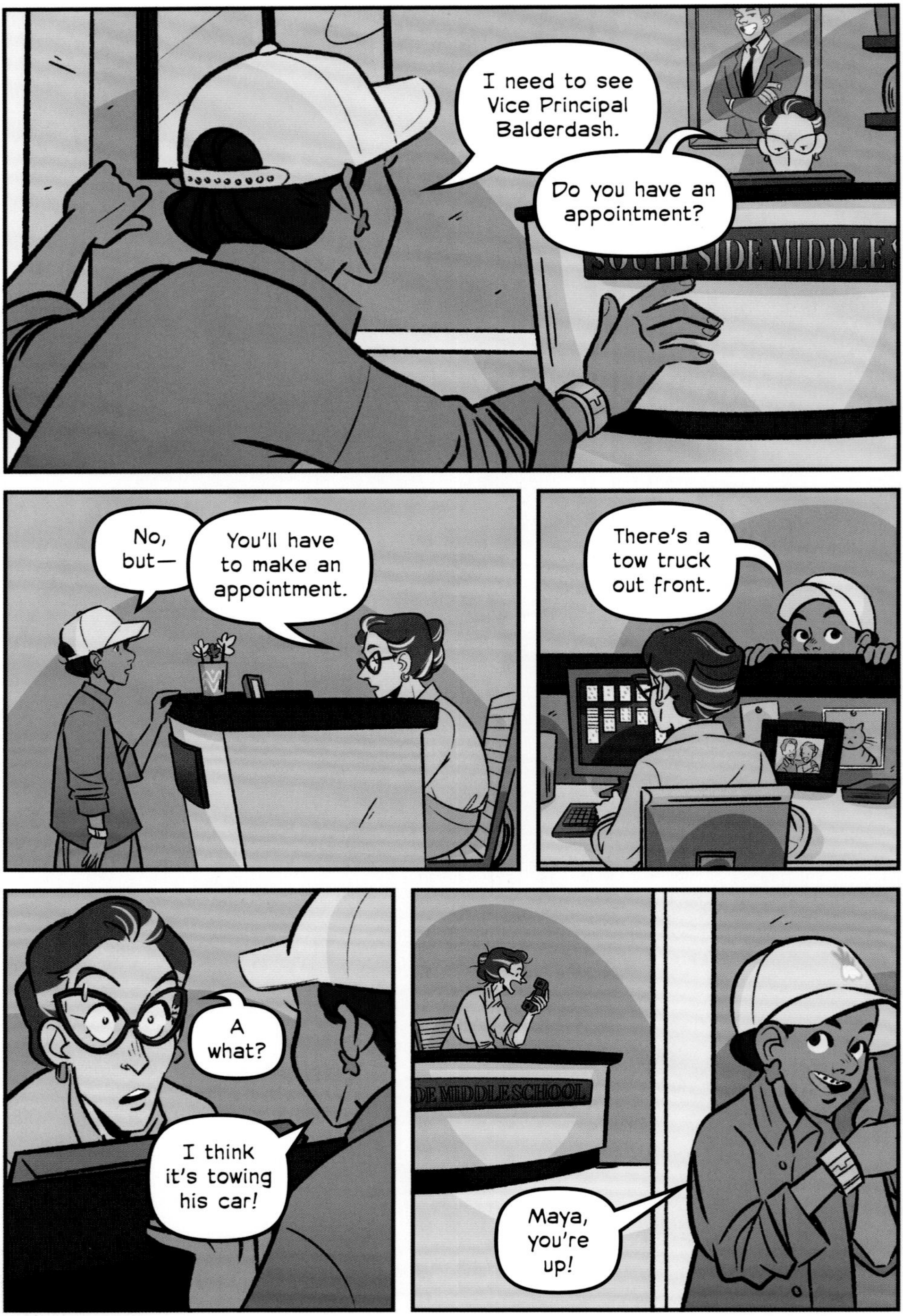
I need to see Vice Principal Balderdash.
Do you have an appointment?
SOUTH SIDE MIDDLE S
No, but—
You'll have to make an appointment.
There's a tow truck out front.
A what?
I think it's towing his car!
DE MIDDLE SCHOOL
Maya, you're up!

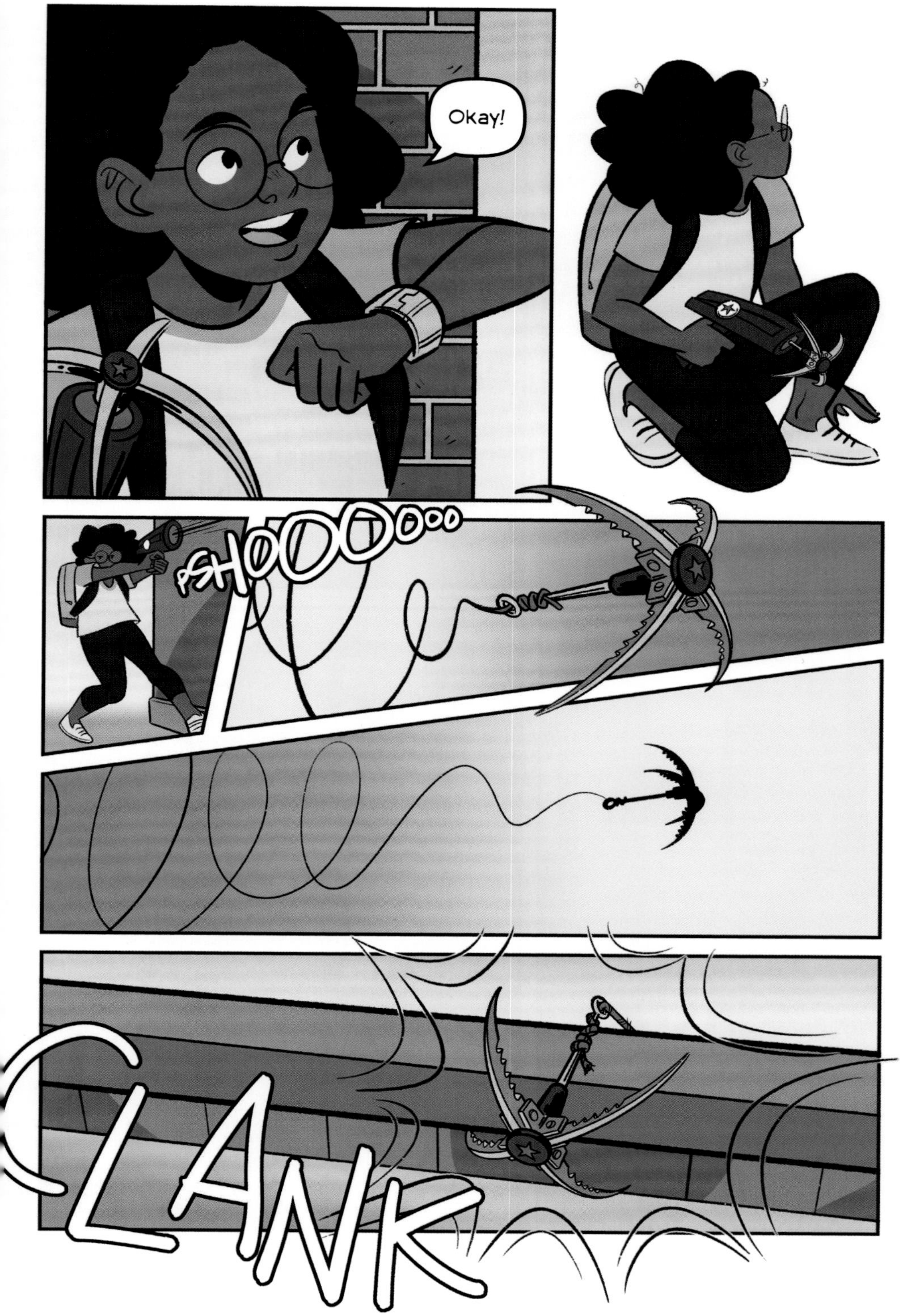
Okay!
PSHOOOOooo
CLANK

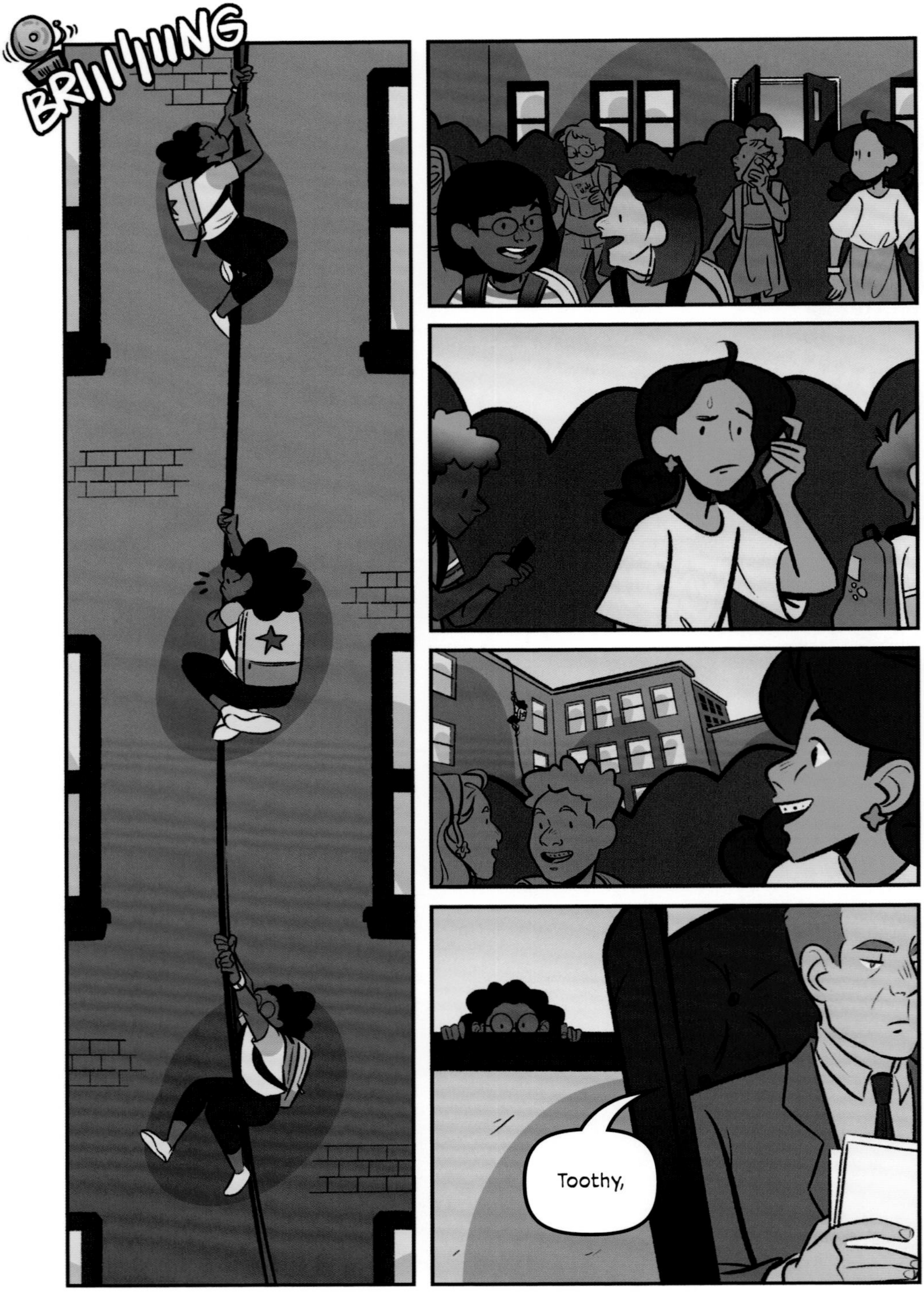
BRIIIIIING
Toothy,

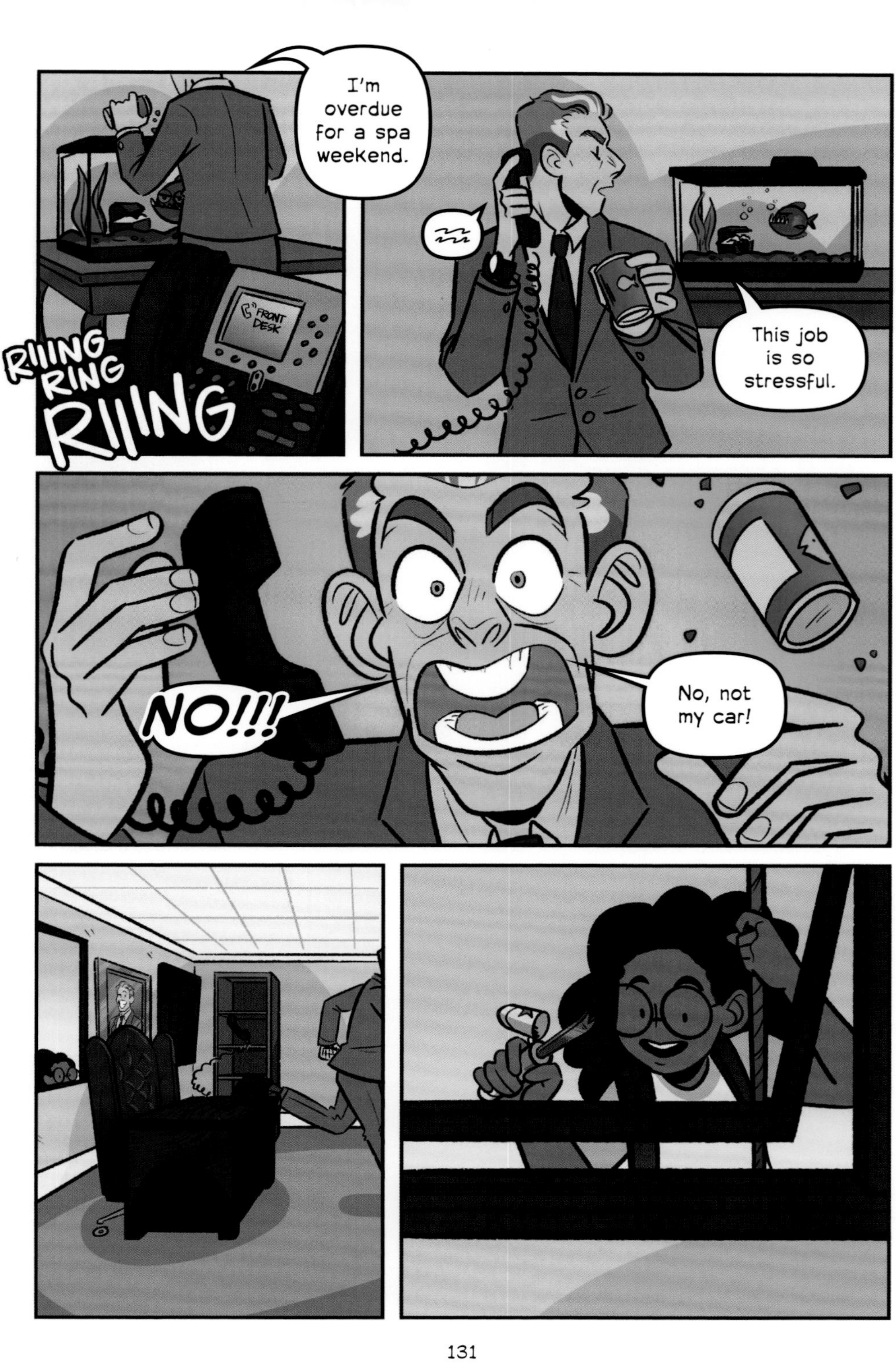
I'm overdue for a spa weekend.
RIIING RING RIIING
FRONT DESK
This job is so stressful.
NO!!!
No, not my car!

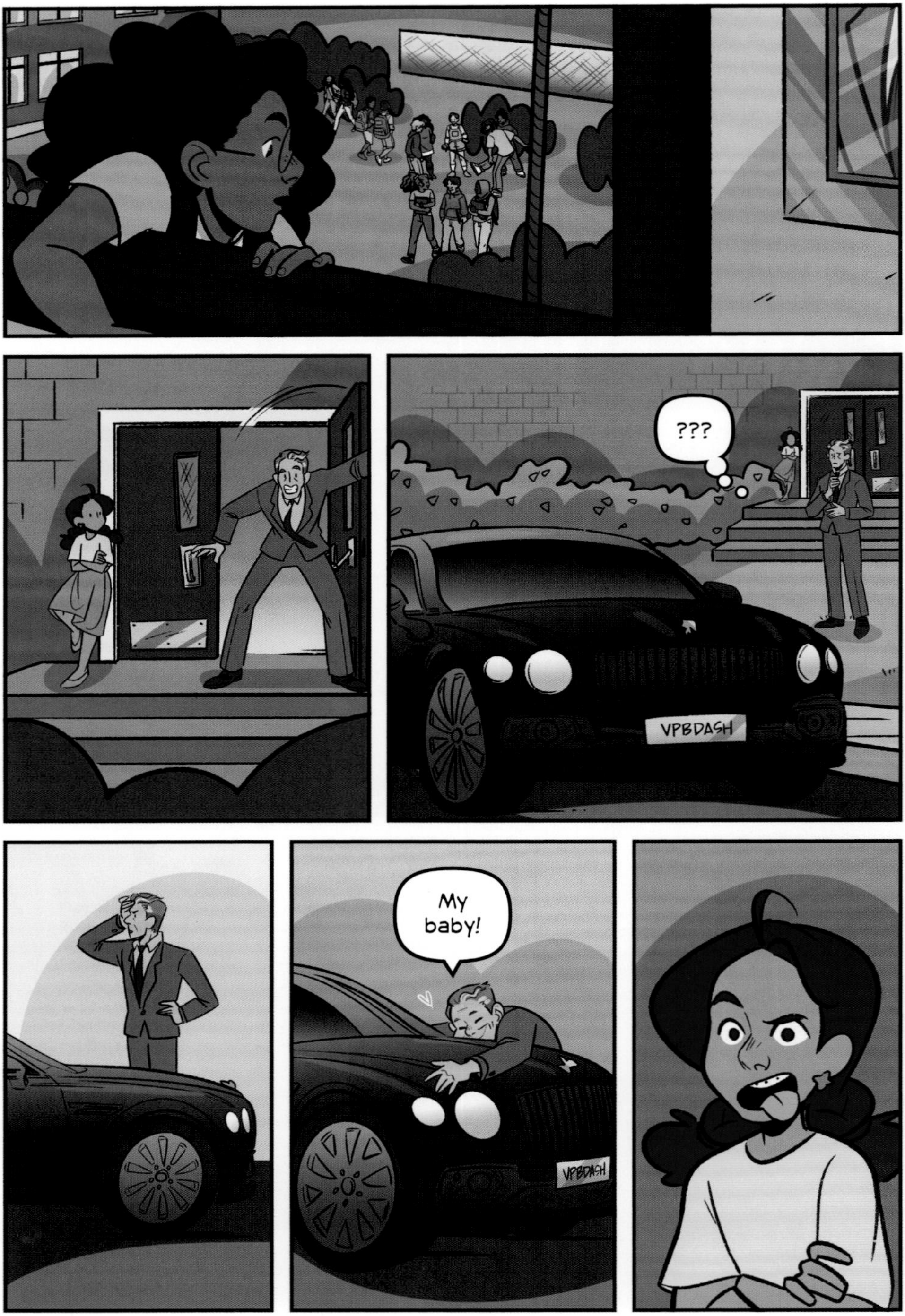
???
VPBDASH
My baby!
VPBDASH

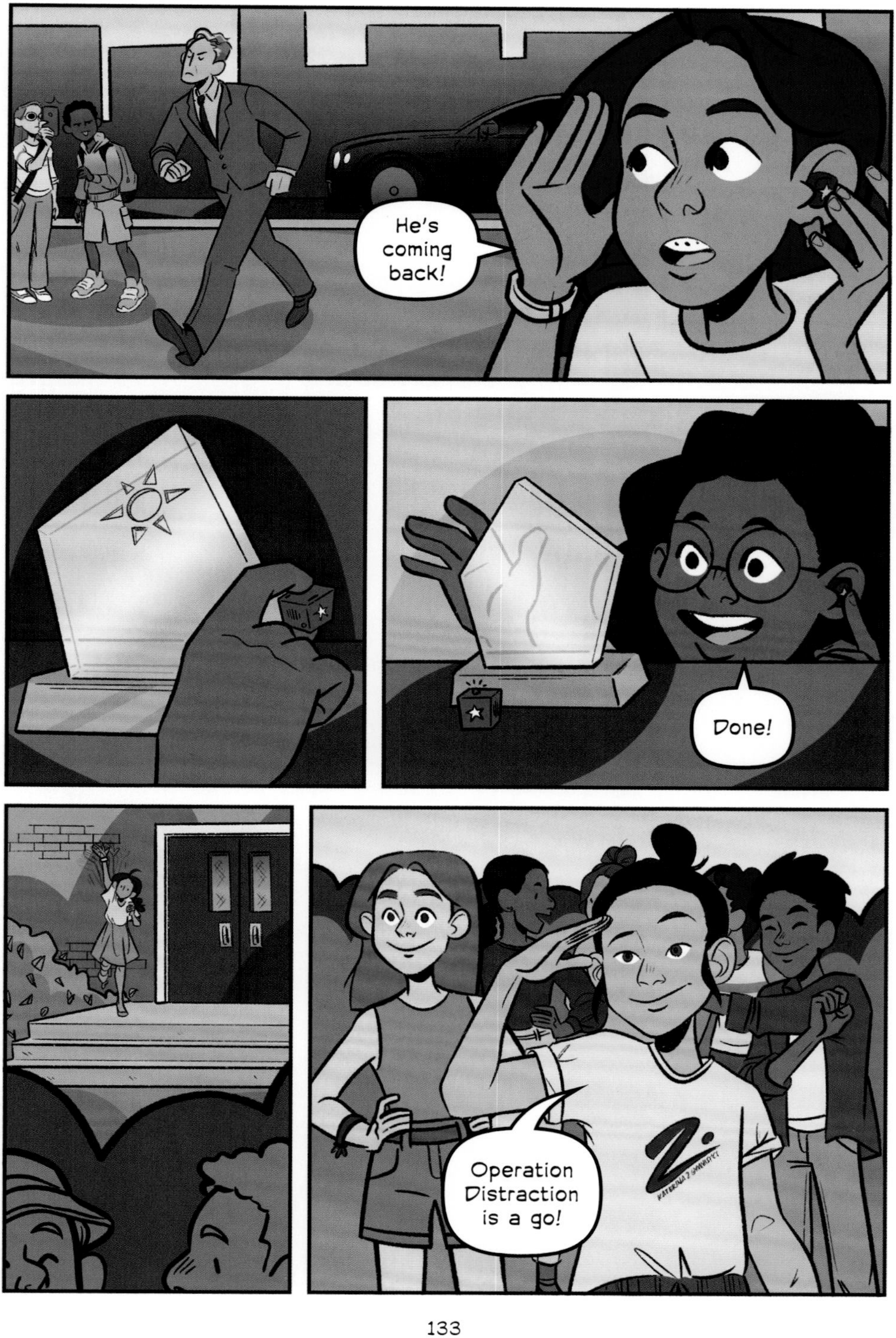
He's coming back!
Done!
Operation Distraction is a go!

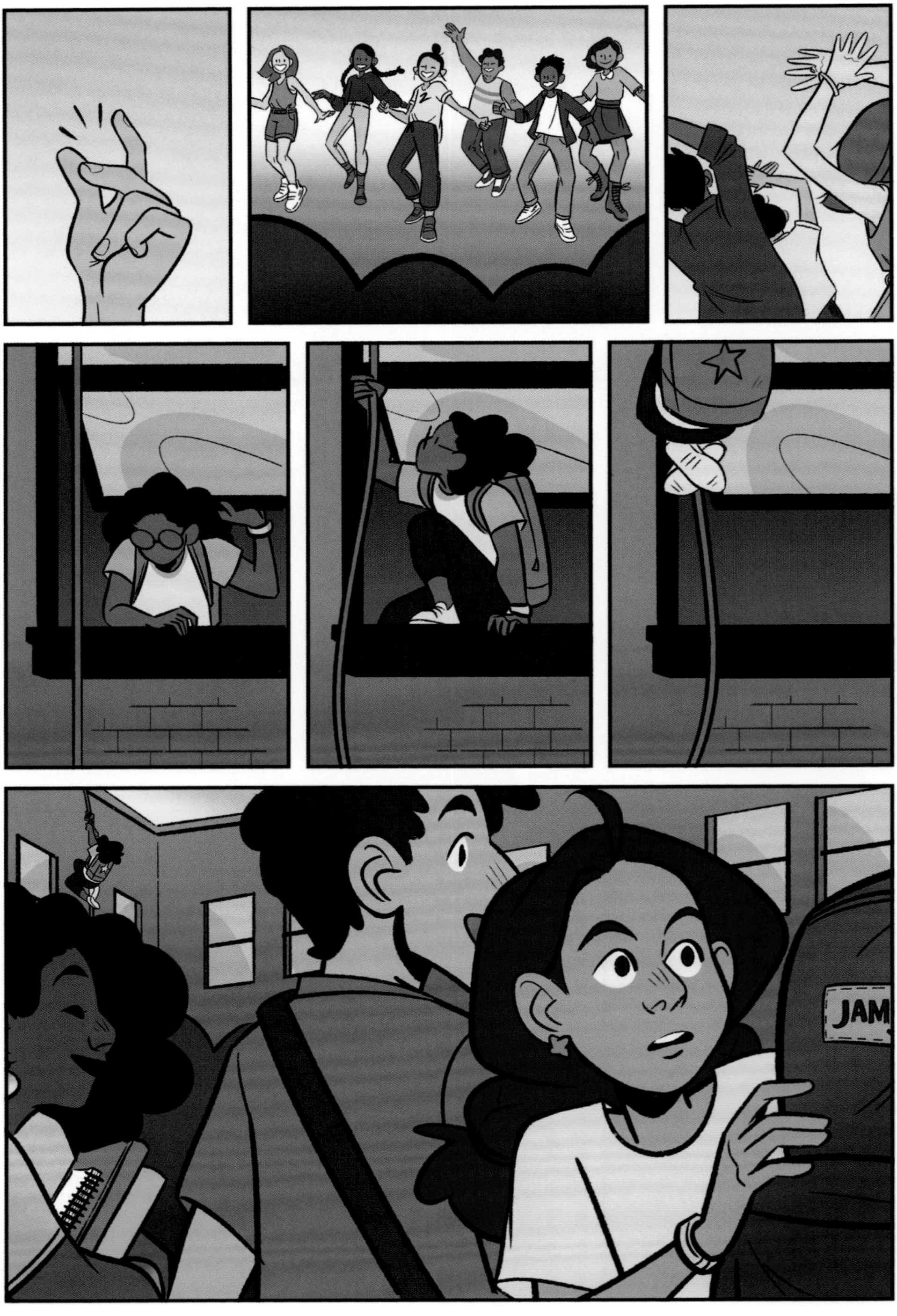
JAM

PROPERTY OF
SSMS
ATHLETICS

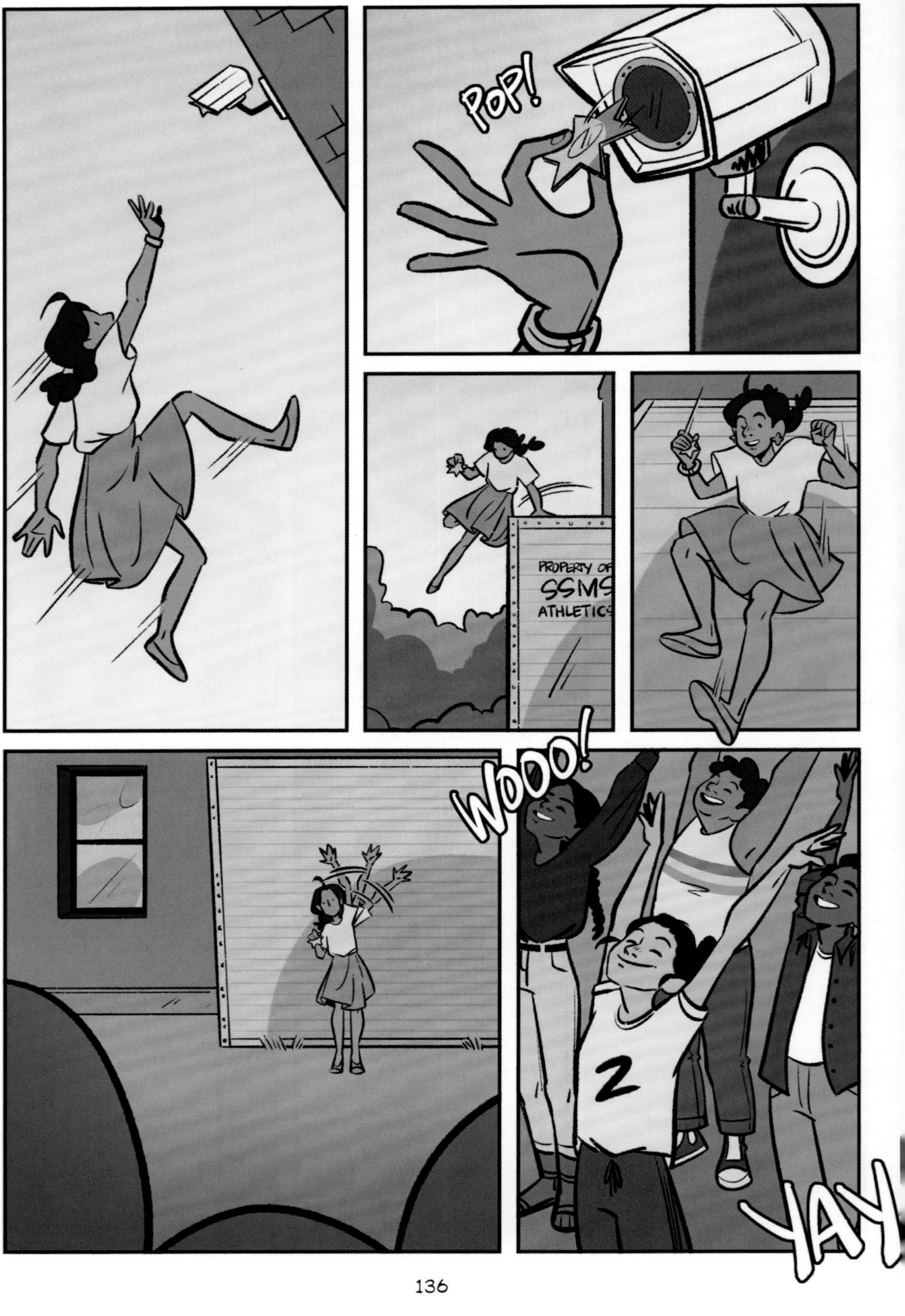
POP!
PROPERTY OF
SSMS
ATHLETICS
WOOO!
YAY

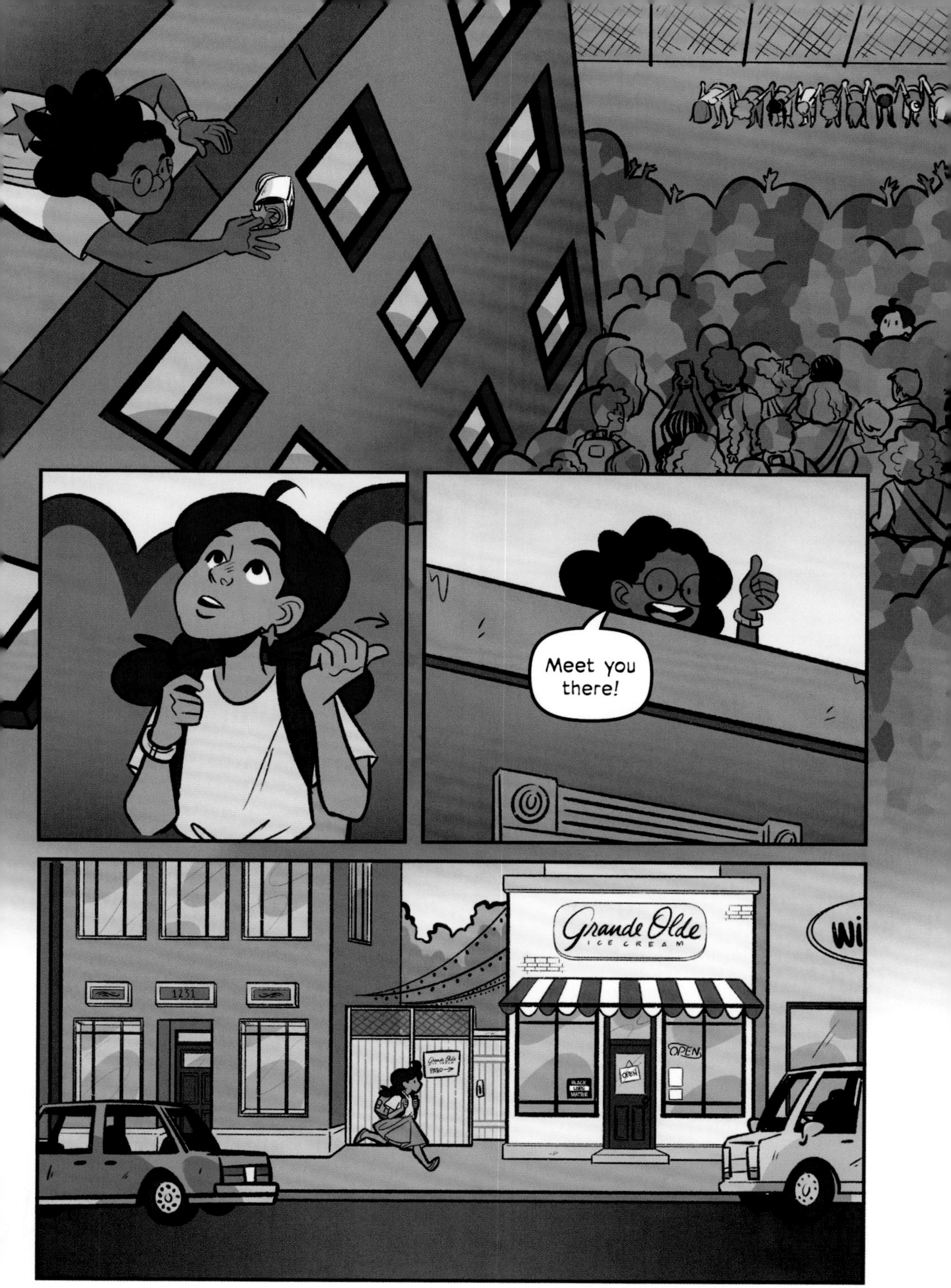

Meet you there!
1231
Grande Olde
ICE CREAM
OPEN
OPEN

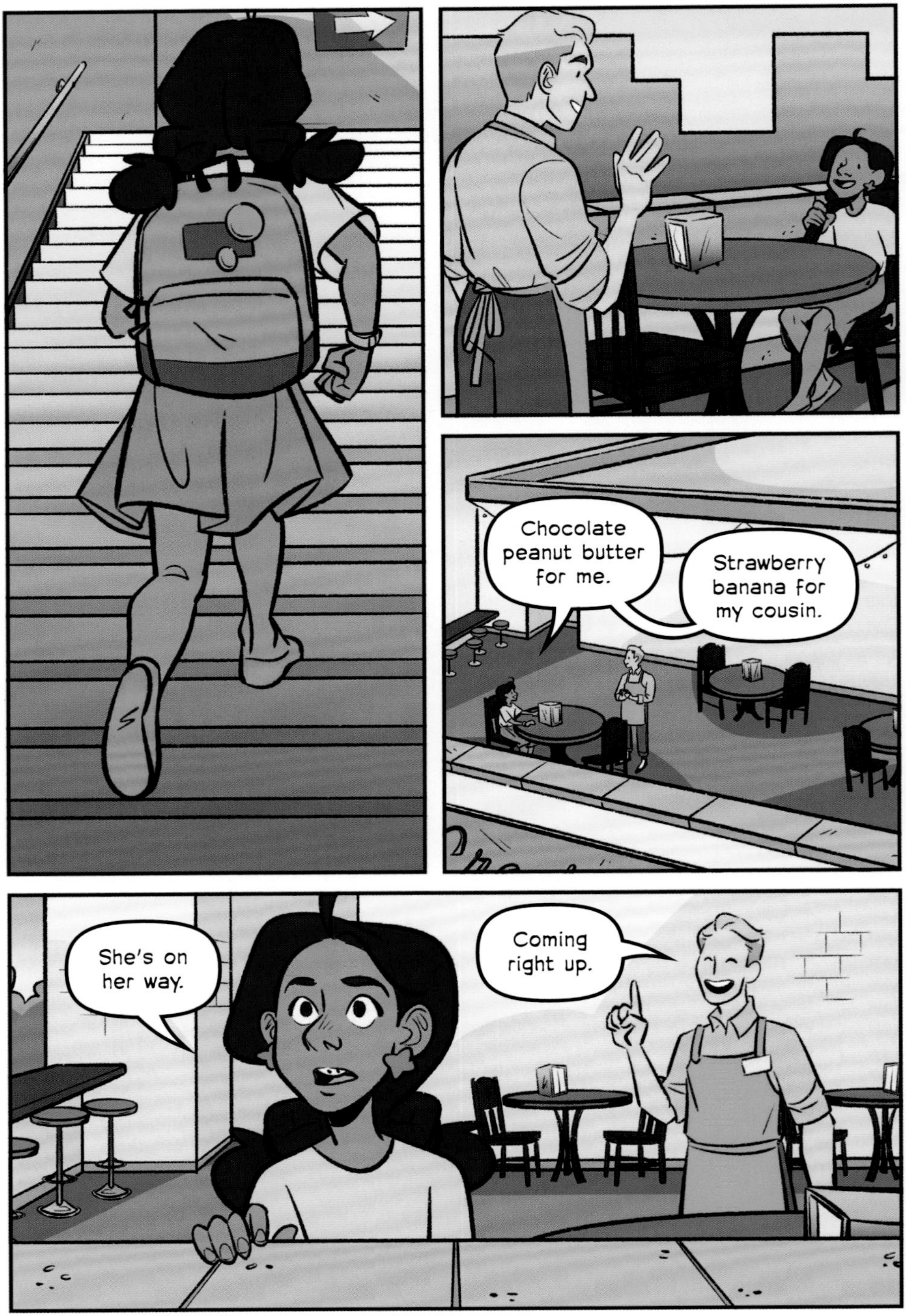
Chocolate peanut butter for me.
Strawberry banana for my cousin.
She's on her way.
Coming right up.

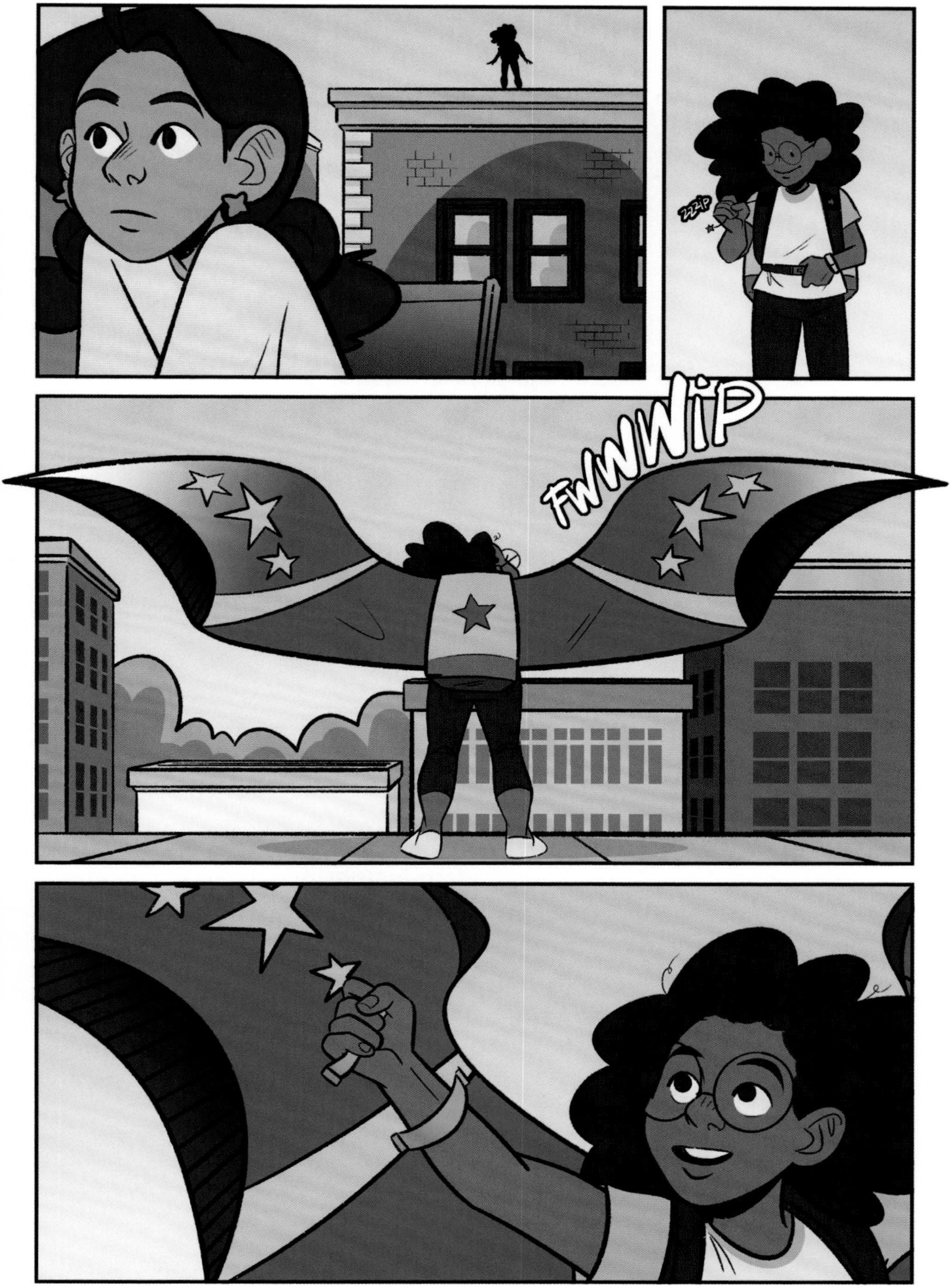
ZZZIP
FWWWIP

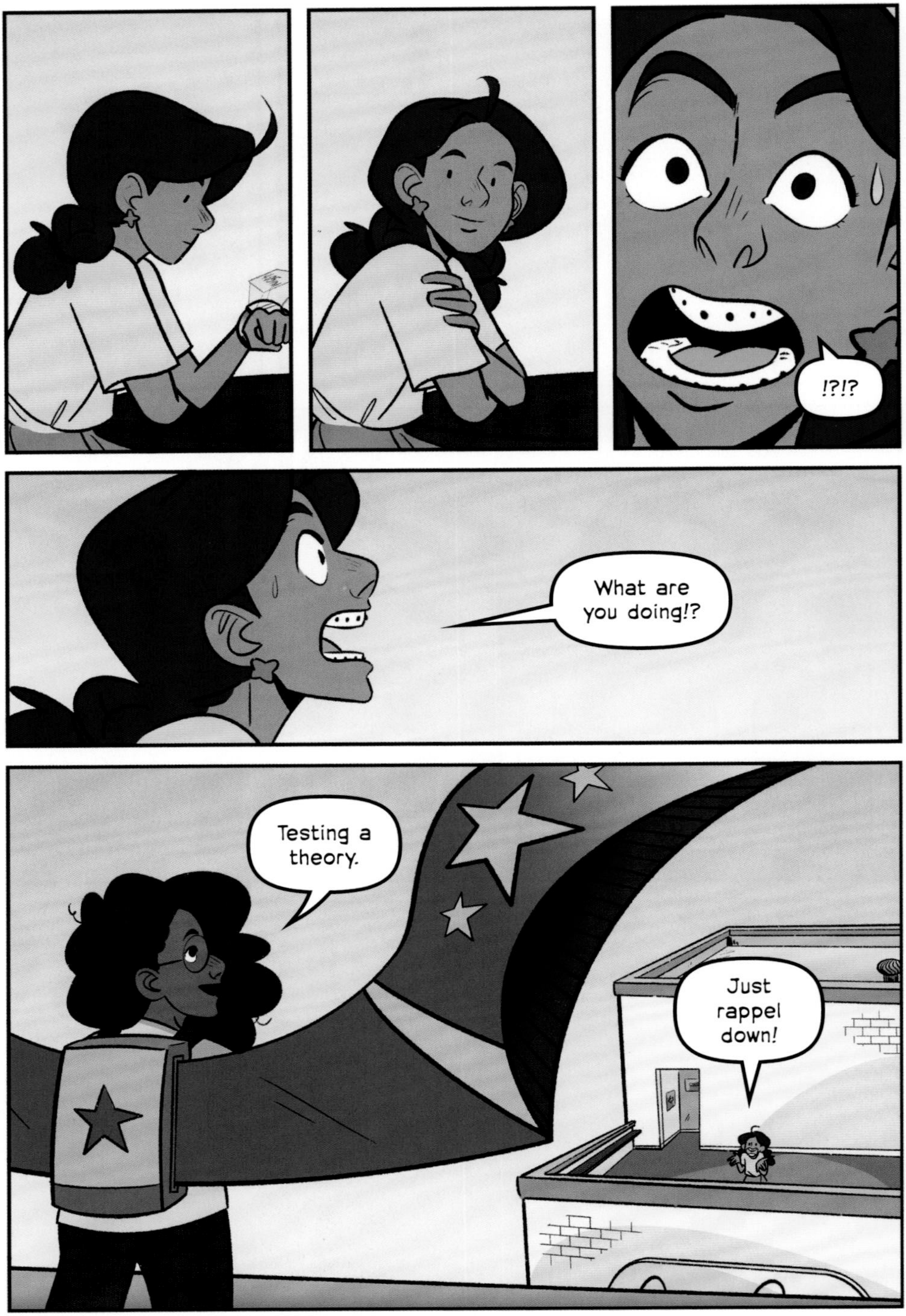
!?!?
What are you doing!?
Testing a theory.
Just rappel down!

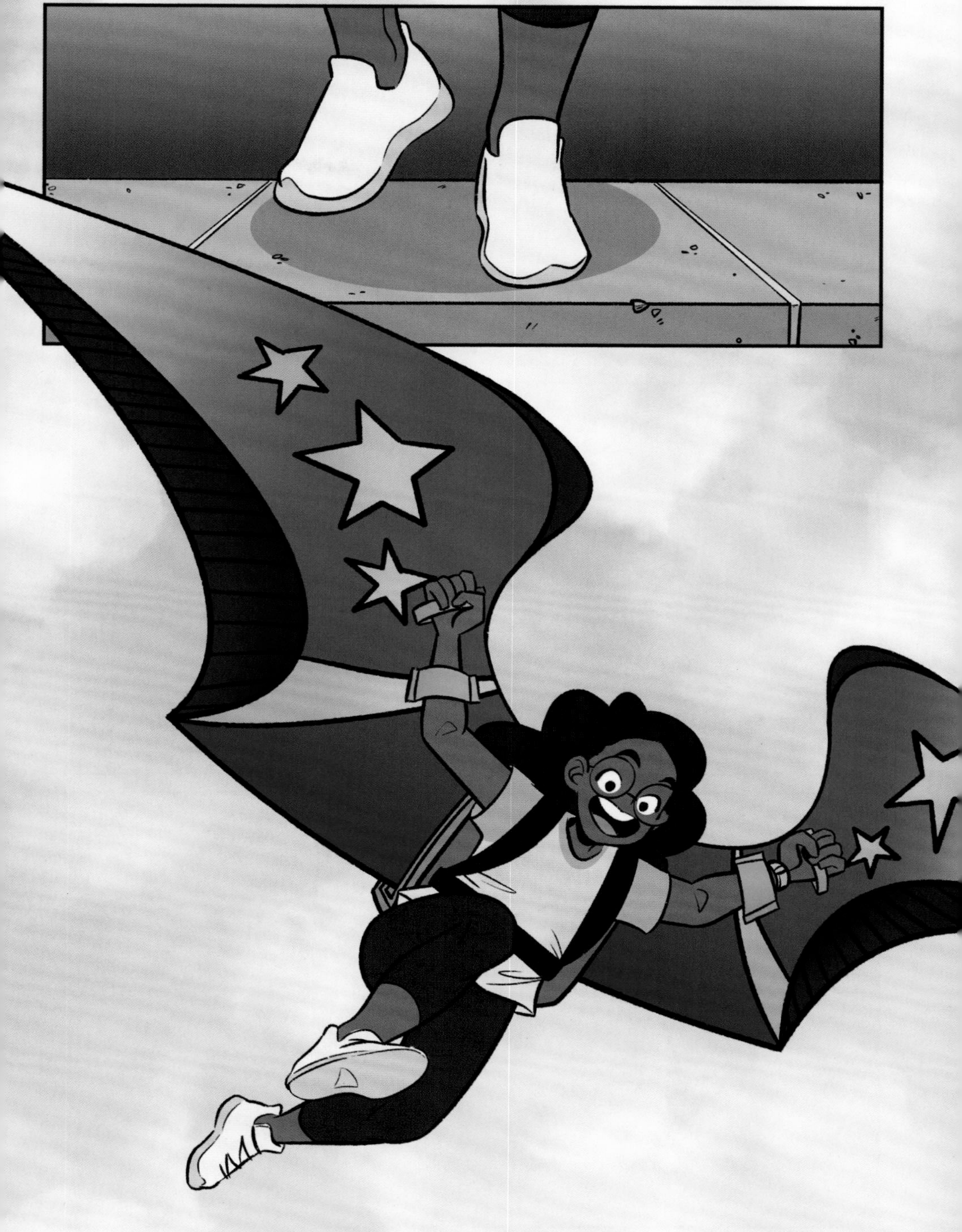

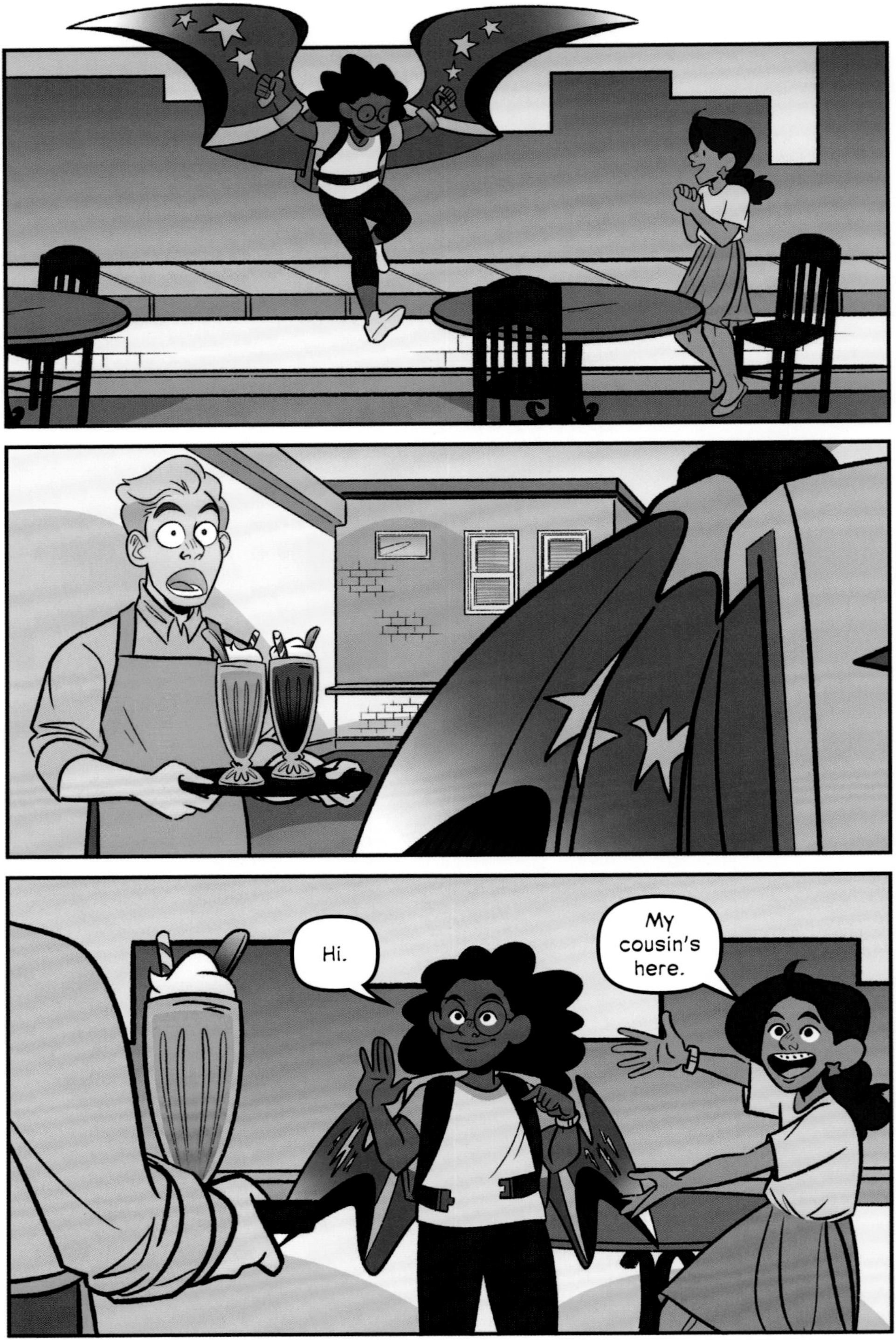
Hi.
My cousin's here.

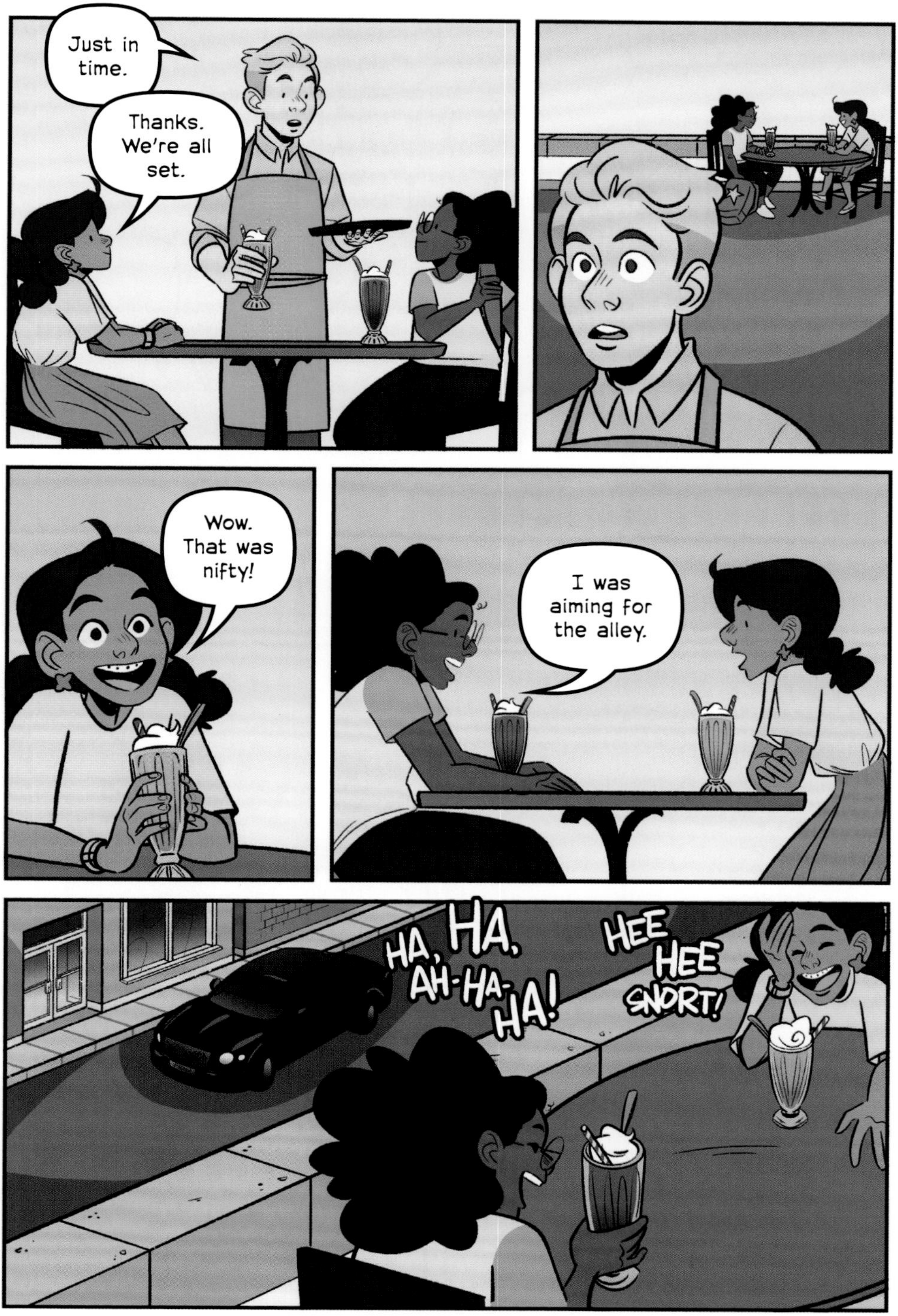
Just in time.
Thanks. We're all set.
Wow. That was nifty!
I was aiming for the alley.
HA, HA, AH-HA-HA!
HEE HEE SNORT!

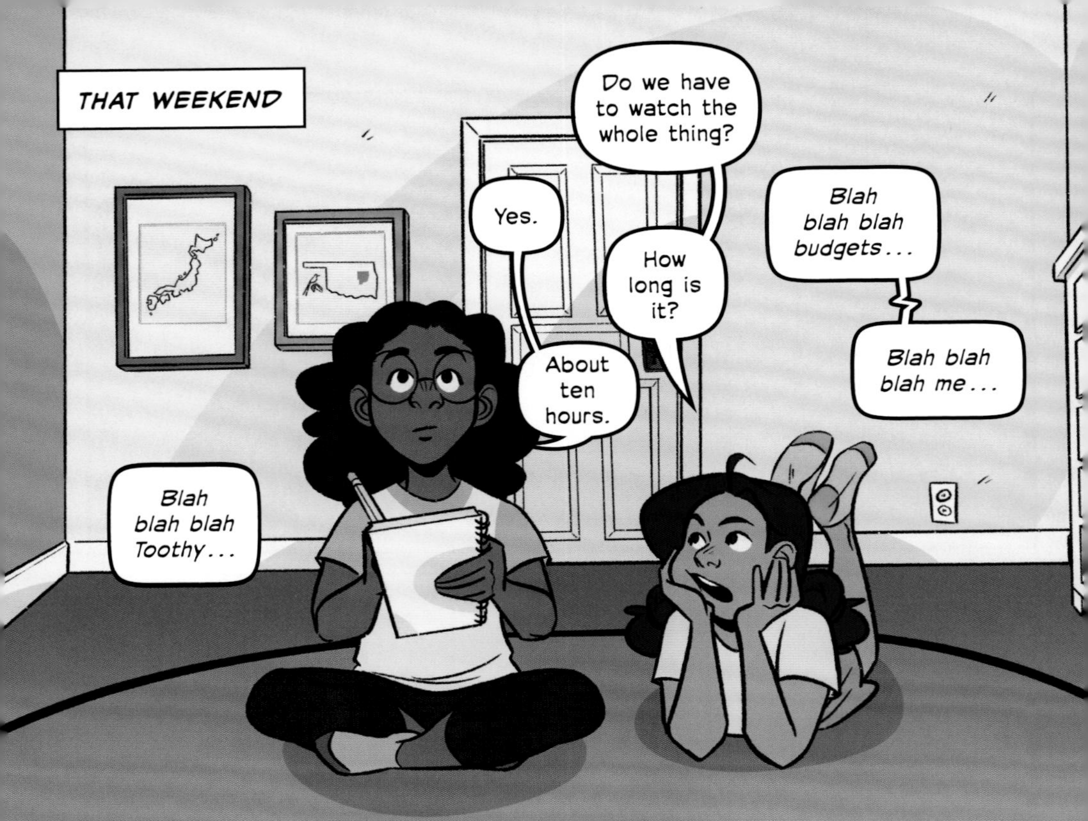
THAT WEEKEND
Do we have to watch the whole thing?
Yes.
How long is it?
About ten hours.
Blah blah blah budgets...
Blah blah blah me...
Blah blah blah Toothy...

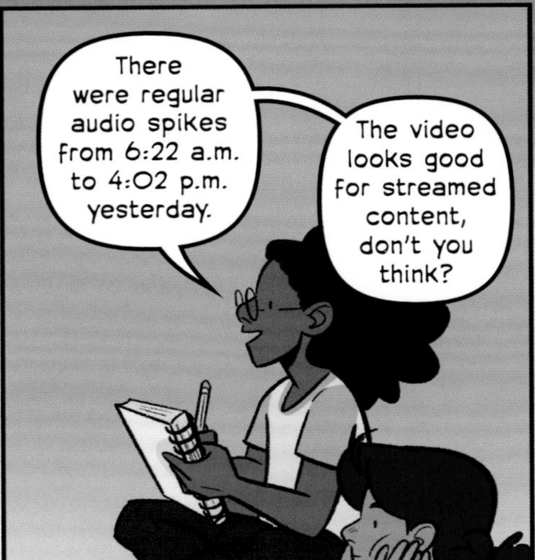
There were regular audio spikes from 6:22 a.m. to 4:02 p.m. yesterday.
The video looks good for streamed content, don't you think?

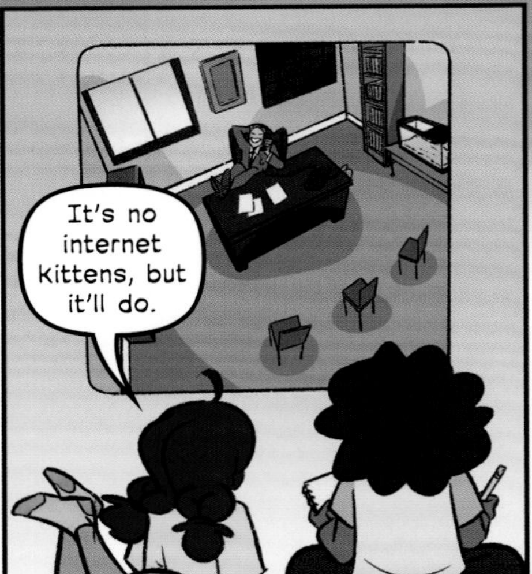
It's no internet kittens, but it'll do.

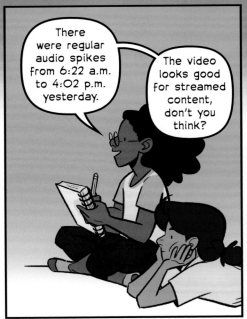

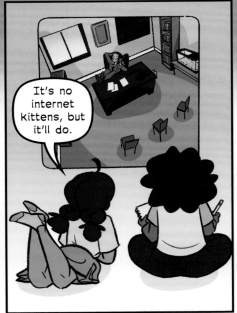

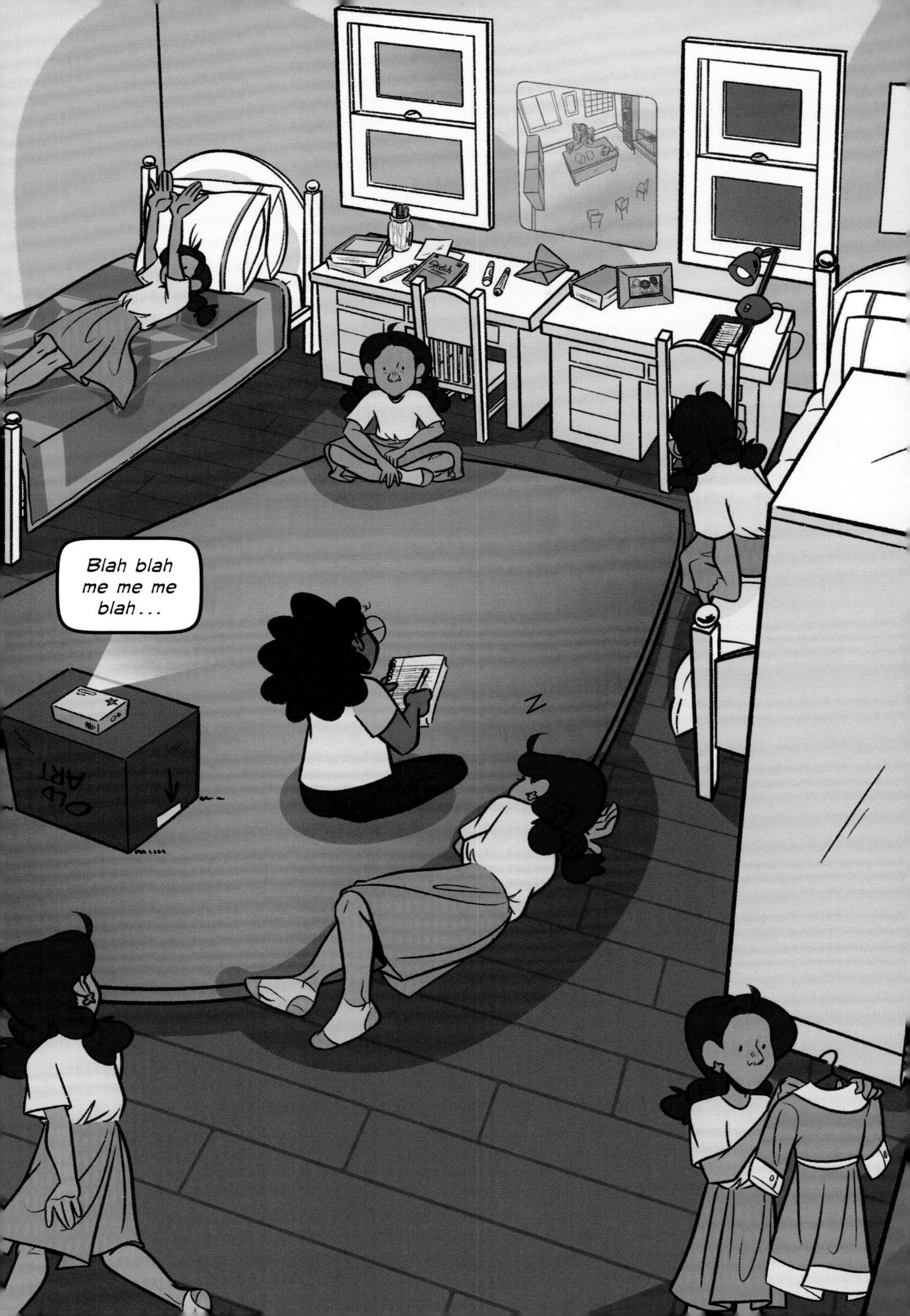
Blah blah me me me blah...

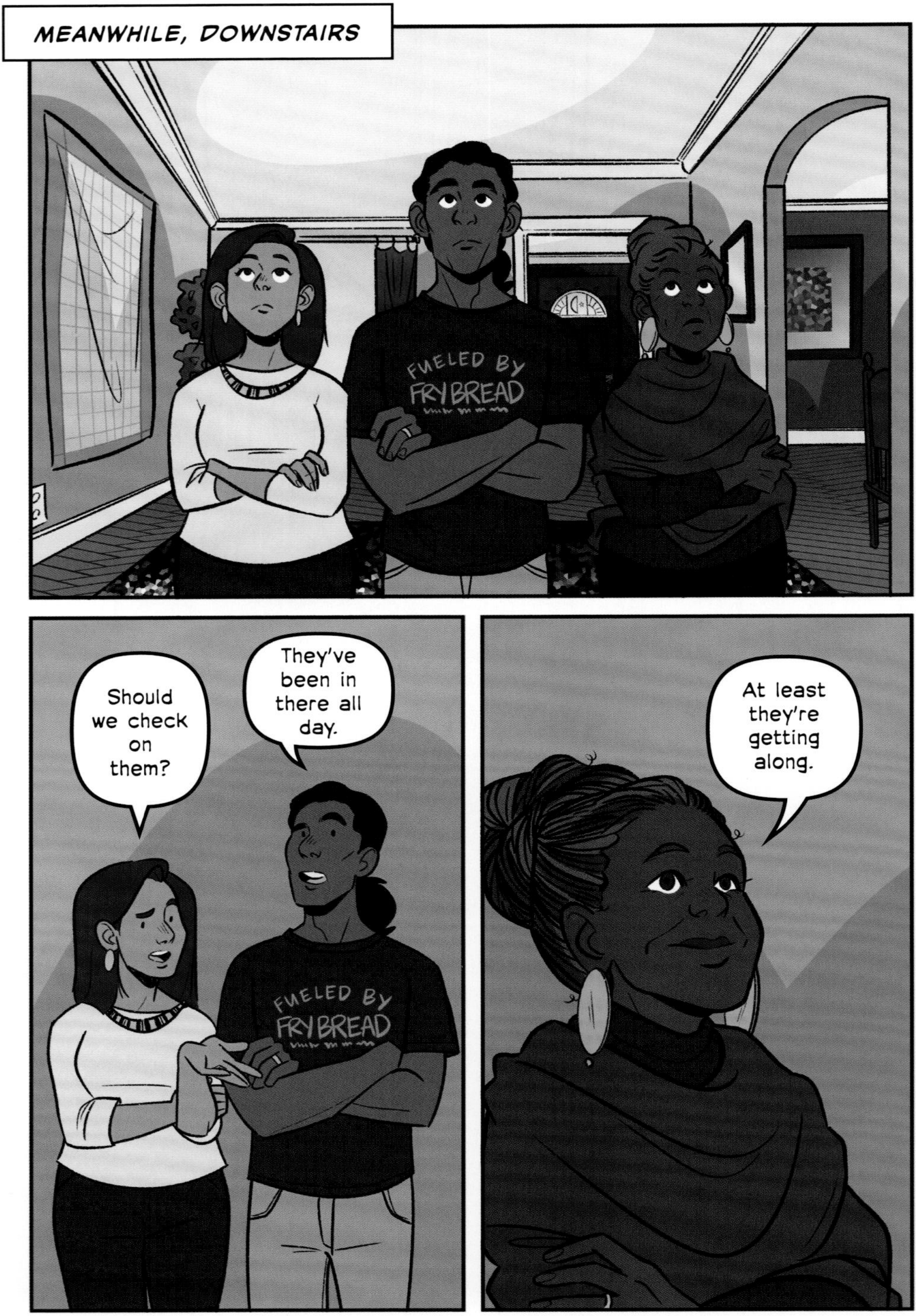
MEANWHILE, DOWNSTAIRS
FUELED BY FRYBREAD
Should we check on them?
They've been in there all day.
FUELED BY FRYBREAD
At least they're getting along.

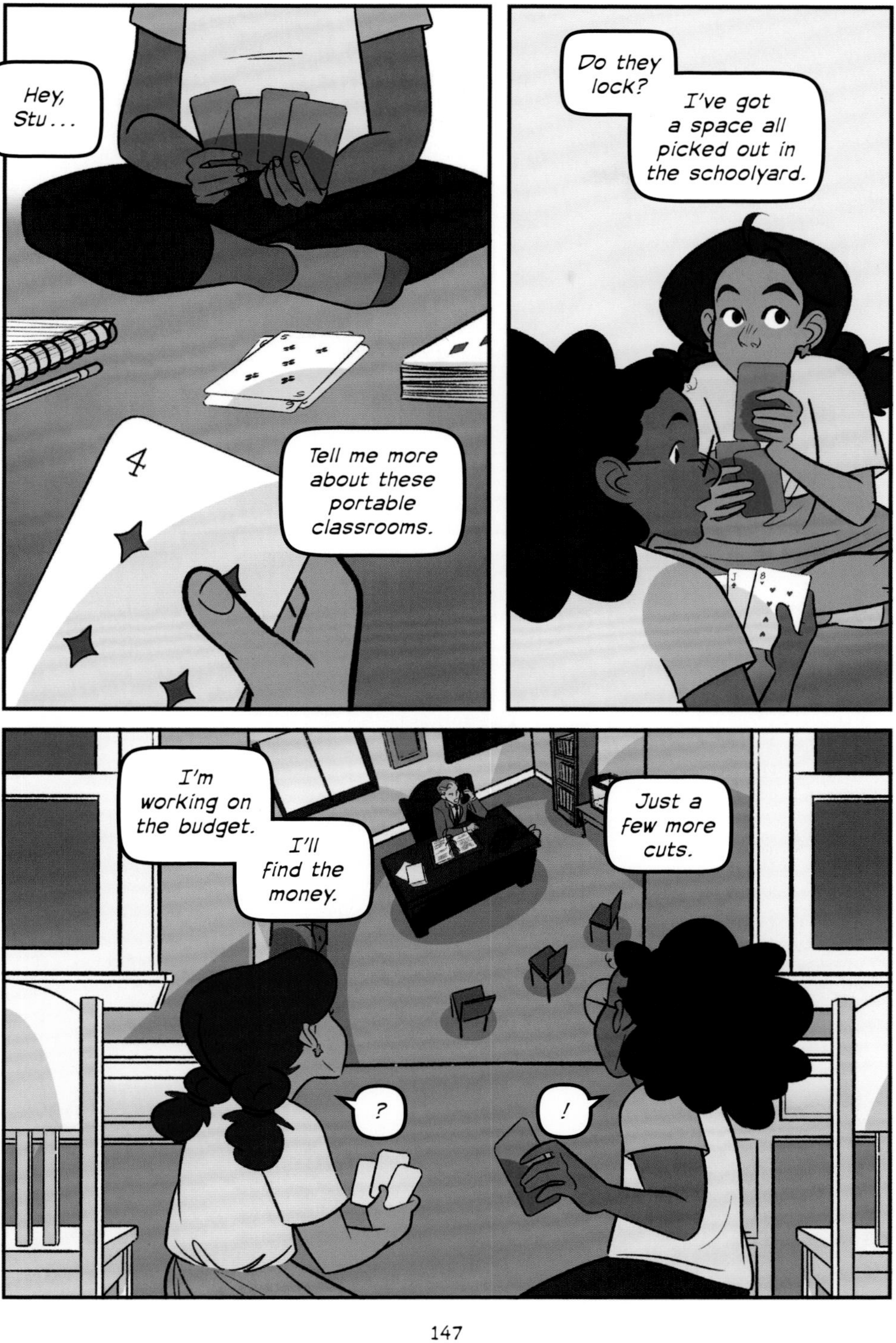
Hey, Stu...
Tell me more about these portable classrooms.
Do they lock?
I've got a space all picked out in the schoolyard.
I'm working on the budget.
I'll find the money.
Just a few more cuts.
?
!

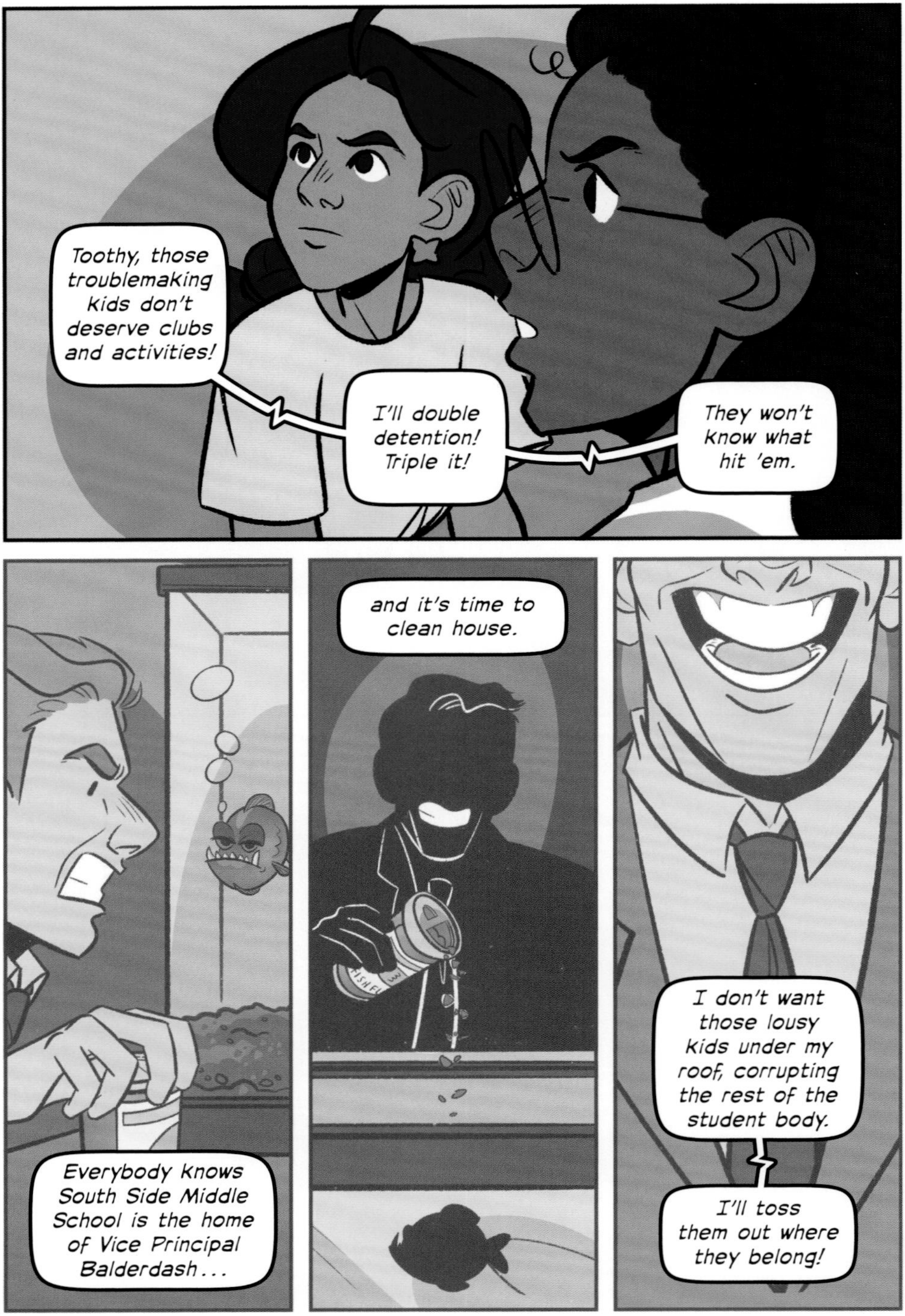
Toothy, those troublemaking kids don't deserve clubs and activities!
I'll double detention! Triple it!
They won't know what hit 'em.
Everybody knows South Side Middle School is the home of Vice Principal Balderdash...
and it's time to clean house.
I don't want those lousy kids under my roof, corrupting the rest of the student body.
I'll toss them out where they belong!

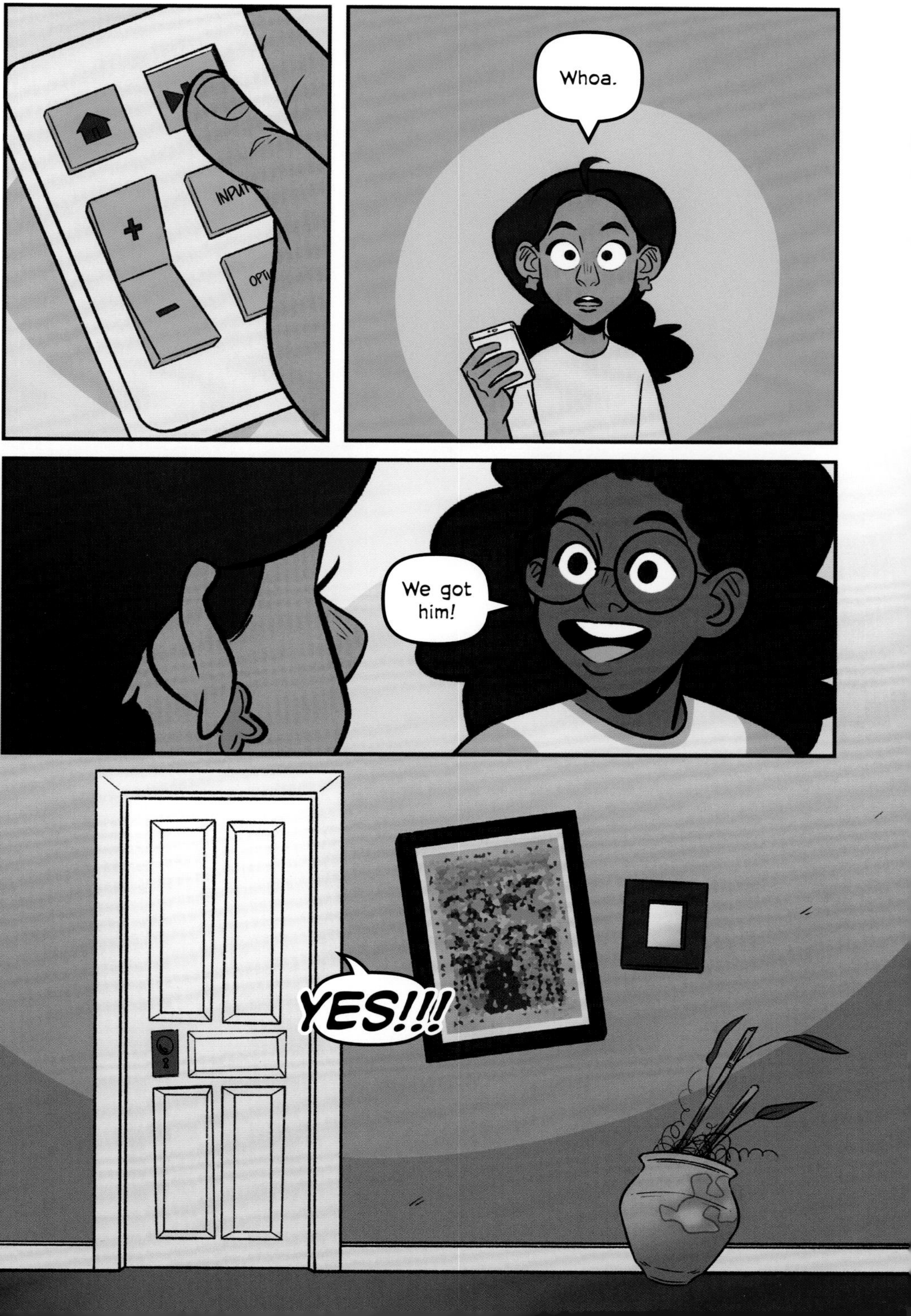

INPUT
OPTI
Whoa.
We got him!
YES!!!

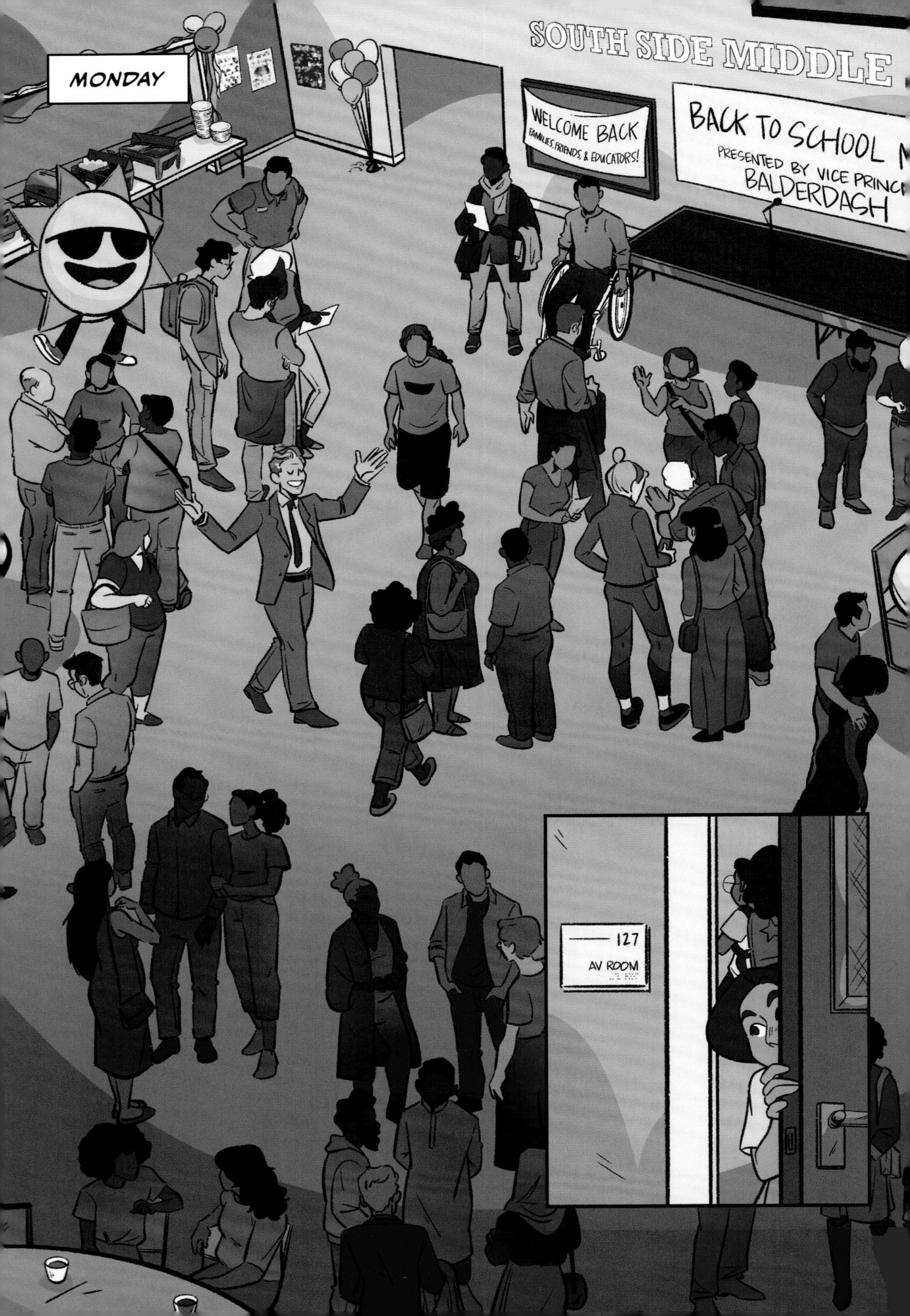
MONDAY
SOUTH SIDE MIDDLE
WELCOME BACK
FAMILIES, FRIENDS, & EDUCATORS!
BACK TO SCHOOL
PRESENTED BY VICE
BALDERDASH
127
AV ROOM

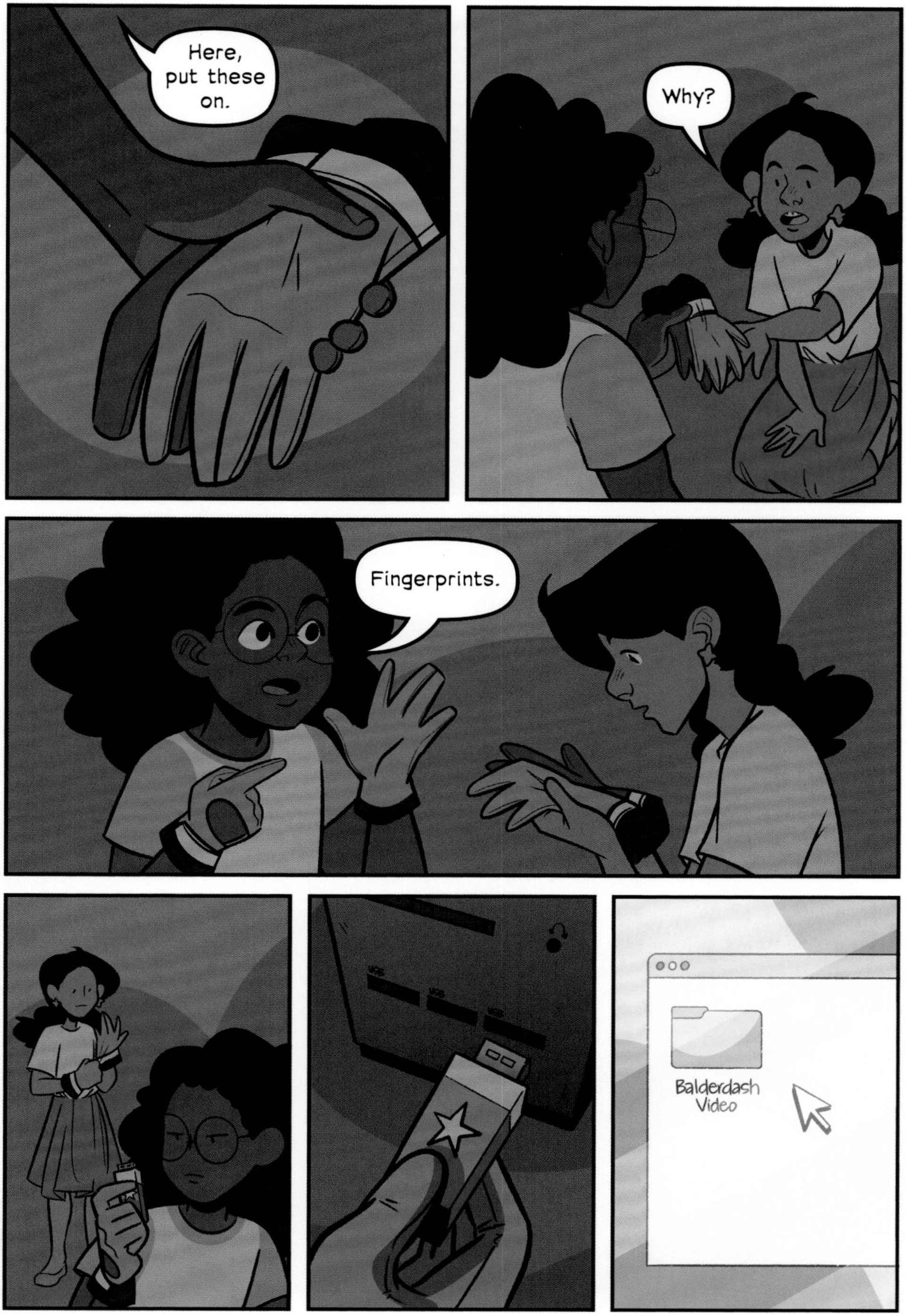
Here, put these on.
Why?
Fingerprints.
Balderdash Video

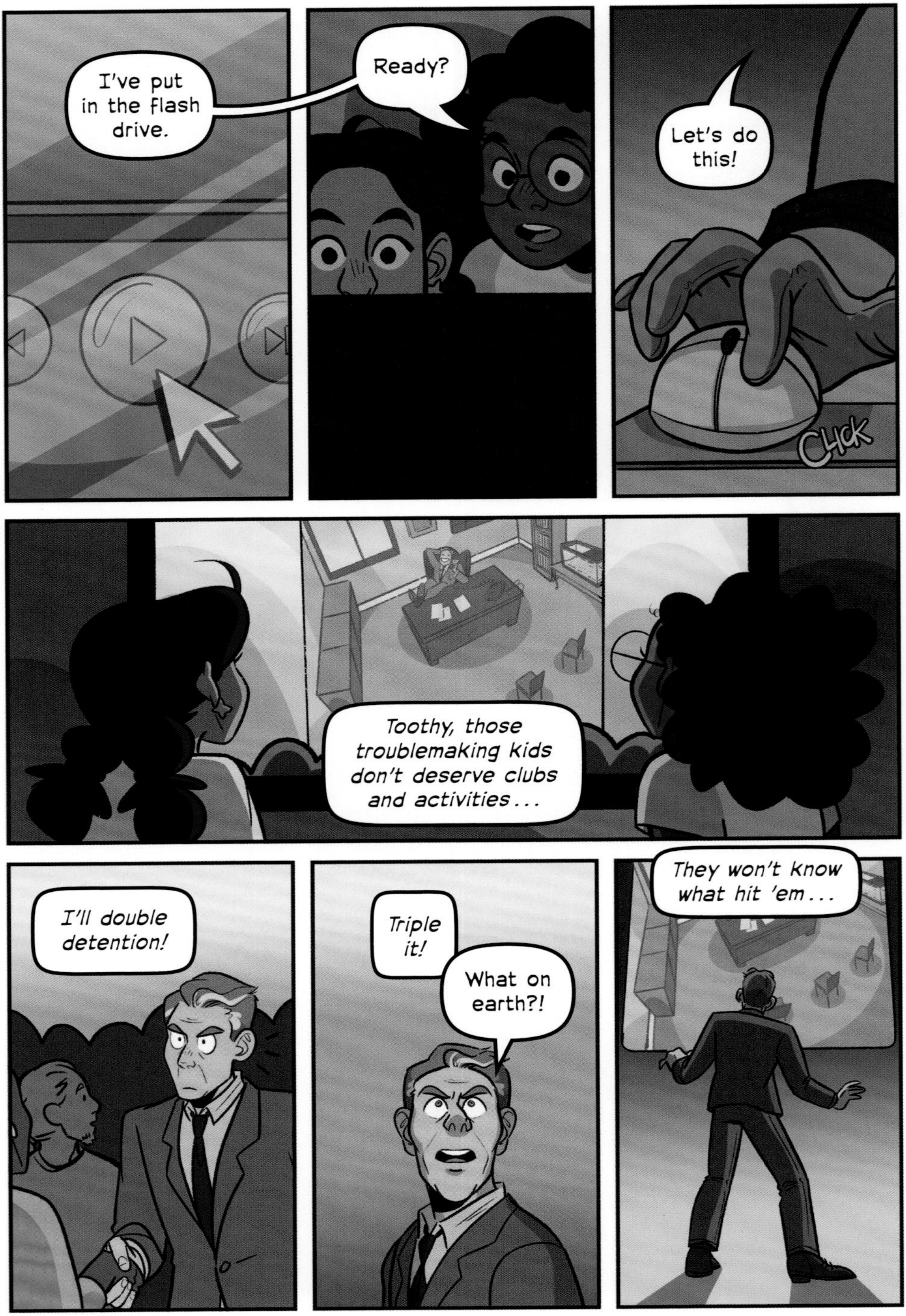
I've put in the flash drive.
Ready?
Let's do this!
CLICK
Toothy, those troublemaking kids don't deserve clubs and activities . . .
I'll double detention!
Triple it!
What on earth?!
They won't know what hit 'em . . .

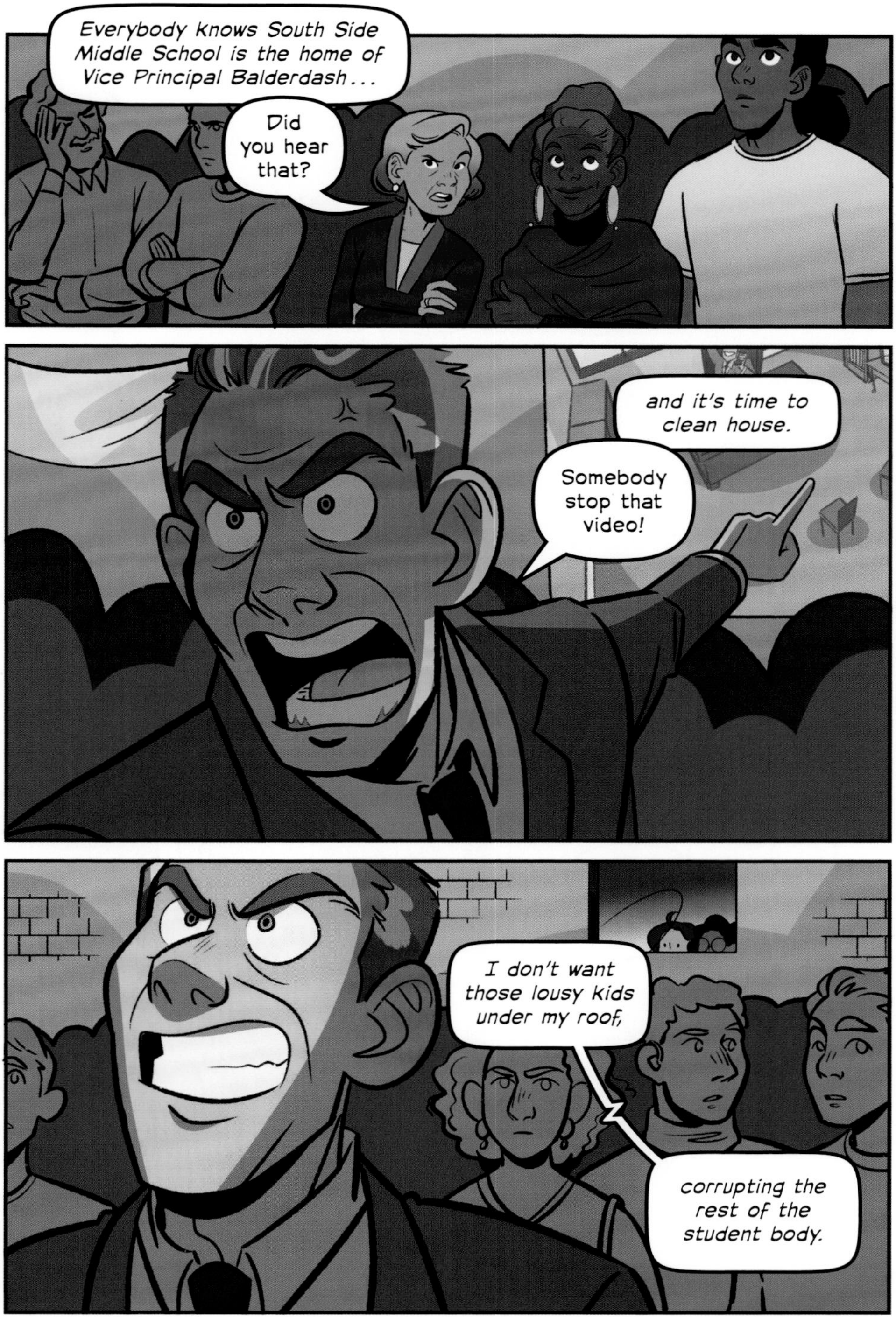
Everybody knows South Side Middle School is the home of Vice Principal Balderdash...
Did you hear that?
and it's time to clean house.
Somebody stop that video!
I don't want those lousy kids under my roof,
corrupting the rest of the student body.

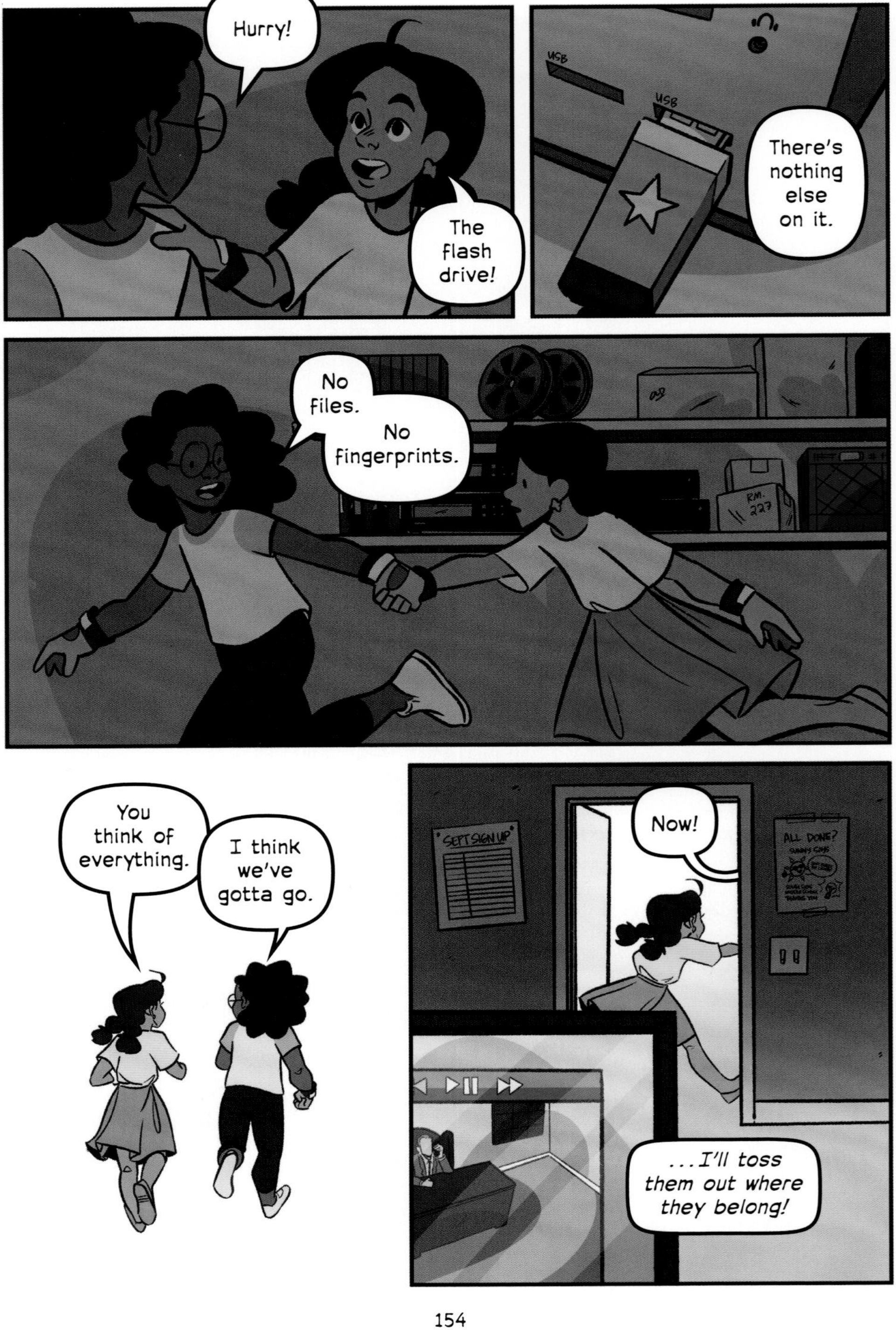
Hurry!
The flash drive!
USB
USB
There's nothing else on it.
No files.
No fingerprints.
RM. 227
You think of everything.
I think we've gotta go.
SEPT SIGN UP
ALL DONE?
Now!
...I'll toss them out where they belong!

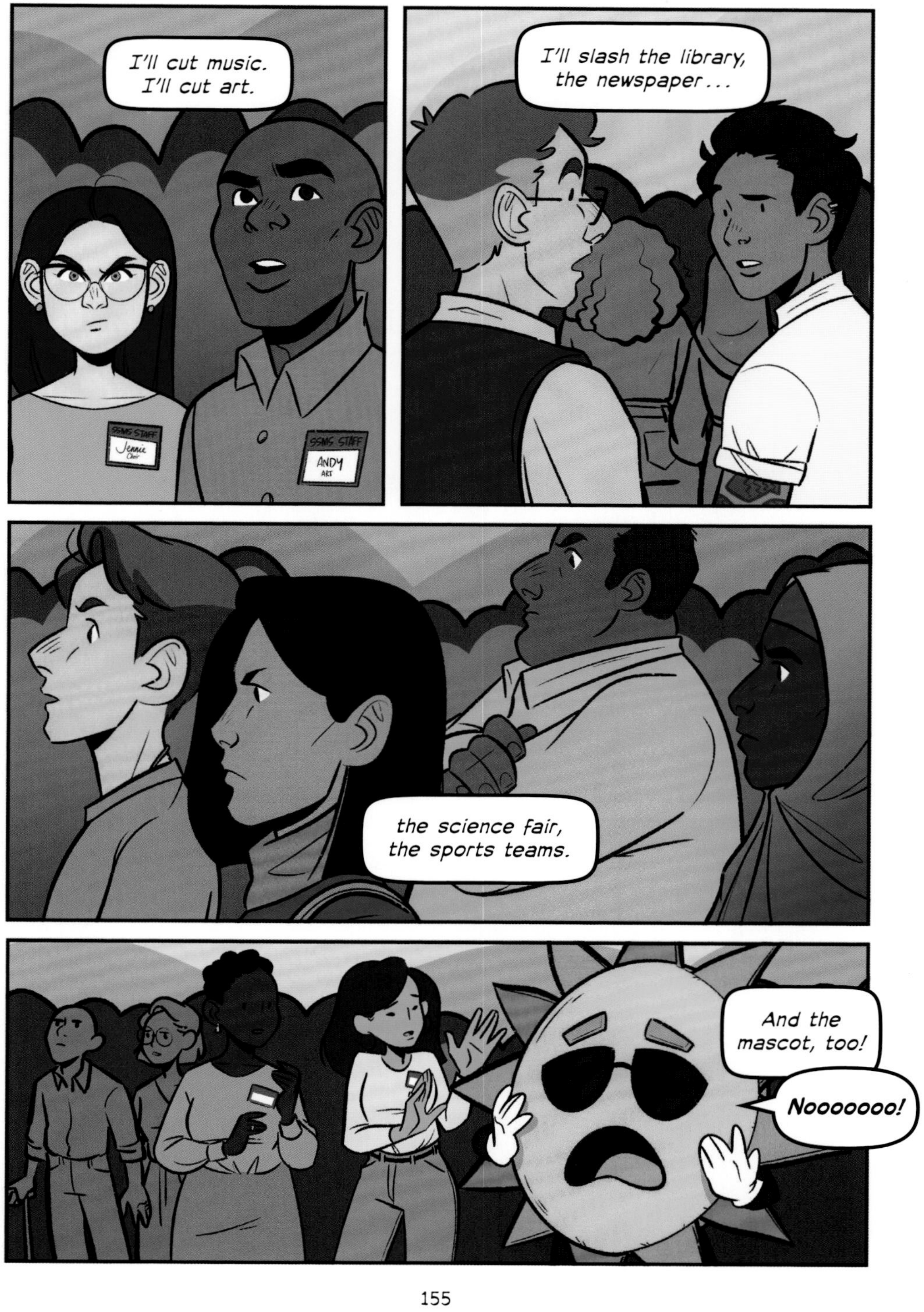
I'll cut music. I'll cut art.
SSMS STAFF
Jennie
SSMS STAFF
ANDY
ART
I'll slash the library, the newspaper...
the science fair, the sports teams.
And the mascot, too!
Noooooooo!

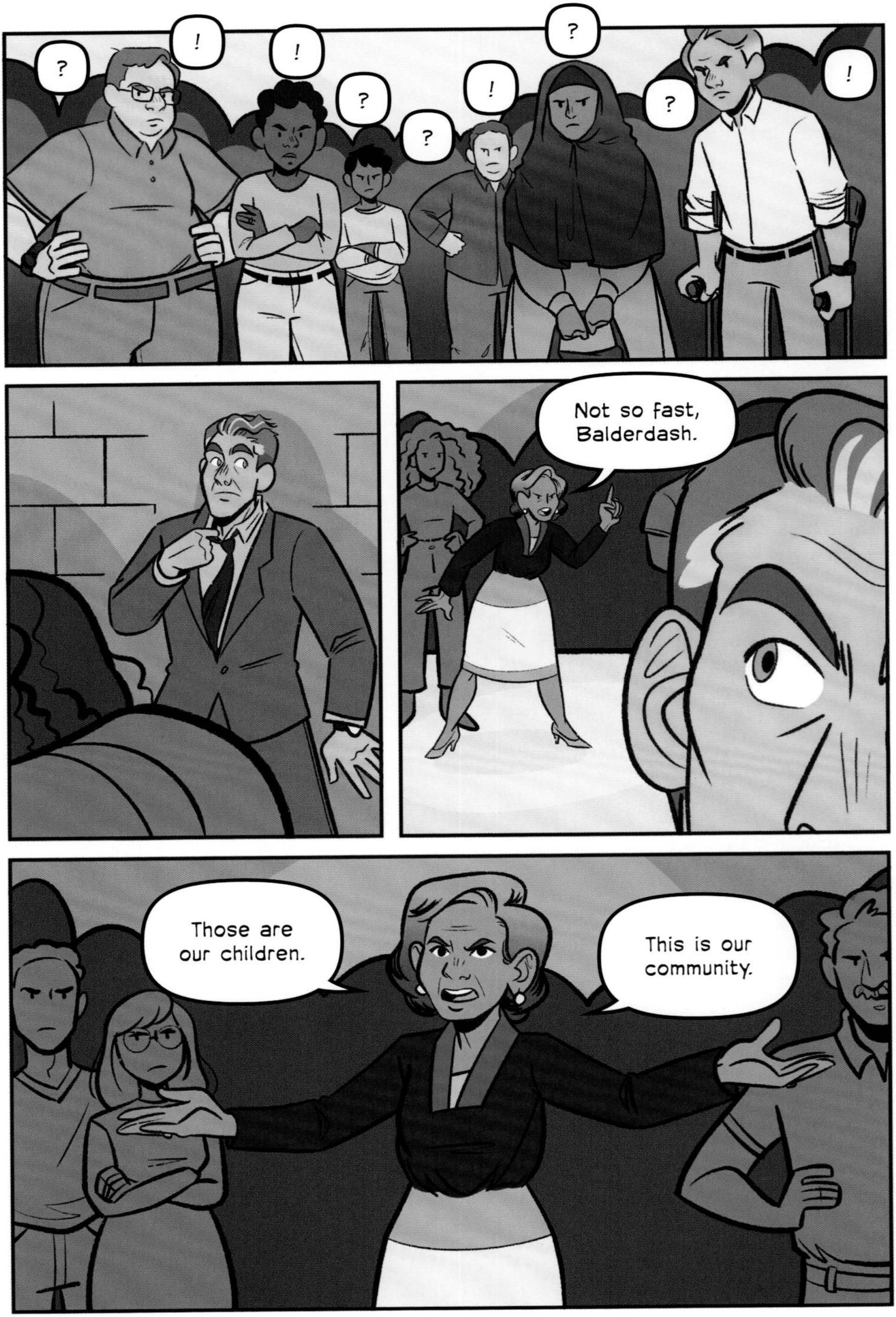
?
!
!
?
?
!
?
?
!
Not so fast, Balderdash.
Those are our children.
This is our community.

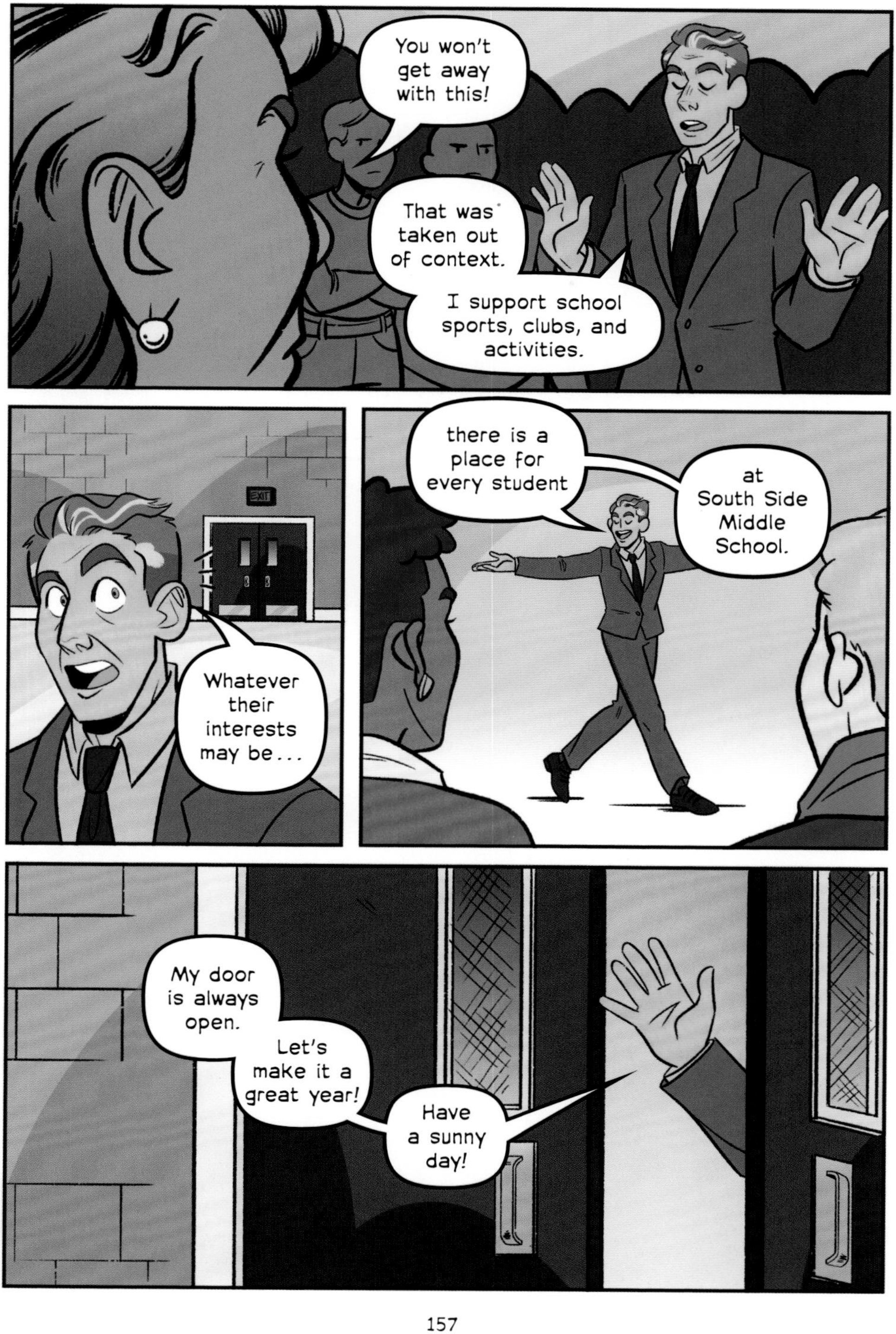
You won't get away with this!
That was taken out of context.
I support school sports, clubs, and activities.
EXIT
Whatever their interests may be...
there is a place for every student
at South Side Middle School.
My door is always open.
Let's make it a great year!
Have a sunny day!

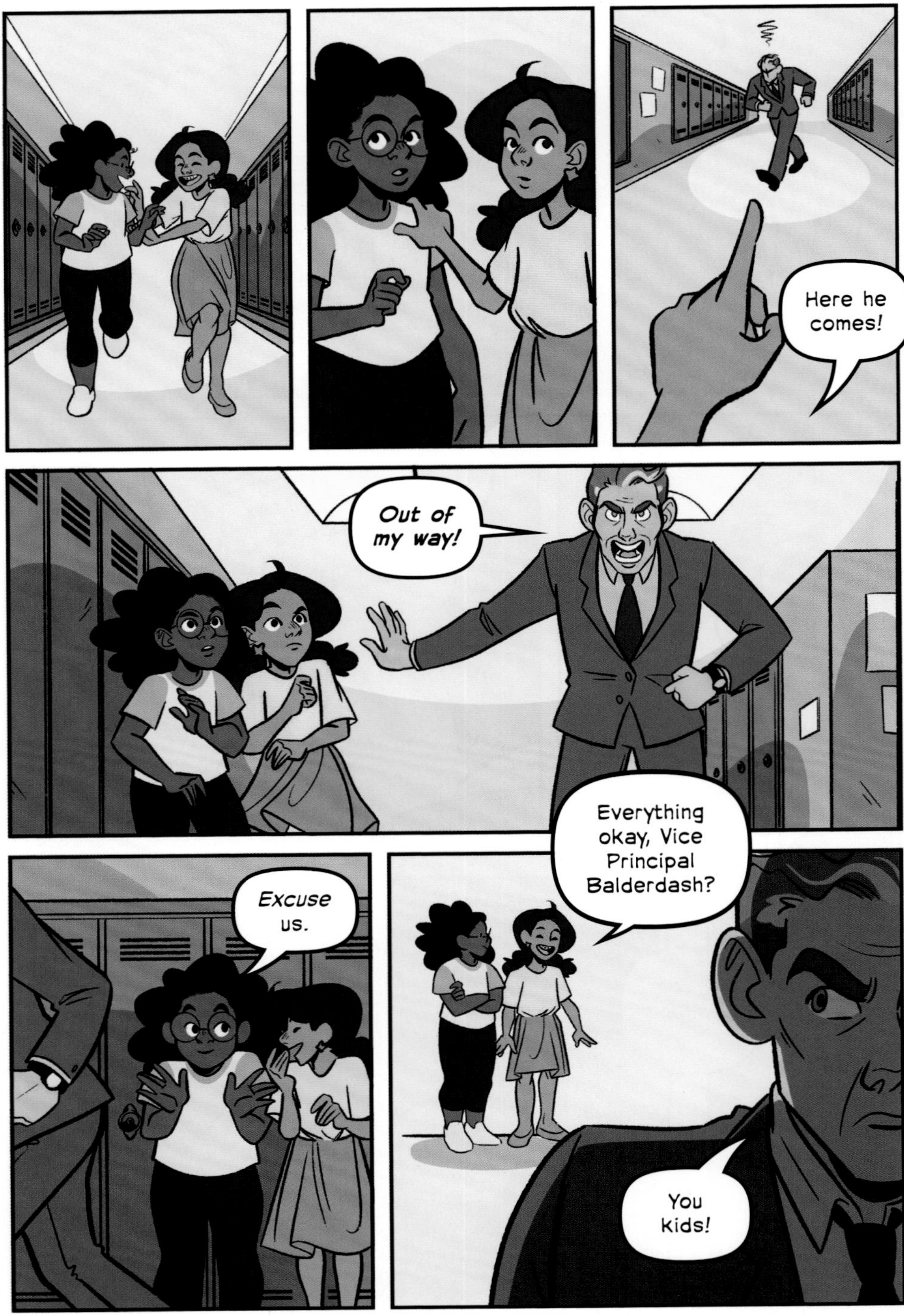
Here he comes!
Out of my way!
Excuse us.
Everything okay, Vice Principal Balderdash?
You kids!

All you blasted kids!
THIS ISN'T OVER!
VOTE!
How dare he talk to my cousin like that!
Nobody messes with *my* cousin.

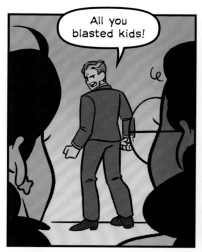

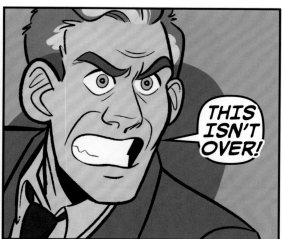

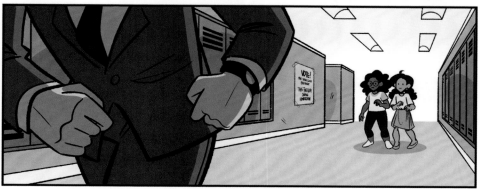

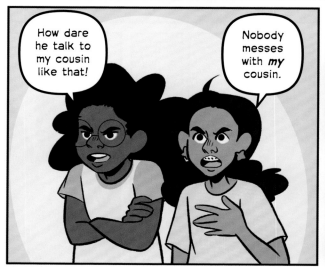

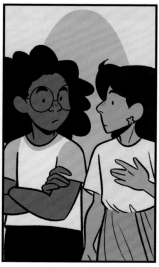

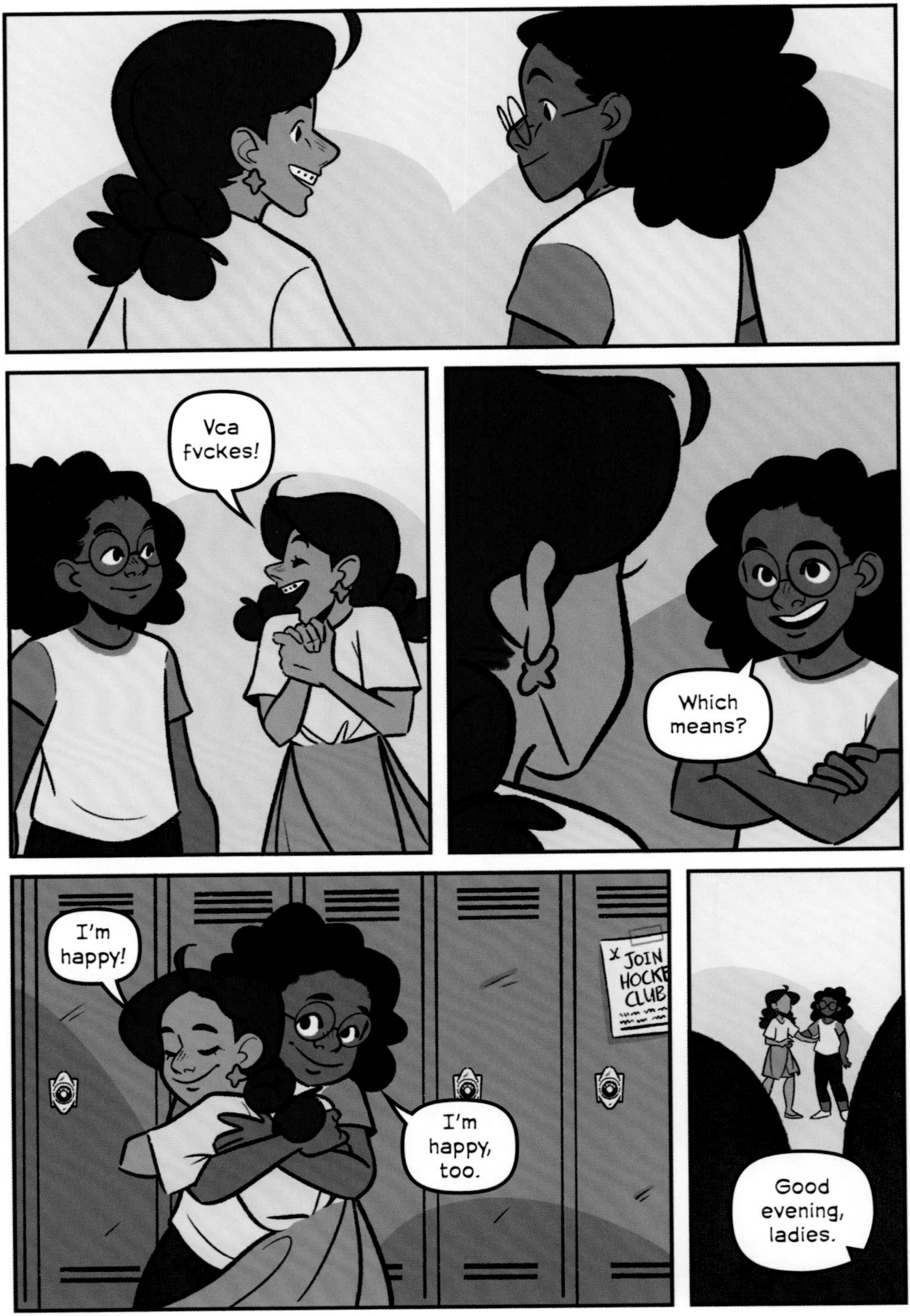
Vca fvckes!
Which means?
I'm happy!
I'm happy, too.
JOIN HOCKE CLUB
Good evening, ladies.

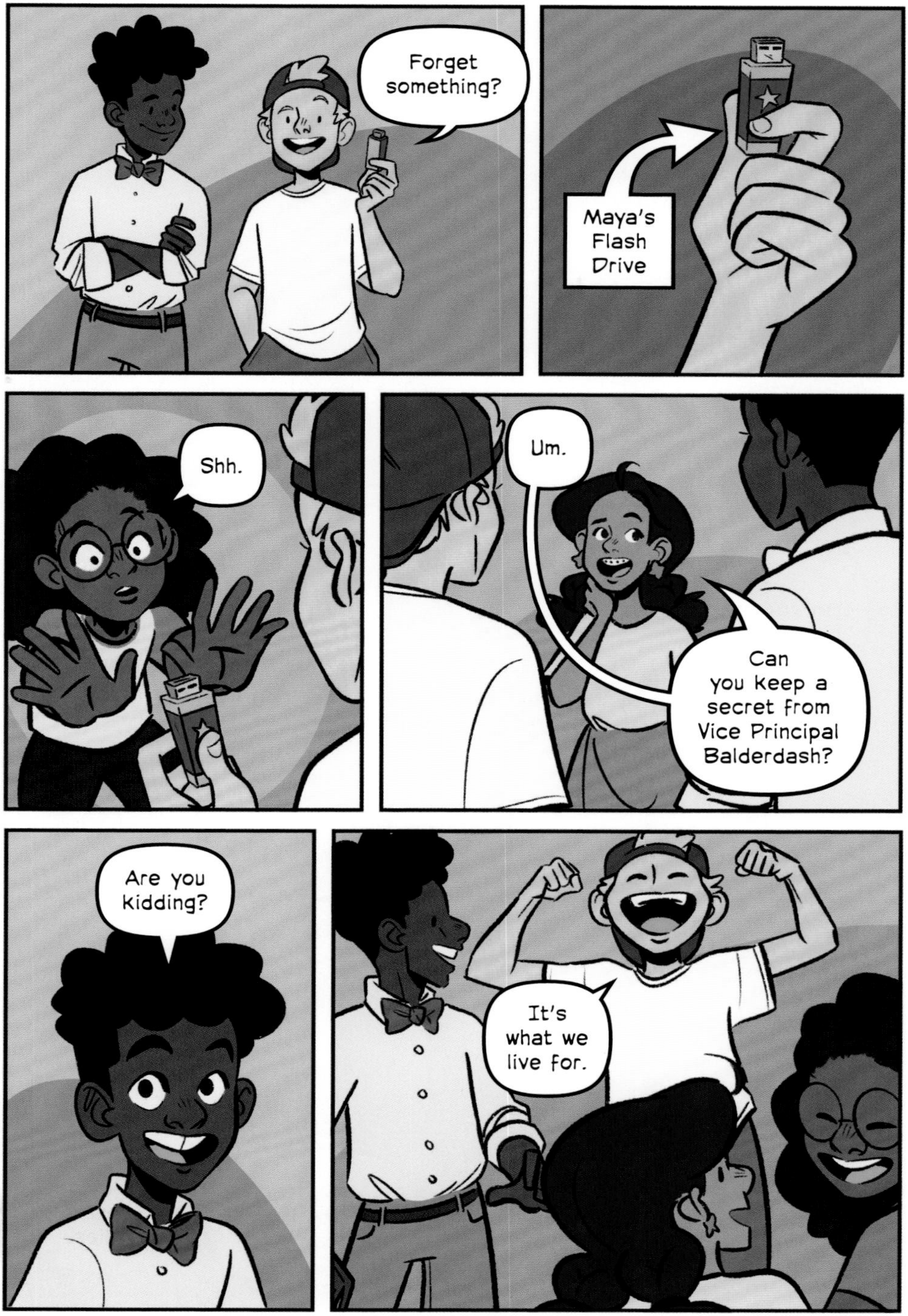
Forget something?
Maya's Flash Drive
Shh.
Um.
Can you keep a secret from Vice Principal Balderdash?
Are you kidding?
It's what we live for.

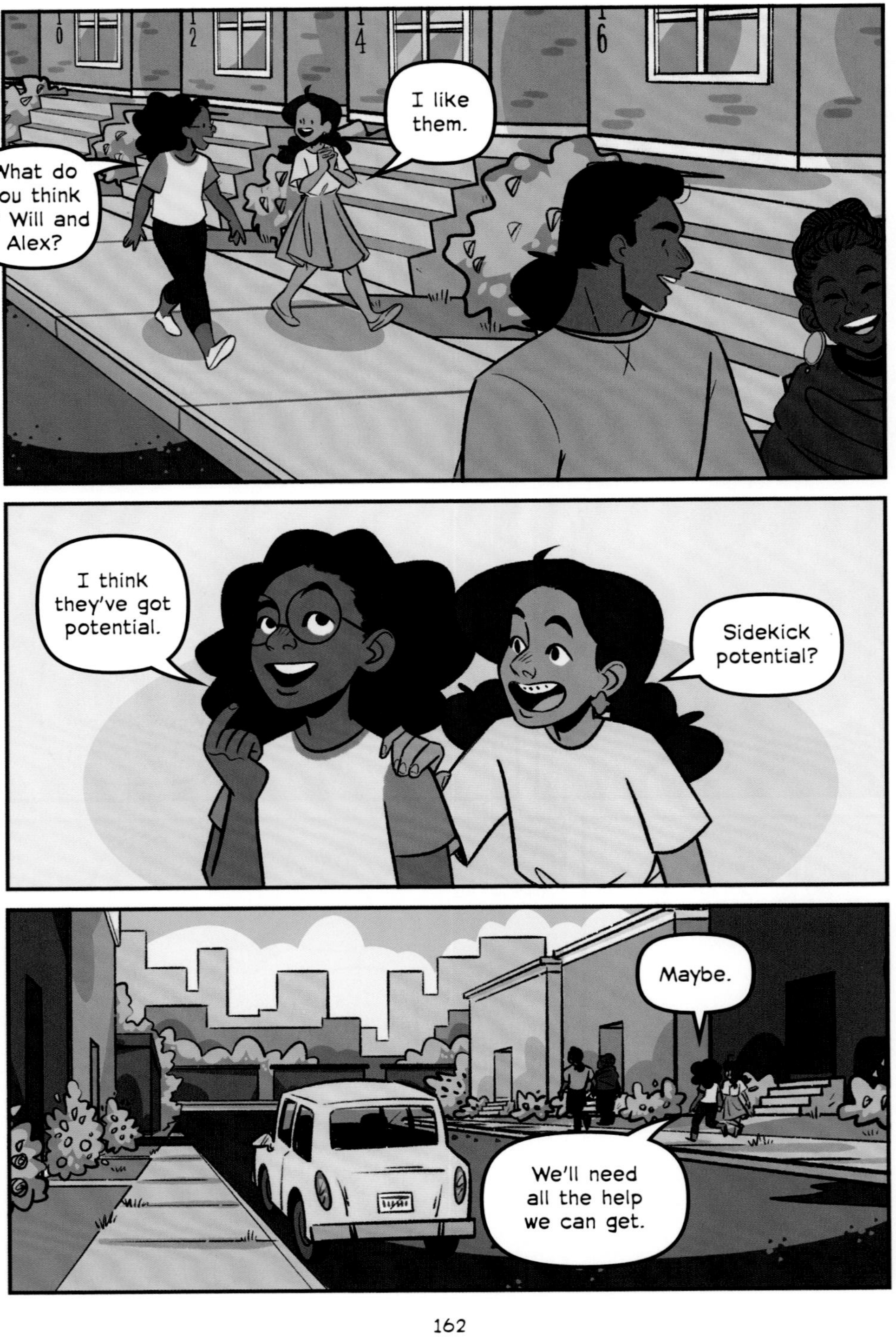
What do you think of Will and Alex?
I like them.
I think they've got potential.
Sidekick potential?
Maybe.
We'll need all the help we can get.

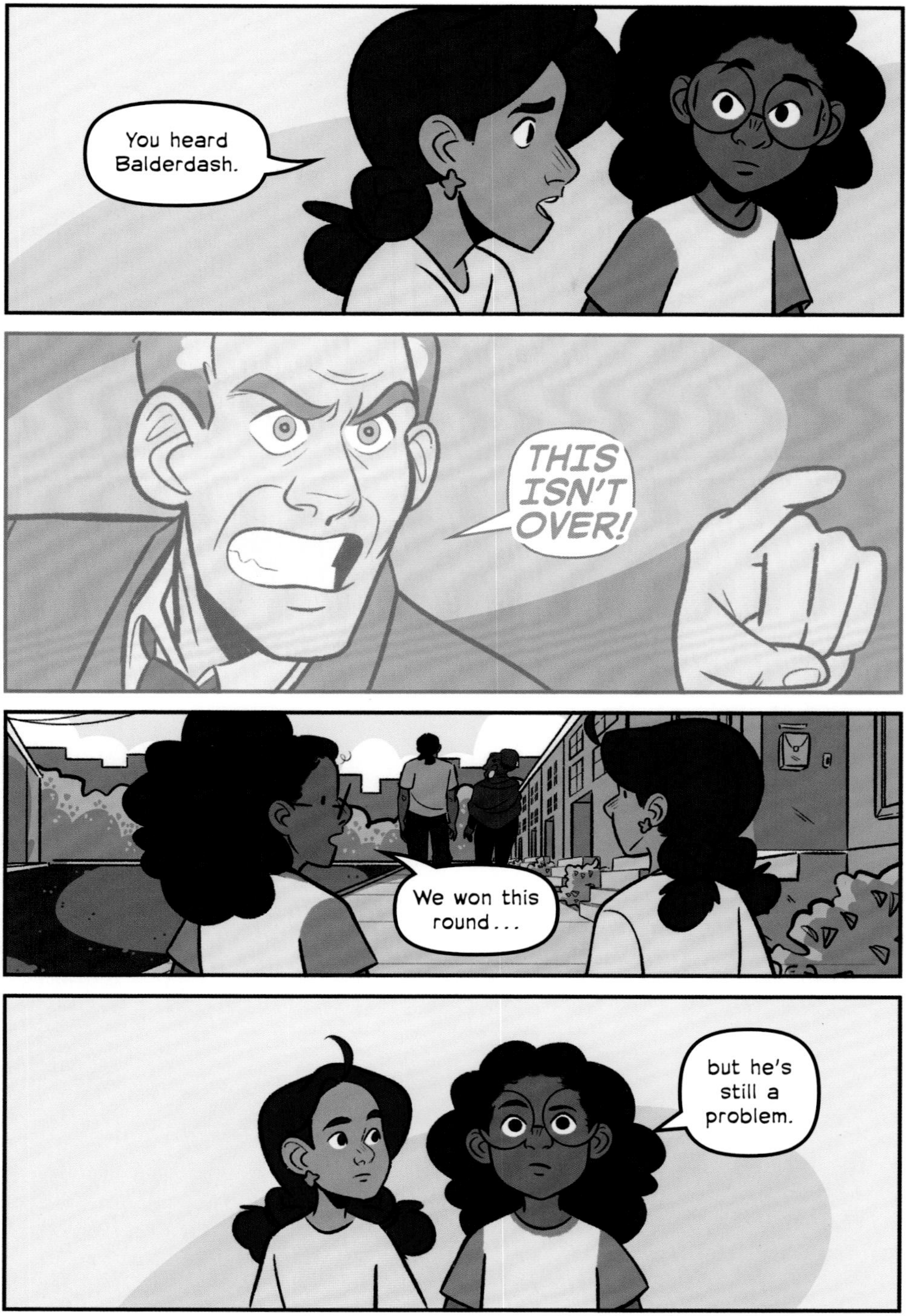
You heard Balderdash.
THIS ISN'T OVER!
We won this round...
but he's still a problem.

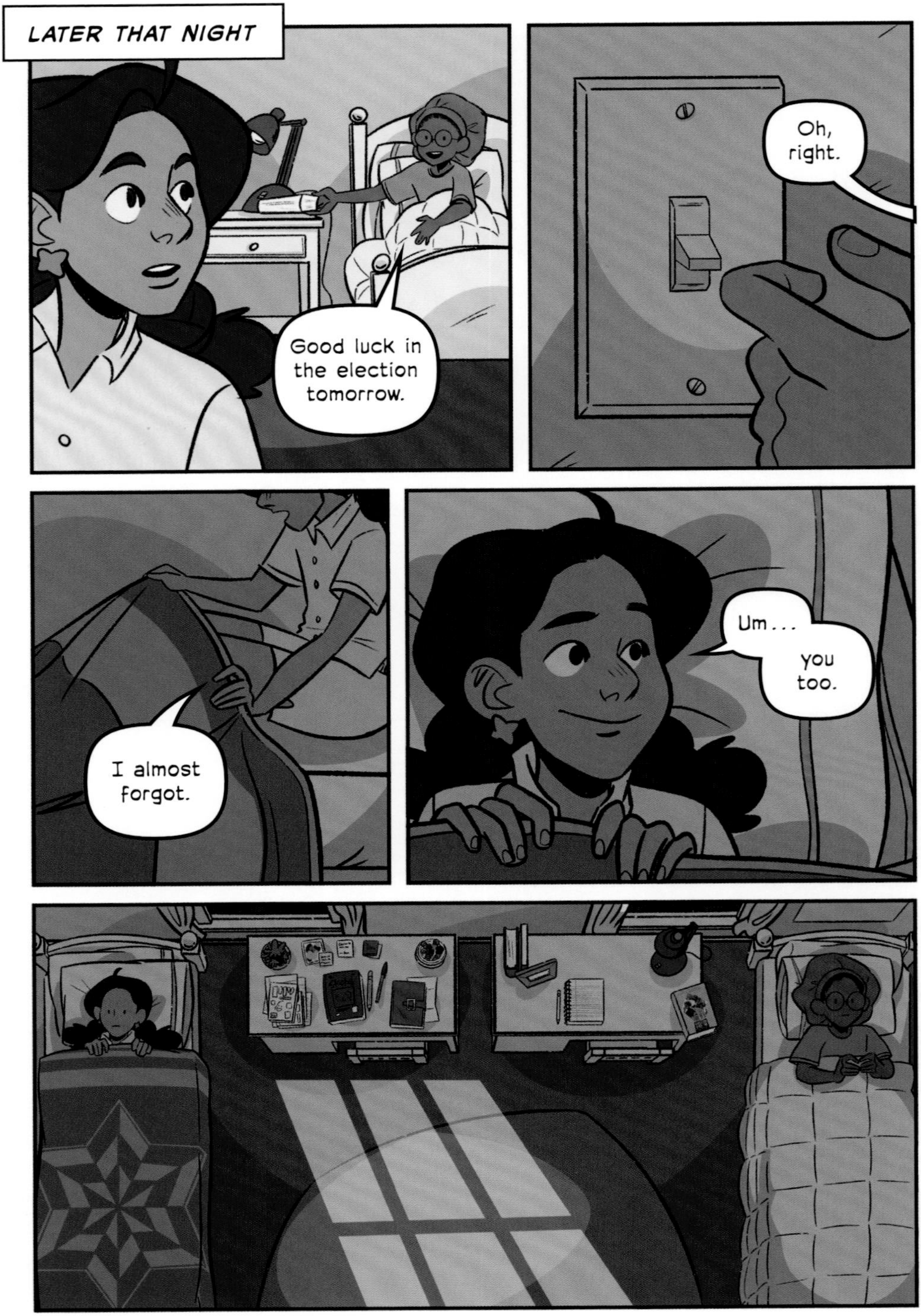
LATER THAT NIGHT
Good luck in the election tomorrow.
Oh, right.
I almost forgot.
Um . . .
you too.

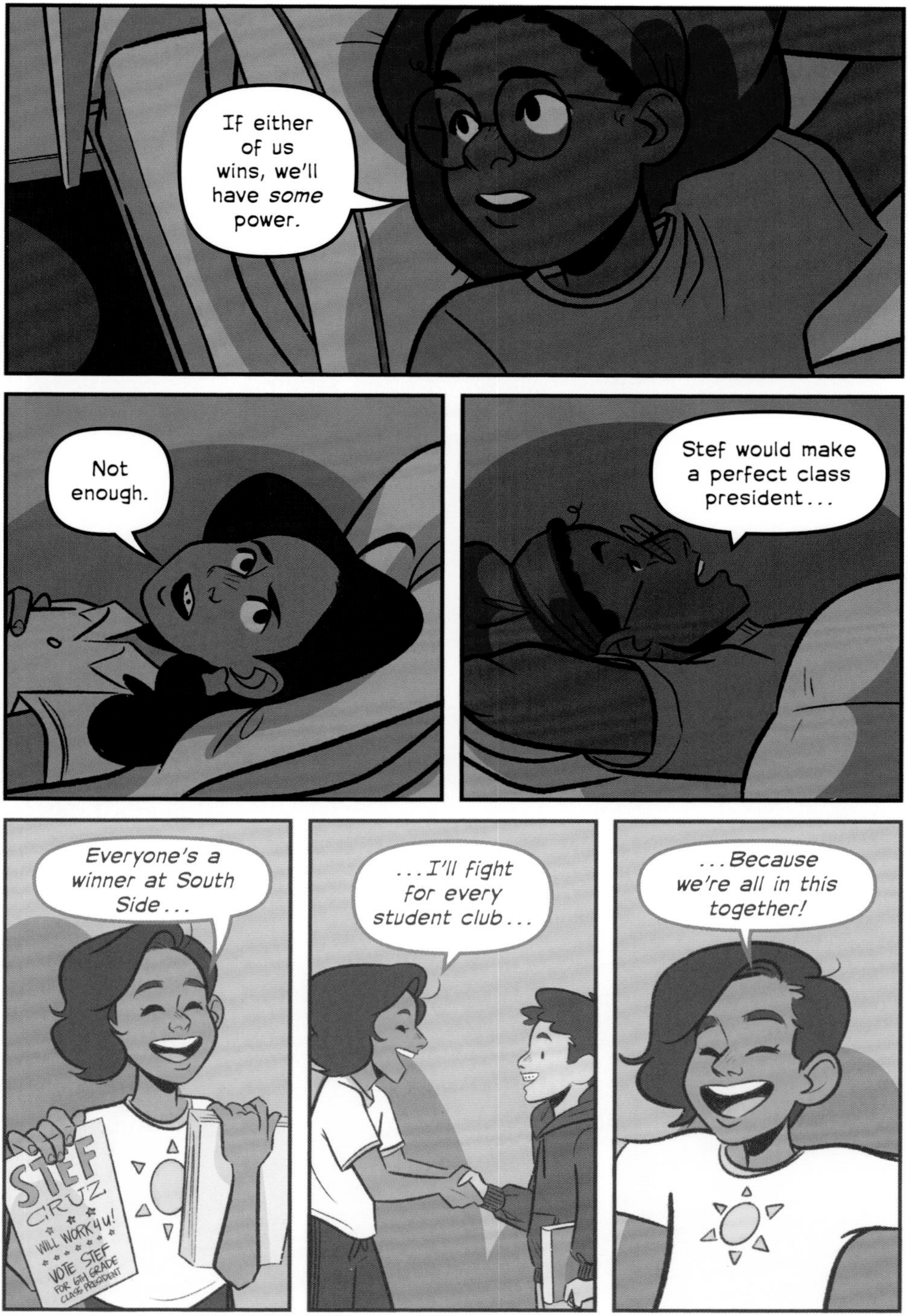
If either of us wins, we'll have *some* power.
Not enough.
Stef would make a perfect class president . . .
Everyone's a winner at South Side . . .
STEF CRUZ
WILL WORK 4 U!
VOTE STEF FOR 6TH GRADE CLASS PRESIDENT
. . . I'll fight for every student club . . .
. . . Because we're all in this together!

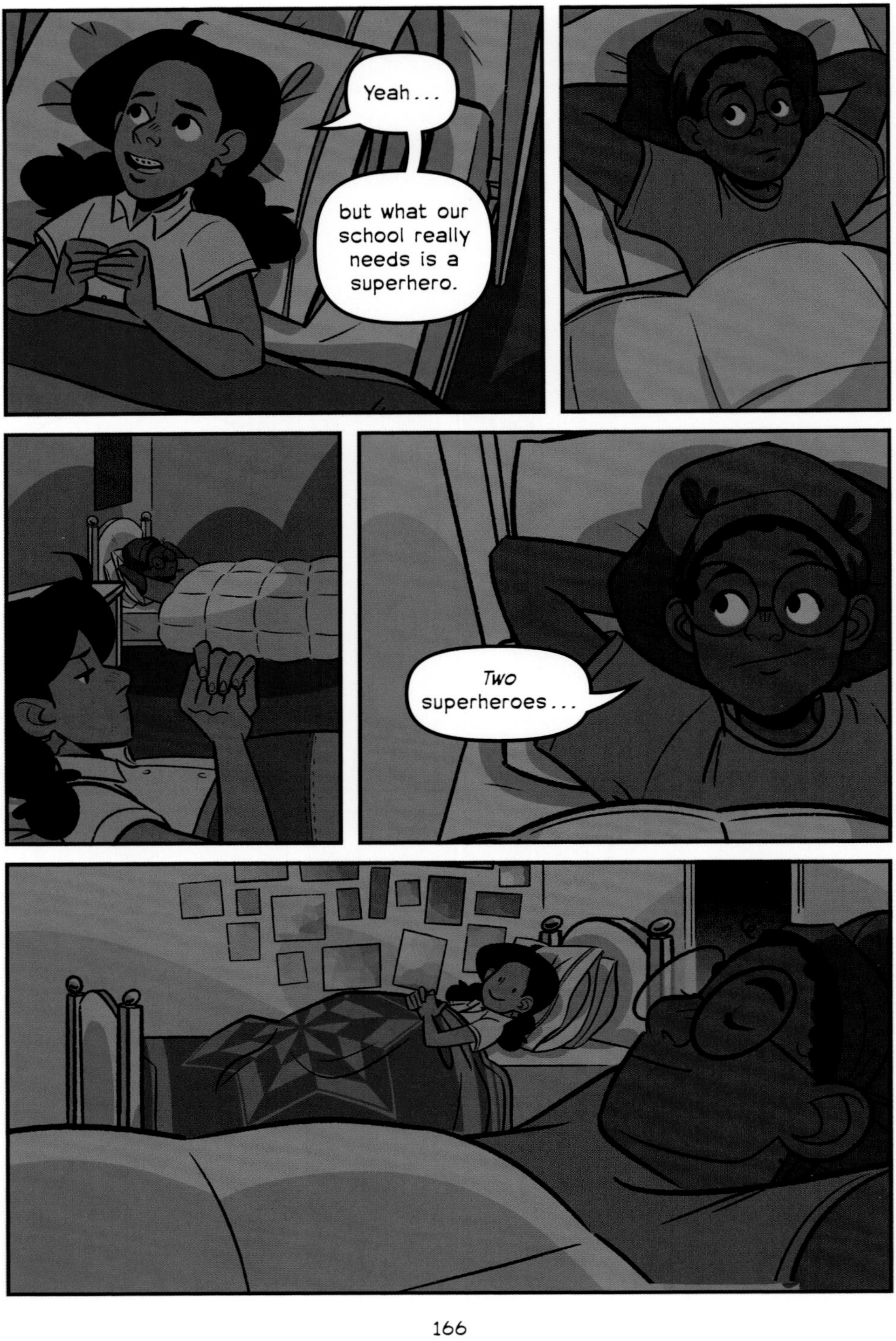

Yeah...
but what our school really needs is a superhero.
Two superheroes...

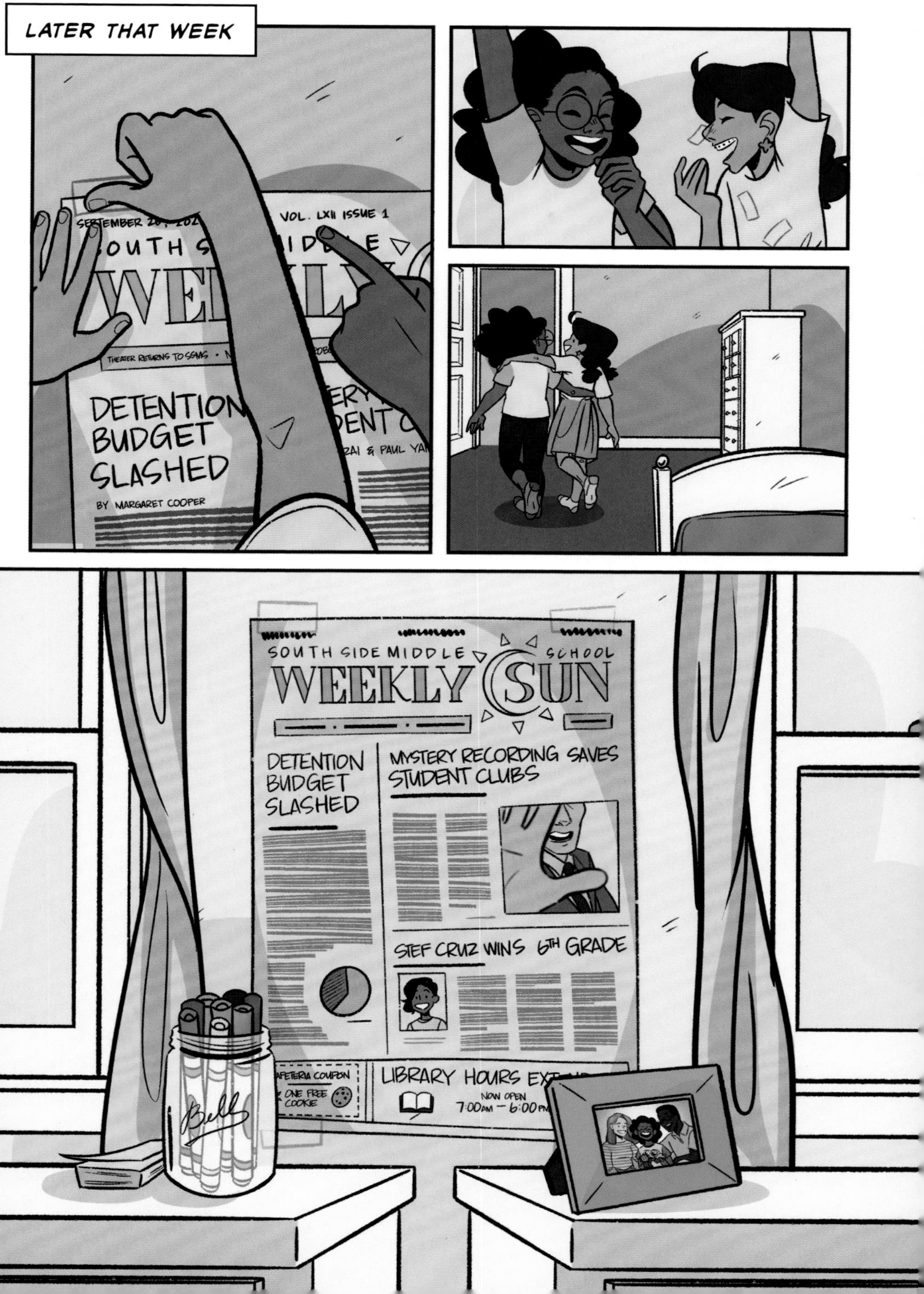
LATER THAT WEEK
VOL. LXII ISSUE 1
THEATER RETURNS TO SSMS
DETENTION BUDGET SLASHED
BY MARGARET COOPER
SOUTH SIDE MIDDLE SCHOOL
WEEKLY SUN
DETENTION BUDGET SLASHED
MYSTERY RECORDING SAVES STUDENT CLUBS
STEF CRUZ WINS 6TH GRADE
ONE FREE COOKIE
NOW OPEN
7:00AM – 6:00PM
Ball

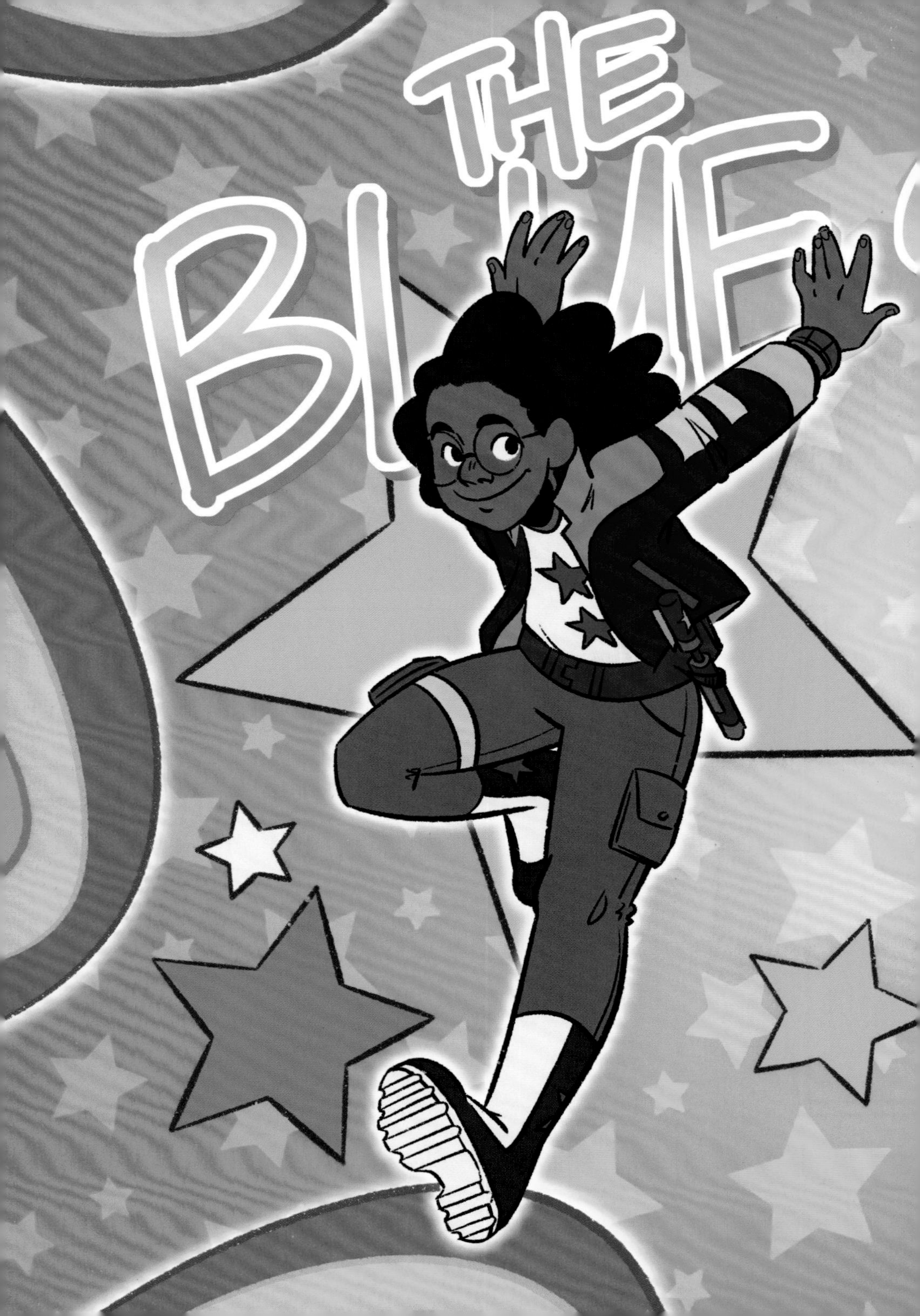
THE